The First Wave

Joshlyn Nicole

Copyright © 2022 by Joshlyn Nicole

All rights reserved.

No portion of this book may be reproduced in any form without written permission from the publisher or author, except as permitted by U.S. copyright law.

Chapter 1

Always Drama

"Hey Daddy, can I come over this weekend?" Kennedy, my twelve-year-old daughter, asked.

This wouldn't be a great weekend for her to come to the house because I had my girl, Chloe, coming into town. Chloe was already on a flight from Cali headed here so I couldn't change our plans. Kennedy's mom was funny about Kennedy being around my girlfriends and I didn't want any drama.

"Uh, this is not a good weekend. I got a lot going on." I said.

"You always got a lot going on. You never have time for me."

"You can't just expect me to be free when you want me to. I'm trying to be more available but being an entrepreneur requires a lot of time and attention."

"I know. I know. I'll just talk to you later."

The phone went dead and I looked at the phone in disbelief that she hung up on me. I put my phone next to my laptop and started typing away, trying to get my mind off that conversation.

I used to play professional football which kept me away from the kids. When I got injured and couldn't play anymore, I got depressed and isolated myself from everyone and everything. That just made the relationship between me and my five kids worse.

I decided to open a few businesses and my time has been stretched thin and now, I barely have time for my kids. I opened a crab and seafood restaurant with my brother. I opened a juice bar with my mom and a bakery with my sister. These businesses kept me very busy.

Now that these businesses were doing well, I could take a step back and manage from afar. And it also gave me more free time. Instead of enjoying that time, I decided to start a new project which is a YouTube channel with my brothers and sister.

It ain't easy working with family but we're making it happen. If only I could get a better relationship with my kids and finally settle down, life would be perfect.

My Pops wants me to take over the record store and restaurant that has been in our family for years but I'm not sure I want to take on that responsibility. The record store has been in business for fifty years and has survived gentrification. It's the only thing in the neighborhood that reminds us of our old hood. It was nothing like going to the record store and playing those vinyl records. Pops had the opportunity to sell it but it has been in the family for two generations and he doesn't want to give it up.

I closed the laptop as the time neared three in the afternoon. It was time to pick Chloe up from the airport. I couldn't wait to see her. Things were getting serious between us and I haven't felt this way about a woman in a while.

I walked out of the house. I stood in the driveway looking at my cars trying to decide which to drive. I hopped in my Jeep since this was Chloe's favorite ride. I answered a call from Chantel as I backed out of the driveway. She's the mom of my ten-month-old baby girl, Life, and it was always drama with her.

"Wassup Ma?" I said.

"Nun. When you gonna come see your daughter?"

"I can come by this weekend."

"Where ya been?"

"Around."

"Well, you know me and Porsha signed up for this reality show."

Porsha is the mom of my three-year-old, Jackson, and my eight-year-old, Layla.

I furrowed my brows. "Now, when did you two become cool?" I asked.

"We squashed the beef to get to the money," Chantel said.

"What's this show about?" I asked.

"It's all about being a baller's wife or girlfriend. My focus is being the fiancée of Ty and Porsha's storyline will be about y'all."

"She ain't even told me that."

Porsha and I had a rocky relationship, to say the least.

"It ain't gonna be no drama," Chantel said.

I chuckled. "You ain't nothing but drama."

"Shut up, Rell. Porsha wants to promote her new salon and to make a little money."

"But at what cost? All money ain't good money. All y'all see are dollar signs and shopping sprees. They might have y'all looking crazy on this show. I like to keep my life as private as possible and now y'all are about to expose everything."

"You just don't want that little girlfriend of yours to know how much of a dawg you are."

"I've changed."

Chantel laughed. "Yeah right."

"I'm serious. I want to be a better man and settle down."

"I'll believe that when I see it."

"I'll talk to you later, Chan. I got to call Porsha."

"Aight later."

I ended the call and called Porsha.

"What ya want?" Porsha asked sounding annoyed.

"Yo, what is this I'm hearing about a reality show?"

"Me and Chantel been filming for a few weeks now and it should be airing in a couple of months."

"And you weren't going to tell me?"

"I ain't gotta tell you shit."

"But you using me as a storyline."

"Boy, I'm barely talkin' 'bout you. Your name was just my way on the show. I'm promoting my business and dating a baller, if you must know."

I shook my head. "Oh yeah. How long y'all been dating?"

"Not that long, like six months."

"Who is it?"

"You don't need to know."

"Who is it?"

She got quiet and then answered me. "Chauncey."

Now I was pissed. Chauncey used to be my boy and we were teammates at one point. "You ain't serious. This better not be the same Chauncey I know."

"He's a good dude."

"You dating my best friend and putting this on a show?"

"Chauncey told me y'all not cool like that."

"P, you know better than this. I considered that dude a brotha. I noticed him moving funny and I had to step back. You wouldn't like it if I got with your best friend whether y'all cool or not."

"What do you want me to do?"

"It's whatever."

I ended the call. I couldn't wait to go out later and let loose. I ain't talked to Chauncey in months but we had to talk about this.

Chapter 2
Should I?

Chloe was waiting outside when I pulled up to the airport. She looked fine as hell in black skintight leather pants and a crop top. I hopped out of the car and wrapped my arms around her.

"You look good," I said.

She smiled. "Thanks, baby. It's so good seeing you."

I put her suitcase in the back as she climbed into the passenger seat. I got back into the car, pulled away from the curb, and joined the heavy airport traffic.

"When are you moving here?" I asked.

"I don't know. I love Cali." Chloe said.

"Don't you want to be here with me?" I asked.

"Of course, but I have a life back home too. I just can't pack up and leave."

"I understand."

"You seem down."

"Nah, I'm straight."

"Where are we headed?"

"I gotta get Marley from school and then we'll go out to eat."

My older sister, Deja, was tragically killed eleven years ago and left behind two kids, Mariah and Marley. Their dad had custody then he got sick and passed. So, Moms got custody of them but Marley was getting into trouble so he's with me. He's doing a lot better since he moved in with me.

"Where are we going to eat?" Chloe asked looking out the window.

"I found this new steakhouse. I think you're going to like it." I said.

"I'm starved so I can't wait. Do your baby mommas know I'm in town?" Chloe asked.

"Nah but I ain't letting nobody come over this weekend so there's no drama," I said.

"I don't want to come between you and your kids."

"It's one weekend. I can make it up to them. Their mommas gotta stop trippin.'"

"Are they always like this towards your girlfriends?"

"Hell yeah. They're like that to each other. Can't have them in the same room for long before shit pops off. I just found out Chantel and Porsha teamed up."

"Why?"

"For some reality show."

"Ah, that's why you're down?"

"I like having a private life. There's so much drama between me and the baby mommas and I don't want that exposed."

"Your name is hardly in mess."

"Exactly and I want to keep it that way. The only reason they're talking about me now is because you're internet famous."

"They tried so hard to find dirt on you."

"I don't want those problems."

"As someone who's been drug through the mud, I don't wish that on anybody."

Chloe got started in the entertainment industry as a dancer and now she's a rapper. Our relationship has created quite the buzz on gossip blogs.

"Them people don't know you fa real," I said.

"And that's why I don't pay them no never mind. The hate is paying my bills." Chloe said.

I pulled into the high school carpool lane. Marley said something to one of his friends and ran to the car.

"Sup?" Marley said climbing into the car.
"Sup, how was your day?" I asked.
"It was straight."
"You want me to grab you something to eat? Me and Chloe are going out."
"I can order food later."
"Nothing over fifty dollars. You like to rack up when you order food."
He laughed. "Aight. I'll be cheap today. Soccer tryouts are next week."
"You gonna play soccer again?"
"I've been thinking about it."
"You haven't played in a long time. I think it would be good for you."
"Mariah wants me to play. It's something we did together."
"She's a good player too."
"She's a dope athlete. She makes me miss the sport when I see her play."
"You got to try out. It's time to dust off those cleats."
"I'll think about it, Unc."

―*elle*―

Chloe and I were now sitting in the restaurant waiting for our food. Chloe was chomping down on her appetizer and I was drinking.
"What ya want to do this weekend?" I asked.
"I'm hosting a party at this nightclub, Lust, tomorrow night," Chloe said.
"What ya want to do during the day?"

"I want to check out this food festival and art museum."

"We can do that. Have you been painting more?"

"I've been trying. I got to visit your seafood restaurant and your Pops' soul food restaurant while I'm in town."

I smiled. "Pops loves it when you come by."

"Have you given any more thought to taking over and letting Pops retire?"

"It's so much going on. I don't have time for another business."

"It's time for Pops to retire and enjoy the fruits of his labor."

"He likes working. He wouldn't know what to do with himself if he wasn't working."

"He's getting older and can't work as much as he used to. There's so much history with that restaurant, it would be a shame to let it go. You got to keep the business alive."

"Pops done got in your ear, huh? He's getting you to convince me to take over the restaurant."

"We had a conversation when I was here a couple of weeks ago. He seemed so sad about possibly losing the restaurant. I just felt so bad."

"I'll think about it but I have so much going on. You know I'm trying to get this YouTube channel off the ground?"

"How is that going?"

"We got to find time to film and start posting on the channel."

"Are you still doing a football summer camp?"

"Yeah, me and a couple of people are finalizing everything now."

"I told my girlfriend about it and she wants her son to do it."

"I'll give you the info as soon as I have it."

The waiter sets our food on the table. Chloe pulled out her phone to take videos and photos of the delectable food.

"Let me try yours."

She stuck her fork in my plate and tried the medium-rare Wagyu steak.

"Dang, that's good. I'm trying to stay away from red meat." Chloe said.

"Why didn't you tell me? I wouldn't have tempted you with a steakhouse restaurant."

She giggled. "The salmon is bomb. Try it."

I tried a piece of the salmon and tasted smokiness, lemon, and garlic. "I like that."

"Where are we going tonight?"

"I want to take you to this lounge. I think you'll like it."

"As long as I can drink and shake my ass, I'll love it."

Chapter 3

Do Better

It was a wild night and I woke up the next day with a mean hangover and no recollection of the previous night. Chloe was fast asleep with the covers pulled up to her neck.

I looked at the time and it was ten in the morning. I knew I wouldn't be able to see my baby girl, Life, today and I didn't want to hear Chantel's mouth.

I climbed out of bed and stumbled to the kitchen. Marley was seated at the bar staring at his phone eating cereal out of a mixing bowl. If I wasn't so messed up, I would be fussing about it.

"Morning," I mumbled.

"Morning," Marley said without looking up from his phone.

"You want me to make you some breakfast?" I asked.

"I'm good."

I poured myself a glass of water and found my painkillers. I joined Marley at the bar. I took a couple of pills with the water. Man, I drank entirely too much yesterday. Hell, I was still drunk.

"Can I go to the movies with my friends today?" Marley asked.

"Yeah, I'll drop you off at the mall. Who's all going to the movies?"

"Mariah and some of our friends."

"What! Nana's letting Mariah outta the house?"

"I was just as shocked. She usually don't let her go anywhere."

I called Chantel to get it over with.

"Hey Rell," Chantel said.

"Hey. I can't come by today. I got a lot going on." I said.

"Just be real and say your bitch is in town and you don't have time for your daughter," Chantel said.

"C'mon Chantel, you ain't gotta do all that," I said.

"You ain't seen your daughter in a month. It's always one excuse after another with you." Chantel said.

I didn't even realize it had been a month until she said it. I had to do better.

"Just be patient with me. I'm trying."

"You ain't trying. You've been partying all night with your bitch and now you can't see your daughter."

"I just have a lot to do today."

"And your daughter is not important? She's not a priority, huh? I ain't begging you to be in her life. She's good without you."

Then I heard a click. I put the phone down and rubbed my temple.

"Dang, she's mad," Marley said.

"It's my fault. I gotta do better when it comes to my kids. Junior ain't even talking to me right now."

Junior is my fifteen-year-old son and we used to be so close now I ain't talked to him or seen him in three months.

"I talked to Junior the other day. His momma kicked him out and he's staying with his cousin." Marley said.

My jaw dropped and I looked at him to see if he was serious. "You serious? When did this happen?"

"A week ago," Marley said.

I called Marie, the mom of Kennedy and Junior.

"Hello," Marie said out of breath.

"Marie, wassup?"

"I'm at the gym."

"You kicked Junior out?"

"I told him he couldn't stay in my house and not follow my rules. He's been skipping school and in all types of nonsense. He said fuck you and your rules and left. I haven't heard from him since and he hasn't been in school."

"And when were you going to tell me?"

"You're so busy, Rell. I can hardly get in touch with you."

"Ma, you know how to reach me. I didn't know you were having issues with him. You should have told me."

"I thought I could handle it on my own."

"Let me see if I can get in touch with Junior and I'll call you back."

I ended the call with Marie.

"Marley, call Junior," I said.

Marley called Junior and we waited for him to answer.

"Yo, what's good?" Junior said.

"It's all good. What's good with you?" Marley asked.

"Getting to a bag," Junior said.

"I feel ya. Your Pops want to talk to you."

Junior sucked his teeth. "I don't want to talk to him."

"I want to talk to you," I said.

Junior got quiet and Marley checked his phone to make sure he was still on the line.

"Wassup Pops?" Junior finally said.

"Nah, don't wassup me. What's going on with you?" I asked.

"Nothin'," Junior mumbled.

"Your mom said you ain't following her rules," I said.

"She got a million rules."

"And you need to follow them. Where ya staying?"

"I'm staying with my cousin."

"Pack your shit. I'm coming to get you."

"Man, I'm good where I'm at."

"No, you're not. You need to go back to school. Text your address to Marley."

"I ain't going back to school."

"We gotta talk and figure this shit out."

"Pops, I gotta go."

"Send Marley your address. I'm coming to get you in a little bit."

He ended the call without saying anything else. I shook my head not believing things in my life were this out of control. I put my head in my hands and took several deep breaths.

"He'll come around," Marley said noticing me stressing.

"What's he up to? What nonsense is he involved in?"

Marley shrugged but I knew he knew something. Marley and Junior were like brothers and told each other everything. Chloe walked into the room wearing her red silk robe.

"Morning y'all," Chloe said.

"Morning," we mumbled.

"Who died?" Chloe asked.

"It's been a hectic morning," I said.

"You want me to make some breakfast?" Chloe asked.

"Yeah, if you want to."

She opened the refrigerator door. "I'm so happy you have groceries for once."

"I went grocery shopping just for you."

"Why y'all so down?"

"I had to tell Chantel that I couldn't see Life today and it's been a month since I've seen her. And Chantel thinks I'm not seeing her because you're in town. But, for once Jamal, Jarrod, and Jayla are free to film a couple of videos. I gotta figure out how to make time for everything."

"You gotta put the kids above everything. I'm sure the kids miss you." Chloe said.

"Yeah, I gotta do better. And Junior left home. He don't want to follow his mom's rules."

"How old is he again?"

"Fifteen."

"He's just a baby. Where is he?"

"He's staying with a cousin. I gotta bring him home. I don't know what he's up to. He hasn't been at school in a week."

"You just finding out?"

"Yeah, Marie didn't want to bother me and thought she could handle it. I know I get in my zone but I don't want people thinking they can't call me. I'll drop everything for my family if they need me."

"I'm going to take a shower," Marley said grabbing his phone and bowl.

"Send me that address when he sends it to you," I said

"Aight." He put the bowl in the sink and ran up the steps.

"What ya making?" I asked Chloe.

"French toast, eggs, and bacon."

"That sounds good."

"You had fun last night?" Chloe asked.

"I don't even remember the night."

"I was looking at photos and videos on social media and it looked like we had a good time."

"Chantel must have seen the same photos and videos because she was trippin' this morning."

"It don't take much for Chantel to trip."

I chuckled. "You right."

"Speaking of Chan, she's all in my messages talking crazy."

"What's she saying?"

"She's just calling me a bum bitch, ho this ho that, the usual shit people say about me."

"I'm sorry."

"I got tough skin, baby. I can handle it."

An incoming video chat from Layla appeared on my phone.

"Hey Layla," I said answering the call. Seeing my baby girl put me in a better mood.

"Hey Daddy," Layla said. She smiled and showed me her missing front teeth.

"What ya doing?"

"I'm just in my room. We're about to meet Uncle Chauncey for lunch."

"Oh really?"

She covered her mouth realizing she slipped up. "No, I didn't mean to say that. I'm about to do yoga with my friend."

I smiled at her little lie. "Are you still doing gymnastics?"

"No, I want to take swimming lessons but Momma won't let me."

"Why?"

"She said it would mess up my hair."

"I'm going to sign you up for swim lessons. I'm sure you can get your hair braided or something."

She grinned.

"How are you doing in school?"

The grin quickly disappeared and she looked away from the camera. "Good."

"Don't let me find out otherwise. Where's Jackson?"

"He's sleeping." She ran down the hall to his room and Jackson was fast asleep in his race-car bed.

"Aw, let that baby sleep," I whispered.

She ran back to her room and lay on her bed. "When are we going to see you?"

"Soon like next weekend."

We talked for a few more minutes until Porsha told her to get ready for the day.

"She's a sweetheart," Chloe said.

"Yeah, she is. She's a Daddy's girl." I said.

Chloe placed a plate and a cup of orange juice in front of me. I wait for Chloe to join me before I dig in.

"Is it good?" Chloe asked.

"Hell yeah. Everything you cook is good."

She smiled. "What you up to today?"

"First, I gotta find Junior and then film a couple of videos for the channel. What ya doing?"

"I'm going to the studio. My first album is almost complete."

"You've worked so hard on this project."

"Yeah, it was harder than I thought it would be but I'm excited for my fans to hear the music."

"Your single Needed Me is dope. I can't wait to hear the rest of the music."

"You really like my music?"

"You know I'm going to keep it real with you. If I didn't like it or thought it was trash, I would tell you. We have to meet up this afternoon to go to the food festival. Tomorrow we'll go to the art museum. It'll be less crowded on a Sunday."

Chapter 4

Never Around

Marley and I were in the car and headed to the mall. I just dropped Chloe off at the studio. My phone rang and it was Moms calling.

"Hey there," I said.

"Hey, what you up to?" Moms asked.

"Nun really. What ya doing?" I asked.

"I'm at the juice bar working."

"How's it going?"

"Business is slow this morning."

"By lunchtime, it'll pick up."

"How come I haven't met this Chloe woman? I saw some photos and I'm not too sure about her."

"She's a good person."

"Uh-huh. Why you keeping her a secret?"

"I'm not. Y'all don't need to meet everybody."

"Your dad met her."

"We went by the restaurant and he was there. That's how they met."

"Why you ain't brought her to the juice bar?"

"We just ain't have time to get out that way. She's usually working when she comes to town."

"What kind of work?"

"She's an entertainer."

"What does that mean? Why you being so vague?"

"She's a rapper."

"Interesting."

I don't like telling Moms my business, she was so judgmental. I was hesitant to bring Chloe around my family.

"Why you ain't seen Life? Chan called me crying and cursing up a storm."

"I've been busy."

"You can't be too busy for your kids. You're finally home after being on the road for years. They need you, Rell. Money don't mean nothing when they ain't getting quality time with you."

"I'm working on being a better dad to them."

"I gotta get back to work. I just wanted to check on you."

I ended the call.

"Did you know Nana let Uncle Ted move in?" Marley asked.

Ted is Moms' older brother.

"Nah, I didn't know that. Why wassup?"

"Mariah told me she don't feel comfortable around him. He's been looking at her and touching her."

I almost crashed hearing that. Mariah is twelve years old, a child. Deja trusted us to look after her babies and this shit happens.

"Did she tell Nana?" I asked.

"Nana don't believe her."

"Did she tell Eric?"

Eric is Moms' husband and the father of my baby brother, Jamal, and youngest sister, Jayla.

"No, she just told me and Nana. I don't know what to do. That's why I'm telling you."

I called Eric.

"Wassup Rell?" Eric asked.

"Not too much, Eric," I said. "What you up to today?"

"Nothing. I'm at the crab restaurant helping out. We got two big catering orders."

"I gotta tell you something."

"Hold on. Let me get outta this kitchen."

I drummed my finger on the steering wheel and waited for him to get somewhere quiet.

"What's going on?" Eric asked.

"Yo, Marley just told me some shit I can't believe," I said.

"What?"

"Uncle Ted's been touching Mariah."

"Fuck! I'll kill him. I told your momma not to move that clown in. I'm about to talk to Mariah right now."

"She's with you?"

"Yeah, I'm taking her to the mall to hang with Marley and their friends."

"We're on the way to the mall now."

"I'll see y'all in a little bit. We gotta talk about this shit in person."

I hung up and tried to focus on driving but my mind was elsewhere.

"Why didn't Nana believe her?" Marley asked.

"I don't know. Her and Uncle Ted are really close. She probably didn't want to believe it."

"Can you tell me about my momma?"

"Do you remember her at all?"

"I remember some things, not a lot. I was only three when she was killed."

It was hard for me to talk about Deja. It's been eleven years and I'm still not over it.

"Your mom was the most beautiful person ever. She had a heart of gold and loved everybody. She's always been my biggest supporter and kept me encouraged. I could have definitely been there for her a little more. She loved to dance and she had the brightest smile. Mariah looks a lot like her."

"Is it true we had a sister?"

"Yeah, that's true. Your momma was pregnant when she was killed. Aaliyah lived for a month before joining Deja."

Marley wiped his eyes with his hand.

"You okay?"

"I'm just mad he took my mom away. I see the pictures and wish I could have gotten to know her. I miss my dad too. I feel like me and Mariah gotta go through this life alone now. It's just us against everybody."

"Y'all are never alone. Y'all got a whole team behind y'all. We can't replace Deja and Michael but we're here for y'all. We love y'all."

Marley smiled and looked down at his lap so I didn't see him upset.

I pulled into the apartment complex where Junior's cousin lives. Junior was standing out front with a group of young men. I didn't like seeing him like this. I worked hard so my kids didn't have to be on the streets like this.

I rolled down my window, got his attention, and waved him to the car. He didn't look happy to see me. He said something to one of the young men standing there and jogged to the car. His mood instantly changed when he saw Marley.

"Yo wassup Marley?" Junior said giving him dap.

"What's good, bro?" Marley asked.

"Working."

"Working?" I asked.

"Pops, it ain't nothin'. I'm gettin' to the money." Junior said.

I didn't know this Junior. "I need you to get your shit and get in this car."

"Pops, you embarrassing me."

"You ain't seen embarrassed. You don't need to be out here like this."

He looked around him and then looked at me. "Aight, give me a sec."

He jogged back to his friends. I pulled into a parking space. I watched Junior hand a gun to a young man. He pulled baggies and cash out of his pockets and gave those things to another young man. I couldn't believe what I was seeing. I've been so busy with life that I've neglected my kids.

"Marley, you knew he was doing this?" I asked.

Marley looked out the window instead of answering me.

"You out here too, huh?" I asked.

"Not anymore," Marley said.

"How did I miss this?"

"You ain't never around."

Chapter 5

Bombshell

Junior, Marley, and I walked into the mall to meet Eric and Mariah. I had a real conversation with Junior and Marley and I hope they get it.

Eric and Mariah were seated in the food court. I gave Junior and Marley money to get food. I sat next to Mariah and across from Eric. Mariah leaned her head on my shoulder and cried. I put my arms around her and rubbed her on the back.

"It's okay, baby girl. We got you." I said.

"I don't want to go back," Mariah said.

"You can come stay with me," I said. I looked at Eric. "Why is Ted staying with y'all anyway?"

"There's something me and your mom haven't told you or your siblings."

"What?"

"We're separated. I got my own spot and I haven't been around the house much. That's why she moved Ted in. She felt like she needed a man in the home."

"Y'all getting a divorce?" I couldn't get over that part.

"Yeah. It's been a good twenty years."

"What happened?"

"It's time for us to go our separate ways. You get tired of putting up with the same old shit."

"You stayed longer than I thought you would."

Eric chuckled. "You and Deja gave me hell when I first came around."

I smiled reminiscing on all the pranks Deja and I played on Eric trying to get rid of him.

Mariah sat up in her chair. "What did y'all do?"

"They were mean and bad as hell. They used to play pranks on me." Eric said.

"And you never got mad at us," I said.

"I knew you were used to it being your mom and dad and you didn't want to accept it was over. And Deja didn't want another stepdaddy."

"I would do anything to have Deja by my side right now," I said.

"She's still with you," Eric said.

Marley and Junior joined us at the table.

"Y'all need to watch out for Mariah. I'm trusting y'all." Eric said.

"Yes sir," Marley said.

"What movie y'all going to go see?" Eric asked.

"We don't know yet," Junior said.

"I gotta get back to the house," I said.

"I'll bring the kids home and text you when I'm on the way," Eric said.

I looked at the kids. "Be on y'all best behavior. No nonsense while y'all at this mall. Y'all hear me?"

"Yes sir," they chorused.

I stood. "I love y'all. See y'all later."

Jayla was the first of my siblings to arrive at the house. Jayla walked into the kitchen side-eyeing Chloe who was helping me set up the lights and cameras.

"Hey Jay," I said.

"Hey Rell," she said. She set her tote bag on the counter.

"What ya making?" I asked.

"I'm going to make a heart-shaped cake and cookies that look like flowers."

"Go ahead and set up. My videographer, Erin, is on the way."

"Erin?" Chloe questioned.

"Yeah, I told you about her," I said.

"Are you going to introduce us?" Jayla asked looking at Chloe.

"My bad. Chloe, this is my sister, Jayla. And Jayla, this is my girl, Chloe." I said.

"Your girl? You're claiming this one?" Jayla remarked.

There was a knock at the door and I welcomed the distraction. It was Erin and my video editor, Tanya. I showed them to the kitchen. Chloe looked jealous as I introduced everyone.

Erin and Jayla worked together to set up for the first video. Tanya and I worked together on the computer to set up the channel and create different graphics for the channel. Chloe stood near us just watching.

"What's the name of the channel?" Chloe asked.

"The J's Cooking Show," I said.

The doorbell rang.

"I'll get it," Chloe said.

Jamal, Jarod, and Chloe appeared in the kitchen seconds later. I dap up my bros and introduced them to everyone.

"You look familiar," Jamal said to Chloe.

"I'm a rapper," Chloe said.

"You're KoKo?" Jamal asked.

"That's me."

Jamal gave me a sly grin and I could only shake my head.

"What y'all cooking?" I asked my brothers.

"I'm cooking ribs and a whole chicken," Jarrod said.

"I'm going to cook a few different things for a college meal ideas video," Jamal said.

"How's school?" I asked Jamal.

"I changed my major," Jamal said.

"Again? I know Eric is pissed."

"He just wants me to get a degree at this point."

"What did you change it to?"

"From criminal justice to IT."

"What's your plan?"

"I don't have one yet."

"Are you filming today?" Jarrod asked me.

"Nah, I'm on director's duties today," I said.

"Where's Marley?" Jamal asked.

"He went to the mall with Junior and Mariah," I said.

"You and Junior back on good terms?" Jarrod asked.

"Not really. He left home and I'm making him move in with me. He ain't happy about it. He's been in the streets hustling." I said.

"Why? It's not like he's hurting for money." Jamal said.

"He dropped out of school too," I said.

"I remember when I dropped out of school but Pops wasn't having it," Jarrod said.

"Did he tell you why he dropped out?" Jamal asked.

"He don't like school and wants to make money," I said.

"With all of these businesses, he could have easily gotten a job," Jarrod said.

"That's what I told him. He never needed to touch the streets." I said.

"Gotta get tough on him," Jarrod said.

"Quiet on the set. We're about to film the first video." Erin said.

We all tuned in to watch Jayla film her cake video. Jayla is super shy, so seeing her get out of her shell was cool. She has loved baking since we were kids. I'm glad she gets to do what she loves every day.

Chapter 6

Who's Chloe?

We had been filming for three hours and Jamal still needed to film his video. We were waiting for Jarrod to finish his whole chicken video. We were chilling in the living room spread out on the two couches.

"This is exhausting," Jayla said.

"It's going to be worth it," Erin said.

"Uncle, we home!" Marley called into the house.

"We're in the living room!" I called back.

Marley, Junior, Mariah, and Eric walked into the room. Everyone said hi to one another.

"How was the movie?" I asked.

"Good," Mariah said. The kids went upstairs.

"Have you told them?" Eric asked me.

"Nope," I said.

"Told us what?" Jayla asked.

"Me and y'all mom got to talk to y'all," Eric said.

"Is it bad?" Jamal asked.

"No, but it's best we tell y'all this news together." Eric looked at me. "Rell, I'm going to go by the house and get Mariah's things."

"Where is Mariah going?" Jayla asked.

"She's moving in with me," I said.

Jayla, Jarrod, and Jamal gaped at me waiting for more information.

"What's going on?" Jarrod asked.

"We're going to go check on everything," Erin said sensing this was a private matter.

Erin, Tanya, and Chloe left the room.

"Uncle Ted was inappropriately touching Mariah," Eric said.

Jayla gasped. Jarrod jumped up.

"Where is he? That's fucked up, G. She's a baby!" Jarrod yelled.

"I went by the house looking for him and he was gone. I'm sure y'all mom told him what happened and he left." Eric said.

"Is Mariah okay?" Jayla asked.

"She's just happy that we believe her and she doesn't have to go back to Nana's house," Eric said.

"Momma didn't believe her?" Jayla asked.

"She thought she was making it up," Eric said.

"That's sad," Jayla said.

"I guess since it's just us, I can tell y'all the other news," Eric said.

"I don't want to hear any more bad news," Jayla said.

"I moved out of the house," Eric said.

"What does that mean?" Jamal asked.

"Me and Momma are separated and living in our own places," Eric said.

"Are y'all divorcing after all these years?" Jayla asked.

"It's looking that way. We tried therapy and making it work and it's time for us to go our separate ways. I'm not going to lie, her taking her brother's side disgusts me and puts a nail in the coffin. I've never been more ready for a divorce."

"That's how I felt when I got a divorce from Ashley," Jarrod said.

"Are you happier?" I asked him.

"It's been six months since the divorce and I'm happier. It was a bad situation from jump, probably why our marriage only lasted two months. Coby hated having her as a stepmom and I knew I had to end it."

"Yeah, I'm glad that situation is over. Ashley was a hot mess." Jayla said.

"I agree," I said.

"Daddy, you ever getting married again?" Jayla asked Eric.

"Nah, I don't think so," Eric said.

"Let's talk about the elephant in the room," Jayla said.

"What?" Jamal asked.

Jayla looked right at me. "Who is Chloe and why are we just meeting her?"

"She's my girl and she lives in Cali," I said.

"She's a stripper," Jayla said.

"She is?" Jarrod asked.

"Was. She hasn't danced in a couple of years." I said.

"She's mad young for you," Jayla said.

"She's twenty-five. She ain't a baby." I said.

"She's fine as hell. You always fucking with bad bitches." Jamal said.

"Excuse me," Eric said.

We laughed. Sometimes we get carried away in front of Eric and he has to remind us he ain't our little friend even though we're grown as hell now.

"How did y'all meet?" Jayla asked.

"At the club," I said.

"How long y'all been together?"

"Dang you on your FBI shit right now. We've been talking for six months."

"So right after you and Chan broke up?"

"Me and Chan broke up a year ago when she was pregnant."

"You ain't ready to settle down?"

"Yeah, I am."

"And you think she's ready to be a wife? She's young and living her best life."

She brought up a good point. I never even thought about the fact Chloe is probably not ready to settle down. We haven't even talked about it.

"I had to look this girl up and boy is she drama," Jarrod said.

"Let me see," Jayla said.

Jarrod handed her his phone. She scrolled through the phone trying to get all the gossip on Chloe.

"That's her past," I said, "Hell, I got a past too."

"I don't like this girl for you," Jayla said.

"You gotta give her a chance," I said.

"I don't know. She seems like nothing but trouble."

It was now five in the afternoon and we were done filming. Chloe, Mariah, Marley, Junior, and I were headed to a food festival.

"I'm so ready to try the different foods at this festival," Chloe said.

"Me too. There's a donut truck I want to check out." I said.

"I always go back to Cali fifty pounds heavier."

I chuckled. "I gotta get back in the gym. Being surrounded by food all day got me slacking."

"You look good with the weight."

"I gotta lose this gut and get back in shape."

"I gotta get in the gym too to prepare for this summer tour."

"You should let me train you."

"You go hard in the gym. I ain't ready for that."

I laughed. "I ain't gonna do you like that."

"Are you still training people?"

"I stopped for a while but now I'm looking for new clients."

"Well sign me up because I'm tired of being out of breath while performing."

I circled the parking lot looking for a spot. We hopped out of the car. The kids walked ahead of us. We purchased our wristbands and walked into the park.

I powered on my camera and started vlogging the experience. Chloe grabbed a map so we knew which tents and food trucks to check out.

"I want to go to the taco truck," Mariah said.

"You like tacos?" I asked.

"I love them."

I smiled because Deja loved tacos too. It seemed she ate a taco a day. We went out for tacos anytime she was sad and it always brightened her mood. Her dad had a popular taco stand and he had the best food.

We walked around to find the taco truck. Mariah looked over the menu and got a grilled chicken taco and a fish taco. We waited to the side for the food.

"What y'all want to try?" I asked.

"I want to visit the Jamaican food truck and the donut truck," Marley said.

"Pops, you gonna buy me something to drink?" Junior asked.

"Yeah, you want some water?" I asked.

"Henny," Junior said.

Marley and him cracked up laughing like he told the funniest joke.

"You better not be drinking," I said.

"I was looking at this map and this truck has liquor ice cream, slushies, and cupcakes," Junior said.

"We have to try that," Chloe said.

"What age did you start drinking?" Junior asked Chloe.

"Fourteen," Chloe said without thinking. "No, I was twenty-one."

"Yeah right," Junior said.

Mariah's food was ready ten minutes later. We grabbed the two containers of food. Each container had three tacos, packets of hot sauce, and a small container of salsa. I pan the camera over the food.

"I want to try a fish taco now," Chloe said.

"Try one of mine," Mariah said.

"You're so sweet. Thank you." Chloe said.

I grabbed a fish taco and gave half to Chloe. I turned on the camera and got a video of her trying the taco and then she filmed me trying the taco.

"That's good," Chloe said.

"I don't even like avocado but I don't mind it in the taco," I said.

Chapter 7

Take Over

Early the next day, Tanya came by the house to edit videos. Tanya wanted to edit the vlog first because she said it would be easier.

"Y'all got a lot of good footage. I think this vlog should be the first video on the channel. My husband loves watching vlogs like this." Tanya said.

"Should we put it up today?" I asked.

"Nah, we'll wait until tomorrow. We want to post on Mondays and Saturdays. Filming in the restaurants and the bakery would be a good idea. It'll be good promo and good content for the channel."

"I agree. My Pops is ready to do a video." I said.

"I would love to see a video of how to make his barbeque chicken and ribs."

"That's the video he wants to do. We just have to find time to film it."

I watched Tanya as she edited the food festival vlog. She was focused and very detailed as she trimmed video clips and added effects to the video.

I powered on my laptop and went through my many emails. The doorbell rang and I ran to get the door. I opened the door and Pops stood there smiling.

"Hey Pops," I said hugging him.

"Hey, son. What you up to?"

He walked into the house and I closed the door.

"Working on the channel," I said.

We walked into the kitchen and sat down at the bar. Tanya and Pops said hi to one another.

"Where are the kids?" Pops asked.

"They're still asleep," I said. "When me and Chloe got in at three in the morning, they were playing video games on the couch."

"Where's Chloe?"

"She went to the studio to work on her album."

"When does she leave?"

"Tomorrow. She gotta get back home and get ready for the tour."

"How y'all making it work? You're here and she's there and y'all always busy."

"It's hard but we make time for one another."

"What are you doing about the school situation with Junior?"

"I'm still trying to figure it out. He don't want to go back to school but he don't have a choice. I'm trying to see if there's a way he can get his GED and be done with school. At his age, I was in talks with colleges for football scholarships. I know he ain't into sports but I gotta find him something to do. I don't want him out in the streets."

"No parent wants that. When Jarrod was out there getting into all sorts of trouble, it was hard on me. All I could do was pray and talk to him. I'm happy he finally got his act together."

"I feel bad I wasn't there for Junior like I should have been. I was on the road busy with life. Then I got injured and took time away to heal and get my mind right. It wasn't my intention to neglect the kids in the process."

"Stop beating yourself up, Rell. Your kids still need you and you can still be there for them."

"You heard about Eric and Moms?"

"Yeah. He's a good guy. I'm surprised they made it to twenty years. Your mom is a lot to deal with."

"Tell me about it."

He chuckled. "And Eric told me what happened with Ted and Mariah. He reported it to the police and found out Ted was accused of raping a fourteen-year-old."

"That's fucked up. I hope they find him and put him under the jail."

"I wish your mom did a better job at protecting her."

"Moms ain't never looked out for none of us. It was always you and Eric protecting us. Moms ain't affectionate and loving like most moms and she chose a lot of things over us. I'm happy to see her healthy and clean but she's the same old person."

Pops nodded his head. "I've accepted that she's never going to change. She is who she is."

"I gotta get to that point."

"I talked to my doctor last week and I gotta slow down. I'm praying the restaurant will survive without me being there every day."

"What's wrong with you?"

"I'm getting old."

I knew that there was more that he wasn't telling me. I had to find out what was wrong with him on my own.

"I know I've said that I don't want to take on the responsibility of the business but I'll help you out."

He smiled from ear to ear. "Thank you so much, son."

"I'm going to bring Junior by the restaurant so he can see how hard we all work and maybe he can take over in a few years. I would rather him run the business than run the streets."

Chapter 8

Passion

Chloe and I strolled the art museum looking at the different artwork along the walls. Pops was at home watching the kids.

"How was the studio?" I asked Chloe.

"So good. We finished the album."

"You have a release date?"

"Not yet. I'm excited about my first project and hope it doesn't flop."

"Your singles are charting so I can only imagine what the album will do."

We both stopped in front of a painting of a person holding a gun to their head. There was a puddle of red paint by the person's foot with a list of things like pain, trauma, and heartache.

"Man, I've been there," I said.

"Me too," Chloe said, "Life gets to be a lot sometimes and I question if I can handle it."

"You're a strong-ass person, Chloe. I always wonder how you handle it."

She wiped away a tear. We walked away to the next painting of a person appearing broken and trying to put the pieces of themselves back together.

"These paintings got me in my feelings. I feel this one too." Chloe said.

"You got to start painting more and releasing that pain. I bet it'll make you feel better."

"This has definitely motivated me to start painting again."

We kept walking around the art gallery admiring all the beautiful work. We decided to go to the pizza place next door once we were done at the art museum. We sat down at a table waiting for our order. I held her hand.

"You okay?" I asked.

"Sometimes I think about my life and get sad," Chloe said.

"Why?" I asked.

"It's some shit I regret. I know you're not supposed to regret because things happen for a reason. But I gave myself to so many people that didn't deserve me." Chloe said.

"You're young, baby girl. You have a lot of growing to do. You just gotta take those painful moments as lessons and move differently. Your past doesn't define you."

"All people do is bring up my past. I'm tired of all this shit being constantly thrown in my face. I made a lot of mistakes in my life but I'm trying to be a better person."

"You don't owe nobody shit. This is your life. You're the only one who has to wake up in your skin and walk this path. You can't let people who don't know you get to you."

"I overheard y'all talking about me. Your sister doesn't even know me and she doesn't think I'm right for you."

"Who cares? If I fuck with you, I'm not going to stop because my sister has an issue. She's judgmental like my mom."

"You never talk about your mom."

"We're not close. I love her because she's my mom. If it wasn't for Pops and my stepdad encouraging me, I wouldn't have played professional ball. My mom has been a hater all my life. She's always been a functional crackhead. I don't know how my stepdad put up with her for so many years."

"My mom overdosed when I was young and I grew up in foster care. I remember the day I found my mom facedown in the room. I was ten years old and I didn't understand."

"I'm sorry. You've been through so much, Chloe. Brighter days are ahead."

They called our number. I went up to the counter and grabbed the two pizzas and order of bread sticks. I took everything to the table. We grabbed hands and I said grace. I took a pizza slice out of the box, took a bite, and put the slice on a napkin.

"Is there anything you regret?" Chloe asked.

"I regret not being there for my sister when she needed me most. There's not a day that I don't think about her. I think I'll feel guilty about that forever."

"I'm sorry for your loss. I lost my sister two years ago and I regret not getting close to her."

"You mind me asking what happened to your sister?"

"Car accident. She has a seven-year-old daughter that her husband is raising alone. I stay in touch with her and let her know I'm here for her."

"Where does your niece live?"

"Maryland. I visit as much as I can. I'm just happy her dad is letting me be a part of her life. I want to be a good example for her."

"What's going on with your other projects?"

"I paused everything for the music. I don't know how you're juggling so much but it was too overwhelming for me."

"It's a lot running multiple businesses."

"How do you manage?"

"It keeps me busy and my mind off of things."

"Which business is your favorite?"

"I love Juicy Boil because I'm doing this with my brother and we created it together. I remember him telling me his vision and what he wanted to do and I was happy to help him make it happen. And Eric has been a great chef at the restaurant. He left a Michelin-star restaurant to work with us. That spot means a lot to me."

"You know I do nails?"

"Yeah?"

"I've been thinking about opening a nail salon."

"My baby momma, Porsha, has a hair and nails salon and she's constantly talking about how hard it is. But she's passionate about it so it's worth it to her."

"I'm still trying to find my passion."

"It's not music?"

"I don't know. I like making music and it's a nice release but it doesn't make me happy."

"I was passionate about football until I got injured. I found a new passion in philanthropy and it makes me happy to give back."

Chapter 9

Payback

The next day, I went to lunch with Porsha. We had to get on better terms with one another so we could co-parent. I'm so tired of arguing and fighting with Porsha. It ain't hurting nobody but our kids, Layla and Jackson.

I walked into the restaurant and found Porsha sitting in a booth near the back of the restaurant. And to my surprise, Jackson was sitting beside her.

"Daddy," Jackson said.

I walked over to the table and picked him up.

"Hey there," I said.

I haven't seen my baby boy in two months. I looked at Porsha. "I didn't know you were bringing him."

"He didn't feel like going to school."

I slid into the booth and sat Jackson beside me. Porsha passed him the kids' menu and crayons.

"I need you to get Layla from school and watch the kids. I have a couple of late clients today." Porsha said.

"I got you," I said.

"Layla's going to be excited to see you. It's been months since we've seen you."

"I've been busy but I'm going to come around more. What time you gonna get them?"

"Around eight or nine o'clock."

"I gotta take my girl to the airport."

Porsha rolled her eyes. "She's still here? That's why you've been ignoring Lay's calls?"

"I always answer her calls or call her back. Don't go there."

The waitress walked over to the table and took our order.

"Are you really with Chauncey? You don't think that's confusing to the kids. They considered him an uncle at one point." I said.

"They don't even know about us."

"Don't lie. Lay already told me y'all went to lunch."

"Are you here to check me about my personal business or are you here to talk about co-parenting?"

"It becomes my business when you involve my kids in some bullshit. I don't know what you two trying to prove but it's fucked up."

"Look, I don't check you about your bitch so don't check me about what I got going on."

"You serious? You stay on my ass about Chloe."

"Because she's a ho and I don't want her around my daughter."

"And I don't want Chauncey around my kids."

She rolled her eyes and took a sip of her drink. "Now, let's talk about co-parenting. I can't keep doing this alone and it's not cool for you to come around when you feel like it. I am tired of making excuses for you and wiping the tears from their eyes. You need to figure out how to be a better father because right now, you slacking and you're not a good dad to Lay and Jackson."

I looked down at the table because she was so right. I let so many things get in the way. I turned my back on them when they needed me most. I cherish the bond I have with Pops and my stepdad, Eric, and I want to have that type of bond with my kids.

"I'm slowing down and I'm going to make them my focus. Not letting anything come between me and my kids again." I said.

"You just disappeared."

"I started creating business after business because I didn't want to be home or alone with my thoughts. I ain't had a moment to sit still in forever. I'm always on the go, used to being on the road, and always training. Then, I was down for months trying to heal from the injury.

I spent those months alone with only my thoughts and it drove me crazy. Once I healed, I learned I would never be able to play again and that fucked me up. I was training so hard and pushing myself to get back on the field. Learning I just wasn't healthy enough crushed me. I've been looking for peace and trying to figure out my life since then."

"Football was your whole life."

"It was all I knew and nobody was there for me when I was down but Chloe. Somebody I considered a brother talked wild shit about me in interviews."

"That's why you and Chauncey fell out? He said you were trippin' off the pills."

"He was the one that started the rumor I was addicted to drugs. Dudes can be right next to you smiling in your face wanting what you got. That's the reason he's with you now."

Porsha was taken aback. "You think he's using me to get back at you?"

"I don't know his intentions, but you need to be careful."

She nodded her head taking in everything I said.

I decided to change the topic. "How's the salon doing?"

"We've been in business for almost three years and it's going better than ever. I've worked hard for this moment. I have celebrity clients now and coming out with hair products."

"All the shit you wanted to happen is finally happening."

"Right. I wake up and can't believe my dreams have come true."

I fell in love with Porsha because she was ambitious and a go-getter. She's been working to have a beauty shop for years. Our relationship was a rollercoaster. We broke up for a while, got back together, had Jackson, got engaged then broke up again. It just never worked between us.

The waitress brought the food to the table and made sure we were good before walking away. Jackson sat up on his knees to reach for the food. I put the chicken finger basket in front of him. I said grace and we began eating.

"See, why can't all our conversations be like this?" I asked.

"Because you be on that rara shit all the time," Porsha said.

"I just had to see wassup with you. I ain't talked to you in a while and now you fucking with this clown."

"Stop being disrespectful. What happened between y'all has nothing to do with me."

"You don't think you owe me any loyalty? You got us out here looking crazy."

"Don't nobody know. And you've had me looking crazy on a few occasions. You'll be with me then be posted on the blogs with some random bitch. And I never said anything. I let you keep me a secret like I meant nothing to you. Most people didn't even know we were together. You've always been disrespectful to me and I took it and now you wonder why I'm not loyal. You're crazy and outta your mind if you think I owe you anything. I've had every chance to expose you and I haven't."

"I'm sure you're about to do just that on the show."

She looked away and I knew I was right. This show was going to flip my world upside down and I'm not ready for the backlash.

"I never meant to do you dirty, Porsha. I was being selfish and never thought about how my wild actions affected you. You've been around since high school. You were by my side when Deja died. Our relationship has always been complicated. You let me do me as long as I came home to you. I know you probably didn't want that but I was wilding. You know I got nothing but love for you. I don't want to keep fighting with you."

Porsha grabbed a napkin and wiped her tears. I held her hand as she got herself together.

"What's wrong?" Jackson asked.

"Nothing. Mommy is okay. I'm just happy." Porsha said.

"You're crying," Jackson said.

"I'm crying happy tears." Porsha looked at me. "Rell, I appreciate you saying that. You never told me how much I meant to you. We were best friends before the relationship drama."

"You know me better than anybody. That's why I questioned why you're with the enemy. You ain't never cross me like this."

"It's complicated, Rell. We started talking and I liked him. I ain't trying to hurt you."

"As much as I hate that dude, I want you to be happy. So, if he makes you happy, I'll back off. You're a beautiful person and I think you deserve better, Ma."

Chapter 10

Tell Me

Chloe and I were chilling in my bedroom as Jackson slept soundly in the bed. I sat on the edge of the bed and watched Chloe pack her suitcase.

"What you do today?" I asked.

"I took a dance class, did a couple of radio interviews then had lunch at your Pops' restaurant."

"I'm sure he was happy to see you."

"Yeah. He's always cool and he kept thanking me. I guess he thought I had something to do with your decision to take on the business. I'm like Rell is too hard-headed for me to convince him to do anything."

I laughed. "What do you think about moving here?"

"I love it here but Cali will be home for now. There's a lot of trouble here and I've seen this city chew people up and spit them out."

I smiled. "You strong enough to handle it."

"I don't know. What you do today?"

"I checked out a couple of schools with Junior and got him registered at this alternative school."

"Did he like the school?"

"He didn't like any of the schools we went to. I just picked the best one for him. He's not old enough to do the GED program so we found this open campus school where he can take more courses and get done quicker."

"That's a good option for him."

"And he'll be working with me and Pops. The goal is to keep him so busy he don't have time for the other shit."

"Right."

"I also went to lunch with Porsha."

"And how did that go?"

"We had a little argument but things turned around. I realized I hurt her and I felt bad."

Chloe looked up. "How did you hurt her?"

"I was doing me and not caring about our relationship."

"So, you cheated?"

I hated to even admit this. "Yeah, a few times."

"You seem the closest to Porsha out of all your baby mommas."

"We've known each other since high school. She's been by my side through a lot."

"Is there a chance y'all could get back together?"

"Nah, it has never worked between us. We have finally closed that chapter and want to move on."

"Why didn't it work?"

"We were both just busy. She was working hard to open her salon. I was on the road playing ball. We just didn't have time for one another."

"How did you meet Chantel?"

"She used to bartend at this club I went to all the time."

"What happened between y'all?"

"Entirely too much."

Chloe laughed. "How long were y'all together?"

"Two long years."

"You never talk about Marie."

"I ain't fucked with Marie in twelve years since Kennedy was born. She remarried years ago and stayed out of the way. She's a good momma to Kennedy and Junior."

She smiled.

"Now tell me about your exes," I said.

"Man, all you got to do is search me and they all come up."

"You really messed with all those people they linked you with?"

"Nah, some of them were just friends. My last guy was Ty, the baller."

"You kidding?"

"No, why?"

"That's who Chantel is dating. Now I know why she's trippin'."

"She can have him."

"What happened?"

"He was a liar. I can't prove he cheated but I'm sure he did. We were only together a year and I had to call it quits. Before him, I dated rappers, labelheads, and ballers."

I nodded my head not sure what to say. Now I had to wonder if the golddigger rumors about her were true. She seemed genuine and like she had changed. She's not open about her exes and this is the most she has told me. I guess because all of her business is on the web, she doesn't feel the need to open up about it.

"What do you like about our relationship?" I asked.

"I can be myself. I can be Chloe. I don't have to be KoKo around you. KoKo is a character and I get tired of playing her at times. I want people to get to know the real me. You don't pay attention to the shit on the web and blogs. I can tell you're genuine and a good person.

I feel like we're both trying to heal from shit and grow into better people. And that's how we connected. Not a lot of people know I grew up in foster care, that my sister was killed, or any of those personal things I've told you. I felt comfortable enough to open up and tell you those things."

If this wasn't real, she was putting on a good act.

"Let me check on Junior to make sure he ain't snuck out."

I left the bedroom and walked down the steps to the living room. Junior was lying on the couch watching a movie. I sat down in the recliner and reclined the chair back.

"Wassup son?" I said.

"Pops, I gotta tell you something," Junior said not looking away from the television.

Now I was scared to hear what he had to say.

"Sit up, pause the movie, and talk to me," I said.

Junior sat up and found the remote to pause the movie.

He looked over at me. "You can't get mad."

"I'll try but I don't know what you 'bout to tell me."

"You want the really bad news or just the bad news first?"

"Boy, just tell me."

"I got court in a week."

I sat up in the recliner. "What did you do?"

"They're saying armed robbery but I ain't have a gun or weapon on me."

"Does your mom know?"

"Nah, I had my cousin come get me and I never told her."

"You have a lawyer?"

"I got a public defender."

I shook my head. "Boy, you asking for a life sentence."

"I didn't want you to be mad at me so I didn't tell you."

"Nah, I'm angrier that you didn't tell me. Now I only got a week to get you out of this."

"I thought I could handle it. The public defender wants me to take a plea deal and I don't know what to do."

"Have you admitted anything to anyone?"

"Nah, I ain't stupid."

I side-eyed him. "When did you start getting into all this nonsense?"

"I hated school so I would skip class and go to my cousin's house. I saw him with all this money and nice things. I wanted the same."

I looked at him confused. "But you come from money. You look crazy out there."

"I wanted my own money."

"You could have come to me and I would have given you a million tips and ideas to make money...legally."

"I was mad at you because you weren't around and never had time for us. It was like we meant nothin' to you. I didn't want to ask you for nothin'."

"This past year was rough for me."

"It was rough for me too, Pops. Momma divorced Kareem and he only fuck with his own kids and not me and Kennedy. And we couldn't see or call you so it was like we had nobody."

"I'm sorry, Junior. I can admit that I've been selfish, and I want to do better. Give me a second chance. I want to make it right."

"I love you, Pops."

I was shocked to hear that. I stood and hugged Junior. His shoulders shook as he cried. This past year that I've been distant, Junior needed me most.

"I love you, son. It's all going to work out."

He pulled away from the embrace and wiped his eyes. "Do you know why I needed the money so bad?"

"Why?"

"I got a baby on the way. She was too far along to get an abortion."

I didn't know what to say. "You're fifteen, Junior. You ain't ready to be a dad. Can't believe you out here fucking with no protection."

"I didn't have it on me, Pops."

"You and the girl cool?"

"Not really."

"She giving you hell?"

"Yeah."

"Buckle up, Junior, it's just getting started."

Chapter 11

Back Together

I picked up everyone from school and went to a taco restaurant with Chloe. We had to combine two tables so we could all sit together. Chloe sat across from me and Layla sat next to me.

Marie was on her way with Kennedy. Kennedy got suspended for fighting and Marie wanted her to stay with me for a few days.

I picked up the menu.

"Figure out what y'all want," I said.

"Everything. I'm starved." Marley said.

"Me too," Junior said.

The waitress introduced herself as Cassi and took our drink order. I watched her sashay away and Chloe glared at me. The waitress was fine as hell and thick, I couldn't help myself.

"What?" I said to Chloe.

"You know what. You ain't slick." Chloe said.

I could only smirk. I looked over the menu with Layla and Jackson. They were both picky eaters and trying to figure out what to order them was hard.

"Do y'all like corn?" I asked them.

"No," Jackson said.

"Yes," Layla said.

"Y'all want a burrito, taco, or quesadilla?" I asked.

"No," Layla said.

"Taco," Jackson said excitedly.

"What you want on your taco?" I asked Jackson.

"Chicken and cheese," Jackson said.
"That's it? No lettuce, tomatoes, or guacamole?"
"Yuck," Jackson said.
"Layla, does your brother eat tacos?" I had to make sure because Jackson says a lot of things and then the food arrives and it's not what he wanted.
"He eats soft tacos all the time," Layla said.
"Layla might like nachos. They have one here with chicken, rice, and corn." Chloe said.
"You like rice?" I asked Layla.
"Yes," Layla said.
Now that I knew what to order for them, I looked at the menu for myself. Cassi returned to the table with our drinks. I helped Jackson put the straw in his cup.
"Are y'all ready to order?" Cassi asked.
"Y'all know what y'all want?" I asked.
"Yeah," Marley said.
We went around the table telling her what we wanted. We handed back the menus and Cassi walked away.
I spot Kennedy and Marie walking into the restaurant. Kennedy had her head down and was dragging behind Marie. Marie and Kennedy walked to the table and I looked at Kennedy funny for having on sunglasses.
Marie gave Chloe the once over and said hi to Junior. She then looked at me.
"It's been a long time. How are you doing?" Marie asked.
"I'm good. I got some shit to tell you." I said.
"Oh boy."
"Kennedy, why you got those shades on? It ain't no sun out." I said.
"Go ahead and show your dad," Marie said.
"No, it's embarrassing," Kennedy said.
"Let me see," I said.
She slowly took off her glasses and her right eye was swollen.
"Damn," Marley and Junior said.

"Looks like you got in a fight with Hulk," Mariah said.

"It was two girls," Kennedy said.

"That ain't cool. Who are they? I want to meet them at the park." Mariah said.

"We're not going to do that," I said standing up, "Marie and Kennedy, let me talk to y'all."

We walked to the back of the restaurant and stood near the restroom.

"What you got to tell me?" Marie asked.

"You 'bout to be a grandma," I said.

She gasped and put her hand over her mouth. "Shut up! Tell me you're joking. Junior got a girl pregnant?"

"Yeah, he said she's about seven months."

"Wow, the baby is almost here."

"That's not it."

She puts her hand over her chest. "I can't take anymore."

"He's fighting a case."

I had to hold her up.

"Rell, are you serious? I didn't even know he got arrested."

"His cousin was handling everything."

"That damn Melo ain't nothing but trouble. What's his charge? Does he have a lawyer?"

"Armed robbery. I got him a lawyer and he's going to get back to me when he gets the facts and evidence."

Marie sighed deeply. "Let me go talk to Junior."

"Order Kennedy some food too."

She walked away and I looked at Kennedy.

"Why did you get suspended if two girls jumped you?" I asked.

She shrugged. "They said I started it and that's not true. I was in class and they were in the way as I walked to my seat. I kept saying excuse me excuse me. They wouldn't move. I tried to go around them and they would get in the way. I pushed past them and they jumped me. Nobody even tried to get them off of me. Everybody just had their phones out recording."

I didn't want to fuss or lecture her. She was upset enough and it wasn't her fault. I hugged her.

"It's okay, Kennedy. I hate to see your eye like this. I'm just glad you're okay. Let's go eat." I said.

I grabbed her hand and we walked back to the table. She sat across from Mariah. Junior and Marie were standing in front of the restaurant. It seemed things were getting heated so I walked outside to diffuse the situation.

"Yo Pops, Moms is trippin'," Junior said.

"I'm trippin' because I want the best for you?" Marie said.

"What you want me to do? I can't unfuck the bitch and I can't take the charges away." Junior said.

I stood in between them as Marie lunged at him.

"This ain't the place to have this discussion. Junior, go back inside and watch how you speak to your mom." I said.

"She needs to watch how she speaks to me," Junior said.

I cut my eyes at him.

He threw up his hands. "My bad." He walked back into the restaurant knowing not to say anything else.

"That boy is too disrespectful," Marie huffed. She started pacing and I'd never seen her this upset.

"Let me handle him. I know all of this is hard to take in. You can't approach him crazy and expect him to listen." I said.

She took a deep breath. "You're right. I just wonder what I did wrong."

"You did nothing wrong. You can't blame yourself for his wrongdoings."

"Kennedy and Junior took the divorce harder than I thought they would."

"Junior told me Kareem stopped fucking with them."

"Yeah, he turned his back on them. I hate that for them but I can't control Kareem. He chose not to be as involved because those aren't his kids and he has that right."

"But it's fucked up. He's known them since they were little. If he cared for them like he said he did, he wouldn't have done them like that."

"I've gotten onto him about it but he doesn't care. He's hurt and wants to hurt me. It's been a year since we divorced and I'm happier and at peace with the situation."

"You looking good too. You done lost weight."

"I've been in the gym, trying to get back fine."

"You can't get back what you never lost."

She blushed and playfully touched my arm. "You're the same old charming Rell."

I could feel something happening here and I had to change the topic. "Listen, I'm here for the kids. If you ever need me, don't hesitate to call. I know I ain't always been available when you needed me but I'm home and I got nothing but time."

We had a nice time at the restaurant and I was now taking Chloe to the airport.

"That food was good. I'm ready for a nap." Chloe said.

"Yeah, I'm stuffed," I said. I cranked up the car and pulled out of the parking space.

"What ya thinking about?" Chloe asked.

"I'm happy I got almost all of my kids with me. I wish Deja was here to see Mariah and Marley."

"She's watching over them, no doubt. Did they ever catch that sicko Ted?"

"They caught him in Tennessee."

"Is your mom still supporting him?"

"Yeah, and I don't get it. If any of my siblings do anything that fucked up, I'm cutting them off. I think the drugs fried her brains."

"I'm releasing my album in two months."

"You having an album release party?"

"Two, one here and one in Cali."

"I'll be there. What do you want to do for Valentine's Day? Will you be here?"

"Yeah, I will be here since I have performances that Friday and Saturday."

"I'm going to plan something special for us."

"I can't wait. I had a good time this weekend. I know our schedules were crazy but we still spent a lot of time together."

I grabbed her hand. "Yeah, it was definitely a good weekend." I winked and she giggled.

I got an alert on my phone that someone withdrew six thousand dollars from the company's checking account. This account was used for all the businesses.

"What's wrong?" Chloe asked.

"Somebody just took six thousand dollars out of my account," I said.

"Uh-oh. Who has access to the account?" Chloe asked.

"This is the business account. All purchases and withdrawals are approved by me, so I don't know what's going on. This just ruined my whole mood."

"You can't be in no bad mood around me."

She gave me a sultry look and flicked her tongue.

I smiled. "You right. I never asked you but what are your thoughts on marriage?"

"It's not a goal for me right now."

"Do you ever want to get married?"

"I haven't thought about it. You want to get married?"

"One day. I'm thirty-five, not getting any younger, and would like to one day settle down."

"What are you looking for in a wife?"

"Go-getter, love my kids, and someone who understands my schedule can get a little crazy at times."

"Does looks matter to you?"

> "I would be lying if I said it didn't. I got to find you attractive and you got to have a good personality to match. I've met a lot of beautiful people with ugly souls."

Chapter 12

Who Did It?

It was six o'clock in the evening when we walked into the house. I lay Jackson and Layla on the couch. Mariah, Marley, Junior, and Kennedy walked upstairs to get ready for the night.

I sat at the bar in the kitchen. I logged into my laptop to see how well our first video was doing. I was shocked to see our views in the thousands. I guess having Chloe in the video helped.

Now I had to figure out who took the money from the account. I called Jarrod first.

"Wassup bro?" Jarrod asked.

"What's good, bro?" I asked.

"Not too much. What you up to?"

"I just dropped Chloe off at the airport."

"Y'all getting serious?"

"I really like her. I'm not sure if she feels the same way."

"I think she does. I was at Pops' restaurant when she visited and she was talking about you. She seems to care about you but only time will tell."

"True. Did you make any purchases today using the company card?"

"No, I haven't. I sent you a couple of things to approve though."

"I haven't had the chance to check my email."

"When are you going to upload the next video? The vlog was dope."

"We'll upload the next video on Sunday. It's going to be your whole chicken video."

"How do you think it's going to do?"

"I think it's going to do great. Food videos are so popular right now."

"I talked to Moms today. I'm worried about her because she was talking a little crazy. I think she's taking this separation hard."

"I can't feel bad for Moms. She don't give a damn about Mariah and is protecting her abuser."

"What ya talking 'bout?"

"She's still in contact with Ted. She hasn't reached out to Mariah since she moved in with me."

"See I didn't know all that. That's foul. She told me she ain't seen Ted."

"I don't know if she's seen him but she's still talking to him."

"That's crazy."

"I'm going to let you get back to work. I'll check the emails you sent me and get back to you."

"Aight, talk to you later, bro."

Next, I called Jayla.

"Talk fast, bro. I have two cake orders to get done."

"Hey to you too, sis."

"You know it gets crazy around here."

"You made any purchases today?"

"No, I've been too busy to do anything. What's going on?"

"I'm trying to see who withdrew six thousand dollars from the company account."

"Damn, that's a lot of money. You know I wouldn't take that much money without you knowing."

"I know I've been busy today and emergencies happen. I'm just trying to figure out who took it and why."

"You talked to Rod or Momma?"

"I just talked to Rod and haven't had a chance to talk to Momma."

I heard someone telling her something in the background.

"Bro, I have to go. Let me know when you find out."

"I got you. I'll talk to you later."

I called Momma next and the call went straight to voicemail. I decided to call Pops. I was getting pissed and needed to calm down.

"Hey son," Pops said.

"Sup, Pops?" I said.

"What's wrong"

"Somebody took six thousand dollars out of the company account."

"Somebody? You don't know who did it?"

"Jay and Rod said they ain't do it and I can't get in touch with Moms."

"You better call the bank and report it as fraud. You got to make a police report too."

"Damn, I ain't got time for all of that. I gotta chuck this as a loss."

"Nah, you can't just consider six thousand dollars a loss. That's a lot of money. You need to check with Jay and Rod and see if anyone else at the restaurant or bakery has access to the account like a manager or something."

"They better not be letting anybody see or touch the company card."

"It's possible somebody did it without their knowledge."

"Now, I got to review the security footage at all these spots to find the truth. I hate this shit."

"Did your girl get to your card? I like Chloe but she's known for taking a man's card and racking up."

"That didn't even cross my mind. I don't think Chloe would do that. She's changed a lot of her old ways."

"You can't put nothing past anyone."

"You right. Me, Junior, and Marley are going to be at the restaurant tomorrow so they can see how everything runs. I know this will keep them busy and out of trouble."

"I can't wait to work with them. You know I'll get them in line."

"I know, Pops."

"I got to get back to it. Go ahead and call the bank. I'll talk to you later."

"Aight, love you, Pops."

"I love you, Rell."

I put my phone down exhausted from all these calls that got me nowhere. Junior walked into the kitchen.

"You took a shower?" I asked.

"Yeah," Junior said.

"You act like you saw a ghost. What's wrong?"

He stood by the refrigerator and crossed his arms. "I got another baby on the way."

"You what?" I hopped out of my seat. "Are you serious?"

"Yeah, Quana just texted me that she's giving birth next week and wants me there."

"Did you know she was pregnant?"

"Nah, she just texted me."

"How you know that's your baby?"

"She said she ain't been with nobody else."

"You believe her?"

"Yeah, she ain't never lied to me. She's having a little girl next week."

"I want to wring your neck but that won't change shit. What are your plans? How you gonna take care of two babies?"

"I don't know, Pops. That's why I was hustling to make money."

"I got a better plan that won't lead to more trouble."

"What's that?"

"You got to help raise and provide for two babies. Go to school and work and stay outta the way."

"Quana doesn't want the baby and wants to put her up for adoption."

"Lawd! If it ain't one thing, it's another with you."

"Pops, I don't know what to do in this situation."

"If this is your baby, you are taking full responsibility for the baby. We can set up a nursery and everything."

"I ain't ready to be a dad."

"It's too late for that. You should have used a glove and you wouldn't be in this situation now."

Junior hangs his head not liking my advice. "I'm going to bed."

"Tell that Q girl that you want your child. And make better decisions going forward."

"Aight. Night, Pops."

"Good night."

He walked back upstairs looking defeated. I couldn't believe at thirty-five I was about to have two grandchildren. I can't believe Junior was this irresponsible after all the talks we had.

I sat back down at the bar. This day has been a mess. I called the bank. I wanted to lose my mind when I heard it was a fifteen-minute wait to talk to a representative.

Chapter 13

Nobody Knows

It was the next morning and I have already dropped the kids off at school. I just left the police station after filing a police report for the stolen money. I still haven't been able to get in touch with Moms.

I walked into the Juicy Boil with Kennedy. Kennedy sat at a table. Jamal and Rod were in the kitchen and I went there to chop it up with my brothers.

"Jamal, I thought you had classes on Tuesday," I said.

"I dropped that class," Jamal said.

"Why?" I asked.

"Professor was a bitch. What you up to today?" Jamal asked.

"I had to go to the police station," I said.

"Why?"

"Somebody stole thousands from me and I gotta get to the bottom of it."

"Damn, did this person think you wouldn't notice?"

"I guess so or they didn't care. I gotta see Life today. I need to stop by the bakery and juice bar to check on things."

"You got a busy day."

"Yup. Yo boy is about to be a grandpa too."

"You lying? Who's pregnant?"

"Junior got two girls pregnant."

They both stopped what they were doing to look at me.

"Damn, he's been busy," Rod said.

"Too busy," I said, "And one of the girls is not ready to be a mom so he's going to have full custody."

"He ain't ready for that," Jamal said.

"He better get ready. These babies are coming and he gotta be there for them." I said.

"Why these girls ain't get an abortion?" Rod asked.

"He said they found out too late," I said.

"I'm calling bullshit. They know his daddy is rich and think this is their ticket outta the hood." Jamal said.

"Daddy's rich but Junior's broke," Rod said.

"Exactly. They ain't seeing it like that. I'll help but that's his responsibility." I said.

"He gotta get a job," Rod said.

"He's working with Pops," I said.

"Him and Pops are going to clash," Rod said.

"Pops ain't going for it. He better get his attitude in check before he even walks in there. We're making Marley work too. His grades are slipping and he got to get back focused." I said.

"Kennedy's eye looks better. I couldn't believe the photo you sent me." Rod said.

"Marie sent me the video and it was an ugly fight. She held her own against two girls though." I said.

"Let me see the video," Jamal said.

I pulled out my phone and pressed play on the video.

"Those are two big girls," Jamal said.

"Kennedy had one before the other jumped in. She definitely held her own." Rod said.

"Y'all need me to help with anything before I leave?" I asked.

"Nope, we're good. We're just cleaning the seafood and got the sauces boiling." Rod said.

"And Rod you haven't let anyone use the company card, right?"

"Nah, I haven't. I keep it in a safe in the office. And the office is locked once everyone gets in."

"I might have to review security footage."

"Just let me know."

I dap up my brothers. "Aight y'all, have a good day. I'm going to try to come back for dinner."

I walked to the front of the restaurant. Kennedy was watching videos on her phone.

"Come on, Kennedy," I said.

She waved bye to Jamal and Rod and followed me out of the restaurant.

We climbed into the car and I made my way to the bakery. Kennedy looked out the window.

"You okay?" I asked.

"Yeah," Kennedy mumbled.

"We need to talk."

"About what?"

"Boys and sex."

She looked embarrassed, not ready to have this conversation. "Why?"

"Because obviously, I didn't prepare y'all enough."

"Why you say that?"

"Your brother has two babies on the way."

Her bottom lip dropped. I'm surprised Junior kept this away from her since they talk about everything.

"Do you have a boyfriend?" I asked.

"No."

Whew, thank the Lord for that. "Have you done anything with a boy?"

"No."

"Has mom talked to you about sex?"

"Nope, but my stepdad said it hurts and can kill me."

I tried not to burst out laughing. Kareem, her stepdad, was a trip and probably said that to scare her and it looks like it's working. "I just want you to wait. I don't want you to be pressured to just give it away to anybody. You're special and you're worth it."

She nodded her head. "How old were you when you lost your virginity?"

"I was too young. I was twelve and I didn't know what I was doing."

"Is it going to hurt?"

I cringed not wanting to talk about this even though I brought it up. "The first time, it might hurt. Hopefully, you find a guy who's gentle with you. How are you taking the divorce?"

"Momma wasn't herself for a while because Remy put her through a lot. I've known Remy since I was three and now he acts like me and Junior don't exist. It makes me sad."

"I hate he's doing y'all like this. I know how close y'all were."

"Not as close as we thought. He took me to father-daughter dances when you couldn't. He's been there for us through everything and now we can't call him."

I hated that the relationship between my kids and I was so strained. I remember when Junior and Kennedy would call Remy before they called me.

"I hope he comes around for y'all."

"I don't need him now."

I smiled. "I know I've been absent, Kennedy, but I'm here now and you can count on me for whatever."

"I know, Daddy. I love you."

"I love you too."

I parked in a parking space in front of the bakery. Kennedy reached out and hugged me. I kissed her on the cheek. My baby girl is twelve now and growing up. We climbed out of the car.

I opened the door to the bakery and Kennedy walked into the shop and I followed her to the front counter. Jayla was on the register checking customers out. Her team was busy behind her preparing orders and baking.

"It smells so good," Kennedy said. She walked over to the display case and marveled at all the desserts. I stood in line and waited for my turn to talk to Jayla.

"Hey bro," Jayla said. Kennedy popped up. "And Kennedy." Jayla came around the counter to greet us. "Kennedy, your eye looks so much better."

"Yeah, I don't need sunglasses today," Kennedy said.

"What y'all up to?" Jayla asked.

"Just checking on everyone," I said. "I see you're already busy."

"We haven't caught a break lately and I love it."

"I gotta ask you something. You can't flip out."

She crossed her arms ready to flip out. "What is it?"

"Does anyone on your team have access to the company card?"

She raised an eyebrow. "Are you assuming that someone here has something to do with the stolen money?"

"I'm not assuming anything. I'm asking a question."

"It's too early for this, Rell."

"Damn, you trippin', Jay. I'm just asking a question."

"No one has access to the card but me. You don't have to investigate shit around here. I barely ask for anything and I damn sho wouldn't steal from you."

"At some point, I'm going to check the surveillance footage here."

She rolled her eyes. "You're wasting your time. None of us in this shop have anything to do with the stolen money. Why don't you ask that gold-digging bitch where the money is?"

"Whoa! Why you going there?"

"She just posted a new photo with a Birkin. She seems like the likely suspect."

"You trippin', Jay. You and Sam must be going through it again."

"Fuck outta here, Rell. I just don't like that you're acting like we got anything to do with the stolen money."

"I see you having a bad day so I'll talk to you later."

She went back to the register to take an order.

"Can we get something?" Kennedy asked.

"We'll go somewhere else with better customer service," I said.

Jay cuts her eyes at me. And Kennedy looked at us confused.

"Come on. I know a better spot." I said.

Jayla wanted to get smart with me but didn't want to do that in front of the customers.

A customer looked at me. "I don't want to get in y'all business but this is one of the best bakeries in the area."

Chapter 14

Shady

I knocked on the door of Chantel's condo. Her man, Ty, came to the door in just his boxers. I tried not to get mad but I told Chantel I was on the way. You would think she would tell her dude so he would be dressed for company.

"Didn't think we would ever see you around here again," Ty said.

"I've been working," I said, "Y'all got Life ready?"

"Chantel getting her ready now."

Chantel walked toward us holding Life with the diaper bag on her shoulder. She handed Life to Ty even though I was standing right there. I didn't want to cause a scene so I remained cool.

"Let me get her car seat. I think it's upstairs." Chantel said.

Chantel ran up the stairs to get the seat. I watched Ty talk to Life and realized she was more comfortable with him and hadn't looked in my direction once. It's been two months but I didn't think she would forget about me. There was a time she called me Dada and reached for me when she saw me.

It sucked not having a better relationship with my kids. I'm determined to make this right and be better for all my kids.

Kennedy and I stood awkwardly outside the door. Chantel returned a few minutes later with the bright pink car seat in tow. She handed it to Kennedy.

"Me and Ty are going out tonight. I need you to keep her overnight." Chantel said.

"That ain't a problem. Can I have my child now?" I asked.

Ty kissed Life on the cheek before handing her to me. I shook my head. Chantel has only known this man for six months and got him this close to our daughter.

"Nah, that ain't cool, Playboy. Keep your lips off my daughter." I said.

"Don't be mad that another dude doing what you're not doing," Chantel said.

"You couldn't wait to throw that in my face. Just call me when you're on the way to get her."

I got Life buckled in her seat and Kennedy calmed her down as she began to fuss.

"I'll sit back here with her," Kennedy said climbing in the backseat.

I closed the door and climbed into the car. I took a deep breath. Man, I've grown so much. A younger me would have handled that differently and swung on Ty.

I backed out of the driveway and headed to the juice bar. To my surprise, Moms wasn't at the juice bar. I decided to talk to the manager, Boss.

"Wassup Boss?" I said giving him dap.

"Not too much, Rell," Boss said.

"Have you seen Moms?" I asked.

"Nah, I ain't seen her since Sunday."

"Did she work yesterday? I know you're off on Mondays."

"Nope. On Sunday, she said she felt sick. When she didn't come in on Monday, I had to come in. Now, she ain't answering my calls."

I wondered why Moms was acting so shady. "How's business?"

"It's a little slow lately. I'm used to being at the Juicy Boil and we're busy nonstop."

"I appreciate you helping out. Moms was getting overwhelmed handling this by herself." I said.

"She didn't realize how hard it would be to run a business," Boss said.

"How are the employees?" I asked.

"I found out why the turnover rate is so high here."

"Why? We have folks get hired one day and gone the next."

"They don't like Moms. She talks to them crazy and she's very disrespectful. I saw it for myself and I had to check her."

"That's Moms for you. She don't know how to talk to people. I gave her the juice bar because I wanted to keep her busy and she was interested in juicing at the time."

"It's a nice little spot. I don't understand why it's not getting more traffic."

"Maybe you can help us bring more traffic to this spot. You helped us out with Juicy Boil."

"I already have a few ideas."

"Let me hear them."

"I want to add more juices to the menu. I want to have one special juice a month. I also want to add smoothies and food items to the menu."

"Hmm, that could work. What kind of food items?"

"Smoothie bowls are popular now. We could add sandwiches and wraps to the menu. I also want to add healthy shots to the menu."

"Boss, you're onto something. I've been trying to get Momma to expand the menu but she wasn't having it."

"And we need to revamp the place and make it more inviting. I want to make the front counter a bar area."

"Boss, make it happen. I trust you and can't wait to see this business grow. I've been thinking about closing this spot."

"Nah, don't do that. I'm gonna get us some good money out of this spot first."

"You still training people at the gym?"

"Always. You getting back into it?"
"I'm thinking about it."
"We saved your spot so whenever you're ready, come back."

Chapter 15

Time Flies

I was back home on the living room floor watching Life crawl around. Kennedy was lying on the couch playing video games. Tanya was in the kitchen editing videos on the computer.

My phone announced an incoming video call from Chloe. I smiled once I saw her face.

"Hey baby," I said.

"Hey. What you up to?" Chloe asked.

"I'm just hanging out with Life and Kennedy."

"Aw, I'm so happy you're getting back involved in their lives. Just keep being there for them."

"I missed so much time with them."

"Don't focus on that, Rell. Focus on the time you have with them now. I'm sure they're just happy to be around you."

"I'm 'bout to be a grandpa."

Her jaw dropped. "You lying."

"Junior got two kids on the way."

"Twins?"

"Nope."

"Oh boy. I know you're not happy about that."

"No, but I can't change it. I just gotta support him and make sure he takes care of his responsibility."

"How does Junior feel about everything?"

"Angry because he doesn't want to be a dad."

"I don't know anybody that wants a kid at fifteen. Shit happens and you just have to handle it."

"Exactly right. He laid down now he got to stand up."
"True."
"What you up to today? You dressed a little sexy."
She stood and panned over her body. "You like?"
I bit my lip. I had to hold my tongue and not say anything inappropriate in front of the kids. "Man, I wish you were here right now."
She smiled. "I'm headed to a photo shoot."
"Those pictures better be for me only."
"I'm going to send you some pictures only for your eyes."
"What does that mean?" Kennedy asked.
I coughed and Chloe laughed.
"It doesn't mean nothing. You don't ever send a boy pictures. You hear me?"
She looked at me confused. "Okay."
"Text me baby before I have to explain anything else," I said.
"Okay. Call me later."
"I got you."
"I love you."
"I love you too."
She puckered up her lips and I pretended to kiss her. Kennedy looked at us in disgust. I ended the call and put the phone in my pocket. Life banged her blocks together and giggled.
I looked at the television. "What game is this?"
"Horizon Zero Dawn. Mariah put me on and I like it."
"How are your grades looking?"
"Good. I got all A's."
"That's what I'm talking 'bout. You like school?"
"Yeah, I like school just not my current school. There are a lot of bullies."
"Didn't you switch schools?"
"Yeah, and I hate this new school. I miss my old school and my old friends."
"Your mom told me you got into a STEM school."

"For next school year. I have to get through this school year first."

"It's almost over."

"I want to homeschool for the rest of the semester."

"I'll talk with your mom and see what we can do."

She smiled. "I would like that."

"You ready for lunch?"

"I'm starved."

"I'll go make something."

I picked up Life and walked into the kitchen. I put her in the highchair. It was Jackson's old high chair and I'm glad I kept it.

I went into the refrigerator and pulled out the containers of food that Chantel packed for Life. She had strawberries, pulled chicken and half a peanut butter banana sandwich for her. I warmed up the chicken and put the food on a plate. I put the plate on her tray. She ate the food and kicked her little feet.

I looked through the fridge for something to eat.

"Tanya, how's it going?" I asked.

She looked up. "I'm editing Jayla's heart-shaped cake video. Trying to get the video out before Valentine's Day."

"How's Rod's video doing?"

"Good. He has 11K views and counting. It helps that he's good-looking."

I took chicken breasts and asparagus out of the refrigerator. I went into my cabinet and found a bag of brown rice. It was an easy meal that I could whip up.

"Tanya, you need anything to drink?" I asked.

"If you have water, I'll take that."

I handed her a bottle of water. I pulled out my skillet and pot and started making lunch.

Life banged her hands on her tray and got more food on the floor than in her mouth. I'm so glad to be spending time with her today. It's been way too long since I've seen her.

"How old is she?" Tanya asked.

"Ten months," I said.

"She's a cutie. They grow so fast. My daughter just turned one and I'm still shocked that she's one."

"That shock doesn't go away. I'm shocked I have a fifteen-year-old and I remember when he was this age."

Chapter 16

Somebody Lying

The kids and I walked into Pops' restaurant slash record store. Mariah and Kennedy stayed up front looking through the records. I had Life strapped to my chest in her baby carrier.

Junior and Marley followed me to the kitchen. Pops was busy cooking with a team of cooks around him.

"Hey Pops," I said.

He looked up and finished what he was doing before greeting us.

"Where are the girls?" Pops asked.

"They're out there looking at the records," I said.

"Y'all ready to learn about the business?" Pops asked.

"Yeah," Marley said.

Junior doesn't say anything. Pops gave us a tour around the kitchen showing us how they prep and make certain dishes. I've always admired how hard Poppa, my grandpa, and Pops worked for this business. There was so much history here and being back in the kitchen with Pops was nostalgic.

"Y'all know how to prep?" Pops asked.

"Nah," Marley said.

"Yes sir and no sir," Pops said.

"Man, I ain't come here to work. Pops said you were showing us around." Junior said.

"This is me showing y'all around. Now wash y'all hands." Pops said.

They walked over to the sink. I saw them goofing off and sprinkling each other with water.

"Hey. Act like y'all got some sense." I said.

They walked back over to us. Pops gave them both a cutting board and knife.

"Have y'all used a knife before?" Pops asked.

"Not for cooking," Junior said.

Pops just gave him a no-nonsense look. He put a green bell pepper on Junior's cutting board and an onion on Marley's board.

"What you want us to do?" Marley asked.

"Cut them with the knife," Pops said.

"I don't need to do all this to run a business," Junior said.

"You need to first see how the business works," Pops said.

Marley chopped the bell pepper in half. "Done."

Pops and I laughed.

"I'll cut one side and show you how it's done," Pops said. Marley moved to the side and watched Pops finely dice the pepper.

"I can't do that," Marley said.

"Just try. And Junior, why haven't you started?" Pops asked.

"This is stupid. I'm trying to run the business, not work in the kitchen."

"I need everyone to leave the kitchen for five minutes," Pops said to his staff.

Uh-oh. I told Junior not to come in here with the attitude. The staff hurriedly left the kitchen. I bounced Life up and down as I noticed her trying to wake up.

"When you in my business, you do as I say," Pops said.

"Man, I would rather get a job at the mall than deal with this shit," Junior said.

"All of this because I told you to cut an onion?"

"I ain't signing up to be no cook. I want to run shit."

"You ain't running shit but your mouth."

"Fuck this. I'll get a job at the mall." Junior looked at me. "Can we go, Pops?"

"Listen to Pop-Pop. You have two kids on the way. One day you're going to be over operations. But right now, you're starting here. We all start somewhere." I said.

"I ain't starting here." He walked away and Pops removed his belt.

"Get back over here NOW!" Pops said.

Junior looked back and knew he was serious. He knew not to try it. He walked back to the cutting board and Pops showed him how to cut the onion.

"I'll leave y'all to it," I said.

I walked out of the kitchen. I looked around for Mariah and Kennedy. My heart skipped a beat when I didn't see them. I called both of their phones and they didn't answer my calls. I walked back into the kitchen.

"Aight y'all, I gotta find Mariah and Kennedy. When y'all get done, call me." I said.

An employee rushed into the kitchen. "There's a big fight happening outside."

Junior, Marley, and I rushed out of the kitchen. Outside the restaurant, there was a huge crowd. It's crazy how in a split second, chaos ensued. We walked outside to see what was going on. At the center of the chaos, were Mariah, Kennedy, and two girls fighting. I'm pretty sure these were the same girls from the other fight Kennedy had.

I groaned when I saw all the camera phones out. I didn't want another video of Kennedy fighting on the internet. Pops walked out of the restaurant and tried to restore order. Marley and Junior broke up the fight. Kennedy lunged forward. I grabbed her and pushed her to the side.

"We don't do this," I said.

She stood behind me and caught her breath.

"Fuck you, you raggedy-ass bitch!" Mariah yelled.

Marley got in front of her, held her back, and put his hand over her mouth to quiet her. Mariah still had a tight grip on this girl's hair.

"Mariah, let her go!" I yelled.

Mariah finally let her go and I pushed Mariah behind me.

"Nothing else to see. Y'all need to go home." Pops said to the crowd.

I opened the door to the restaurant and pushed the girls inside. Mariah puts her hair back into a ponytail. We sat down at a booth.

"Are y'all crazy? Why would y'all bring that drama here?" Pops asked.

They both looked down at the table. They knew by his tone that he was pissed and it was best not to say anything.

"Let me handle this, Pops. Y'all get back to work." I said. Junior, Marley, and Pops went back to the kitchen.

"What happened?" I asked.

"One of the girls, Cindy, came in here. She saw me and started talking crazy. She said she beat me up and called me scary." Kennedy said.

"And that's when I told her she wouldn't have done nothing by herself," Mariah said.

"So, Cindy and Mariah were going at it and arguing. One of the workers said we were too loud so we took it outside." Kennedy said.

"We went two doors down so we weren't in front of Pop-Pop's restaurant," Mariah said. "We were standing in front of the pizza shop. A lot of kids from Kennedy's school hang out there. This boy, Chez, came out of the shop and said bet y'all can't beat her or something like that. Kennedy was like we should go and leave it alone. I told her we should show them what we're about and not back down."

Kennedy continued the story. "Cindy's cousin, Diamond, came out of the pizza shop saying I see you brought back up this time. I didn't want to fight but Mariah told them let's go to the park since the park is up the street."

"Chez went back into the pizza shop and told everybody it was about to be a fight. And everybody came out wanting to see this fight." Mariah said.

"We started running to the park. When we got outside Pop-Pop's restaurant, Mariah swung on Cindy." Kennedy said. "Diamond jumped into the fight and that's when I jumped in."

"And we beat their asses too. Their corny asses thought they had the up on somebody when they jumped Kennedy." Mariah said.

I rubbed my temple. What was I going to do with these kids?

"I don't like y'all handling it like that. Anything could have happened and it could have gone left quickly. I'm all for self-defense but I don't want y'all picking fights. Kennedy, you have to go back to that school and Mariah won't be there. They might try you again and I don't want that to happen." I said.

"I wish they would. All she got to do is call me and I'm there." Mariah said. She was feisty and on go like her mom, Deja.

"I don't want to go back to that school," Kennedy said.

Life cried as she wiggled in the carrier. I took her out of the carrier and dug through the bag for her bottle. I cradled her in my arms and she grabbed her bottle ready to eat.

"Why can't she come to my school?" Mariah asked.

"That's not a bad idea. I gotta talk to her mom first." I said.

"Can we get something to eat?" Mariah asked.

I gave her money. "Get me a rib plate with mac and cheese and green beans."

Mariah and Kennedy walked to the front counter to order the food.

My phone lit up with an incoming call from Boss.

"Wassup Boss?" I said.

"Hey. Your mom just came by acting weird. She took all the money out of the register saying she needed to go to the bank. I just sent everyone home and closed the shop."

"That's insane. She never makes deposits during business hours."

"I tried to call her to see what's going on and the call went straight to voicemail."

"There's no money anywhere, not even the vault?"

"She said she loaned the money from the vault to Jayla."

"Oh really?"

"I'm looking through the office now. I heard from one of the employees that she always sneaks money out of the register."

I was so disappointed to hear this. "Boss, she ain't never going to change." It was a huge risk giving Momma the responsibility of running her own business but she convinced me she had changed and would be able to handle it.

"I need to review security footage there and see what's going on. Is the company card there?" I asked.

"Yeah, it was just sitting on top of the desk," Boss said.

"Which means anybody could have gotten it."

"It's usually in the safe. I don't know what your momma got going on."

"She knows better than to be this sloppy. I appreciate you calling and letting me know what's going on."

"Of course.

"How much do you think she took?"

"We haven't even had a chance to count the money. We started with three thousand, six hundred and seventy-two dollars."

"I should probably be seeing a four-thousand-dollar deposit in the account."

"Right."

"Let me call Jayla and I'll hit you back."

I called Jayla and she wasn't in the mood to talk.

"What do you want?" Jay asked.

"Did Momma loan you any money?" I asked.

"No," Jay said.

Somebody was lying and I was pissed not having answers. I never thought my family would do me dirty or steal from me. I worked hard to put us all on so there was no need to steal money. I pray my family ain't behind this theft situation.

"She just said she loaned you some money," I said.

"She ain't loaned me money in a long time since I needed help with my rent," Jay said.

"I'm just trying to figure things out. Everybody saying something different."

"I told you to stop investigating me. I ain't got shit to do with that stolen money."

"Why you so defensive about this? I can't ask you one question without you popping off. You got me thinking you know something and not telling me."

"Look, I don't know nothing about the money. I just had an officer come in here and grill me about this shit. I'm tired of it."

"How was I supposed to know you just talked to the police? I can't afford a six-thousand-dollar loss."

"What ya mean? That's nothing to you. You're rich."

"And I want to stay rich. If somebody took a dollar from you, you want it back. I want my money back. This hurts all of us, not just me."

"I get it but you're trippin'. You're questioning us, blowing us up about this, and coming to my business being rude."

"I don't expect you to get it, Jay. You ain't made it to this level of success yet."

"I can't stand your rude ass. I gotta get back to work."

I ended the call. Jay and I always bump heads. We weren't close but I will always look out for her and make sure she's good. She was bartending at the strip club and wanted more out of life. That's why we started the bakery.

I got a notice that four thousand dollars was withdrawn from the account. I was expecting a deposit.

"Fuck!" I said.

"What's wrong, Daddy?" Kennedy asked.

I looked up and saw the worried expressions on Kennedy and Mariah's faces. They had returned to the table with food.

"Nothing. Just something with work." I mumbled.

I was supposed to go to the bank and get a new account but I haven't had the time. Now whoever was stealing from my account once again. I've never been more pissed in my life.

Chapter 17

Invasion

When we returned to the house, police officers were in the yard and there was yellow tape by my garage. I looked at my cars in the driveway with flat tires and broken windows.

"What the hell?" I said.

I pulled up to the house and parked behind a police car. I got out of my car livid.

An officer walked up to me. "Sorry sir, this is an active police investigation."

"This is my house," I said.

"I need to see an ID," he said.

"I got to reach for my wallet," I said.

He nodded his head. I pulled my wallet out of my pocket and handed him my license.

"Thank you, Mr. Duncan."

"What happened?"

"We got a call from a neighbor about a robbery in progress. The neighbor couldn't see any faces but noticed a couple of them had weapons so he didn't approach them. By the time we got here, they were gone. We think it may be someone you know. They didn't cause a lot of damage besides the broken windows and flat tires on the cars and small damage to the property. They seemed to know where things were. Are there any handguns in the home?"

"Yeah, I have a gun."

"We need to know if that handgun has been stolen. We need you to do a walk-through and let us know what's been taken."

"Aight. I got to get my kids out and we can do the walk-through."

"Do you have another place y'all can go? We don't advise you to stay here tonight."

"Yeah, we got another place to go."

Luckily, I still had my townhome. I was getting ready to move out of this house and working with a realtor to find a more secure place. I walked back to the car and opened the back door.

"Somebody broke into the house. I need y'all to pack y'all bags. We're going to go to my other spot for the night." I said.

"Who did it?" Mariah asked.

"I have no clue but we're going to find out," I said.

They climbed out of the car. I took Life out of her seat and held her in my arms. A few police officers followed us into the home. My door was on the floor. There was clear forced entry at the front door and a broken window.

The television and the gaming systems were gone out of the living room. I started listing things that I noticed were missing. An officer was writing it all down and I was typing a note on my phone.

Next, I noticed my expensive ass computer and camera missing from the kitchen. Luckily, Erin had everything on SD cards and flash drives. It would have been devastating to lose all that footage. The thieves also took cookware, food, and my expensive knives.

I walked through every room. They took clothes, shoes, jewelry, televisions, computers, and my gun. I talked with a police officer at length about the stolen goods and robbery.

I could look at security footage from my phone. The officers and I tried to pinpoint the time so we could get footage of the incident. An officer guessed that this happened around six this afternoon.

We forwarded to that time and two black SUVs with tinted windows pulled up to the house. About eight people jumped out of the vehicles. They all had their faces covered. A couple of them smashed the windows of my sports car and another was going in my Jeep. Another person was breaking the front window of the house. And I could see another one fidgeting with the front door. The person at the door stood back and kicked in the door.

That explained why my door was off the hinges. I had to get someone out here to put the door back on so we could secure the place.

I switched to the inside camera and they all split up and took things from different rooms. Watching this only made me more upset. I worked hard for my shit.

Chapter 18

It's Time

After such a draining and long day, I followed the kids into the townhome.

"This is nice, Daddy," Kennedy said.

"I hope they find the clowns that broke into our house," Marley said.

"Don't worry about that. We're going to get to the bottom of it. Y'all get settled in. I'll be in the living room with Life." I said.

I kept walking through the house as the kids ran upstairs. I sat on my velvet couch in the living room and turned on the television. I lay Life beside me. I don't know who was after me or why but this shit had to stop.

A call from Chloe popped up on my phone. I didn't want to talk to her but answered the call anyway.

"Hey," I said.

"I just saw a blog that you got robbed. Are y'all okay?"

"We're good. We weren't there, thank God for that. The kids were shaken up."

"I'm sorry that happened to you. I pray they find who did it."

"Somebody stole more money from my account. This time four thousand dollars."

"Is this the same person that stole the six thousand dollars?"

"The police think so. I gotta go to the bank and get this straightened out."

"Your sis is being shady and saying I had something to do with the robbery."

"You serious?"

"Yeah, she commented on a blog that I was behind the robbery and set you up."

"Ignore it. She's been in a bad mood all day."

"I know you've seen the posts and articles about my past. You're probably wondering if I have anything to do with the stolen money and robbery. I ain't into that scamming shit anymore and it was one of the biggest mistakes I've made. There was a point in my life when I was hurt by so many and I wanted payback. But that was my past and I was young and dumb. I ain't the same Chloe from back then."

"You don't have to explain that to me, Chloe. I already know that. I don't think you're behind any of this shit. It'll all come to light soon."

"I'm tired of being judged for my past. It's like no one will ever see me differently. I'm always going to be a stripper ho and scammer to people."

"Don't let it get to you, Ma."

I heard her sniffles.

"Are you crying?" I asked.

"I'm so happy you're getting to know me. I appreciate that. It just makes me so emotional."

"Don't let this internet shit get to you."

"I'm going to call you later. I gotta get myself together. You've had a hard enough day."

"If you need me, I'm here. Did something happen today?"

"I had a producer try it today. He won't let me have two of my songs. My team is working on it but I'm stressed. I want my first album to be perfect."

"And it will be. You're talented, Chloe. It's all going to work out. Let your team handle it and don't stress about it."

Junior ran into the room with a panicked expression on his face. "Quana is having the baby!"

"Oh shit," I said.

"What's going on?" Chloe asked.

"Junior's girl is in labor," I said.

"Prayers to y'all. Call me later."

"I will."

I ended the call. "Let me call Eric to see if he can come over and watch the house."

Junior paced the floor. I called Eric and he agreed to come over.

"Watch Life for a second," I said.

Junior sat on the couch. I ran upstairs. Mariah and Kennedy were in one of the bedrooms lying on the bed watching television.

"Hey girls, me and Junior gotta go to the hospital," I said.

"What's wrong?" Kennedy asked.

"Q is having her baby," I said.

"Can we come?" Mariah asked.

"You guys can come once the baby is born," I said.

I kissed them on the cheek and walked down the hall to the next guest bedroom. Marley was on his laptop listening to music.

"I'm 'bout to head to the hospital with Junior. Eric is coming over to watch the house. If you need anything, call me."

Chapter 19

She's Here

Ten hours later, Quana gave birth to a baby girl via emergency C-section. Ava is here and she's beautiful. It was ten in the morning and it has been a long night. Junior, Marie, and I were in a different room from Quana watching Ava sleep. Our lawyer was on the way to make sure all of the paperwork was filled out correctly.

"I can't believe I have a little girl," Junior said looking at Ava.

"I can't either. She's beautiful and I think she looks a lot like you." Marie said.

"I gotta do right by her. I want to see her get big."

"Just stay away from that nonsense and focus on school and work," I said.

"I'm staying outta the streets. I got little ones depending on me."

"And you need to listen to Pop Pop so you can run the business one day."

"I'm going to do better."

"Yo Marie, I need Reem's number," I said.

"I'll text it to you," Marie said.

"Kennedy wants to go to school with Mariah."

"She's been talking about changing schools for months now."

"I would like it if they went to school together. They'll have one another for whatever."

"Is she going to move in with you?"

"That's up to you. I think the drive is too far for you."

"Is your new house going to be for the same school?"

"Yeah, it's in the same area. My realtor got me a nice spot. My new house is gated and the neighborhood has security."

"Mansion, huh?"

"Yeah, and it's nice. It has a guest house so Junior and his little ones will have their own space."

"I'm proud of you, Rell. You work so hard."

That meant a lot coming from Marie. She's always been the hardest on me to make sure I'm living right and doing right by my kids.

Our lawyer, Benson, walked into the room. We talked about the full custody agreement and the legality of everything. We just had to wait for the DNA results to finalize everything. A nurse came in to take Ava to the baby nursery for testing and observation. Benson left some time later.

"I got to get to work," Marie said.

"And I gotta go to the bank," I said.

"Y'all leaving me?" Junior asked looking terrified.

"You got it. I'll be back as soon as I can." I said.

Marie and I walked out of the room.

"Can you believe our baby got a baby?" I asked.

"No, I can't believe it. I'm trying to support him but I know he has such a long road ahead. I'm worried he's not ready." Marie said.

"He gotta get ready. The baby is here now. I hope he stops all the other foolishness and gets his life back on track." I said.

"I've spent so many nights worried about that boy and if he would make it back home."

"I got it now, Marie. Let me do all the worrying."

She smiled. "I know you got it. You're a great dad."

We went our separate ways at the parking deck. I called Eric when I got in the car.

"Sup Rell?"

"Sup Eric? You got everybody to school?"

"Yeah, just waiting on Chantel to get Life."

"She was supposed to get her a couple of hours ago. What happened?"

"She said she's running behind."

"You need me to come home? I got to run to the bank and sign for this house."

"Nah, handle your business. I took the day off."

"I appreciate you, Eric."

"Of course. I'm always here for y'all."

We talked for a few more minutes before we ended the call. I pulled out of the parking space and made my way to the bank.

As soon as I got to the bank, two thousand dollars was withdrawn from the account. What the hell was going on? I've had a total of twelve thousand dollars stolen from me. And Momma still hasn't deposited that four thousand dollars she took from the juice bar into the account. I tried to calm myself before going into the bank, but I was livid.

I was glad my usual banker, Tony, was free. We decided to go into the office to talk.

"Man, I'm mad as hell right now," I said.

"Tell me how I can help you," Tony said.

"Like I told you on the phone the other day, someone is taking money out of my account. I reported the charges and filed the police report. A phone rep told me the account would be locked and no one would be able to touch the money but it's still happening."

"Okay, let me take a look at the account. We will set you up with a new company account and get all funds transferred to the new account."

"And this time I don't want nobody else on the account. No authorized users or nothing. I want to be the only one over this account."

"So, you want to remove Jarrod, Jamal, Jayla, and Janet from the account?"

Janet is my momma, if you're wondering.

"That's correct," I said.

We sat around for what seemed like hours getting everything corrected. I felt so much better when I left the bank. I'm just hoping we can get to the bottom of this and I can find out who stole the money from my account.

Chapter 20
A Real One

I'm on the way to my new house to meet my realtor, Keisha. I wasn't ready for the stress of trying to sell one place and get moved into another but my kids' safety comes first and this move has to happen immediately.

I answered a call from Rod.

"Wassup bro?" I said.

"Just calling to check on you. You've had a crazy twenty-four hours." Rod said.

"Yeah, I have but ain't nothing I can't handle," I said.

"I heard Q had her baby," Rod said.

"She did and Junior is scared out of his mind."

"We know that feeling but he's going to be aight."

"I just left the bank. I got a new account so get rid of the card you have. I don't have authorized users and I'm the only owner of this account. I don't want anyone else having access to this account so whatever you need, I'll order it for you."

"I understand, bro. If someone stole twelve bands from me, I wouldn't let nobody even see the new card."

"I'm glad you understand. Jay ain't been understanding shit and giving me a hard time."

"That's Jay for you. She's crazy like Moms."

"It ain't cool. Wish she would chill out sometimes."

"Her and Sam going through it. He cheated again."

"She ain't going to leave him so why does she care?"

"She deserves better but she keeps putting up with his shit."

"Her issues with Sam ain't got nothing to do with me. She needs to stop taking her anger out on me. Ya feel me?"

"I feel ya. What you up to?"

"Headed to the new house. I'm keeping a low profile with this place. No parties or nothing."

"I can't wait to see it. From the pictures, it looks perfect for you and the kids."

"It is. It even has a pool and a nice big backyard. I can't wait for the kids to see it."

"How many bedrooms?"

Eight."

"That's a lot of house."

"I need the space. We're going to have a game room, an office space, and turning the basement into a gym. You and your baby boy, Coby, are invited whenever. I know he's going to love the game room."

"You know we're coming over."

"What's going on between you and Allison?"

"Ain't nothing, bro. I'm too busy and she ain't like that."

"Y'all were together for a lil minute too."

"Yeah, almost a year. The grind don't stop for no one. Feel me?"

"I feel ya. How's the day going?"

"We 'bout to open for lunch in a little bit. We got two big groups coming in so it's going to be a busy day."

"I'm going to stop by for dinner. Also, Erin and I want to come to the restaurant and film for the channel."

"Just let me know when. We can film before the business opens."

"That's a good idea. I gotta get a new camera first."

"I'm still mad they broke into your shit, bro. I remember when a group of teens broke into my car and stole my gun and laptop."

"It's fucked up. I'm ready to see who's behind all this shit."

"Me too, bro. When does Junior go to court?"

"Friday."

"How is it looking?"

"Michael is trying to get them to drop the charges but it can go either way at this point."

"What's the punishment?"

"Since it's his first offense, it can be probation, fines, or some type of program."

"How does Junior feel about that?"

"You know Junior. He acts nonchalant about everything. I know he's worried about how it's going to go but wants to be a tough guy."

"I know how that is. I spent many years in and out of the system."

"I'm glad you turned it around, bro. I hated visiting you in there."

"Roughest two years of my life. I even had to miss Deja's funeral and that killed me. That was a rough time for me."

"It was rough for me too. But we're better than ever. And Deja is with us and watching over us."

"I feel her next to me at the most random times. Whenever I feel low, I hear her encouraging me and telling me to keep going. I had a dream about her last night. We were just at a park talking about life. I miss her every day."

"I still feel guilty, bro. I was away on the road and couldn't be there like she needed. One day, she called me crying and saying she was ready for a change. She was pregnant and just wanted better for the kids.

I knew she was serious this time and we made plans for her and the kids to come to Texas and stay with me. It was going to be her opportunity to restart her life and get away from that crazy dude. She wanted to work in social services and get her life in order. On the day she was supposed to board a plane -" I paused and choked back tears. It was still so hard to talk about this.

"On the day she was supposed to change her life, her coward-ass boyfriend shot and killed her with Mariah and Marley in the next room. It still makes me so angry. And I think about how Aaliyah fought for an entire month to live and she didn't survive that attack either."

"I always think it's so unfair Deja didn't get a chance to live out her dreams. Even though this clown will rot in prison, he still has his life when he violently took hers. Deja was such a beautiful person. She didn't deserve that, no one does."

"I'm thinking about the day I had to go to the house. As soon as I found out she got killed, I got a flight to Atlanta. It was me and Pops that packed up the house. We saw all the blood tracked through the house – a bloody handprint on the living room wall. Deja died fighting and protecting her kids."

"I recently read up on the court case and it gave me chills."

"It was hard sitting in court and hearing it. Deja was my best friend. She supported me through it all. Always had my back. She was a real one. Me, you, and her were the three Musketeers."

"I remember when y'all ain't want me to tag along with y'all."

I chuckled. "Pops made us bring you anyway."

Chapter 21

Be There

Keisha, the realtor, was in the kitchen when I arrived at the house. My kitchen was huge with a walk-in pantry and state-of-the-art appliances. Keisha and I took a tour around the property. I was sure that this was the place that I wanted. We toured the guest house beside the house, and I knew Junior would love his new space.

This house was perfect for my family. I have already hired interior designers and movers and was ready to make this move. I looked around at the house, the guest house, the pool, and the huge backyard. All of my hard work paid off.

Keisha and I walked back to the kitchen. She stood on one side of the island and I stood on the other.

"What do you think?" Keisha asked.

"I love it. You picked a good one." I said.

She smiled. "I'm glad you like it. As soon as I saw it, I thought of you. Are you thinking about selling or renting the townhome?"

"I think I want to rent it out but I'm not sure."

"Give it all the thought that you need."

I filled out paperwork to finalize the sale. After about twenty minutes of going over paperwork, I had a new house in my name and keys to an eight-thousand-square-foot mansion.

I climbed back in my car and made my way to the townhouse. Eric said Chantel still hasn't picked up Life and I can't reach her.

I opened the door to the house. Eric was on the couch watching sports highlights on the television. Life was sitting on the carpeted floor playing with her toys. I walked into the kitchen and made a snack.

"Where's Kennedy?" I asked.

"That girl is still asleep," Eric said.

I looked at my phone to check the time. "It's almost one o'clock. She's going to sleep the day away."

"She stayed up late worried about Junior."

"How late?"

"She was up until four in the morning."

"Jeez. Has Chantel reached out yet? I've been calling and calling and she's not answering."

"Nah, she hasn't reached out to me."

"This isn't like her."

"I think she's hungover and still asleep. She sounded drunk when I talked to her at six this morning."

"Oh, she had a wild night out? That explains everything. Have you talked to Moms?"

"I can't get in touch with her. We're trying to serve these divorce papers and no one knows where she is. I'm ready to move on with my life."

"You got a new lady already?"

"I'm talking to someone but it's hard when you're still married. Now we can't find Janet so who knows when this divorce will happen."

"She left the restaurant on Sunday and said she was going to deposit four thousand dollars in the account and that hasn't happened. All of this shit is making it hard to keep these businesses afloat. After I pay the bills and employees, I'm going to be left with nothing."

I sat on the couch beside Eric with my turkey sandwich in my hand.

"Just keep going, Rell. This ain't going to break us. Your businesses are doing well and you'll get that money back. And you know Boss is going to turn things around at the Juice Bar. You got to be patient."

"How do you like working at Juicy Boil?"

"It feels like home. I've been a chef at a few restaurants and this has been the best experience. I like coming up with new recipes and being able to cook what I like to eat. And people are so appreciative and always say they love my food. It's a cool environment to work and your brother, Rod, is on top of everything. It makes me so proud to see how far y'all have come."

"We're just glad you came to work with us. I never thought you would leave that Michelin-star restaurant for us."

"I wanted to support y'all, it was a no-brainer for me."

"Have you talked to my Pops lately?"

"We talk all the time."

"Did he mention any health problems to you? He's being very secretive about it."

"He mentioned outpatient surgery but he didn't say why."

"Really? He told me his doctor wanted him to slow down. I wonder what's going on with him."

"I'll talk to him. You know your Pops don't like to open up about things like that."

"I know it. He might talk to you."

"You took care of everything?"

"Yup, got a new bank account and a new house. I got to fix up the old house and put it on the market."

"Me and Janet trying to sell our old house too."

"I thought Moms was staying there. Where is she at if she's not there?"

"I don't know. She told me I could sell the place. It's one less thing to fight about in divorce court. I went by the place and all of her things were gone. I'm spending so much money to fix the place up."

"I can't believe y'all selling the house. Guess it's really real."

"It's bittersweet. We've been in that house for fifteen years."

"You need to check your daughter too."
"What Jay do now? Y'all have always butted heads."
"She's just trippin'. Just make sure she's okay."
"Trippin' how?"
"She became irate when I asked her questions about the stolen money and she's accusing Chloe of setting up the robbery."
"I'll have a conversation with her. I think her and Sam are having problems again."
"Rod said the same thing."
"I wish she would leave that dude alone."
Kennedy stumbled down the steps.
"Hi, Papa and Daddy," Kennedy said.
"Hey, baby," I said.
"Hey, Kennedy," Eric said.
Kennedy sat on the couch beside me and rested her head on my shoulder.
"Your mom agreed to let you change schools."
"Yes! Do I move in with you or stay with Mommy?"
"That's up to you."
"I want to be with you."
"I heard you and your mom been bumping heads lately."
"She just doesn't understand. It's hard to talk to her."
"She thinks you don't like the rules and being rebellious."
"She's strict with me but let Junior do whatever. She won't let me go anywhere."
"Where do you need to go at twelve?"
Kennedy rolled her eyes. "See? You don't get it either."
"I just wanted to know where you want to go."
"Movies, mall, or even the library. She always says no."
"She wants to protect you. You don't need to go anywhere alone. Little boys and girls getting snatched up like crazy. It ain't safe."
"I'm going to make a bowl of cereal now." Kennedy stormed out of the room.

I shook my head. "What am I going to do with these kids?"

"Keep being the amazing father you are," Eric said.

Chapter 22
Let's Talk

Chantel finally came at two in the afternoon to get Life. Eric has left and gone home.

"What took you so long?" I asked packing Life's bag.

Chantel adjusted her sunglasses on her face. "I don't want to talk about it."

I walked to the front door and handed her the bag. "You good? Sound like you want to cry."

"I'm good."

"If you need me to keep Life until you get it together, I can."

"I'm fine."

"Come on, Life. Mommy's here."

Life crawled to the front door and I picked her up.

"Daddy will see you soon baby." I kissed her on the cheek and handed her to Chantel. "Do you need the car seat?"

"Nah, I got her a new one so you can have the other one."

She walked to her car and got Life buckled in her seat. She waved in my direction and climbed into the car. She pulled away and I walked back into the house. I joined Kennedy on the couch.

"In a few minutes, we gotta go and get everyone from school," I said.

"Will I get a chance to see my new school?"

"Tomorrow, we're going to do a tour and get you registered."

"When do I start?"

"We'll get all of that information tomorrow."

I got up from the couch, gathered my keys and wallet, and put on my jacket.

"Let's go, Kennedy."

We left the house and got in the car. I picked up Mariah and Marley from school. I decided to go to the Juicy Boil for dinner. The restaurant was crowded but we found a booth.

"How was school?" I asked once we were seated at the table.

"It was straight," Marley said.

"You paying attention?" I asked.

"Yeah," Marley said.

"Doing your work?" I asked.

"Yeah," Marley said.

"Did Pops give you your work schedule?"

"I work on Tuesdays and Thursdays when I don't have practice or games."

"When do you start?"

"Next Tuesday."

"You think you want to one day own a business?"

He shrugged. "I don't know. That's Junior's thing, not mine."

"What's your thing?"

"Music."

"Really? Do you sing or rap?"

"Rap. And I like making beats."

"That's dope. You know I support you." I looked at Mariah. "How was your day?"

"Good. We're getting ready for Friday's game. Are you coming?"

"I'll be there."

A waiter walked over to get our order. My phone vibrated on the table with an incoming video call from Junior.

He was lying in a hospital bed cradling Ava in his arms. I showed the screen to Marley, Mariah, and Kennedy. They talked with Junior for a little bit and were so excited to see the baby. I took the phone from Mariah.

"How's it going, son?" I asked.

"She can eat," Junior said.

I smiled. "She got an appetite like you then."

Junior laughed. "Moms just left and we had a good conversation. We didn't have to get loud with one another and it was just cool to talk to her."

"That's good. I'm glad y'all sat down and had a conversation."

"Are y'all coming by the hospital?"

"Yeah, as soon as we're done with dinner."

"Did you talk to my lawyer, Mike, yet?"

"Yeah, we're trying to get everything together for Friday. They're not trying you as an adult and you better thank God for that."

"Am I looking at any time?"

"We're pushing for community service or probation. It's all up to the judge."

"I would rather serve time than be on probation."

"Don't say that. We would rather have you out here than in there."

"I heard from my cuz that probation is hell."

"You just got to follow the rules and stay out of trouble. As long as you're working and going to school, you ain't got to worry about being in trouble."

"I'm going to stay outta the way."

"Did Pops give you your schedule?"

"Yeah, he only put me on for three days."

"That's all you need. I don't want you slacking in school. As long as you do well in school, you will get an allowance."

"School is boring, Pops."

"I don't care how boring it is, you still gotta finish."

Chapter 23

No Contact

Friday is here!

The DNA test confirmed that Ava is Junior's daughter and she was cleared to go home early this morning. Marie was at the house with Kennedy and Ava while Junior and I were in court.

I sat in the front row as Mike and Junior stood in front of the judge. I didn't know how this would go but I'm praying Junior is coming home with me.

I listened as the judge gave options for the case. If he pleaded guilty, he would get six months of probation and sixty hours of community service. And if he pleaded not guilty, he could risk taking this to trial and losing. We chose to plead guilty. Junior wasn't happy about probation.

We walked out of the courtroom. I went to the counter to pay his fines and fees. We walked out of the courtroom with probation papers in hand. Junior pouted the whole way home. Marie and Kennedy were so relieved to see him.

"What's wrong, Junior? You don't seem too happy." Marie said.

"I don't want probation," Junior mumbled.

"It's only six months. You can stop smoking for six months." I said.

"I'm going to bed. Can y'all watch Ava?" Junior asked.

"Yeah, we got the baby," Marie said.

Junior walked out of the house to the guesthouse.

"The movers should be here in thirty minutes. I gotta go to the police station and review the footage. Eric said he's going to come by in a little bit." I said.

"Okay, I'll hold it down until Eric gets here," Marie said.

"And Porsha is bringing Jackson by. I'm keeping Jackson and Layla this weekend."

"I ain't seen Porsha in so long."

"She said she's going to be on her best behavior."

"She better be. And I was watching the news and it looks like Ted posted bail."

I looked at her shocked. "What judge thought it would be a good idea to grant him bail?"

"I have no idea. I was just as shocked watching the story. The sicko shouldn't be back on the streets."

"I wonder who paid the bail."

"Well, your mom was walking out of the building with him."

That shocked me more than hearing he got bail. "You gotta be kidding me."

"No, here's the story."

She showed me the article and the photo of him leaving jail. I couldn't believe a judge granted him bail. This had to be a mistake. I've never been more furious. There's no reason this dude should even be free right now.

My phone rang with a call from Mariah's school.

"Hello," I said into the phone.

"Hi, Mr. Duncan. I have a Janet Duncan here wanting to check out Mariah Duncan. I don't see her name on her paperwork so I was seeing if she's authorized to pick up Mariah."

That confused me. What was Momma doing at the school? I haven't seen or heard from her but she appears at the school.

"No. She's not allowed to have contact with Mariah."

"Okay. She and Ted Cain are adamant there's a family emergency."

I couldn't believe they were this bold. "There hasn't been an emergency. Please keep them away from Mariah."

"Yes sir. We will have them escorted off the campus."

"Thank you."

I ended the call. I felt panicked and scared. I plopped on the couch hyperventilating.

Marie looked at me worriedly. "Everything okay?"

I got myself together before answering. "Moms and Ted just tried to check Mariah out of school. Thankfully, the school called me and didn't let that happen."

Marie gasped. "You need to go get her. That is way too bold. You can bring her back here and I'll watch everyone while you take care of everything."

Chapter 24

Shocking

Ted was back in custody after attempting to make contact with Mariah. Moms was pissed but I don't care. I'm sure there were evil intentions behind them wanting to check her out even though they said they just wanted to talk and make sure she was okay. Yeah, right.

I was currently meeting with Detective Williams at the police station. We sat in his office and reviewed the security footage from the night of the break-in at my old house.

They enhanced the video and we're hoping we can ID suspects this time. We caught someone removing their mask before getting back into the car. Detective Williams paused the footage and zoomed in. When I saw the face, I was shocked.

"You know him?"

"Yeah, that's my sister's no-good boyfriend."

"Do you know his name?"

"Nah, I don't know much about the dude."

Truth is, I was going to check Sam myself. He better hope the police catch him before I do.

"Will your sister be cooperative with the investigation?"

"Probably not."

"He's the only one we have a clear image of. We did find blood at your place where they broke the window so we'll test that and see what we come up with. We recovered a computer and a handgun. Someone tried to pawn these things at a local pawn shop but he ran before police got there. I will follow up with your sister, Jayla, and see if she can offer any information."

"You think she was involved?"

"I don't know what to think until we find the suspects and question them."

Sam had only been to the house a few times before I told Jayla to stop bringing him over. I didn't like him and I didn't want to be around him. It doesn't surprise me that his shady ass was behind the robbery.

"I have even more shocking news."

"Yeah?"

"We found out who took the money out of the account."

I scoot to the edge of my chair. Detective Williams has been working hard on both cases. I knew he would get to the bottom of everything.

"Who did it?" I asked.

"Janet Duncan."

I jumped out of my chair. "My own momma? What the hell? How do you know?"

"We have been investigating and reviewing security footage at the restaurants. She's seen on camera taking money out of the registers at the bakery, crab restaurant, and juice bar. Now that's not unusual because we thought she was in charge of balancing the registers and making deposits. After talking to Jayla and Jarrod, we found out that wasn't the case and they do that themselves."

"This is wild. How did y'all link her to stealing money from the account?"

"We have surveillance footage of her at the bank withdrawing the money."

"This was probably going on for a minute and we didn't notice."

"We looked her up and she has a lengthy criminal history."

Moms was a scammer and drug dealer way back when so her being behind this shouldn't shock me. But I wanted to believe she changed so it is shocking.

"What happens next?" I asked.

"We are finishing up the investigation and gathering all the evidence. We have to obtain an arrest warrant and we'll go from there."

Now I was left wondering why my momma would cross me like this. I know she's been moving funny lately but I never expected this.

"I appreciate y'all working so hard on these cases," I said.

"Of course. Thanks for coming by, Jarrell."

I shook his hand. I walked out of the police station not sure how to feel. I climbed into my car and called Pops.

"Hey Rell," Pops said.

"What you up to, Pops?" I asked.

"I'm at the house chillin'. I wasn't feeling my best so I stayed home."

"What's wrong with you?"

"Ain't nothing. Just a little tired."

"Uh-huh." I didn't believe him.

"How did it go at the police station?"

"You won't believe what I found out."

"What?"

"Momma stole the money from the account and Sam was a part of the robbery at the old house."

"I thought Janet put her scamming thieving ways behind her."

"I did too, Pops."

"I can't believe this. Janet was on the right track. Do you think Jayla knows Sam was behind the robbery?"

"I hope not. Moms already crossed me. I would hope Jay wouldn't do that to me."

"I saw the news. They really let Ted out on bail?"

"His ass is back in jail now. Ted and Moms tried to get Mariah from school."

"I hope they keep his ass this time."

"Me too. It's crazy that I got to press charges on my momma. I don't know how everyone's going to react to that."

"What momma steals thousands from their child? She could have asked you for money and you would have given it to her. She never had to steal from you."

"I always made sure she was straight. And it ain't like she's always been the best momma to us but I did it anyway. She picked running the streets over us a lot of days. I just wanted to believe she put all of that behind her to be a better mom to us."

"I'm sorry, Rell. I know you've wanted your mom to be there for you since you were young."

"She could never be there for me. She made so many promises and she let me down a lot. She did a lot of shit to us but this is a new low. She used to tell me I could make more money on the block than trying to make it as a football player. She didn't think I would make it and wanted me to give up on my dreams to hustle with her. She taught the game to Rod and fucked up his life."

"Yeah, we done been through hell and back with Janet. She might need to sit down for a while to change her life."

"I don't think she wants to change, Pops."

Chapter 25

Backstabber

I was at the Juicy Boil to talk to my bro about everything. Rod and I walked into the office. I closed the door. He had a seat at his desk and I sat in the chair in front of his desk.

"Wassup bro?" Rod asked.

"You won't believe the shit I just found out," I said.

"What?" Rod asked.

"I know who stole the money."

"Who?"

"Moms."

"No fuckin' way. You lying, bro."

"I wish. I talked to Pops and Eric and they were just as shocked. Eric said he noticed money missing from his account too."

"Damn, Moms still scamming out here."

"And she's been stealing from here and the bakery."

"Man, that explains why we've been short lately. I thought my cashiers weren't giving out the proper change or something. Why the hell is she stealing all this money? She's making enough bread not to do that."

"I wish I knew, bro. It still doesn't make sense to me."

"I'm sorry, bro."

"I've been dealing with Moms' shit for years. Can't believe she stooped this low."

"Me either."

"And I found out someone close to us was involved in the robbery."

"Word? Who?"

"Sam."

He looked at me with his bottom lip on the ground. "Jay's Sam?"

"Yeah, that Sam."

"You think Jay had something to do with it?"

"I don't know. I haven't even called to talk to her about it. I'm still trying to make sense of this shit."

"This is wild. I need a shot." He pulled a bottle of Henny and plastic shot cups from his desk drawer. He poured four shots and we both took two back.

"What happens now?" Rod asked.

"They're working on a warrant for Momma. I was telling them I wasn't sure about pressing charges. It ain't up to me. The prosecutor wants to pursue charges and throw Momma under the jail. She got a record and they've been waiting for her to slip up. It's outta my hands at this point."

"Don't feel bad about it, Rell. Just think Momma didn't give a fuck about taking food out of your kids' mouths."

"I just thought we were finally getting on the right track. We've been fighting for years. I was so mad she had you believing that you couldn't be anything but a dope boy. She had you out on the block young as hell. When that shit went down, she wasn't there and left you to take the blame. She didn't show up to court, bail you out, or nothing."

"Yeah, she turned her back on me. We ain't seen eye to eye since then."

My phone lit up with an incoming call from Eric.

"Wassup Eric? I'm here with Rod." I said.

"Hey, Rod," Eric said.

"Wassup?" Rod said.

"I just talked to y'all mom and she was distraught. She said she took the money to help Ted."

"That's how he got the bail money, huh?" I asked.

"Exactly," Eric said.

"Why the hell is she trying to help this rapist?" I yelled.

"I'm just as angry, Rell. She took six thousand dollars from me. I just left the police station. Y'all mom is in serious trouble."

"I can't feel bad for her," I said, "She wasn't thinking about any of us, just her brother Ted."

"You know Ted is not really her brother? That's somebody she ran with back in the day." Eric said.

Rod and I looked at one another in disbelief. My whole life felt like a lie.

"Y'all there?" Eric asked.

"We didn't know that," I said.

"My fault. I thought y'all knew. That's why I didn't understand why she moved this shady dude into the home. I know they messed around in the past but she told me she was done with him. Now I see he's been around the whole time."

"Like she's really with this dude?" Rod asked.

"Yeah," Eric said, "I guess she's always been with him and I played the fool. I loved her and didn't want to leave her. When she told me she would change, I believed her. She told me she would leave the streets behind and focus on the family. She would leave the street shit alone for a little bit then go right back."

"I didn't even know y'all were going through all that," I said.

"It was hell being married to Janet but we tried to make it work for years."

"Have you talked to Jayla?" I asked.

"Nah, I can't reach her. I stopped by the bakery and she wasn't there. I went by her place and she wasn't home."

"That's odd," Rod said, "You think she heard about Sam being behind the robbery?"

"Probably. He was arrested an hour ago." Eric said.

"Damn, they working fast," I said.

"Crazy thing is he was wanted for another robbery that happened last month. They're going to put two and two together and charge him for breaking into your place too." Eric said.

"Where did Jay find this character?" I asked.

"She knows how to pick them," Eric said sarcastically.

"Is Moms going to turn herself in?" I asked.

"Nah, she thinks this will go away so she's hiding out. I told her she might as well face the music. She admitted a lot of shit to me. Her and Ted had plans of leaving the state and pimping Mariah. I'm glad the school called you because we would be having different conversations right about now."

"Moms is sick in the head," Rod said.

"What kind of Mom would do all of this? It's fucked up. Moms tried to do the same to Deja. That's why we had to stay with Pops for a while and she had to do so much to get us back." I said.

"I didn't know she tried that with Deja," Eric said.

"Moms has done a lot of fucked up things to me, Rod, and Deja. Jam and Jay got lucky they didn't go through the same hell." I said.

"I'm headed to your place now, Rell," Eric said.

"I'll be there in a couple of hours. I gotta go see Boss at the juice bar." I said.

Chapter 26

Funny Business

I walked into the juice bar. Music was playing, people were actually sitting in the restaurant, and there was a line at the register. The whole atmosphere was different and I'm glad Boss could help me.

Boss was in the kitchen meeting with the staff. I looked up at the menu and new things have been added.

My phone vibrated in my pocket and I smacked my teeth when I realized it was Chloe calling. She called several times today but I didn't feel like talking to anyone. I decided to get it over with and answer the call.

"About time. I've been trying to call you all day." Chloe said.

"My bad. I've been busy today. Wassup?"

"Just making sure you're good. I saw they made an arrest in your robbery."

That's right. It only took them a little time to connect the dots and charge Sam for the robbery at my house.

"Yeah, that's Jay's boyfriend," I said.

"Interesting."

"I've had a day, Chloe. I gotta talk to you later about it."

"Just call me when you can. I know how you get. Just know I'm here for you. I'll be there next week for Valentine's Day."

"I appreciate you, Chloe. I'll talk to you later."

Boss walked over to me as I ended the call with Chloe.

"Wassup Boss?" I said giving him dap.

"Wassup Rell?" Boss said.

"I like what you're doing here. I ain't seen this much traffic in a while."

"A new gym opened up down the street bringing a lot of traffic our way."

"How's the new manager?"

"Roger is dope and the employees like him."

"You think we need another manager?"

"Not right now. The team we have is perfect."

"Guess you heard about Moms."

"Yeah. I didn't think she would be the one behind all of this. Have you talked to her?"

"She's only reached out to Eric. She stole six thousand dollars out of his account."

"What did she need all this money for?"

"To take care of Ted's legal fees. I thought this clown was my uncle. He was someone Momma used to run with and I guess her man. They were trying to pimp my niece."

His head spins. "Am I hearing shit wrong right now?"

"Nah, you heard me right. I've been trying to understand this shit all day. I'm surprised you didn't know since Moms tells you everything."

"I knew Ted wasn't her brother but I didn't know the history. I'm glad you were able to save Mariah and give her a safe home."

"If Marley didn't tell us, we wouldn't have known anything and they would have done worse things to her."

"Let me give you some good news."

"Yeah, I need it."

"Honey is coming home in two weeks."

"Congrats, bro. I know the kids are excited."

"They can't wait to have her home."

Honey is Boss' wife and she's been locked up for the past ten years on drug charges. Boss has been holding the family down and caring for their four kids.

"We gotta throw a party," I said.

"She just wants to go bowling," Boss said.

"I'm going to rent out the bowling alley for y'all."

"You ain't gotta do that."

"I want to. Y'all good people and I'm glad she's coming home."

"I'll let you know the date. Wassup with you and Chloe?"

"We still kicking it. Why?"

"I saw a photo of her and some rapper and thought something was up."

"Nah, we good." I tried not to act surprised but I haven't seen this picture. "I'm coming back to the gym, Boss."

"You got a new client?"

"Yeah. She's on a weight loss journey so I'm going to help her with diet and exercise. I'm excited to get back to it."

"I'm training a few athletes right now."

"That's wassup. I'll let you get back to it. I just wanted to check on things."

"Of course. I'll talk to you later."

We dapped and I walked out of the juice bar. I sat in the car and scrolled through social media looking for this photo of Chloe.

I went to this popular blog page and saw the photos of Chloe. In one photo, she was hugged up with this dude and in the other photo, she was sitting on his lap. Seeing the photos made me sick to my stomach. I went to the comments section and people questioned if we broke up. I exited the social media app and called Chloe.

"Hey, babe," Chloe said.

"Who is this dude?" I asked.

"Let me guess you saw the blog."

"Yeah, I'm trying to figure out what's going on."

"It's nothing. It was for a music video for his new song. The blogs are making it a bigger deal than what it is."

"Just keep it real with me, Chloe. I don't want to be blindsided."

"It's not what it looks like, Rell. You know this is my job. You said you were cool with it but now you trippin'."

"Nah, I ain't trippin'. I was just confused about why you didn't tell me about this music video."

"You don't tell me about every little project you're working on."

"How would you feel if I was with some woman and it was plastered all over the blogs?"

"That's fair but I don't control the blogs. I don't know what they'll post."

"You didn't clear shit up either."

"Hell, I just saw the post when a friend sent it to me."

I didn't know if she was lying but something didn't seem right.

"Aight, I'm 'bout to hit the road. I'll talk to you later." I said.

Chapter 27

No Manual

It was early morning on Saturday and Chantel just brought Life to the house. Porsha brought Layla and Jackson last night. It would be the first time having all my kids under one roof.

Chantel and Porsha were going on a trip for the reality show and I would have the kids for a few days. I walked back to my bedroom with Life in my arms. I carefully placed Life in the bed and lay beside her. I grabbed my phone off the nightstand. It was four in the morning and I couldn't go back to sleep.

I was shocked to see a text message from Jayla.

> Jayla: I had nothing to do with it. Me and Sam haven't been together in a month. I'm stepping away from the bakery for a while. I'm sorry.

I called Jayla and it went straight to voicemail. I didn't want her to think I blamed her for what Sam did. I certainly didn't want her to leave the bakery. I don't know if I can find a good enough baker to help us out in the meantime.

Just as I was about to sleep, I got a call from an unknown number. I decided to answer and it asked me to accept charges. I had no clue who could be calling me from jail.

"Bro!" Jamal said.
"What the hell did you do?" I asked.
I was shocked as hell to get this call from Jamal. He's never been in trouble before.
"Don't tell Dad," Jamal said.
"Are you really in jail right now?" I asked.
"Yeah bro, over some bullshit. They said I got to wait to see the judge on Monday."
"What's the charge?"
"DUI. I fucked up and -"
"We'll talk about it later. Keep your mouth closed and don't talk about shit to them folks. Tell 'em to talk to your lawyer. I'll make sure you're taken care of."
"You think I have to sit in here all weekend?"
"Nah, I got you. Just chill out and I'll see you a little later."
"I love you, bro."
"I love you, Jam."
The call ended and I still couldn't believe what happened. I called my lawyer, Chris, who has handled criminal cases for my family before. He jumped right on it and promised me that he could get Jamal bonded out of jail today. I definitely couldn't go to sleep now so I turned on the television.
Life woke up at five in the morning for her bottle. I scooped her up and walked downstairs to the kitchen. I grabbed a bottle from the fridge and sat on the couch in the living room. I held her in my arms as she drank her bottle. I turned on the television to cartoons.
Junior walked into the house with a crying Ava.
"Good morning. What's wrong with her?" I asked.
"I don't know. She's been crying for an hour now." Junior said.
He sat beside me and put Ava next to him as she wailed. Junior was drained and unfazed as he held his head in his hands.
"Hold her in your arms, Junior," I said.

"She don't want that," Junior mumbled. "I ain't good at this, Pops. This is why she should have been put up for adoption."

"Don't say that. She's just fussy. You take Life and I'll get her."

He happily grabbed Life from me. I picked up Ava, held her over my shoulder, and rubbed her back. She stopped fussing and sucked her thumb. Junior looked shocked that I calmed her down.

"She hates me," Junior said.

"You got to be gentle and patient." Ava let out the loudest burp. "See? That's what's wrong with her. How are you feeding her?"

"I just prop up the bottle to have a little time to myself."

"Boy, you better start holding her and feeding her. She's too young for all of that."

It was weird to see Junior so disconnected from Ava. I don't know if he'll ever create a bond with Ava.

"I work today. Can you watch her?" Junior asked.

"Yeah. I got a full house too."

"Everybody here?"

"Yup, I got everybody. How's your other girl doing?"

"Good. She's ready to have the baby."

"Y'all back together?"

"Nah, I got a new girl."

I looked at him surprised to hear that. "Oh really? When did this happen?"

He laughed. "It's new, Pops but she's good people."

"She goes to school with you?"

"Nah, she dropped out."

"She working?"

"Yeah, she works at some hot wing spot. She got a little girl."

"How old is her daughter?"

"Two."

"That's a lot of responsibility, son."

"That ain't my kid."

"You can't look at it like that. When you get with a woman with a kid, you're taking on that responsibility too."

"She got a daddy. I got a lot going on with my own situation to take on someone else's situation."

"You got a lot of growing to do, Junior. You need to chill for a little bit and be by yourself."

He leaned back on the couch with Life resting on his chest. "I'm chillin', Pops."

"You need condoms?"

"Pops!"

"Don't be embarrassed now. You need to be careful."

"I ain't went through the million condoms you already gave me."

"How's school?"

"I just started, Pops. It's straight so far. It don't feel like school. I can smoke weed right out front and they don't say shit."

"You better not be doing that."

"I'm just saying, they cool at this school and they don't be sweating us."

"How's the work?"

"It's easy."

"Are you even going to classes?"

He laughed. "I ain't going to lie to you. I skipped a couple of classes."

"I'm going to take a belt to your behind if you keep this up."

"Pops, I'm too old for that."

"Keep trying me and you'll see."

Chapter 28

Change Is Hard

Pops came by later to watch the house while I went to get Jamal from jail. I couldn't even tell Pops that Jamal was locked up because he would surely tell Eric and I wasn't ready to deal with that yet.

It was ten in the morning and I was waiting outside the jail for Jamal. Chris was able to get him bail so he didn't have to sit all weekend. After ten minutes of waiting, Jamal walked out of the building and climbed into the car. He looked exhausted.

"Do you know where your car is?" I asked.

"I don't know. They towed it and took me to jail. Have you told my dad?" Jamal asked.

"Nah, you're going to tell him. Were you really driving drunk?" I asked.

"I just left a party and thought I was good to drive," Jamal said.

"You realize you're not old enough to be drinking, right?"

"It ain't even the drinking that got me in trouble. I was smoking and smelled like weed. They searched the car looking for drugs. Then they wanted me to do this test to see if I was good to drive. I told them I wasn't doing it so they arrested me."

"Why you ain't do the test?"

"Because I was fucked up. Ain't no way I was going to pass. Either way, I was getting locked up."

"What were you thinking?"

"I wasn't thinking. I was having a good time."

"Well, you're in a lot of trouble now. DUI ain't your only charge. You were also charged with drinking underage and they found a fake ID on you. And it sounds like you were acting like an ass to the police with that obstruction charge. Bro, you racked up some charges last night and got lucky we knew a judge who could get you out."

"The cops were acting like assholes. They asked me if I stole the car and then asked if I had a right to drive the car."

Eric bought Jam a Porsche Panamera as a high school graduation gift. Not a lot of nineteen-year-olds driving cars like that.

"That's messed up, Jam. You know that they put in the report that you charged at officers?"

"I don't remember shit, to be honest. They came up to my window mad aggressive. And I was aggressive back because I was irritated. Fuck them pigs."

I shook my head. Jam had a lot to learn. "You work today?"

"I got to call out. I ain't get no sleep and I'm tired."

"You want to get something to eat?"

"Nah, I'm good. Am I going to jail?"

"Jam, it looks pretty bad right now. We're going to do what we can to keep you out of jail but the judge has the final say so."

"What about my car?"

"We gotta figure out where it's at first."

"Dad is going to be pissed."

"Hell yeah. That's an expensive whip. I feel bad for you, bro."

I put in my gate code and I pulled into my driveway. I finally got my sports car and Jeep back after the repairs and they looked good as new. I parked my Cadillac Escalade next to the Jeep.

"Can I take a nap before you invite Dad over?" Jam asked.

"Yeah, go in the guesthouse. Just knock. I think Junior is still there. I'll bring you over some clothes."

"Thanks, bro, for everything."

"Don't mention it."

He climbed out of the car and walked over to the guesthouse. Moments later, Junior let him into the house.

I climbed out of the car and walked up the walkway. I took a deep breath before walking into the house. Layla and Jackson were running around playing tag. Pops was lying on the couch with Ava on his chest. Life was on the floor playing with a ball.

I sink into the recliner.

"Where are Marley, Mariah, and Kennedy?" I asked.

"They're upstairs playing video games," Pops said.

"How are you feeling, Pops? You seem like you're under the weather." I said.

"I'm getting over a cold," Pops said.

"Why don't you want me to know what's wrong with you?"

"I don't want you to worry. Everything is finally catching up to me."

"What does that mean?"

"I got to take care of myself."

"Oh." I could tell he didn't want to talk about it so I let it go. "Have you talked to Moms?"

"She called me out of the blue yesterday. She's in a lot of trouble and I guess she needed someone to talk to. I've been through this so many times with Janet."

"Does she feel bad?"

"It was hard to tell. She just seemed worried. She doesn't have any money for a lawyer because she spent all that money on Ted's legal fees and defense team."

"Did you know that Ted wasn't her brother?"

"I found out years ago when I caught them in bed messing around."

"Whoa."

"Imagine how I felt."

"Wasn't she married to Eric at the time?"

"Yeah, and I had to tell him I caught her in the act. I didn't tell him who. I just told him recently who it was and he was so mad that I didn't tell him then. He's a good guy and he stayed despite all of her bullshit."

"He thought she would change."

"I left the moment I realized Janet will always be Janet. Those types of people are draining to be around. You want so much better for them and they're comfortable where they're at."

"Has she always been this way?"

"She's been like this since I met her at fifteen. Always in the mix, hustling, and not caring about much. She grew up in the streets. I never even met her folks. She was hurt by so many people that she didn't know how to let people in or know how to love another person. It's certain things you can't teach people."

"She was doing so good and staying out of trouble. I figured she was finally done with that life and changed her life. I didn't want to give up on her but I'm finally done with her."

"You're going to be okay, Rell. I know you've wanted her to come around and be better but we can't change people. That's just who she is."

"You right."

"Where's Jam?"

"He's in the guesthouse sleeping. He had a long night."

"What happened?"

"Guess I'll tell you now. I didn't have to pick Jam up from a friend's house."

"Where was he then?"

"Jail."

Pops sat up on the couch careful not to wake Ava.

"Why? What did he do?"
"DUI."
"He's nineteen!"
"He got a lot of charges. I don't even know how to tell Eric."
"What's his other charges?"
"He got aggressive with the cops so they charged him with obstructing an officer and disorderly conduct. He also got charged with minor in possession of alcohol and possession of a fake ID."
"Oh boy. I'm surprised they gave him bail."
"Money talks."
"When does he go to court?"
"Friday."
"Eric is going to kill him and kill you for not telling him."
"I know but I wanted to take care of it. Moms stole a lot of money from Eric and I didn't want him to stress about bail money."
"I'll call him and tell him to come over. How's Jam feeling?"
"Tired. He was too high and drunk to remember the night."
"Sounds like he had a wild night."
"Hell yeah. He's paying for it now."

Life crawled over to the recliner. I picked her up and she rested her head on my chest. Pops took his phone out of his pocket and called Eric.

"He'll be over here around noon," Pops said once he ended the call.

Junior walked into the house.

"Jam sleep?" I asked.

"Knocked out," Junior said.

"You ready to go to work?" Pops asked.

"Yeah," Junior said.

"Go see if Marley is ready to go," Pops said.

He ran up the steps.

"Pops, you working today? You don't seem like you're in any condition to work." I said.

"Nah, I'm going to drop them off and go back home to rest," Pops said.

"If you need me to take them, I can."

"No, I got it. Your Pops ain't handicap."

"How's your girl, Stephanie?"

"We're good. Better than ever."

Stephanie and Pops have been together for five years now. Stephanie is around my age and thirty years younger than Pops. I didn't expect them to last this long.

"Y'all ain't getting married?" I asked.

"That ain't what we want," Pops said.

Layla and Jackson walked into the room.

"What y'all up to?" I asked.

"Nothing. We want to go outside." Layla said.

"We'll go outside in a little bit. Go upstairs and see what's taking Marley and Junior so long." I said.

Layla ran up the stairs and Jackson pulled toys out of the toy box.

"He reminds me so much of a younger you," Pops said, "Junior is your twin when it comes to looks but Jackson acts just like you."

I smiled. "Junior gets his personality from his moms."

Layla ran into the living room.

"They wouldn't let me in the room. Said they'll be down in a minute. It smelled like smoke." Layla said.

"They better not be smoking in my house," I said.

I sat Life on the floor and raced up the steps. I could smell the weed before I even got to the door. I barged into the room. Marley and Junior were leaning out of the window smoking a blunt.

"Dang Pops, you can't knock," Junior said.

"Put it out right now!" I yelled. Junior put out the blunt. "Are you two crazy?"

"Calm down, Pops."

"Don't tell me to calm down. You in my house smoking. You got a huge backyard and I wouldn't have even caught y'all. But y'all want to be bold and disrespectful and smoke in the house. We got babies here."

"Unc, that's our bad," Marley said.

"Marley, you better be careful following behind Junior. He's just going to get you in trouble." I said. "Both of y'all go downstairs so y'all can get to work on time."

I didn't feel like dealing with them right now. I followed them down the steps.

"We're ready," Junior said.

"Junior, you know if they drug test you, you're going to fail and you're going to juvie," I said.

"I don't care about going to juvie," Junior said.

Pops stood up and handed Ava to me.

"You need to care. You got kids to think about." I said.

"I don't care about these kids. You made me do this." Junior stormed out of the house.

"I got him," Pops said following him.

Marley looked at me. "Later, Unc."

"Have a good day at work."

He walked out of the front door.

I couldn't get through to Junior and it bothered me. He was going down this destructive path and I couldn't stop him. Mariah and Kennedy walked down the steps.

"What y'all doing?" I asked.

"We were playing the game but now we're hungry."

They walked into the pantry and raided the closet for snacks. That reminded me that I had to go to the grocery store. I walked back into the living room where Jackson was lining up all his toy trucks and cars.

I put Ava in her bassinet. I stared at her sweet face, sad that her parents couldn't be there for her. Marie and I were eighteen when we had Junior. I went away to college and Marie stayed here in Atlanta and went to a community college. We made it work. I know Junior would come around once he processes everything.

"Y'all hungry?" I asked Layla and Jackson.

"Yes," Layla said.

"What y'all like to eat?" I asked.

"Chicken," Layla said.

I texted Eric to pick up some food. My phone vibrated and it was Rod calling.

"Yo Rod," I said.

"Yo Rell, have you seen Jam? He was supposed to work today and I can't reach him. Eric said he can't reach him either."

Jam had me doing all his dirty work. "Jam got into a little trouble."

"Is he okay?"

"Yeah, but he can't come to work today."

"Man, I hope baby bro is good."

I couldn't hide the news from Rod. "He got locked up. Don't tell Eric though. He's on the way here and I'll tell him when he gets here."

"Locked up? What did he do?"

"DUI and resisting arrest."

"Eric is going to be so pissed."

"And his car was impounded."

"Man oh, man. Not the Porsche. Jam got himself in a jam."

I chuckled. "You talked to Jay yet?"

"Nah, she dodging my calls and texts. Eric told me he talked to her and she's good and just wants to be left alone."

"I gotta find a baker for the shop. The manager, Reese, told me it's been hectic without Jay being there. They need help right away."

"I'll post the job listing."

"I appreciate that, bro."

"Just hold ya head, bro. Better days are coming."

I smiled because Rod knew exactly what I needed to hear. "I've been stressing, Rod."

"I know you have."

"Junior don't want nothing to do with his baby girl and I can't make him bond with her.

"Just take over, Rell. Let him process it and come around in his own timing. A lot of people don't bond right away with their kids. Just step in and be there for Ava until he's able to do so. I gotta get back to work, bro. Erin is coming by later to film for the channel."

"That's happening today? Y'all need me there?"

"Nah, we got it. My staff is excited to film the video."

"I can't wait to see the final video. I'll talk to you later."

Chapter 29

In A Jam

Eric was at the house thirty minutes later with three bags full of food with chicken, sides, and sweet treats. He set everything on the counter. I called Mariah and Kennedy down to eat. I fixed plates for Jackson and Layla. Eric and I stood in the kitchen once the kids were settled at the table.

"So, what's going on? Where's Jam?" Eric asked.

"You can't get mad," I said taking a bite of my chicken wing.

"Where is he?"

"He'll be over here in a second."

"What are you not telling me?"

You couldn't put anything past Eric.

"I had to bail him out of jail." I flinched as he threw up his hands.

"You what?" His voice made the kids look in our direction.

"What's wrong?" Mariah asked.

"Nothing. Everything's okay." I said.

"What kind of trouble is he in?" Eric asked.

I ate some mashed potatoes before answering him. He was making me nervous. "DUI, underage drinking, possession of false identification, disorderly conduct, and obstructing an officer. Other charges are pending."

Eric paced the floor. "Are you serious?" He looked around for cameras as if this was a prank. "Tell him to get in here now."

I called Jam.

"Hello," Jam said groggily.

"Come to the house," I said.

"Dad's there?"

"Yeah."

"You told him?"

"Yeah."

"Fuck! I'll be there in a second."

I ended the call and turned to Eric. "He'll be here in a second."

"Why did you keep this away from me?"

Here we go. "I was going to tell you but I wanted to get all the information and get him home first."

"You got him a lawyer?"

"Yeah, it's Chris Walton. I'll send you his information."

"Y'all kids are going to be the death of me. Rell, you can't keep me in the dark about these things."

"I know. That's my bad."

"Where's his car? I didn't see it in the driveway."

Damn, where was Jam to take some of this heat off of me? "It's impounded."

Eric shook his head and he was getting more pissed by the second. "You know who has the car?"

"Yeah, they're talking about five hundred dollars to get the car."

"Jeez. Send me their information too."

"I can take care of it if you want."

"Nah, you're already paying for the lawyer. I'll take care of it."

There was a knock at the door. I ran to get the door. Jam stood there in the sweatpants and T-shirt I gave him.

"It smells good," Jam said walking into the house. He was in better spirits but I knew Eric was about to ruin his good mood.

We walked into the kitchen.

"Hey Dad," Jam said nervously.

"Don't hey Dad me. What were you thinking to get behind the wheel while you were drunk? You have to stop making these dumb decisions." Eric said.

"Dad, I went to a party and had one drink and smoked one blunt. I was fine to drive." Jam said.

"Your ass shouldn't be drinking at all. Why were you at a party anyway? With the way your grades are looking, you need to be in your room studying."

"Rell, you got a painkiller?" Jam asked.

"Yeah, I got you," I said.

I went into the hall bathroom and got the pills for him. He got a bottle of water out of the fridge and took two pills.

"Dad, I know you're angry but yelling ain't going to solve none of this," Jam said.

Eric lunged in his direction and I stepped in front of Jam.

"Come on y'all, let's not do this," I said.

Eric walked away and took several deep breaths.

"Jam, you acting like this whole situation is no big deal. You went to jail and got all of these charges." Eric said.

"It's already done, Dad. I can't change what happened." Jam said.

"Tell me what happened," Eric said.

"I went to a party with my boys. It was on campus and I should have walked back to my apartment but I wanted to go to the store and it was only a block away. I figured I could make it up the road." Jam said.

"While high and drunk?" Eric asked.

"I wasn't thinking," Jam said.

"What happened next?" I asked.

"I was heading back home and saw the lights behind me. I kept going then I decided to stop. The officer, Officer Fox, was pissed that I didn't stop right away. I was trying to get my car to campus because I knew I was going to jail. I just told the officer my bad, I ain't see the lights."

"I know he ain't go for that," I said.

"Nah," Jam said. "Fox then said he smelled weed and asked if I had anything on me. I told him no and he asked me to get out of the car. I got out of the car and Fox looked at the car suspiciously. He asked me if it was my car and I asked him if it had come back stolen. He thought I was getting smart with him and that's when shit went left. He wanted to search the car and I told him he didn't have to do that because nothing was in the car. Then he started talking about probable cause."

"Did you have anything in the car?" Eric asked.

"Nope. But his ass wouldn't let me go. He then said he stopped me because I was driving erratically and not in my lane. You can tell he pulled that shit out of thin air. Another officer, Officer Walt, pulled up and he's like we want to do a few tests to see if you're good to drive. And I told them that I was right at the school and I could walk the rest of the way to my apartment.

They ain't hearing shit. I told them I wasn't taking a test and Officer Walt said I would be under arrest if I didn't take the test. And I just remembered cursing them out and being thrown to the ground. I don't think I was resisting arrest or trying to fight them pigs." Jam said.

"Son, you're lucky to be alive," Eric said.

"Why you say that?" Jam asked.

"I feel like I haven't properly prepared you for situations like this. There's a lot of us that have been shot down or mistreated by the police." Eric said.

"They let your ass get away with a lot," I said.

"Fuck those pigs. They can kiss my ass." Jam said.

"Not in front of these babies," I said.

"My bad, Rell. I hate that they think they can say whatever or treat us any type of way because they got a badge." Jam said.

"You got to own your part in this shit too," Eric said getting frustrated with Jam.

"I ain't do shit," Jam said.

"The charges say otherwise. You ain't even supposed to be drinking let alone driving under the influence. Wait until your school hears about this arrest. And we still got to get your car. We got a whole mess to clean up because you had one wild night of partying." Eric said.

Jam sat at the bar with his plate of food. I could tell he was done with the conversation. Eric and I joined him at the bar.

"I changed my major," Jam said.

"Again?" Eric asked.

"Yup."

"Do you even want to finish college?"

"I don't know, Dad."

"What's wrong with you? You seem like you have a lot on your mind."

"I feel torn when it comes to this situation with Momma. Me and Jay's experience with Momma is totally different than Rell, Rod, and Deja's experience. She was an okay mom to me and Jay."

"You don't have to pick a side," I said.

"I think it's messed up what she did to you and Dad. I feel like I don't know her like I thought I did. I know you guys always said she was different with me and Jay but I didn't get it."

"Have you talked to her?"

"I talked to her yesterday. I didn't want to believe what I heard. But she told me what she did and why. I feel angry that she played a part in what happened to Mariah. They ruined baby girl's life and she got to heal from that shit."

"Is that why you were drinking and getting high?" Eric asked.

"Nah, I was going to have a good time regardless. But I went a little too hard because it was a lot to take in at once."

"I'm sorry, Jam. I wish you would have talked to me. I know this is a lot on you and Jay. Jay's going through it so bad that she had to step away from the bakery." Eric said.

"I haven't talked to Jay. I can't reach her." Jam said.

"She ain't talking to no one but Eric," I said.

"I don't want to see Momma behind bars. I know she got to pay for what she did but it's a lot to process." Jam said.

"I know how you're feeling, Jam. I was willing to chuck it as a loss and part ways with Moms but the prosecutor has other plans." I said.

"I wouldn't have been mad at you for pressing charges. You do so much for all of us." Jam said. "I'm just angry that my life was a lie. I thought we were some perfect blended family and we weren't. A lot was going on that me and Jay were kept in the dark about."

"Don't try to make sense of all of this right now. You're going to drive yourself insane." I said.

"I wouldn't be mad at you if you took a break from college. Even Jay realized it wasn't for her. I just want you to be happy and to do what you want to do. This is your life now and you got to figure it out, son." Eric said.

Chapter 30

Glazed

It was later in the day and I was on the couch in the living room surrounded by my kids watching a movie. I never felt more at peace than at this very moment. Layla laid her head on my stomach. She was growing up so fast and I wish there was a way to stop time.

"Kennedy, who you texting with that smile on your face?" I asked.

"Daddy," Kennedy said embarrassed.

"You don't want to tell me nothing anymore," I said.

"I'm just looking at funny videos," Kennedy said.

The front door squeaked open.

"We're home," Marley said.

Marley and Junior walked into the room.

"How was work?" I asked.

"It was straight," Marley said.

"I worked the register today," Junior said.

"You like that more than working in the kitchen?" I asked.

"Yeah, I can see all the fine girls coming into the restaurant."

I shook my head. "You want Ava?" He looked at her resting on my chest.

"Nah, you got her. I'm going to go take a shower." Junior said.

"Come back over to watch the movie and have family time."

"Okay. I'll be back."

Marley walked up the stairs and Junior walked out of the house. A message from Chantel popped up on my screen. I figured she wanted to know about Life but of course, she wanted to start drama.

```
Chantel: Tell yo bitch to stop texting my man!
Me: What?
Chantel: I just caught Ty texting Chloe.
Me: What's that got to do with me?
Chantel: It's cool. I'll handle it.
```

I knew that this wouldn't end well. I called Chantel and she sent me straight to voicemail. I text Chloe.

```
Me: You texting your ex now?
Chloe: What you talking about?
Me: You and Ty texting?
Chloe: He reached out to me.
Me: What y'all got to talk about?
Chloe: Let me hit you back later. In the studio.
```

Now, I was pissed because I didn't like how she was moving. Hugged up with some dude and now she's texting an ex. I was trying to trust her but everything was telling me that something was up. I wasn't going to trip right now. I was just going to enjoy the rest of my night.

Junior joined us for family night an hour later. I could tell something was up the moment he walked into the room. His eyes were glazed and he was out of it.

"You smoked?" I asked.

"Nah, I was chillin'," Junior said.

"Let me holla at you in the kitchen."

I handed Ava to Kennedy and walked into the kitchen. I stood by the refrigerator and Junior leaned over the counter.

"I ain't stupid, ya know?" I said.

"I know, Pops," Junior said.

"What did you take?"

"Nothing."

"What did you take? Don't make me ask again."

"I popped a pill."

I shook my head. "You're heading down a dangerous path. Your nana battled addiction and look at her life. I don't want that for you."

"Pops, I'm trying to deal with all this shit without losing my mind."

"Drugs ain't how you deal with it. I'm here for you, Junior. All you got to do is let me in. I know you got a lot of shit on your plate. You ain't got to figure this out alone. Just get off the block with Melo and stay away from the drugs."

He took a water bottle out of the fridge. His shoulders began to shake and I grabbed him in my arms.

"I don't want to live, Pops. I wake up every day wanting to end this shit."

"I've been there, Junior. I promise you that it's going to get better. Don't worry about the babies right now. Me and Momma got it. Just focus on getting your life together. You have such a bright future and I don't want drugs to dim it. I love you, Junior."

I just held him and let him cry. I wanted to cry with him but I held it together. I felt horrible that I wasn't there for him when he needed me. I know I can't keep beating myself up about it, but I felt so guilty.

"You got this, Junior. I'm by your side always and we're going to figure this out."

"Can I go back to the guesthouse?"

I was worried about him. "Chill out with us for a little bit."

I witnessed drugs change Momma into a monster. Her addiction made her selfish and cold-hearted. She didn't care how she got it. She hurt the people closest to her for her next fix. Tried to pimp out her daughter for drugs. Had her teenage son on the block dealing the same drugs she got high off of. It took over her life.

I didn't want to witness addiction ruin Junior.

Junior looked at me. "Pops, I don't want to keep waking up and fighting to live. I'm getting tired."

"Just hold on, son. I promise you things are going to get way better."

Chapter 31

Don't Worry

On Monday, I was in the car with all my kids taking them to school. Kennedy was nervous about her first day at the new school. Junior was in the passenger seat with his headphones in his ears staring out the window. He didn't want to go to school but I was making him go anyway.

"Daddy?" Layla said from the backseat.

"Yeah, baby?" I said.

"Can we get crab legs tonight?" Layla asked.

"Yeah. I'll get Uncle Rod to bring us some for dinner. Him and Coby are coming by the house tonight."

I pulled in front of Layla's school. She kissed me on the cheek and hopped out of the car. One down, six more to go. I took a sip of my coffee and made my way to the middle school.

"Kennedy, you need me to go in with you?" I asked.

"No Daddy, please stay in the car," Kennedy said.

I chuckled. "Why you so embarrassed by me?"

"I don't want people to know you're my dad."

"I ain't that popular here as I was in Texas and Ohio."

"Kids still know about you though," Marley said.

"Really? Y'all heard kids talking about me?"

"Yeah," Mariah said, "I think it's cool to have a famous uncle."

"I'm glad you're not embarrassed by me."

"Daddy, I want people to get to know me for me," Kennedy said.

"That's fair," I said.

Ava started crying which woke up Life. Now I had two crying babies in the backseat and I was in the middle of traffic.

"Get their bottles outta the bag," I said.

"They're so loud," Mariah said covering her ears.

Kennedy and Marley found their bottles and fed them. I looked over at Junior who remained unfazed about everything. I'm sure he was high. I don't know what to do with Junior.

I dropped all the kids off at their schools and was now at Pops' restaurant to film a video.

I took the stroller out and fastened Ava and Life into the double stroller. I took Jackson out of the car and stood him on the ground. I made sure the car doors were locked and we walked into the restaurant.

Connie, a manager at Pops' restaurant, watched the kids. I walked into the kitchen. Erin, Marissa, a videographer, and Pops had already set up the cameras.

Pops was excited to film this video where he would be showing how he cooks six of his most popular foods.

Marissa held up a camera and I started the other camera. Pops showed us how to cook the barbeque ribs first. He was such a natural in front of the camera. It was cool seeing this side of him. He hasn't been feeling well and I've been worried about him.

We filmed for about an hour and then took a small break. Stephanie, Pops' girlfriend, walked into the kitchen.

"Hey Steph," I said hugging her.

"How ya doing, Rell?" Steph asked.

"I'm good. How ya doing?"

"Good. You got to come by the house more."

"I know. It's been crazy lately. I told Pops I'll be there this weekend for Sunday dinner."

"He would love that."

Steph hugged Pops. She dug in her bag and pulled out a paper bag with a pharmacy name on the front. She handed the bag to Pops.

"What's that?" I asked.

Steph looked like she was about to say something but Pops gave her a look.

"It ain't nothing," Pops said, "Let's get back to filming."

"Steph, can I talk to you out here?" I asked.

Pops whispered something in her ear.

"Sure, Rell."

We walked out of the kitchen as they continued filming. We stood by the front counter.

"What's going on with Pops?" I asked.

"He's just been under the weather," Steph said.

It was something she wasn't telling me. "Is it serious?"

"Don't worry about it, Rell. I'm taking care of him."

"Is it cancer?"

"He just needs to rest, change his diet, and exercise. He's getting older and needs to take better care of himself."

I looked away. When I got injured, it was hard to sit still and focus on healing. Honestly, it was the hardest year of my life. Pops loves to work and this business has been his baby for the past twenty years after Poppa passed. I know it would be hard for him to let someone take over but for his health, I hope he scales back and relax.

Steph rubbed me on the back. "Your Pops is one stubborn man. He just needs to listen and take a break."

"What can I do?"

"Get someone else in control of the restaurant. You know he ain't ready to let go but I think if we can get someone in here that he trusts will run the business correctly, he'll finally sit down."

"I'll work on it, Steph. I'm worried about him."

"I know, baby. He's been stressing about you, Junior, and Rod and missing Deja too."

I smiled. "Deja was his baby girl. I didn't know he stressed about us."

"Your Pops will always worry about you and Rod. Y'all used to come by the house just because, now we hardly see y'all. He misses cooking for y'all and chilling with y'all on the porch."

"I'm going to do better, Steph. I've neglected a lot of people over the past year as I tried to get my life together. I'm going to make it a habit to be at the house every Sunday."

Steph smiled. "He would love that."

"You got to meet the great-grand."

"She's here? Y'all got her out the house already?"

"Yeah, I had to come check on the filming."

"Let me meet baby girl."

We walked to the back of the restaurant where Connie was watching the kids. Jackson was coloring on a menu. Life was asleep in the stroller. Connie was holding Ava in her arms.

Steph looked into the stroller at Life. "Wow, Life is a big girl now."

"She'll be one in two months."

"It's been that long? She's beautiful looking just like you with a bow."

I chuckled. "Yeah, she's looking more like me now."

"How are you and her mom?"

"We ain't together. You got to meet my new girlfriend."

She looked at me shocked. "New girlfriend? I didn't even know you and Chantel weren't together."

I smiled. "Yeah, I'll introduce you to her. She'll be here this weekend."

Steph looked at Ava.

"She's so tiny. Her name is Avanna right?" Steph asked.

"Yeah, we call her Ava," I said

"She's a doll. I can't believe you got this baby outta the house already."

"I was thinking the same thing. She's not even a week old." Connie said.

"Let me go wash my hands," Steph said. She walked away and disappeared into the kitchen.

I sat next to Jackson. "I appreciate you, Connie."

"Of course. It gave me something else to do."

"How's your little girl?"

"Madison is five going on thirty."

"Is Travis coming around more to see her?"

Connie rolled her eyes. "Travis is still being Travis. I just washed my hands of that situation. I feel bad that she doesn't have her dad, but my dad is an amazing grandpa and father figure."

"I see how Junior is with Ava and I wonder if he'll ever come around."

"He's so young. I think he'll come around. Travis is a grown-ass man dodging his responsibility. He done had two more kids and don't take care of them either."

"Man, that's messed up."

"Just keep being an amazing grandpa to Ava."

I cringed hearing the word, grandpa.

"You better accept that you're somebody's grandpa."

Steph walked back to the table and sat next to Connie. Connie handed her the blanket and Steph put the blanket over her. Ava didn't even cry when she was passed over to Steph.

"Oh my, she's so precious," Steph said on the verge of tears.

"Isn't she? Almost makes me want another one." Connie said.

"How is Ms. Maddy doing?" Steph asked.

"Sassy as ever," Connie said.

"I made her the crochet bear she wanted. I got to bring it the next time I come by." Steph said.

"She's going to love it. She already likes the little puppy you crocheted for her."

It was time to exit this conversation and check on the filming. "I'm going to leave y'all to it."

Chapter 32

Peep This

It was now lunchtime and I was back at the house after a long morning. Jackson, Life, and Ava were asleep so it was quiet in the house. I grabbed my laptop and checked the channel's analytics. I was shocked at how well we were doing. Every day we're gaining subscribers and views. Rod's whole chicken video was doing the best and Jay's heart-shaped cake video was a close second.

I checked my emails next. Rod had sent me a bunch of resumes and applications for the baker position. I sifted through all of them and narrowed the extensive list to ten applicants. I would let Rod figure out the best day for interviews.

I put my laptop to the side and kicked up my feet. I scrolled through social media and saw a post that made me stop in my tracks. Chloe posted a photo and Ty commented heart and tongue emojis under her post. I'm sure he was trolling but I wondered why he ain't blocked from her page.

A phone call from Marie interrupted my scrolling.

"Hey, Marie," I said.

"Hey, Rell. What you up to?" Marie asked.

"Just chillin' at the house. What's going on?"

"I just got a call from Kennedy's new teacher."

"Already?"

"Yeah, I was shocked too. This was her science teacher. She told me that Kennedy was disrespectful and refused to do the work. It's only the first day and she's already showing out."

I shook my head. "I'll handle it."

"Now, she didn't start acting like this until she got around Mariah."

"Kennedy always had an attitude, what are you talking about? She's gotten smart with me plenty of times and I've had to put her in her place. She knows better than to disrespect her teachers."

"I just want the best people around her."

"Mariah is an honor roll student and star athlete. I'm telling you now that she ain't influencing Kennedy. You got to trust me, Marie."

"I'm a little worried about Junior popping pills and Kennedy acting out."

"You act like they weren't doing all of this with you. Junior's drug habit started long before he got in this house."

Marie sighed heavily. "You're right. I'm sorry for coming at you like this. I don't understand these two anymore."

"Nah, I get it. We're both feeling the same way."

"I gave Remy your number and he said he would call you."

"I've been calling him and it goes straight to voicemail."

"He ignores my calls too. I want to talk to you about something else."

"Yeah?"

"I want you to be careful with that Chloe chick. I'm seeing a lot of things on social media, and I don't like it."

"Marie, I peep it too. It'll all come to light soon."

"She better not hurt you, Rell."

"Baby, I'm going to be good regardless. What you doing for Valentine's Day?"

"I've been talking to someone so we're going out to dinner."

"Oh yeah? You're so low-key when you're dating. I don't know until I get the wedding invite. Chantel and Porsha can't wait to rub it in my face."

"They love giving you hell."

"And you like to see it."

Marie chuckled. "Those two are something else. I can't wait to see their new show."

"I ain't ready to see it."

"When does it air?"

"Next month. They've been filming for about six months now."

"Is Porsha really dating Chauncey? Is she doing this to piss you off?"

"You tell me, Marie. I don't know what's going on with them."

"It's too messy. Chauncey was like your bro. I was arguing with him the other day about this."

I smiled. "Ma, you still got my back?"

"Always. Tell me how you're really doing?"

She knew me so well. I can tell her how I felt without her judging me or telling everyone my business. "Ma, I'm hurt. Everybody's shady and trading lanes. I worked hard to build this life and my own family and friends are tearing me down. I've been thinking about Deja lately and I miss her. I think about how Moms did her and I can't be shocked she did this to me."

"Rell, you got to deal with what happened and heal from it. It won't go away just because you don't want to think about it. One day, you got to sit down with your mom and tell her how you feel."

"I ain't ready for that. I don't want to see her again."

"You need to tell her how you feel. You've been sweeping your true feelings under the rug for years. You've let her come back into your life without holding her accountable and acknowledging her wrongdoings.

You gave her money, a business, and countless opportunities. And look at how she did you. She stole from you and tried to pimp Mariah. She's toxic, Rell. Just because she birthed children doesn't mean she's a mom and you can't make her be a mom."

I wiped away the tears because she was so right. Moms has never been a mom to me and has hurt me a million and one times.

"I gotta figure out how to deal with this shit," I said.

"Therapy."

"Nah, I don't want to do that."

"Healing is a journey, babe. It's not going to happen overnight."

Chapter 33

Wasn't There

Eric walked into the house around five in the afternoon with Junior, Kennedy, Marley, Mariah, and Layla following him. I sat on the living room floor surrounded by Jackson, Ava, and Life and their toys. It has been a long day and I was exhausted. The kids filed into the living room.

"How was school?" I asked.

"Good," Mariah said. She had on her soccer uniform with grass stains all over her.

"You went to soccer practice, I see."

"Yeah, I need to take a shower."

"Go ahead." She ran up the steps.

"Junior and Marley, y'all need to do y'all homework." Junior and Marley walked into the kitchen and sat at the table to do their homework.

"Eric, can you watch the kids for a second? I need to talk to Kennedy." I said.

"Yeah, I got you."

He took off his shoes and sat on the floor. Kennedy and I walked upstairs to my room. She sat in my office chair at my desk.

"How was your day?" I asked.

She shrugged.

"You know why I need to talk to you?" I asked.

"No idea," Kennedy said.

"Your attitude, that's why."

"I don't have an attitude."

"Why do you go to school?"

"To learn and do my work."

"So, why you disrespecting your teacher?"

"She came at me first. She made a huge deal because I sat in the back of the classroom. She wanted me to sit up front because I was new. I just told her I was straight."

"That's all you said?"

"I mean we went at it for a second and she called Mom saying I was being disrespectful."

"It sounds like you were being disrespectful. You don't go at it with an adult."

Kennedy rolled her eyes.

"You want to go back to your old school?"

"No."

"Then straighten up. Fix that attitude and do what your teacher tells you to do."

"I'm not going to just allow somebody to disrespect me because they're an adult."

"That's fair. But you shouldn't be going at it with an adult. Let me or your mom handle it."

"Fine."

"Do you have homework?"

"Yeah."

"Go downstairs and do your homework."

I followed her downstairs to the kitchen.

"Lay, come do your homework," I said.

"Coming," Layla said.

I sat down at the table and rolled up my sleeves.

Kennedy took her folder out of her backpack and threw her bag to the floor. I chose to ignore her attitude. Layla walked over to the table with her folder in her hands. She sat beside me and I helped her with her homework. Marley and Junior were drawing on scrap paper and not doing their work.

"Y'all need help with y'all homework?" I asked.

"We're just taking a break," Marley said.

"Y'all ain't done nothing to take a break." And then I took a good look at them. "Are y'all high?"

They both burst out laughing even though I didn't tell a joke.

"I knew something was up," Eric said from the living room.

"They were like this when you picked them up?" I asked.

"Yeah, they were out of it and acting weird. I already thought it was strange that Junior was at Marley's school."

I looked at Junior. "Did you go to school today?"

"Yeah, I just met up with Marley after school," Junior said.

"How did you get there?"

"I got a ride from my girl."

"And then y'all smoked?"

"You got me," Marley said.

"It was just y'all or were y'all with other people?"

"Nah, just us," Junior said.

"Did you say hi to your baby girl?"

"Pops, don't blow my high."

"Marley, you gotta stop following behind Junior. You want to play sports and you know they drug test athletes at your school. And Junior, you're on probation. You need to be careful before your ass is sent to juvie."

"Pops, why you always preaching?"

"I'm preaching because I don't want y'all going down the wrong path. The hardest thing in my life was seeing my bro behind bars. I'll be damned if I see y'all behind bars or lose y'all because of this street shit. I grew up differently than y'all. We weren't rich and I watched Pops work a couple of jobs to make ends meet. And Moms was either out in the streets getting high or locked up.

Moms didn't give a damn about me, Rod, or Deja. We're really from the bottom and had to hustle to survive. Y'all don't know about that struggle. There's a lot I wanted to keep from y'all but y'all found the shit anyway. Y'all need to stay focused. All y'all see is the glitz and glamour and think it was easy getting to this point. I worked hard to get where I am."

"School ain't gonna get me where I'm trying to go," Junior said.

"Where you trying to go?" I asked.

"I'm trying to get to the money. Pop Pop only paying us nine dollars an hour and that ain't no money."

"Y'all both get an allowance. I'm sure you're getting more than enough money. Your momma done spent so much on Ava and she's straight for the next few months. You don't have to worry about those extra costs so why do you need so much money?"

"Drugs," Kennedy coughed.

Kennedy and Mariah laughed. The fact that my other kids knew Junior had a problem meant that this was serious and I needed to get him help.

"Shut up, Ken," Junior said.

"Let's be real, how much you spending on drugs?" I asked.

Eric walked into the kitchen holding Ava in his arms.

"She needs a bottle?" I asked.

"Yeah," Eric said.

"The pink bottles in the fridge are hers. The polka dot ones are Life's bottles."

Eric went into the refrigerator to get the bottle.

"I don't want to talk about how much the drugs cost. I got a problem. I know it." Junior said.

"Do you want help?" I asked. "Because I can pay all this money to help you and you go right back to the drugs."

"Daddy, I need help with this sheet," Layla said.

"I'll help you," Eric said sitting beside her at the table.

"I don't know what I want," Junior admitted.

I looked at Marley. "Is this the same path you want to go down?"

"I've seen Junior struggle with a lot, Unc. I've been here for him more than you have. You keep making him out to be a bad kid. I ain't easily influenced. I like getting high but I ain't shooting up or popping pills." Marley said.

"Marley, tell me how I was supposed to be there when Junior didn't want me there?" I asked.

"Pops, you know why we fell out," Junior said.

"Because I told you to stop acting up in school and you felt like I couldn't tell you nothing."

"It's the fact you only show up when it's convenient for you. But, when I needed you, I couldn't call you."

"None of us could," Layla said sadly.

I know I could have been there more for the kids. I'll always regret putting everything over them. We weren't living in the same state and I couldn't travel back to Atlanta for every little thing.

Anytime I had time off, I came home to spend time with them. I spent the off-season here in Atlanta and tried to see them as much as I could. Drama with the moms and girlfriends caused a rift and led to me not seeing them at times.

"Y'all act like I have never been in y'all lives. I had a nontraditional job that had me away for weeks at a time. But every off-season, I was here. Y'all mad because I missed a few parties, recitals, games, or ceremonies. I wanted to be there but I couldn't. This past year I went through a lot recovering from an injury. I had to figure out my life after being forced to retire from football. I know I was distant and I'm sorry. I still think it's unfair for y'all to act like I was some deadbeat and wasn't here for y'all at all."

Man, this shit hurts. I tried to do right by them and didn't always get it right.

"Y'all dad works extremely hard to provide for a lot of people. Once he realized his main source of income, football, was no more, he had to figure it out. He opened up different businesses that took up a lot of his time. He wasn't purposely abandoning y'all, he was trying to make sure you guys had the best life possible." Eric said.

"I wasn't smart with my money when I was younger. I bought unnecessary things and people demanded a lot of money from me. I was on the verge of being broke and had to come up with a plan." I said.

"Y'all dad is here now and he has more time to spend with y'all," Eric said.

"And he would rather spend his time with KoKo," Kennedy remarked.

"That was one weekend," I said.

"You love her more than us," Kennedy said.

I raised an eyebrow unsure where this was coming from. "I don't love anyone more than I love my kids. Y'all mean the world to me."

Kennedy dropped her pencil and cried. I pulled her onto my lap. Kennedy is my oldest girl and was such a Daddy's girl so I know my absence affected her. Yeah, she was grateful to have Remy when I couldn't be there, but she would have liked to have me too.

"Whelp, that got deep fast," Marley said.

"You started it by implying that Junior is on drugs because I wasn't there for him," I said.

"I didn't mean it like that, Unc."

"And you aren't the reason I'm on drugs. I missed you a lot Pops and I'm glad you're here now." Junior said.

"Go give your Pops a hug," Eric said

Junior got up and hugged me. I kissed him on the cheek. "I love you, son."

"I love you too, Pops."

I'm glad my kids and I sat down to have this difficult conversation. When I showed back up in their lives, I was hoping we could move on and act as if nothing happened. But my kids deserved to know why I was absent and they needed me to understand their pain.

Chapter 34

Unsure

Rod and Coby showed up an hour later for dinner. Eric was still here helping me out with all of the kids. Junior and Marley set the table in the dining room for dinner. Rod, Eric, and I gathered in the kitchen to sort out all the food.

"How's it going, bro?" Rod asked.

"It's been a long day," I said.

"What happened?"

"I realized Junior is addicted to drugs. I offered to help him but he doesn't want help."

"Sadly, you can't help him unless he wants it."

"I know. I also had a tough conversation with the kids and I got to hear how they felt about me being distant."

"That's good y'all talked about it. I hope they realize you were just trying to provide a better life and weren't staying away on purpose."

We set the food on the table. The kids gathered around the table to eat. Ava and Life were fast asleep in their cribs upstairs. Eric, Rod, and I took our food to the kitchen and sat at the bar.

"Coby's getting big," I said.

"Too big. Every day he wears a new size." Rod said.

"Is he into sports?" I asked.

"No, you can't train my son for football," Rod said.

We laughed.

"Bro, I was just checking. Marley and Junior ain't interested." I said.

"He's in the band, bro. He doesn't like playing sports." Rod said.

"How was work?" I asked.

"It was cool. Pops came by to hang out with me." Rod said.

"Stephanie told me he's sick and refuses to rest."

"Really? He seemed fine to me."

I looked at Eric. "Do you know what's wrong with Pops?"

"It's not my place to say. Stephanie is right about him refusing to rest. He's being stubborn." Eric said.

"Rod, we need to spend more time with Pops. I've decided to spend Sunday afternoons with him." I said.

"I'm down for that. I pray he gets better." Rod said.

Eric looked down at his phone and I could tell he got bad news.

"Wassup?" I asked.

"Jam got suspended from school," Eric said.

"That's possible in college?" Rod asked.

"It's just something they do before they make the final decision to kick a student out. We have to appeal so he doesn't get expelled. I talked to his lawyer earlier and he warned me this would happen." Eric said.

"What is Jam saying about all of this?" Rod asked.

"He's seemingly unbothered and nonchalant about this situation. Luckily, he has an off-campus apartment, so he doesn't have to leave his place." Eric said.

"Is he facing jail time?" Rod asked.

Eric sighed. "The most time he's facing is two years."

"They can drop some of the charges and take into account he doesn't have a criminal history," I said.

"I'm trying to remain optimistic but after going through this with Rod, I know how it can go," Eric said.

"But I was facing decades behind bars, and I only got two years once they dropped a couple of charges for lack of evidence. You never know how it'll go." Rod said.

"That's true too. I worry about Jay and Jam so much. Jay is not doing well and it worries me." Eric said.

"I still can't get in touch with her," Rod said.

"Me either," I said.

"She's upset about this situation and feels responsible. She needs a little time to herself. I'll tell her to reach out to y'all."

"Whenever she's ready. We just want to make sure she's good." I said.

"She really liked this boy for some reason and she's hurt and heartbroken," Eric said.

I looked at my phone and saw a message from Jam asking to crash at my place for a few days. I was confused but I told him yeah and told him his dad was currently at the house. He texted me back that he'd wait a couple of hours before coming over. I'm sure something was up and I would be in the middle once again.

"I checked out y'all channel and y'all got something special. It's nice seeing all of y'all together." Eric said.

"Tanya is an amazing editor," I said.

"My favorite video is Rod's whole chicken video," Eric said.

"Everybody is loving that video," Rod said.

"Jam got a video coming out later this week. He's so good in front of the camera." I said.

"And he's funny as hell," Rod said.

"I can't wait to see his video," Eric said.

"Has anyone talked to Moms?" I asked.

"Nope," Rod said.

"Nah and her number is disconnected. I'm sure she's hiding from the police." Eric said.

"She's making it worse for herself. She might as well turn herself in." I said.

"I told her the same thing," Eric said.

"What's going on with the divorce?" I asked.

"It's hell right now. She's demanding alimony. Probably trying to get money for her case. She already stole from me so I don't want to give her a dime." Eric said.

"I thought she was going to sign the papers and go," I said.

"She saw that Eric had a new chick," Rod said.

"That's what it is. But she's been with Ted without me knowing it, making everybody believe that's her brother." Eric said.

"Yeah, that's foul. That's why I don't trust bitches." I said.

"They ain't all the same," Eric said.

"You and Chloe having issues?" Rod asked.

"I've been peeping shit and she says it's nothing but I don't believe her," I said.

"She acts single," Rod said.

"You see it?" I said.

"That's why I always ask if y'all good," Rod said

"I thought we were, bro. Now I'm not too sure."

Chapter 35

Stop Trippin'

There was a knock at the door at eleven at night. I opened the door to Jam's smiling face.

"Dang bro, what took you so long?" I asked.

"Trying to avoid seeing Dad," Jam said.

He walked into the house carrying two duffel bags. We sat at the bar in the kitchen.

"Tell me what's going on," I said.

"I'm homeless. I don't have an apartment." Jam said.

My eyes widened at this revelation. "You serious?"

"Deadass. The lease was up a couple of months ago and me and my roommates didn't renew. I've just been crashing at friends' places or getting hotel rooms when I could. Now that I don't have school and can't be on campus, I need somewhere to stay."

"You can crash here but you gotta tell your dad. I don't want to be in the middle of this."

"I don't want to tell Dad."

"Why didn't you get a new spot? You got money to get your own crib."

"I was going to drop out, bro. Instead, I decided to change my major and stick it out."

"Jam, it seems that you hate college."

"It ain't for me."

"What do you want to do?"

"I want to be a YouTube star."

I rubbed my temple. I didn't want to discourage him but his new career plans worried me. "Are you going to make a channel?"

"Yeah. I still want to do the cooking channel with y'all."

"Go for it. You're good on camera and I'm sure people will watch your videos. It's not as easy as you think so be prepared to work hard."

"Can I use your editor?"

"Nah bro, figure that out on your own. It'll give you some new skills to learn instead of taking the easy way out."

"Well, can I ask her questions if I need help with editing?"

"Yeah, but she ain't editing your videos. What's your channel going to be about?"

"Vlogs. My life is lit and I think people would find it interesting."

"You're such a party boy. You party more than me."

"Dad says I party too much."

"He ain't wrong. Look at the situation you're in now."

"I can't have a good time?"

"Yeah, but you have to be responsible."

"I'll do better, bro."

"I need you to talk to Junior. I think he'll listen to you."

"What you want me to talk to him about?"

"Drugs."

Jam sighed. "I already told him to stop popping those pills. I'll talk to him again."

"Now, call your dad."

"It's late as hell."

"I'm sure he's up."

Jam pulled out his phone and called Eric.

"Hello," Eric said groggily.

"You sleep? I'll call back in the morning." Jam said.

"Nah, I'm up. What's going on?"

His smile turned into a frown. "I'm going to stay with Rell until they make the decision about school."

"Why?"

"I just need to get away from campus."

"I understand that. It's going to get better, Jam."

I couldn't believe Eric fell for this.

"I know, Dad."

"Yo, tell your dad the truth," I said.

Jam cut his eyes at me.

"What's going on now?" Eric asked.

"I don't have an apartment," Jam said.

"Where have you been staying?" Eric asked.

"With friends and at hotels."

"Man, if it wasn't so late, I would pull up on you and wring your neck."

That's the Eric I know. He didn't play any games.

"Dad, I'll talk to you later." Jam hung up the phone as Eric fussed at him.

"Yo, he's going to kill both of us," I said.

Jam shrugged. "I'll deal with it tomorrow."

"You want the upstairs or downstairs guest room?"

"I'll take the downstairs one. I appreciate you, bro. You're always here for me."

"Of course. Love ya, man."

"Love you, bro."

We hugged. He walked down the hall to the guest room. I cleaned up a little bit before heading upstairs to my room. I got comfortable in my bed and called Chloe.

"Hey Rell," Chloe said.

"Hey. What you up to?"

"I'm getting ready to go to the club for a walkthrough."

"Dang, you been at the club every night for the past two weeks."

"It's nothing, babe. I gotta eat."

"Who is this Isaac dude?"

"Isaac is my best friend. He's been coming with me to my bookings making sure I'm good."

"He got his hand all over your ass. What's that about?"

"It's just a picture, babe. It doesn't mean anything. You got to stop trippin' about every little thing."

"I know I'm not crazy. If you want to do you, just let me know."

"Here you go."

"I ain't stupid. And my baby moms been telling me shit about you and Ty."

"Why is she so worried about me? And tell your sis to stay out of my messages too. She needs to worry about her felon-ass baby daddy."

I raised an eyebrow. "Baby daddy? What you talking 'bout?"

"Don't you know your sis is pregnant?"

I sat up in bed. "You serious? How do you know this?"

"I'm cool with Sam's brother, Shawn, and he told me. Shawn called me telling me his bro was locked up and Sam was worried how his girl was taking everything because she's pregnant."

"When did you become cool with Sam's brother?"

"I was being petty and trying to piss your sis off."

"You're always in some mess, Chloe. I don't want you beefing with my sis. That puts me in a bad position."

"I ain't beefing with her. She got enough going on and I ain't trying to stress her even more. Word on the street is Sam got another girl pregnant."

I couldn't get over the fact that my baby sis could be pregnant. I wonder if Eric knows.

"Did Jay confirm any of this?" I asked.

"Yeah. When I brought it up, she said her and her baby would be fine."

"When's the last time you talked to her?"

"That was earlier today. She was mad that I became cool with Shawn to spite her."

I shook my head not believing any of this. I didn't like drama or being in messy situations.

"You gotta squash this, Ma," I said.

"It's already squashed. I got something on her and she's leaving me alone."

"What about you and Chantel?"

"It's on sight with that bitch."

I held my head in my hands. I knew this could end badly and I needed to find a way for them to squash this and move on.

"What happened?" I asked.

"She's been talking recklessly so I just have to show her."

Chantel has gotten into it with so many people in my life. I'm sure she stirred up some mess and Chloe ain't going for it.

"I hope she knows how to fight with all that mouth. My girlfriend, Alexis, is coming with me too."

"It ain't gotta get to that point."

"I'll send you what she sent me and you'll understand."

We talked for a few more minutes before I ended the call. I ran down the steps to the guestroom. Luckily, Jam was still up and watching television.

"Wassup bro?" Jam asked.

"You comfortable?" I asked.

"Yeah, I'm good."

"Is Jay pregnant?"

He sat up in bed. "What are you talking about?"

That meant Jay hadn't told anyone. "Nothing. I was just wondering."

Jam side-eyed me. "You know something I don't?"

"Not really. Don't bring it up to Jay or Eric."

"Of course. How did you find out?"

"My girl told me."

"They still arguing? Jay told me about her and Chloe going at it a couple of days ago."

"Chloe said it's done now."

"I hope you're taking up for Jay because Chloe has said and done some things."

"Jay can handle her own, bro. She started this shit. You can't talk crazy to everybody."

"She was only looking out for you."

"I don't need nobody looking out for me. I got me."

"You really think Chloe going to be your wife?"

"I'm just having fun. This ain't nothing serious."

"Every time you have fun, a baby appears nine months later and then there's drama."

I smiled. "I'm being careful, bro. You and Jay don't have to worry about me. It's my job as big bro to worry about y'all."

Jam smiled. "I just want the best for you."

Chapter 36

Trouble

The morning brought more drama my way when Chantel came by the house to get Life.

"I need to talk to you," Chantel said putting Life back down on the living room floor. Jackson and Ava were also on the floor playing. The other kids were at school. I buckled Ava into her swing.

Chantel and I walked into the kitchen to talk.

"How was your trip?" I asked.

"Good. I don't want to talk about that." Chantel said.

"Wassup?"

"You need to get that bum bitch, Chloe, out of your life."

"Why you gotta dog her like that?"

"I'm being serious, Rell. I don't like you most of the time but I still care about you. That girl is nothing but trouble and a liar."

Now, I was concerned. If everyone was warning me, could there be something that I wasn't seeing?

"What did Chloe do?" I asked.

"She's been sending Ty nude photos. I found the photos when I was looking through his phone. Ty said the photos are old but I'm not stupid." Chantel said.

I dropped my head. I knew something was up.

"She's a low-down snake. Ask your pops if she ever offered to suck his -"

"Not in front of the kids."

She looked away. "Rell, she's not who you think she is. You need to leave her alone."

"She'll be here on Friday and I'll have a conversation with her."

Chantel rolled her eyes. "Sounds like you still want to be with her."

"Why am I supposed to just believe you when you've lied a million times too? I would rather talk to her myself and see wassup."

"You think she's going to tell the truth?"

Chantel pulled out her phone and showed me messages, videos, and photos. It was a lot to take in. Chloe said hurtful things to Chantel and even brought up Life. Chloe sent pictures to Ty and looking at the screenshots Chantel showed me, it looked like they met up a time or two. Chloe also admitted to a few shady things.

"Now you see the type of person she is," Chantel said.

"Yeah, that's wild. I can't believe she brought Life into the drama." I said.

"She's a hateful person."

"Thanks for bringing this to my attention."

There wasn't much else for me to say. I felt numb. I was getting used to people I trusted most doing me dirty so this didn't shock me. This was one of those times I needed Deja. I needed to hug her, see her, and hear her say everything would be okay. I sat down at the bar and Chantel rubbed me on the back.

"You okay?" Chantel asked.

I said nothing because I couldn't put my feelings into words. Chantel hugged me and I wrapped my arms around her. I didn't realize how much I'd missed Chantel until this moment. We've had so many fights and arguments that I forgot what made me fall in love with her. And she was looking fine today in this skintight dress.

I looked into her eyes and kissed her on the lips. I was shocked she kissed back and didn't push me away. She looked at me and smiled at me slyly. I went back in for another kiss and sat her on my lap. I rubbed her ass as she bit my lower lip. I was only thinking about one thing. I caressed her body as we kissed.

"Daddy," Jackson said.

We both snapped out of it.

"He's behind you," Chantel whispered.

She fixed her dress and hopped off my lap. She paced the floor.

"What have I done?" She said.

I looked at Jackson. "Wassup lil man?"

"Juice please," Jackson said.

"Okay, Daddy will bring you juice."

He ran back to the living room. I got up and got him a juice box from the fridge. I took the juice box to Jackson. He was on the couch holding a toy truck and watching a movie. I walked back to Chantel.

Man was I pissed. We could have had a great time.

"Sorry," Chantel said.

"Don't apologize. We didn't even do nothing." I said.

"We could have. I'm engaged and you're in a situation."

"Don't stress it, Chantel. They're not going to know about this."

She stopped pacing and looked at me. "I thought I hated you."

I smiled. "Can't nobody hate me."

She smiled. "I miss you sometimes, Rell. Then I remember how hell those two years were and that we were no good together. I've missed our friendship and just laughing with you."

"You changed on me, Chantel. You started creating drama and being mad all the time."

"That injury changed you, Rell. You weren't a nice person for a long time. It seems like you're finally getting back to yourself."

"I feel like myself again. I'm not as angry. When I got injured and had to retire, I felt like I lost control of my life. I was abusing alcohol and painkillers and I wasn't myself. That's why I tried to distance myself from everyone and everything to get my life together. I hurt a lot of people during that dark period of my life. I lashed out at those closest to me and I'm still trying to repair all these relationships. I'm sorry, Chantel."

She covered her mouth with her hands and the tears fell from her eyes. "Did I hear you correctly?"

I wrapped my arms around her. "You heard me right. I can't keep making excuses. I made fucked up decisions and hurt a lot of people."

She kissed me and I wiped her tears.

"Hey, you two, break it up," Jam said walking into the kitchen.

I completely forgot about him being here.

"Okay, I really have to go," Chantel said.

Jam gave me a sly smile.

"It ain't what it looks like, bro," I said.

"Hey, you ain't got to explain that to me," Jam said.

I helped Chantel get Life's things and walked her to the car. I watched her drive away before going back into the house.

"What y'all got going on?" Jam asked.

"It ain't nothing. We were just talking." I said.

"Uh-huh." He found the biggest bowl in the cabinet and made a bowl of cereal. "You want that old thang back, huh?"

"Nah, it ain't about that. I want to get in a good place with everyone." I said.

"Sure, bro."

I chuckled. "What you up to today?"

"I have a meeting with my lawyer. Dad's coming by in a little bit to pick me up."

"Y'all on better terms?"

"Not really but that's Dad."

"He just wants the best for you."

"Yeah, I know. Can you help me with my channel?"

"What you need help with?"

"Getting everything up and running."

"Yeah, I'll help you. Let's go to the computer."

He grabbed his bowl and we walked into the living room. I put Ava in her bassinet as I noticed she was drifting off to sleep. Jackson was still on the couch watching television. I sat at the desk in the corner. Jam grabbed a kitchen chair and sat beside me.

"You still creating an office in this big ass house?" Jam asked.

"Yeah, I'm just being lazy. All of this is going to be moved upstairs in that empty room. Prince, our interior designer, will come by and help me get this place together."

"I like this spot better than the old place."

I showed him the ropes of YouTube and he seemed overwhelmed when I was done explaining everything.

"That's a lot," Jam said.

"You can do it, Jam," I said. "Film your first video and I'll help you get started."

"I don't know what to film."

"Film a day in the life vlog and see what happens. I got a camera you can use." My phone rang. "Excuse me for a second."

"Go ahead."

I put the phone on speaker. "Hello."

"Hi, is this Mr. Duncan?"

"Yes?"

"Hi, this is Yolanda Sparks, the principal at Freedom Middle School."

"Yes, how are you?"

"I'm great. How are you?"
"I'm fine."
"We have your daughter, Kennedy, in the office."
I sighed. "Yes?"
"She seems to be having a hard day. I pulled her out of the classroom for being disruptive. I asked if she wanted to stay or go home and she wanted to go home."
"Being disruptive in what way?"
"She was talking in class, wouldn't get off her phone, and was disrespectful to her teacher."
"Does she want to talk to me?"
Yolanda asked Kennedy and I heard her say no.
"I'm on my way to get her," I said.
We talked for a few more minutes before I ended the call.
"Fuck!" I said.
"What's going on with her?" Jam asked.
"Nothing a belt can't fix," I grumbled.
"It's about time you get tough on these kids," Jam said.
"I've been sparing them but our folks ain't spare us and we turned out fine," I said.
"Hell yeah. I appreciate all those whoppings because I stayed away from a lot of nonsense to avoid getting one. Yeah, I made a huge mistake that's going to cost me but it ain't have nothing to do with how Dad raised me. I did wrong on my own."
"You're going to be straight, Jam."
"This whole situation got me fucked up."
"I know. But you can't stress it. Just gotta trust it's going to work out. You got a good lawyer. You just have to catch the right judge and you're going to be fine."
He doesn't say anything. I put my arm around his shoulder. His body began to shake as he let the tears fall.
"Bro, you're going to be fine." To see him breaking down made me want to break down too.

"This case. Momma. Jay. It's too much." Jam mumbled.

Moms and Jam were close and I hate this for him. He didn't know about Moms' shady past. He's finding out about all of this now. I know he struggles with missing her and being angry with her. And I know with Jay going through so much, it weighs on him. He's only nineteen and still finding his way in this world.

"Things are going to work out, Jam. Keep moving forward. These dark days ain't going to last forever."

"Hello," Eric called into the house. Then we heard the front door close.

"In the living room," I called back.

"I'm coming," Eric said.

I was glad he was here.

"I don't want him to see me like this," Jam said.

I handed him a tissue. Eric walked into the living room. Jackson ran to him and talked to him about trains.

"Why this big boy got on a diaper?" Eric asked.

"Ask his momma. She says he ain't ready to potty train. Every time I send him home in underwear, she sends him back in diapers." I said.

"When does she think he's going to be ready? He's almost three."

"That's what I told her but she doesn't listen."

Eric put Jackson down and walked over to us.

"You okay, Jam?" Eric asked.

"No," Jam said. Eric didn't say anything more and just hugged him.

"Yo, I almost forgot. I gotta get Kennedy from school. Can y'all watch the house? I won't be long." I said.

"Yeah, we got you. What did she do now?" Eric asked.

"Just Kennedy being Kennedy."

"Wear her tail out right at that school," Eric said.

Chapter 37

Calm Down

I walked into Freedom Middle School with my belt in hand. Kennedy was sitting in the front office.

"Get up!" I said shocking everyone in the office.

Kennedy jumped out of her chair. "No Daddy."

A school resource officer held me back before I could swing the belt. He pushed me into the hallway.

"You serious right now?" I yelled. "That's my child!"

"I'm looking out for you. Chill out."

"Let him go!" a familiar voice yelled.

I looked up and Mariah was walking toward us.

"It's okay, Ma," I said.

She ran over to us with tears down her cheek. She was so dramatic and reminded me of Deja in this moment. Deja was tough as nails with a heart of gold.

"What's wrong?" Mariah asked.

"Go back to class!" the resource officer said.

"Can you let me go? Damn." I said.

He lets me go. I hugged Mariah and wiped her face with the tail end of my shirt. Kennedy was in the office surrounded by staff comforting her.

"What happened?" Mariah asked.

"Kennedy got in trouble and I came to handle it," I said.

She looked at the belt in my hand.

"It's okay, Ma. You can go back to class. I'll see you later." I said.

She looked at me worriedly. "Okay."

I kissed her on the cheek and she walked back down the hall sneaking glances over her shoulder to make sure I was good.

"Can I go back to the office now?" I asked.

"You got to calm down first," the resource officer said.

"I am calm, bro."

"You're a good father, man. I just don't want things to go left. Discipline can easily be seen as child abuse. I know who you are and I don't want your reputation ruined by lies."

I gave him dap. "I appreciate that, brotha."

"You can go back into the office now."

I took a deep breath and walked back into the office. I don't even look at Kennedy.

"Kennedy has expressed concerns about going back home with you so we have called her mom," Mrs. Sparks said.

I looked over at Kennedy. "You serious right now?"

She looked away.

"You ain't got nothing to say? I'll pack everything at the house and you can go back to your mom's house."

I stormed out of the office. I walked back to my sports car pissed. I called Marie as soon as I got in the car.

"I already know. I'm just as pissed as you are." Marie said before I could say anything.

"They're trippin' acting like I was about to abuse her," I said.

"Kennedy acting scared and got them folks worried. I just had to leave a fucking meeting for this shit."

If Marie was cussing, she was angry.

"Try to calm down before you get to the school. We don't want them calling the folks on you too."

She chuckled. "You right."

"I gotta go back to the house because Eric and Jam got somewhere to be."

"I have to go back to work so I'm bringing her to your place."

"Aight. See ya later."

I drove back to the house with my mind on everything. I walked into the house still mad. I walked into the living room and plopped down on the couch.

"Where's Kennedy?" Jam asked.

"Why you frowning like that?" Eric asked.

"Man, y'all won't believe what just happened," I said.

Jackson climbed on my lap. I rubbed his hair as he fell asleep on my chest.

"What?" Eric asked.

"I went up to the school with my belt in hand. When I saw Kennedy, I told her to get up. As soon as I was about to swing the belt, this big ass officer grabbed me and pushed me into the hallway and had me pinned against the wall." I said.

"Why?" Jam asked.

"He didn't want me to get in trouble for child abuse," I said.

"You can't even discipline your kids no more. That's why these kids acting out now." Eric said.

"Kennedy then told these people she was scared to come home so I couldn't check her out," I said.

Eric looked dumbfounded. "Why are they intervening with the way you discipline your child? Spare the rod, spoil the child."

"Dad, you would have caught so many charges back in the day," Jam said.

"Hell yeah. I used to pull up to y'all classes and start whopping ass." Eric said.

"I hated that. And I would get it from Pops later." I said.

"Y'all hardly gave us any issues though. Y'all were good kids for the most part." Eric said.

"Because y'all didn't play. Once you embarrassed me in eighth grade, I stayed on my best behavior." I said.

"Dad, we got to go," Jam said.

"Thank y'all for watching the house," I said.

"Of course," Eric said.

Eric and Jam walked out of the living room. A few minutes later, I heard the front door close. With both Jackson and Ava asleep, it was nice and quiet. I turned on the television to a sports channel and watched sports highlights.

Ten minutes later, there was a knock at the door. I lay Jackson on the couch and ran to the door. Marie stood there.

"Where's Kennedy?" I asked.

"She won't get out of the car," Marie said.

"What did they say?"

"They were trying to tell me about discipline and how to parent. I wasn't going for it. I explained to them the kind of dad you are. I'll be damned if they try to paint you out to be a monster."

"I appreciate you, Ma."

"Of course. I had to get them together."

Marie and I walked to her car. Kennedy was in the passenger seat with her hood over her head. I opened the car door.

"Get out. Your mom has to go back to work." I said.

She reluctantly got out of the car.

"See y'all," Marie said climbing back into her car. She waved and pulled out of the driveway.

I took off my belt and held Kennedy's arms as I hit her on the behind with the belt.

"Please Daddy stop," Kennedy said.

I pushed her away.

"Go in the house." She walked into the house. I closed the front door. "Go wash your face."

She walked into the hall bathroom to wash her face. I sat at the bar in the kitchen. She returned and grabbed a water out of the fridge.

"Come sit next to me," I said.

"I can't sit," Kennedy said.

"I ain't hit you that hard. Come on."

She carefully climbed onto the bar stool next to me.

"I'm sorry," Kennedy said.

"For what?" I asked.

"Acting up in school and telling them I was scared. I didn't know they would be that serious. They were about to file a police report and Mom came to the rescue."

Marie didn't even tell me that. Man, I'm glad she was there to vouch for me.

"And you know I've been sparing you too. You needed a whopping months ago and I've let you slide. I don't want to do that but you ain't listening. You can't be going to school doing what you want. I send you there to learn, that's it. You're a great student so I don't know why you acting out like this."

"I'm going to do better, Daddy."

"You better. You too smart to be acting up like this. Do your work and stop disrespecting your teachers."

"Yes sir."

"You have work to do?"

She nodded her head.

"I'll leave you to it. I'll be in the living room if you need me."

I walked back to the living room. Ava stretched her arms and moved her head from side to side. I picked her up before she let out a huge wail. I walked back to the kitchen to make her a bottle. Kennedy was sitting at the kitchen table taking worksheets out of her bag.

"Mom took my phone. Can you get it back for me?" Kennedy asked.

"You shouldn't have been on it in class," I said.

I poured the water and a scoop of powdered formula into the bottle. I shook the bottle and made sure everything is mixed.

"I hate it here. I see why Junior wants to die." Kennedy said.

I turned around to look at her. "What did you just say? Are you throwing a fit about a phone? You know you're not supposed to be on your phone in class."

I cradled Ava in my arms and put the bottle in her mouth.

"I made a mistake," Kennedy said.

"Your teacher asked you to put it away and you got smart with her. I want to talk about this kill yourself remark."

"I didn't mean it."

"But your brother has been talking about it?"

"Yeah."

"What's so bad about being here? I ain't even that tough on y'all. Y'all wouldn't have made it with Eric and Pop-Pop as parents. Maybe you need to move back in with your mom since you hate it here."

"I'm sorry I said that. I just want my phone."

"You scared your mom going to see something in your phone?"

She looked away. "No."

"What's on that phone?"

"Nothing."

"Do your work."

I walked back to the living room and sat on the couch. I text Marie to go through Kennedy's phone. I'm curious what she's hiding from us. I answered an incoming call from Pops.

"Hey Pops," I said.

"Hey Rell, me and Stephanie can get the kids from school."

"Thanks for reaching back out."

"What time does everyone get out of school?"

"Layla gets out at two-thirty. Marley at three thirty. Junior at three forty-five. And Mariah at four fifteen.

"Middle school get out after high school?"

"Yeah, they start later though."

"What about Kennedy?"

"She got sent home. I'll tell you about it when you get here."

"Send me their school addresses too. I want to make sure we're going to the right schools."

"I'll text you the addresses. How ya feeling?"

"Today was a good day. I feel like myself and I have a lot of energy."

"You worked today?"

"Nope, I took the day off."

"What! You took a day off, you sure you're not sick?"

He laughed. "I gotta take better care of myself. I want to see my little one get big."

Hold up. What?

"Little one? What ya talking 'bout?"

"Uh…" He realized he slipped up and was buying time for a lie.

"Uh, what?"

"I got a little one on the way."

"Stephanie pregnant?"

"Yeah, she's three months pregnant."

This news didn't make me excited. Who wants a sibling at thirty-four years old? His great-grandchildren were going to grow up with this baby. He was too old to be having kids. And he told me he couldn't have any more kids so I was confused.

"Pops, I don't know how to feel."

"I know it's a lot to take in."

"You too old to be having kids."

"Stephanie wanted a child so we made it happen."

"No, she should have found someone who wanted kids too."

"Let's talk about this later. And don't you tell Rod."

Chapter 38

What's New?

The doorbell rang. I looked down at my phone and it was five o'clock.

"Lay and Jacks, that's probably Momma," I said.

I walked to the front door and swung open the door.

"I will never get used to your driveway. I'm going to need new tires." Porsha said.

"I'm going to have someone come out here and pave it," I said, "How was the trip?"

"Draining. It was a lot of drama. Sometimes I regret signing up for this show."

"Are y'all done filming?"

"Yeah, for the show. We have to film the reunion in three months."

"You get a little break from the drama."

"It's going to be nerve-wracking to watch the show and see what scenes made the cut."

"I can't wait to see how much shit y'all talked about me."

I stepped to the side and Porsha walked into the house. Jackson and Layla ran to her yelling Mommy.

"I missed y'all so much," Porsha said.

Junior, Mariah, and Marley were at the kitchen table doing their homework. Kennedy and Ava were in the living room. Porsha said hi to everyone. We stood by the refrigerator to talk.

"You got a full house," Porsha said.

"All the time. You know Kennedy, Marley, Mariah, and Junior stay with me now." I said.

"And don't forget Uncle Jam," Marley said.

"Right. He's here too." I said.

"How's Jam doing?" Porsha asked.

"He's good. Just fighting this case."

"He has to remain positive and know it'll all work out."

"That's what I told him."

"Kennedy and Junior are big kids now. I can't believe it. I met them when they were little."

"Junior's a daddy now."

"You lying?"

"That's his baby in the living room."

"Boy, I thought that was your baby. You really a grandpa?"

"You really thought I had a baby?"

"Hell, I don't know. How did you introduce her to Jackson and Layla?"

"As Junior's baby, nothing else. He's got another baby on the way."

She almost fainted. "I ain't talked to Marie in years, but I need to reach out and make sure she's good."

"I'm sure she'll appreciate that. Y'all ain't never had drama."

"And we used to hang out a lot when the kids were small. She got married and things changed."

"I'll text you her number."

"Let me go talk to Junior because I can't believe this." She walked to the kitchen table and I walked into the living room.

"How's Ava doing?" I asked.

"She's being nosey, trying to figure out who's here," Kennedy said. Ava had her head resting on Kennedy's shoulder and picked up her head, hearing my voice.

"Let me get her."

Kennedy gladly handed her over and I rocked Ava in my arms. After Life, I said I didn't want any more kids, but Ava makes me want another one.

"What ya watching?" I asked.

"A movie," she said.

"Can you pause it and say hi to Ms. Porsha? She hasn't seen you in a while."

"Okay, I'm coming."

I walked back into the kitchen cradling Ava in my arms. When Porsha saw Ava, she gasped and put her hand over her mouth.

"Junior, is that your baby girl? She's beautiful." Porsha said. "Let me wash my hands so I can hold her."

Junior looked up at Ava and smiled when he saw Ava staring right at him. Porsha walked back to the table drying her hands on a paper towel. She sat down and I handed Ava to her. Ava fussed a little, but hearing Porsha's soft and sweet voice, she calmed down.

"She looks like you, Junior," Porsha said.

Kennedy walked into the kitchen.

"Hi Kennedy, you're so tall now," Porsha said.

"Hi," Kennedy said hugging Porsha. She sat at the table beside Mariah.

I stood back and watched Porsha interact with my family. It would have been like this if I didn't mess up. Porsha was always good to my kids and accepted them as her own which is why her and Marie didn't have any issues. The front door opened and closed and I wondered who it was.

"It's me," Jam said.

"And me," Eric said.

They appeared in the kitchen a few seconds later. Jam looked at Porsha and then at me. He caught me earlier with Chantel so I already know what he's thinking.

"Can you hang around for a bit?" I asked Porsha.

"Yeah," Porsha said.

Eric and Jam said hi to Porsha and the kids before we walked to the back porch to talk. We stood on the balcony overlooking the pool and the huge backyard.

"Bro, what you got going on?" Jam asked.

"Ain't nothing, bro. We just chillin'." I said.

"Did I miss something?" Eric asked.

"Rell and Chantel were kissing earlier," Jam said.

"What!" Eric said.

"You couldn't wait to tell," I said. "It was nothing. We were talking and it led there."

"So, you ain't really done with Chantel?" Eric asked.

"No, I am. It was just a moment. I found out some things about Chloe and I got to end it. She's causing too much drama in my life. It ain't worth it."

"Yeah, I heard some of the things she said to Jay and I'm not happy. She threatened to shoot Jay, you know?" Eric said.

"I didn't know that," I said.

"We have some news," Jam said.

"Yeah?" I said.

"They decided to make the resisting arrest charge a misdemeanor and it's now a without force charge," Jam said.

"That's good. A felony would have ruined everything." I said.

"Right."

"I'm assuming the meeting went well."

"It did. I know I'm facing time behind bars so I just have to wait and see. Just like you said, I have to get the right judge on the right day."

"And your mom is in custody. She put up a fight so she's in the hospital." Eric said.

"Y'all saw her?"

"She's not here and she's not allowed visitors."

"Where did they find her?"

"Down south somewhere. They will bring her back to the city to face all these charges. The crazy thing is she signed the divorce papers early this morning. And she texted me that she was ready to die. I didn't think nothing of it until I got the call from the officer."

"What's her condition?"

"Critical."

"That means they fucked her up."

"I wish she would have just turned herself in," Jam said.

"You okay?" I asked.

"I'm hoping she pulls through," Jam said.

"Do Jay and Rod know? And are they okay after finding out?" I asked.

"Yeah, we told them. Rod didn't care. I got to go check on Jay." Eric said.

"Tell her to call me. I want to hear from her." I said.

"I will. When are the interviews for the bakery?"

"Tomorrow. Jam, you think you can watch Ava for me?"

"Yeah, I got you."

I couldn't even wrap my head around the news they told me. I didn't know how to feel.

Chapter 39

Let's Decide

The next day, I showed up at the bakery at nine in the morning. Boss and Rod were already there waiting for me. I dap them up and we walked to the office.

If it wasn't for Boss helping out at the bakery and juice bar, we would have two failed businesses.

"Boss, how's the juice bar?" I asked.

"Better than ever," Boss said. "It's a good team over there and a dope atmosphere."

"You got Honey's official release date?"

"Still waiting. As soon as I know, you'll know. I hope to know a date by the end of the day."

"I'll wait to hear from you before I make any plans."

"How y'all mom doing?" Boss asked.

"Her condition is now stable. She's expected to survive." I said.

"How y'all feeling?" Boss asked.

"I don't feel nothing," Rod said.

"Yeah, same," I said.

"That's the pain talking," Boss said.

"Ain't no pain. That woman ain't shit." Rod said.

"When is the first interview?" I asked changing the subject.

"Nine thirty. I think we need to hire two people. Someone who can help out front and a person to bake and decorate the cakes. They get a lot of orders and that person can focus strictly on getting those special orders done." Boss said.

I handed him and Rod a sheet of paper. "I asked Eric to reach out to Jay. I wanted to see what she's looking for in an employee and what questions we should ask the applicants."

They both took time to read the list of skills and the questions we should ask.

"These are good questions. Some of these I wasn't even thinking about." Boss said.

"Before this interview, let me hear what y'all think about something," I said.

"Wassup?" Boss asked.

"I'm 'bout to end things with Chloe. It's a lot of drama and I ain't never been in the press this much."

"Right," Rod said.

"Yesterday, I slipped up with my baby moms, Chantel."

"Slipped up how?" Boss asked.

"I should say almost. It was a kiss, nothing else."

"She's engaged, right?" Boss asked.

"Yup to Chloe's ex-boyfriend."

"The world can't be that small," Boss said.

"What ya want to know?" Rod asked.

"Should I tell Chloe?"

"Hell nawl," Rod said.

"You ending things anyway so what's the point?" Boss said.

"Chantel's going to tell her dude and I'm sure it's going to get back to Chloe. I want her to hear it from me."

"Now why is Chantel telling? That's going to cause problems for you and her." Boss said

"That's what I told her but she feels guilty," I said.

"You got to convince her not to tell," Rod said.

Juan peeked his head into the office.

"Sorry to interrupt. Someone is here for an interview." Juan said.

"What's their name?" Boss asked.

"Skyy Bennett," Juan said.
"Send her back in five minutes," I said.
"Got it." He walked away.
We joked around for the next five minutes as we got ready for the first interview.
The last interview ended at eleven thirty and I was exhausted.
"Man, they were all so good," Rod said.
"Who y'all like most?" Boss asked.
"I liked Skyy for the front of the house position and Dana for the baker position. Her work was dope." I said.
"I liked Anita for the front of the house and Skyy for the baker position," Rod said.
"Why y'all like Skyy so much? She had an attitude the whole interview." Boss said.
"She's fine as hell," Rod said.
"That don't mean she's qualified," Boss said.
"What's your pick, Boss?" I asked.
"I like Dana for the baker position and Michelle for the front-end position," Boss said.
"Call in Juan and Tess and see what they think," I said.
"I'll go get them," Rod said leaving the office. He returned seconds later with Juan and Tess.
"Aight, we need y'all help since y'all met everyone and had a chance to talk to them," I said.
"Okay," Tess and Juan said.
"Right now, we are stuck between Dana and Skyy for the baker position. Tess, you would work closely with this person so we need your opinion." I said.
"Oh boy," Tess said. She hated being put on the spot.
"I like Dana," Juan said.
"Dana is sweet, creative, and a talented baker. Since she has so much experience, we wouldn't have to train her as much and she could jump right in and that's what we need. Things are stressful without Jay and I think she can handle that pressure." Tess said.
"I guess we have our person," I said.

"And for front of the house, we have Skyy, Anita, and Michelle," Boss said.

"Why Skyy?" Tess asked with a frown.

"That's those two," Boss said pointing at me and Rod. We could only chuckle.

"It's a tough decision between Anita and Michelle," Juan said.

"Dang, you not even considering Skyy?" I said.

"She was mad rude," Juan said.

"I missed her being rude. She seemed cool to me." Rod said.

"Of course you missed it," Tess said rolling her eyes.

We shared a laugh.

"I'm going to go with Michelle. She's mad cool, friendly, and has experience in baking and cashiering so she can do both if we need her to," Juan said.

"Those were my thoughts about Michelle too," Boss said.

"I like Michelle and I think she'll work well with the team," Tess said.

"Time to send out those emails. Find out Michelle and Dana's availability because Jay wants to meet them before we make a decision." I said.

"I got it," Rod said.

"Thank you, Tess and Juan," I said.

They walked out of the office. Rod got on the computer to send out the emails. I checked my phone for messages. I had several missed calls and unread text messages. I opened a text from Pops. Pops hated to text, so I knew it had to be serious if he was texting me.

Pops: **Just got Marley from school. Suspended 7 days for fighting**

"Damn," I said out loud.

"What happened?" Boss asked.

"Marley got in a fight," I said.

"These kids are wilding," Rod said.

"They've had to deal with Moms' shenanigans for the past ten years after Deja's death," I said.

"Can you believe Pops is about to have a baby?" Rod asked.

"Whose Pops?" Boss asked.

"Our Pops," Rod said.

"He's too old to be having a baby. He supposed to be loving on them grandbabies and great grands." Boss said.

"I'm still pissed," I said. "With his health problems, the last thing he needs is a baby."

"I agree with you there," Rod said. "Did you tell Boss how you almost got locked up for child abuse?"

"Oh yeah, I got to tell you this shit," I said.

"Wait! What happened?" Boss asked.

"Kennedy showed out in school being disrespectful and not doing her work. Where I'm from where you showed out is where you get worked out. I showed up at the school with a belt and they had an officer detain me when I was about to swing the belt. And then Kennedy said she didn't feel safe at home like I was abusing her and beating on her. They wouldn't let me check her out and they called Marie. Marie is the reason I'm not in jail. She stopped them from filing those bullshit ass charges."

"Nah, I would have had to smile for my mugshot. She needed her butt whopped for that." Boss said.

"I've been taking it easy on them and they've been running all over me," I said.

"I'm tough on mine but they know I love them. They know when I have to whup their ass, I ain't abusing them." Boss said.

"You already know I don't play no games with Coby. I'm raising him how Pops and Eric raised us." Rod said.

Chapter 40

Think About It

At one in the afternoon, I walked into the house.
"I'm home," I announced.
I'm in the kitchen," Pops said.
I took off my shoes and walked through the house. Pops was sitting at the kitchen table holding Ava.
"Wassup Pops?" I asked.
"Not too much," Pops said.
"Where's Jam?" I asked.
"He went out. How did the interviews go?"
"Good. We think we found two people for the bakery."
"That's good."
"Where's Marley?"
"In his room."
"You handled him?"
"Nah, left that to you."
"Did he tell you what happened?"
"Him and another kid got in a fight with a teacher."
"What! You didn't say all of that in the text."
"I wanted you to get here safely. Marley is lucky they are not pressing charges."
"Shit. Let me get a drink to calm my nerves." I poured two shots of Vodka and took them back.
"Don't you start that heavy drinking again!"
"I'm not, Pops."
I walked up the stairs to Marley's room. I knocked on the door and walked in. Marley sat up in bed.
"You fought a teacher today?" I asked.

"He started with us," Marley said.

"Tell me what happened."

I crossed my arms and leaned against the wall. Marley thought about what to say before starting the story.

"So, boom, we were in math class. Mr. Tune felt like me and Quinn weren't doing the work since we were talking. But we were working and wasn't bothering nobody. Mr. Tune wouldn't leave us alone and coming at us aggressively. After a while, I was like you act like you want to fight or something. And Mr. Tune undid the buttons on his shirt and squared up."

"That's crazy," I said.

"Quinn ran up and swung. I tried to get them apart and Mr. Tune started swinging on me."

"A grown-ass man swung on you?"

"Yeah. That's why he got suspended and I'm sure he's going to get fired. You can read the write-up. I ain't lying."

He walked over to me and handed me a pink slip of paper. I read over the paper.

"As soon as he got aggressive, you should have walked outta the class and reported it. I don't ever want you getting into fights with adults unless you're defending yourself. According to this report, one of y'all called him a bitch, and that escalated the situation. You left that part out."

He dropped his head.

"You didn't think I would read the report? I wasn't born yesterday, Marley."

I walked into his closet and dug around for a belt. I walked back out with a thick leather belt.

"I'm going to go to your school and sort all of this out. I need you to understand that you're in trouble for disrespecting your teacher. That's not cool at all. You understand me?"

"Yes sir."

"I'm about to give you two options for your punishment. Either a whopping or let me have your phone for five days."

"I can't be without my phone for that long."

"Stand up."

I left him in the middle of the floor crying. I joined Pops in the kitchen.

"Sounds like you handled it," Pops said.

"I did," I said sitting at the kitchen table.

"Who's getting the kids today?"

"Eric. He had the day off. You heard anything else about Momma?"

"Nah, I haven't."

And then it was quiet at the table.

"What's your issue?" Pops asked a few minutes later.

"Nothing," I said.

"You don't act like it's nothing."

"Pops, you don't need a kid right now."

"A baby is on the way whether you like it or not."

"You're supposed to be spending the rest of your life enjoying retirement, relaxing, and spoiling the grandkids. Now you 'bout to add the stress of a child to your plate. That doesn't make sense to me."

"I'm grown, Rell. I can make my own decisions. I know it doesn't make sense to you but it makes sense to us. Stephanie decided that she wanted a kid. Yeah, it caught me off-guard but I told her, let's make it happen. She got off birth control and here we are."

"What kind of life can you give this child? You're sick all the time and barely have any energy to do anything."

"Don't go there, Rell. I'm still healthy for the most part. I can't wait to welcome this little one into the world and see their little face."

I shook my head. "Sure, Pops. I still think this is irresponsible."

"I don't tell you how to run shit in your household so don't do that to me."

"Tell me something."
"What?"
"Did you and Chloe do anything?"
"Hell nawl. I wouldn't do you like that, Rell."
"But she wanted to do something?"
"She tried to cop a feel or whatever and I had to send her on her way."
"Why you ain't tell me that?"
"I didn't want you to flip the shit on me like you always do. How did you find out?"
"Chantel told me."
"What! How did she find out?"
"She's been fighting with Chloe and I guess it came up."
"I'm sorry for not coming to you."
"Y'all ain't do nothing?"
"Nothing."
Marley walked into the kitchen.
"Can I make a snack?" Marley asked.
"What ya making?" I asked.
"Noodles and baked chicken."
"That's a snack? Go ahead. The pots and pans are on the stove. Just take out one chicken breast."
"Okay."
"Look at our baby boy chefing it up," Pops said, "I guess working in the restaurant is paying off."
"He's been cooking a lot lately," I said.
"You should let me make a cooking video," Marley said.
"You'll be home so we'll make it happen. We can film tomorrow, just think about what you want to cook." I said.
"I already know," Marley said.
"What?" I asked.
"Four-meat spaghetti."
"What's in it?"
"Ground beef, sausage, shrimp, and pork meatballs."

"That's a heavy meal."

"I think it will be good. You can have a salad with it."

"A salad don't make that any healthier."

Marley laughed. "Can I make it?"

"Yeah, we'll go grocery shopping in the morning."

"I want to visit Momma too."

That statement had me stuck and I didn't know what to say. I haven't been back to Deja's gravesite since they buried her. A piece of me doesn't want to believe she's gone.

"I'll text Rod and I'm sure he can find a time for y'all to go," I said.

"I want you to come with us," Marley said.

"I don't know 'bout that."

He pouted. "Please."

"Let me think about it."

Chapter 41

Bottom Line

The next day, Erin came to the house to help Marley film his video. I had other things to do so Jam stood in my place to help him.

I was headed to a restaurant to meet Reem, Marie's ex-husband. It was the only time he was available and I needed to talk to him. He was already seated at the restaurant when I got there. I sat across from him.

"What's good, bro?" Reem asked.

"Ain't nothing. Wassup with you?" I asked.

"Shit. Same old, same old."

The fine-ass waitress walked over to the table to get our drink order. I read her name tag. *Destiny*. She was short, slim with a phat ass, and had hazel-colored eyes. I was mesmerized by her beauty and physique. Once she walked away, I got down to business.

"I invited you out to talk about a few things," I said.

"Talk to me," Reem said.

"When I was on the road or life got in the way, you stepped up and raised Kennedy and Junior as your own and I've always been appreciative of that," I said.

"Of course," Reem said.

"I'm trying to understand what happened. They feel like you don't fuck with them anymore. Even though they pretend it doesn't bother them, I know it hurts them that y'all are not close anymore." I said.

Reem nodded his head. "Bro, the divorce was rough. Kennedy and Junior were angry and pushed me away.

I know I should have fought a little harder to be there for them. I didn't know what to do."

"Kennedy was a straight-A student who hardly got in trouble and now she's acting out in school. Junior is a dad and addicted to drugs."

Reem looked shocked. "I'm sorry, bro. I'll reach out to them and check on them."

"I appreciate that."

"Man, you just dropped a bomb on me. They started acting out a year ago and we thought nothing of it. Then we realized the seriousness of everything when we found out Junior was hustling and Kennedy had a bad attitude. They were cursing me out, being disrespectful, and trying to fight me."

Now I looked at him shocked. "See? I didn't know all of that. They painted a different picture. I knew you wouldn't just abandon them."

"Nah, I wouldn't. When I ask if they want to hang out, they always say no. I tried to call and they sent the calls to voicemail. It's not like I haven't tried to keep a relationship with them but they act like they don't want me in their lives. I stopped trying to be there for them."

Destiny walked to the table with our drinks and got our food order. We paused the conversation to tell her what we wanted. She sashayed away like she knew we were watching and we were.

I took a sip of my drink. "How's life, bro?"

"Life is good. I'm trying to rebuild my life and get used to the single life. Me and Marie were together for ten years. Those feelings don't go away, ya know?" Reem said.

"Sounds like she wanted the divorce and you didn't," I said.

"I wanted to make things work but she was tired and kept saying she wasn't happy anymore," Reem said.

"How are the kids?" I asked.

"Benjamin, Journey, True, and Faith are all good and getting big. I'm just glad Marie ain't bitter and we can co-parent." Reem said.

"That's good. I'm trying to get to that point with two of my baby mommas."

"It took a lot of work for us to have a good co-parenting relationship. I can admit I was an asshole at first and that made things extremely difficult."

"My baby mommas like drama and fighting with me and my new girlfriends."

"Sounds like some maturing needs to happen."

"They ain't there yet."

"What's going on with you and your girl? I saw you posted on some blog with some young thang."

"Ain't nothing going on. I'm about to be single soon."

"Damn, how long y'all been together?"

"Almost a year."

"The last girl I remember was Chantel."

"I forgot you met her. It's been a couple since then."

"How old is y'all baby girl now?"

"Eleven months and I can't believe it."

"We got to get our kids together."

"I'm down for that."

Chapter 42

Cover Up

After chopping it up with Reem for two hours, I went to the bakery. Today, Dana and Michelle would meet the manager and fill out new hire paperwork. I said hi to the staff and walked to the office.

I was surprised to see Jay sitting behind the desk. She was completely focused as she typed away on the computer and completely focused. She looked up and we didn't say anything. I looked around the room trying to think of something to say.

"Wassup baby girl?" I finally said after minutes of awkward silence.

And Jay breaks down in tears. I closed the office door and rushed to be by her side.

"I don't know what to say, Rell. I feel horrible about everything." Jay cried.

"It wasn't your fault and I don't blame you," I said.

"I still can't believe Sammy would do something like this. I've known him for two years and feel like I don't know him. He's been acting crazy so I've had to lay low so he doesn't find me. I'm moving in with Daddy because the threats are too much."

This reminded me of one of the last conversations I had with Deja. I was worried and scared for Jay but wasn't sure what to do. This situation had me feeling so helpless and I hated that.

"Is it true you're pregnant?" I had to know.

"Chloe told you, huh?"

"Yeah. Have you told anyone?" I asked.

"No, I can't bring myself to tell anyone," Jay said.

"I won't tell anyone. Jay, what happened between you and Chloe?"

"We have history you don't know about."

I pulled up a chair beside her. Jay wiped her face with a tissue.

"What history?" I asked.

"We worked together at the club when she lived here briefly. She was a dancer and I was a bartender. She always wanted Sammy but he never wanted her. And when he picked me, she felt she was better and was always mad and jealous about it."

"You think she got with me to spite you? Is that why you told me to be careful?"

"I don't know her intentions, Rell. I know she's an attention seeker and a known pass-around. I don't have a lot of good things to say about her. And now she's talking to Sammy and Shawn like they're her best friends and the three of them are doing this to hurt me."

There was a knock at the door.

"Who is it?" I asked.

"Rod."

I looked at Jay.

"You can let him in," Jay said.

I opened the door and closed it once he was in the office.

"Damn, y'all having a moment. Feels like I'm interrupting something." Rod said. He sat in the chair across from Jay.

"We're just talking," I said sitting beside her.

"I'm a mess. My life is a mess." Jay said resting her head on the desk.

I rubbed her on the back.

"I just want you to know I'll protect you at all costs. I won't let Chloe come at you crazy or even touch you.

She'll be here this weekend and we're going to talk." I said.

"I thought you were going to have her back more than mine. I know we're not the closest and we fight a lot."

"That doesn't matter. We're family and you're my baby sis. Of course, I got your back."

"You've been hiding out, sis. I've been trying to reach you to make sure you're good." Rod said.

"I appreciate y'all. I just didn't know what to say. So much happened at once and I didn't know how to deal."

"I understand," Rod said.

"I got to tell you something, Rod."

"What?"

"I'm pregnant."

He jumped out of his seat. "You're what?" He sat back down in his chair still in disbelief.

She stood and tightened her shirt and showed off her growing belly.

"You're really grown, Jay. Our baby is having a baby." Rod said, "Is Sam the daddy?"

"Sadly, yes," Jay said.

"He's threatening her," I said.

Rod looked at me. "Me and you got to handle that."

"No, I don't want y'all to get hurt or make the situation worse. I'm just going to stay out of the way." Jay said.

"How many months are you?" Rod asked.

"I'm seventeen weeks pregnant so about four months."

"How long have you known?" I asked.

"I found out last month. It's too late for an abortion so I got to figure things out and get prepared to be a mommy."

"We're here for you," Rod said.

"I thought y'all were going to be mad at me," Jay said.

"Nah, we'll leave the being mad to Eric. He's going to go crazy when he finds out." I said.

"You can't hide it too much longer," Rod said.

"I don't know how to tell Daddy," Jay said.

"There ain't no easy way to tell him. He's already on edge because of this situation with Jam." I said.

"That's true. I'll wait until all that blows over before I tell him."

"How are you feeling about Momma?" I asked.

"I feel sad, hurt, and angry. I feel like I don't know her. She's the only other person to know about the pregnancy. She was excited and it was weird to see her so excited because she's never been over the moon excited about the other grandbabies. I knew that something was off about her relationship with y'all. And now it makes sense as I'm learning everything she put y'all and Deja through. I feel bad that y'all didn't experience the mom me and Jam experienced. I've just been on a rollercoaster of emotions."

"I've been numb since I found out everything from Ted touching Mariah to Moms stealing all this money for his legal fees," Rod said, "When I hear people talk about their mom and the good memories of their mom, I don't have that. Mom reminded us often that she didn't want us. I thank God we were able to escape to Pops' house. To see her be so loving and just a good mom to Jay and Jam was hurtful."

"What's crazy is that I didn't realize what she put us through wasn't normal," I said. "I never thought the harsh way she talked to us was wrong. She treated us like shit and I saw nothing wrong with that. It was always Momma being Momma or we excused it as her being in a bad mood."

"And we blamed ourselves and tried to be better so she could treat us better. That's why I went out on the block with Moms. It was the only time she cared about me and showed some affection. It was short-lived. Once I got caught, she got mad at me saying I wasn't more careful. She was so mad that she cut me off." Rod said.

"Y'all need therapy. What she did wasn't right. No mother should treat their children like that." Jay said.

My phone vibrated and it was a text message from Marie.

`Marie:` **`Finally went through the phone. She has social media accounts and texts with a couple of boys, Mitchell and Paul.`**
`Me:` **`I'll handle it.`**

She then sent a series of screenshots from Kennedy's phone with messages from these boys and her different social media accounts. Man, I was pissed seeing these messages and photos.

"What happened? Your whole demeanor changed." Jay said.

"Kennedy is growing up and it's killing me," I said.

"What she do now?" Rod asked.

"You know Marie took her phone?" I said.

"Yeah, you told me that," Rod said.

"I told Marie to go through the phone and she finally went through it. Kennedy has social media accounts that she's not supposed to have. And she's texting boys. Marie sent me the messages and it's like they're talking in code."

"Let me see. Maybe I can figure it out." Jay said.

I handed her the phone.

"You got to have a real talk with her," Rod said, "A lot of these kids shouldn't be on social media. They're on these sites wilding, talking to whoever, and then meeting up with strangers. It's dangerous especially if you don't know they're on these sites."

I nodded my head taking in what he said. "Yeah, we got to talk about this."

"I don't understand these messages. Why hasn't Marie had the talk with her and let her know how dangerous it is to be on these sites?" Jay asked.

"Marie let Kennedy and Junior do whatever. Bless her heart, she tries to be tough on them but they run over her. It's always been this way."

Chapter 43

Kicked Out

As soon as Kennedy got home, we went upstairs to my room to talk.

"What I do now?" Kennedy asked sitting on the edge of my bed.

"Me and your mom went through your phone," I said.

Her jaw dropped to the ground. "Y'all what? Don't y'all believe in privacy?"

"It should be nothing in that phone you're hiding from me and your mom."

"I'm not hiding anything."

"Why are you on social media? You're not even old enough for an account so I know you're using a fake birthdate."

"My friends are on there."

"I don't care if Jesus was on there. You're not allowed to have social media accounts. The biggest problem is that me and your mom didn't know you had these accounts. You are following and befriending strangers on these sites. You don't know who is behind some of these accounts. Someone can message you pretending to be someone and then you meet up with this person and you're never heard from again."

"That happens?"

"Yes, it happens. That's why me and your mom are against you having social media accounts. You are too naïve to be on these sites."

"I'll delete my accounts."

"No worries. We did that for you. You also posted a photo of yourself in itty bitty shorts and a sports bra. I don't know what you were thinking but never take a photo like that again."

She covered her face with her hands. "This is humiliating."

"Imagine how I felt seeing my twelve-year-old like that."

"Okay, I won't take photos like that."

"I can't believe you posted that photo for the world to see. That was bold of you."

"It was cute."

"Nothing was cute about that picture. Who are Paul and Mitchell?"

"Y'all went through my messages too?"

"We went through everything."

"That's not fair. It's my phone."

"We pay the bill."

"Y'all can keep the stupid phone. I'll get a job and get my own shit."

"Who you cussing at?" She crossed her arms and pouted. "Who are these boys?"

"Friends. That's all you need to know."

"Why y'all talking in code?"

"That's just how we text." I showed her a message. "Y'all took screenshots of my messages? I'm sure you got messages in your phone you don't want me to see."

"I'm grown. Now, tell me what you and Paul were talking about."

She rolled her eyes. "Skipping school to go to the mall. I decided not to do it."

"So, you do have some sense?"

"Are we done?"

I showed her Mitchell's messages.

"You don't want to know."

"I knew it! Y'all were being nasty. I knew those cat and eggplant emojis weren't there for no reason."

"Daddy!"
"Does this mean you're having sex?"
"No, I'm still a virgin."
"And it better stay that way."
"I'm saving myself until marriage."
"Texting like this, I'm not sure."
"Anything else?"
"Why you got an attitude? I'm not even coming at you as crazy as I should be."

"I just think it's insane y'all went through my phone. Just because I'm a child doesn't mean I don't deserve privacy."

"You're twelve and you don't know everything. We got to prepare you for this world. Not everyone will mean you good. We want to protect you as much as we can. And I hope you know that you can't just be sending freaky shit like this to a boy. Now, he's only thinking about you for one thing. I understand you're curious but you need to be careful."

"Y'all can keep the phone if I can't have privacy. I don't need y'all snooping around and being in my business. I don't want the phone that bad."

"I'm going to be in your business until you're of age to make sound decisions. You can't just do what you want to do."

Kennedy sucked her teeth. "I hate it here."

"You want to go back to your mom's house since you hate it here? If you don't want to follow my rules, it's probably best you go back to your mom's place."

"Actually, I do want to go back because you're acting like a bitch."

I knew I heard that wrong. "I act like a what?"

"You heard me." She said this while rolling her neck.

"Go ahead and pack your things. You're going back to your mom's house. I'm not going to be constantly disrespected by you in my house."

"Fine by me."

She stood and I popped her on the behind. She swung at me and I had to grab her fist before it connected.

"Oh, you have lost your mind. Let me show you that you ain't that big and bad as you think." I sat on the bed and pulled her across my knee and gave her an old-fashioned butt whopping. I stood her up. I hated doing this.

"Get your things packed." She limped out of the room and I called Marie.

"Hey," Marie said.

"Hey, I need you to come get Kennedy," I said.

"What happened?"

"I had a conversation with Kennedy about the things we found in her phone. And she's angry we looked through the phone. She was disrespectful and even called me a bitch. And when I popped her, she swung on me."

"Is she alive?"

"Yeah, but she got to go back to your place. She don't respect my rules."

"I understand. I'm about to pick up my rugrats from aftercare. I should be over that way in an hour."

"She'll be outside waiting on you."

"Lawd, don't kick her out, Rell. Just stay calm until I get there."

"I can't make no promises. If she says anything smart, she's going outside."

"Let me hurry to y'all. I'll see you in a little bit."

"Aight, see you soon."

I ended the call and left the room. I passed by Kennedy and Mariah's room where Kennedy was crying as she packed her things. Mariah was sitting beside her crying and helping her pack. I said nothing to them and continued downstairs.

A hush fell over the room. Marley, Junior, and Jam were at the kitchen table. I walked to the living room and checked on Ava in her bassinet.

I lost my cool with Kennedy and I needed to calm down. I plopped down on the couch and watched sports highlights.

Junior walked into the living room and stood over the bassinet watching Ava sleep. He was slowly coming around. He joined me on the couch a few minutes later.

"What's good?" I asked.

"I want help," Junior said.

I took my eyes away from the television and stared at him. "You serious?"

"Yeah. I can't keep living like this."

"The program I found would have you at the facility for thirty days then you would continue with outpatient rehab services for a few months."

He thought about it. "I really got to be gone for thirty days?"

"Yeah."

"Can y'all visit?"

"Yeah, we'll come visit you. I would rather visit you there than behind bars."

He leaned back on the couch. "I'll do it."

I was so proud of him for taking this first step. This was going to be a long journey for both of us.

"I love you, son," I said.

"I love you too, Dad."

He hasn't called me Dad in years. I kissed him on the cheek and he didn't wipe it off. We just chill on the couch watching sports highlights. It was cool to have this moment with Junior. It was like old times.

About ten minutes later, Kennedy and Mariah appeared in the room with her two suitcases and duffel bags. Both Mariah and Kennedy's eyes were red and puffy.

"Ma, you acting like she's moving to another state. You'll still see her at school." I said.

"I'm going to miss her being here," Mariah said.

"You're being dramatic. Y'all go to the same school and will hang out like always." I said.

"You kicking her out?" Junior asked.

"Absolutely. She's talking to boys, showing her body on social media, and has accounts she shouldn't have." I said.

"Can't save you there, sis. Let's go outside and wait on Momma." Junior got up from the couch and the three of them walked outside. Jam walked into the room.

"Where's Kennedy going?" Jam asked.

"She's going back to her momma's house. She keeps saying she hates it here." I said.

"She's just mad she can't do what she wants."

"Exactly. Me and Rod saw Jay today."

"How is she?"

"She's emotional and overwhelmed. Sam is acting crazy."

"What else is new?"

"She got to move in with Eric."

"Dad is going to drive her crazy. That's why I ain't move in with him."

"You ready for court?"

"As ready as I'll ever be. I got to take my car to the shop tomorrow because they damaged it. I got to get a new paint job and everything."

"That's the least of your worries."

"I know."

"Did you quit your job?"

"Big bro was trippin'. I'm going to get a job somewhere else."

"What happened between you and Rod?"

"Rod was trippin' cuz I asked for two weeks off. He said nah and I walked off the job."

"Where are you going to work now?"

"I'll figure it out. I've been applying like crazy and got a couple of interviews next week."

"Have you filmed your first video?"

"Yeah, it's a vlog of me quitting my job."

"Bro, you're crazy. That's why Rod was trippin'. You had a camera in his face."

"Maybe. The video is funny as hell though."

Marley walked into the room.

"How did filming go?" I asked.

"It was fun," Marley said.

"You got to try his spaghetti. I wasn't sure at first but it's good." Jam said.

"I'll get some in a second. Erin sent me a clip of you in the kitchen. You're a natural and you didn't seem nervous." I said.

"I wasn't nervous," Marley said, "And Jam was behind the scenes cutting up."

"That sounds like Jam. He don't take nothing seriously." I said.

"My video dropped today and the girls are wilding in the comments," Jam said.

"I got to check out the video and comments. It's been a busy day. I haven't had much downtime." I said.

"Yo boy getting views and marriage proposals," Jam said.

Chapter 44

Bad Idea

Friday is finally here and it's Valentine's Day. I've been waiting for this day all week. I couldn't wait to see Chloe and have this conversation with her.

At the last minute, Chloe made this a girls' trip and invited three of her friends. Since I made a lot of plans and spent a lot of money, I decided not to cancel anything even though I had plans to end shit with Chloe.

I pulled up to the airport. Chloe and her friends, all dressed in club attire, were standing about and talking. Chloe squealed when she spotted me. She was happy to see me but I wasn't happy to see her. They put their things in the trunk and climbed in. Chloe introduced me to Alexis, Summer, and Tiara.

"What's your problem?" Chloe asked.

"Nothing," I said.

I drove to the hotel that I reserved for us. I didn't say much during the drive there. I told her friends to wait in the lobby as we went to the suite.

I opened the door to the room. Chloe gasped seeing the rose petals on the floor. The rose petals led to the bed. On the bed were flowers, a gold studded teddy bear, a stack of cash, and the new Chanel purse she wanted. Chloe cried seeing everything and then she wrapped her arms around me.

"This is beautiful," Chloe said.

"We got to talk," I said.

"Uh oh. What did I do?"

"I'm going to let y'all get settled in. Come meet me at the hibachi restaurant down the street in two hours. Leave your friends behind so it's just us."

I dropped a kiss on her lips and left her looking confused. I told her friends that it was nice meeting them as I left the hotel.

It was ten in the morning and I needed something to do before I met up with Chloe for lunch so I went to the gym. I will start training my client next week. Marie called me while I was running on the treadmill. I slowed it down and answered the call.

"Hey Ma," I said.

"I see you went all out for your girl, KoKo. I thought you were breaking up with her." Marie said.

"We're going to lunch to have the conversation. I had this planned for a while and it was too much of a hassle to cancel everything."

"I'm going to send you a video of Kennedy and my girls opening the gifts you sent them. And Reem just stopped by and delivered more goodies for them. They're getting spoiled rotten today."

"Did you get spoiled today?"

"Yeah. The guy I'm talking to got a dozen roses and a fruit arrangement sent to my office."

"Is Kennedy still mad at me?"

"Not as mad. She said she might call you later. When is Junior going away to this facility?"

"Next Thursday."

"You think it's going to help?"

"Only if Junior wants to be helped. He told me he was serious and this is a good program. We can only pray for him."

"It breaks my heart to see him spiraling out of control and unable to do anything about it. Junior is the one that taught us all about parenthood."

"I never saw this coming, Marie. We knew he was depressed and tried to get him therapy and it didn't seem to help much. I'm still trying to deal with the fact my son is battling addiction. It's hard to even say that out loud."

"I can't say it at all. I pray he gets better."

"Did Porsha reach out to you?"

"Yeah. It was good to hear from her. I'm proud of how far she has come especially with owning a beauty shop. She also talked about her and Chauncey's relationship."

"Yeah? How do you feel?"

"It's a complicated situation. Porsha seems to be in love and she's not doing this to hurt you. Now, Chauncey is a different story. I think he's using her to get back at you and Porsha is going to get hurt in the end. I ain't trying to ruin her happiness but she needs to be careful."

"I already tried to warn her but she thinks they have a genuine connection."

"I feel for her."

"Have you talked to Chantel?"

"Lawd, you know I can't talk to that little girl. I lose brain cells every time I have a conversation with her."

I chuckled. "Ma, you crazy."

"Rell, your next girl got to be more than pretty."

I sat at a booth near the back of the restaurant waiting for Chloe. She was in the taxi on the way to the restaurant. I was nervous because I wasn't sure how this shit would go.

Chloe slid into the booth across from me five minutes later. She was now wearing a gold glittery mini dress with fur draped over her arm and her hair was straightened and flowing down her back.

"You ain't cold?" I asked.

"I got my fur," Chloe said.

The waitress walked over to the table and got our drink order. I ordered a water and Chloe ordered a vodka tonic. I knew if she had alcohol in her system, this was going to go left.

The waitress walked away to get our drinks.

"Why you acting so cold?" Chloe asked.

"Because I found out a lot of shit about you," I said.

"Like what?" Chloe asked.

"You causing a lot of drama in my life and constantly lying. You act like I'm dumb and can't figure things out."

"What have I lied about?"

"Come on. Don't play dumb. You acting innocent but you threatened to shoot my sister and told my baby momma and baby to go to hell."

"I didn't mean those things. I said a lot of shit out of anger."

The waitress brought our drinks and gave us time to view the menu.

"That ain't cool, Chloe," I said.

"They came at me first and weren't nice to me either," Chloe said.

"And I'll address that with them. Right now, we're talking about you. I know you tried to get with my Pops too."

She dropped her head. "So, this is where it's going? I might as well not order lunch."

"Nah, we can still have a nice lunch."

I got the waitress' attention so we could order. She walked over to us and we placed our order. She walked away to put in our order.

Chloe sipped her drink. "I'm sorry, Rell."

"I didn't fall in love with KoKo. I fell in love with Chloe. I know you have a good heart but you've been hurt so many times in your life. Maybe you need to heal before getting into a serious relationship. You ain't ready for what I'm ready for and that's fine. That's why I'm letting you go so you can be free to do you. That's what you want, right?"

"No, that's not what I want. I'm trying to change, Rell. I made a huge mistake. Your dad was flirting with me and I was flirting back."

I doubted that Pops was flirting with her. Pops is friendly and charming and she probably took him being nice as him flirting.

"It's bigger than the Pops' situation. You're still communicating with an ex that you told me not to worry about. You hugged up with a new dude every night. You look single to me."

"You don't do social media and don't like being posted. I respect your privacy and I'm wrong? That doesn't make sense to me."

"It's not about me being posted on your page. It's about respecting me and our relationship. You wouldn't want my page filled with photos of me hugged up with random women."

"That's the thing, these guys aren't random. They're my closest friends. Rell, you're insecure and can't handle being with a beautiful girl."

Now, I was getting aggravated. "Fuck outta here with that. Just admit you were being disrespectful. You got an excuse for everything but won't own up to shit. You've done a lot of low-down and fucked up things."

She squinted her eyes and glared at me. "What have I done?"

"C'mon now. You don't need a list. I'm going to sleep with an ex and see how you feel."

"I haven't slept with an ex."

"You ain't met up with Ty?"

"We met up but we didn't have sex."

I side-eyed her not believing that for one minute. "Oh aight. This is going nowhere. I wish you the best, Chloe. I'm 'bout to get my food to go."

"You're triflin'. You could have told me this over the phone. You wait until I get here on my favorite holiday to drop this bomb on me. It's fucked up."

"What's fucked up is you wishing death on my baby girl who had nothing to do with you and Chantel's petty beef. You went behind my back and tried to fuck my Pops, your ex, and whoever else. I didn't realize this whole time I was in a relationship with KoKo and not Chloe."

"Rell, please give me another chance. I'll do better."

"Do better for someone else."

She picked up her cup and threw her drink in my face. This woman has lost her mind. I stood and wiped my face with a napkin. She lunged across the table. I steady myself as she swung her fists and threw shit off the tables. I knew this sit-down would end badly but not this bad. I pushed her away and restrained her in the booth.

"Are you crazy?" I asked.

"No, are you crazy? You bum ass bitch!"

All I saw was red and I had to get away before I did something I regret. I turned to walk away and she jumped on my back.

A manager came over to restrain her. I couldn't believe she attacked me. I looked at the camera on my phone and there were scratches on my face.

"Look at my face!" I yelled to Chloe.

"Ah-ha, that's what your ass gets," Chloe said licking out her tongue and mocking me.

The manager escorted us out of the restaurant. Manny, my good friend and owner of the restaurant, walked out of the restaurant. Chloe was a few feet away pacing.

"I'm sorry, Manny," I said. "You know I'll cover the damages."

"Stay away from the crazy chicks," Manny said.

"Who you calling crazy?" Chloe asked.

She ran over to us and started swinging on Manny. I stood in between them and pushed her away.

"You got to chill," I said.

"Let me go!" she said swinging wildly.

I felt a fist in my eye and I just wanted to fuck her up. I let her go and held my eye. I heard the police sirens in the distance and cursed under my breath.

"See the shit you caused?" I said.

I sat on the bench outside the restaurant trying to collect myself. Chloe stood to the side with her arms crossed. Three police cars parked in front of the restaurant. An officer walked up to me.

He looked at my face and winced. "Do you need medical attention?"

"I'm good," I mumbled.

The other officers got out of their cars, one went to Manny and the other went to Chloe.

"I'm Officer Payne. Can you tell me what happened today?"

Then we all turned to Chloe yelling and crying hysterically. She was spazzing out and I'd never seen this side of her.

"I broke up with her," I said.

"On Valentine's Day?" Officer Payne asked. Even he knew that was a bad idea.

"No better day," I joked.

"Was she defending herself or did she attack first?"

"C'mon. I ain't 'bout to hit no woman. She threw a drink and jumped across the table. All I did was push her to get her off me and restrain her. Look at my fucking face!"

"I see it. That's why I asked if you needed medical attention."

"This shit ain't nothing. I played football and got hurt worse than this."

Chloe flipped out when they told her she was going to jail.

"I don't want her to go to jail," I said.

"That's not up to you when she's causing a public disturbance and threatening officers," Officer Payne said.

"Chloe, chill out. Damn." I said.

"Fuck you, Rell. None of this would be happening if your ass wasn't acting like a clown with your punk ass."

The female officer read Chloe her rights and put her hands behind her back.

"What about the fucking marks on me?" Chloe yelled as they were putting the cuffs on her wrists. I stood to my feet ready to go.

As they walked past me, Chloe tried to kiss me and I pushed her out of the way. And I ended up in cuffs too. Manny fussed with Officer Payne and the other officer.

"This shit ain't fair. Y'all got my man in cuffs when he was attacked by this crazy chick!" Manny yelled.

"Yo, get my jewelry and cash!" I said.

Manny took my chain and diamond necklace from around my neck, the cash from my pockets, and the Rolex off my wrist.

"Call Rod and let him know what happened and you can give all that shit to him," I said.

"I got you, bro. We gonna get you out. Just stay calm, bro. Don't let these folks rile you up." Manny said.

Chapter 45

Just Messy

I was booked into jail at noon and didn't walk out until six in the evening. It took them forever to process me and grant a bond. A news crew stood in front of the jail, and I didn't say anything to the reporters. I walked over to Rod's truck and climbed in. He handed me my jewelry and cash.

"It's a shit storm right now," Rod said.

I leaned my head against the window. "What happened?"

"Chloe bailed out an hour ago and she's been on a warpath on social media exposing Jay, Chantel, and you."

"She exposed Jay's pregnancy?"

"Not yet. Just revealing their messages like the family has always been against her and tried to sabotage the relationship. I'm sure she's going to expose a lot more. She's painting you out to be some monster because you broke up with her on Valentine's Day and acting like you beat her ass."

"I don't even do this social media shit but I guess I have to respond to this."

"A lot of people are sticking up for you. I would just lay low. How the hell did things go left?"

"I was just trying to end shit, bro."

"You always end up with these crazy women."

I turned on my phone and looked on social media and saw our mugshots and all the drama. I worked too hard for shit to go down like this. I got a notification that Chantel is going live and I joined the live to see what was going on. And it was Chantel, Ty, Jay, and three other women in a car pulling up to the hotel to fight Chloe. I showed Rod my phone and he just shook his head.

"Jay, better stay outta the way. I can't believe they brought Life to this shit." I said.

I typed in the comments for her to go home. I tuned into the live when Chloe walked out of the hotel in a tracksuit and her hair pulled back into a ponytail. She had Tiara, Alexis, and Summer with her and they were ready for a fight.

There was no talking. Chantel ran right up to Chloe and punched her repeatedly in the face. You could hear Ty behind the phone hyping up the fight. And I could hear Life crying and one of the women trying to calm her down.

"This shit is sad," I said.

Rod pulled into the driveway and I propped up the phone on the dashboard to watch the fight.

"She just got out and is already in more mess. Chantel beating her ass though." Rod said.

"As much shit as Chantel talks, I would hope she knows how to fight," I said.

I read the comments as they scrolled up the screen. Alexis jumped into the fight to help Chloe and one of Chantel's girls jumped into the fight. Jay was standing to the side like she was ready to be tagged in and I was praying she stayed out of it. It was crazy that this was going down live for the world to see.

I exited the live because I couldn't take it. It shouldn't have gotten to this point. I took a selfie, posted the photo, and captioned it Happy Valentine's Day. I wanted people to see what she did to my face but I didn't want to say too much about the situation. Rod and I climbed out of the car and went into the house.

Jam, Junior, Marley, Coby, and Mariah sat at the kitchen table with their eyes glued to their phones.

"Wassup?" I said.

They all jumped up and ran to me and I embraced them.

"I'm okay, y'all," I said.

We gathered around the kitchen table to talk.

"What y'all up to?" I asked.

"We were watching Chantel's live. And Junior was going at it with people in your comments on the new photo you posted." Jam said.

"The fight ended?" I asked.

"I don't know. IG shut down the live. It was getting crazy." Jam said.

"Chantel and her girls were winning," Mariah said.

"Why did you go to jail if she attacked you?" Marley asked.

"Officers being petty. Jam, how was court?" I asked.

"They just read all the charges and gave me a new court date," Jam said.

"Did they drop any charges?"

"A lame-ass traffic charge of failure to remain in lane. Everything else they kept." Jam said.

"It's hell going through the court system. Everything takes so long." Rod said.

"I'm ready for all of this to be over," Jam said.

"They finally brought Moms up the road. She's in a wheelchair and she looked rough." Rod said.

"You saw her?" I asked.

"Eric sent me the video from a news article," Rod said.

"Today's been a wild day," I said.

"Jay just texted me that everybody is good and nobody got arrested," Jam said.

"Good because no one else needs to be bailed out today," I said.

"Chloe's going off on live with a bloody nose and swollen eye," Mariah said.

We all looked at her phone and I winced seeing her face.

"Jeez, she got her ass beat," I said.

"Somebody needs to take her phone. She's been at it for the past two hours." Rod said.

"I'm hungry," Coby said.

"Turn that off, Ma. I don't want you to listen to that. Come on Rod, let's cook." I said.

Rod and I looked through the refrigerator and cabinets and decided to make fried fish and fries for dinner. My phone rang and I sucked my teeth when I saw it was Pops calling. I had several missed calls from him so I decided to face the music and answered the call.

"Wassup Pops?" I asked.

"Stephanie showed me your mugshot. Are you okay?" Pops asked.

"I'm good."

"Why you ain't called and told anybody what happened? I called Eric and he had no idea."

"Rod bailed me out and I'm just getting home. A lot of shit happened today."

"I see. Stephanie showed me some things from the Instagram."

"Pops, don't stress yourself out over this."

"I see your face and I can't help but stress."

"I broke up with Chloe and things went left. It was a huge fight and we both got locked up. I shouldn't have gone to jail but officers said I provoked the situation. And all I did was push her away when she tried to kiss me."

"That's bullshit."

"Exactly, Pops. I could have fucked her up and I didn't."

"It looks like Chantel and her friends handled that for you."

"You saw that too?"

"Stephanie has been keeping up with everything. She's watching Chloe's live right now."

"I wished I would have listened to everybody who told me to stay away and told me she was nothing but drama. Now I see it for myself."

"You want to see the good in everyone, Rell."

"And that only hurts me."

"You gonna be aight. This just proves she ain't the one. Take it on the chin and keep moving. I've been trying to get you and Connie together for years and y'all both are stubborn."

"Well, she was on and off with Travis for a long time."

"She would be a good woman for you."

"I don't know, Pops."

"Well, you just broke up with ol girl so I don't expect you to be thinking about that right now."

"How's your Valentine's going?"

"We're both sick so we're stuck in the house."

"I'm stuck in the house too while Chloe and her girls enjoy the suite I paid for."

"I would have kicked them out."

"I ain't cold like that."

"You still coming by Sunday?"

"Yeah, we'll be there."

"Can't wait to see y'all. I'm glad you're okay, Rell. I'll call Eric and let him know you're good."

"Thanks for checking up on me."

"Always. I love you and I'll talk to you later."

"I love you, Pops. Later."

I ended the call.

Rod and I busy ourselves in the kitchen making fish and fries.

"How was everyone's Valentine's?" I asked.

"I don't even have a Valentine," Rod said.

"Mariah did," Jam said.

Mariah rolled her eyes.

"Yeah, me," I said, "It better not be anybody else."

Mariah cuts her eyes at Jam.

"I'm just playing," Jam said.

"Nah, who is it?" I asked.

"Nobody," Mariah said.

"We had a party," Coby said.

"Did you get lots of candy?" I asked.

"Yes, and Daddy ate some of it."

"My girl was trippin'," Junior said.

"Why?" I asked.

"I didn't have the money to go all out like she wanted," Junior said.

"What she wanted?" I asked.

"She wanted this expensive ass bag and diamond bracelet. I got her flowers, a card, and chocolate. I told her we could go to a nice restaurant and she wasn't hearing it."

"You did right. Y'all haven't been dating that long for you to spend that kind of money. If she couldn't appreciate what you gave her, that's on her." I said.

"I like what you did for Chloe," Jam said.

"Jam, what you do for your girlfriend?" I asked.

"I ain't got a girlfriend."

"Since when? You and Simone have been together forever."

"It's on to the next. Simone got tired of my shit."

"Y'all will be back together next week. Y'all always breaking up and getting back together." Rod said.

Jam laughed. "I think she's done for real this time."

"Marley, you got a girl?" I asked.

"Nah," Marley said.

"He got all the bitches," Junior said.

"They ain't got me though," Marley said.

Junior and Marley fist-bumped and laughed.

"Mariah, you want to tell me about your Valentine now?" I asked.

"Fine, I'll tell you since Jam can't keep his big mouth closed," Mariah said.

"You didn't tell me it was a secret," Jam said.

"His name is Isiah and he's on the boys' soccer team," Mariah said.

"What he got you?" I asked.

"A teddy bear and chocolate. It was embarrassing."

"Why?" Rod asked.

"He asked me if I wanted to be his girlfriend."

I turned to look at her. "What did you say?"

"I told him no. I felt like I hurt him and I feel bad about it."

"You don't need a boyfriend right now. You need to focus on soccer and school. Don't feel bad about it. He'll be okay." I said.

"Rejection is a part of life. You just put a little hair on his chest." Rod said.

"Today ain't go how I expected," I said.

"I knew when you told me you were ending things on Valentine's Day, it was going to be bad," Rod said.

"Not this bad, bro. Like she went crazy."

"She was drunk, I'm sure."

"What's drunk?" Coby asked.

"It ain't nothing you need to worry about right now," Rod said.

Jam walked over and showed me his phone. It was a blog post with a chain of comments between Porsha, Chauncey, and Chloe. It looked like Chauncey and Chloe teamed up to expose me and Porsha wasn't having it. I grabbed his phone and swiped through the slides.

"Damn, he's still talking shit about me," I said after reading everything.

"Who?" Rod asked.

Jam handed him the phone and Rod read the comments.

"Is he in the city?" Rod asked.

"Yeah, he's around," I said.

"He's talking reckless," Rod said.

"All he do is talk," I said.

Next, I called Porsha.

"Rell, you good?" Porsha asked.

"I'm calling to ask you that," I said.

"Today has been rough. Me and Chauncey got into it after he called himself disciplining Layla."

"He put hands on my daughter? I'll kill him."

"He popped her and I told him he ain't supposed to touch her. He said Lay got smart with him. And I told him, I handle her, not him. He didn't like me checking him and went off. It ain't the first time he went crazy but it was the first time it got physical."

"You okay?"

She sniffled. "Yeah, I'm fine. You and Marie were right about him and I was too blind to see it."

"Don't blame yourself, Ma. You deserve better and you know that. Where are the kids?"

"My mom and dad are keeping them tonight. I got to get myself together."

"Stay off of social media."

"Them two clowns want to team up and kiki. I couldn't let that shit slide."

"They know each other?"

"I don't think so. They're being petty to hurt you."

"I appreciate you looking out for me, Ma. I don't want you in the middle of this mess."

"I couldn't let them paint you out to be a drug addict or alcoholic. That wasn't cool."

"You know Chauncey has been saying that same shit for the last year."

"It's crazy because he never talked bad about you to me. And that's why I felt like he was genuine. He would only talk about the good times. Now that he's mad, his true feelings come out. I wouldn't have been with him if I knew that's how he truly felt. I think you should defend yourself, Rell. Everybody's painting a different picture of you and I don't like it."

"They can keep painting. I don't need to prove shit to anyone. As long as y'all know what's good, I'm good."

"I like that about you."

"Porsha, take some time for yourself, and don't stress about this drama. I'm about to order your favorite dinner and send it your way."

"Aw, thanks, Rell."

"Don't mention it. Love you. Be safe."

"Aight, love you too."

I ended the call.

"Man, you and Porsha should be together," Jam said.

"Too late for all of that," I said. "We're better off as friends."

"What did she say about everything?" Rod asked.

"I got to pull up on Chauncey. He popped Layla and got physical with Porsha." I said.

"We doing this today?" Rod asked.

"Nah, tomorrow. I've already had a long day." I said.

"Her and Chauncey still together?" Jam asked.

"They broke up," I said.

"That's why him and Chloe teamed up," Jam said.

"Right," I said.

I grabbed my phone and deleted the photos of my face from social media. I just wanted all of this to die down. I arranged dinner, chocolate, and flowers to be sent to Porsha. A message from Connie made me smile.

Connie: **Thanks for the gifts for me and Sassy! You're the sweetest and I'm happy you're in my life. Hope you're doing okay. Call me when you can.**

"Why you cheesing so hard?" Rod asked.

I looked away. "It ain't nothing."

"It better not be a new girl," Jam said.

Chapter 46

Stay Out

It was the following day and I hardly slept. It was hard to remain quiet as people trashed my name but I knew it was best not to say anything. I woke up to Ava wailing and chewing her fist. I brought her crib into my room to make these early morning feedings easier. I even have a mini fridge filled with her bottles in my room.

I looked at the time and it was only four in the morning. I took Ava out of the crib and grabbed a bottle from the fridge. I sat on the edge of the bed and gave her the bottle. Anytime I think of having another kid, I think of these early morning feedings with Ava.

I checked my phone for messages and all I saw was drama. Once again, Chauncey and Chloe were coming for me. I didn't even want to read any of the negative things. Getting with Chloe was the biggest mistake of my life.

Porsha had posted a photo of the things I got delivered to her house with the sweetest message and that post set off Chauncey and Chloe. It's crazy that me and Porsha had so much love for one another but it just never worked out between us.

I read through blogs trashing my name, calling me a deadbeat, saying I'm broke, and claiming I'm an alcoholic and drug addict. The worst accusation was that I was abusive to women. I've stayed out of the public eye because I liked having a private life and no drama. Now, my life is being torn about and talked about by millions who don't know me.

I couldn't go back to sleep after scrolling through everything. I took Ava in my arms and walked downstairs to the living room. I sat in the dark rocking Ava in my arms. I was having thoughts of ending all of the pain right now. Everything was finally looking up and now it's crashing down again. I was back in a dark place.

I called Rod.

"Yo," Rod said groggily.

"I can't do this shit, man," I said.

"What's going on, bro?"

"I feel like I can't get in control of my life, bro."

"You're in control, Rell. Hold yo head, bro. This is going to be over soon. You know how it is. Trending one week and the next week back to normal. They'll find something new to talk about. Let it blow over. They can't break you."

I tried not to break down in tears but I was feeling weak.

"You there, Rell?"

"Yeah," I mumbled.

"You need me to come over?"

"Nah, I'm good. Let me get myself together and I'll call you back."

"You're not alone, bro. You got me always."

I almost broke down when I heard him say that.

"All of this shit is taking a toll on me, bro. Pops is sick. Moms stealing all this money. Junior's going to rehab. Jay's going through it with life and Sam. Jam ain't himself."

"Yeah, it's a lot going on. We have to stay positive, bro. Everything is going to work out. Don't stress about it."

"I failed as a father, bro. I don't think I'll ever forgive myself for letting them down."

"You ain't failed, bro. You're still there for them and they love you."

I felt the tears coming before I could stop them. I was losing my mind and I couldn't even talk to Rod.

"Bro, talk to me, please. Matter of fact, I'm on the way. Just hold on."

I heard the phone click and I threw the phone beside me. I looked down at Ava's big curious eyes and wondered what she was thinking. I wiped my face and got myself together.

Rod was at the house fifteen minutes later. He used his key and carried in a sleeping Coby. I was sitting on the couch in the dark. Ava was now in her bassinet fast asleep. Rod laid Coby on the other couch in the room and then sat beside me. He noticed the bottle of liquor on the table.

"Damn, you already drinking. It's five in the morning, bro." Rod said.

"I don't want to feel shit," I said.

"Chauncey's talking recklessly and I'm trying to stay out of it. He's saying he was there for you more than me and Jam." Rod said.

"Where did he say that?" I asked.

"I saw a clip on a blog. Guess he went live explaining y'all friendship and that he was there when we weren't."

"He's always talking out his neck. He just wants a response from me. He knows I don't do the social media shit. I told him to pull up to the Juicy Boil."

"What did he say?"

"His punk ass ain't respond. And I'm like cool you got all of this to say but can't have a conversation with me."

"Has Chloe reached out?"

"Nah, fuck her. I ain't got nothing to say to her. I realized I opened up to the wrong bitch."

"You gonna bounce back."

"You see this shit they're saying about me?"

"They don't know you. Let them talk."

"And this reality show starts next week. No telling what Porsha and Chantel said on this show."

"You think they were talking crazy about you?"

"It was at a time we weren't on the best of terms so I'm sure they were."

"They're defending you like hell right now. Even Marie got into it with Chauncey and she stays outta the way."

"Word? I didn't even see that."

"She was calling him out on his shit. He had to delete her comments."

"I don't even know this dude anymore."

"I was thinking about how we grew up and came from the bottom. Man, them hard times made us. Moms was always gone. Pops worked a lot but still spent so much time with us. He always cared for Deja like she was his daughter. I was thinking about our grandpa and all the shit he used to tell us about life. How he kept us in line. Whenever we got in trouble, Pops sent us to Poppa's restaurant to work and Poppa would preach and fuss the whole time."

I smiled. "I miss Poppa. I know Pops misses him too. Poppa always knew I would play pro. He had a jar on the restaurant counter to collect money for my football fees and trips. He told me football was going to be my way out. I wished he could have seen me out on the field playing professional ball."

"He saw you and he's with you. I remember Poppa always telling me that there was nothing good out in the streets. I didn't believe him until I sat in that cell alone facing all that time. And then I realized he knew what he was talking 'bout. Poppa always told me I was better than the street shit. It was more than the money for me. I liked the bond me and Moms had on the block. I didn't expect her to turn against me and testify against me. That was some cold shit."

"Moms always been cold towards us. It took her stealing twenty thousand dollars from me to realize it."

"That's a lot of bread."

"Yeah, I got to bounce back. I just built this shit, man. I get pissed every time I think about it."

"You got to secure some brand deals."

"I done left so many deals on the table because I don't want to be in the public eye. Ya feel me?"

"Yeah, I feel you, but you out there now so might as well take advantage of it. You got a name, you popular, and you got millions of followers. Look at how the channel took off just because you promoted it on your IG."

I nodded my head. Bro was making valid points.

"If you read the comments, they're waiting on you to make another video. Rell, you have so many supporters out there."

"Help me out, bro. You're more into this social media shit than I am."

"You know who else can help?"

"Who?"

"Connie."

Pops and Rod were not letting up when it came to me getting with Connie. "Word?"

"She has side hustle managing social media personalities and influencers. We're going to help you out, bro. You ain't leaving no more money on the table."

Chapter 47

Pull Up

It was later in the day and I was at the Juicy Boil with Jam waiting for Chauncey to pull up.

"What's it like being back here?" I asked Jam.

"I don't miss it," Jam said.

"It was that bad working here with Rod?"

"Hell yeah."

"He ain't let you get away with shit, huh?"

"Nothing."

I smiled. "How's your channel?"

"It's a lot of work. I'm putting out the quitting my job vlog today."

"How many subscribers you got now?"

"I have three thousand and that's because of your shoutout on IG."

"You're going to have way more than that once you start uploading consistently. How's the job search?"

"Just getting ready for these interviews. One of the positions is working at a call center and the other is a retail job."

"The call center gig might be good for you. How much is it paying?"

"Fifteen an hour."

"Hell yeah. Go after that one. You'll gain a lot of skills from that position."

"I'm praying I get that one. It'll get Dad off my back."

"Definitely."

"Have you talked to Moms?"

"Nah, I haven't. Have you?"

"She called me this morning. It was weird. We got into it and she said she didn't want to talk to me again."

Jam was seeing the ugly side of Moms and I felt bad for him. "I'm sorry, Jam."

He dropped his head and doesn't say anything.

"I knew something was up with you but you kept saying it was nothing," I said.

"I didn't want to talk about it. It's like we don't mean nothing to her." Jam said.

"I ain't even got a call, bro," I said.

"It's fucked up. I didn't think I was going to live the rest of my life without my mom and she's still alive." Jam said.

"That's real."

He covered his face with his hands.

"Don't do that here. Let's go to the office." I said.

I ushered him into the office. Rod looked over at us but continued cooking. I closed the door and he sat on the couch and started bawling. Jam was going through so much and I felt bad that I couldn't do more to ease the pain. I stood beside him and rubbed him on the back.

"Better days are coming, Jam. I know it's a lot right now but you will get through this."

"Rell, I ain't built for this shit," Jam said.

"Yes, you are. You are already getting through it and you don't even realize it. When I got injured, I didn't see myself making it through. I was in so much pain and couldn't even walk some days. It crushed me when I found out I would never play football again. Football was my life and I felt incomplete without it.

I was broke when I left the league and had so many people depending on me. I had no idea at the time how I would make it through but I did. I'm facing setbacks again because of Moms and all the drama with Chloe and Chauncey but I know I will bounce back. It looks like you can't handle it but you're handling it.

You're a lot stronger than you think. You know we're all here for you. You ain't in this shit alone. I got you, baby boy, forever. I ain't going to let you fall and not catch you."

He stood up and I held him in my arms and let him cry on my shoulder. There was a knock at the door.

"Y'all good?" Rod asked.

"Yeah," I said.

"Can I come in?" Rod asked.

I looked at Jam and he nodded his head.

"Come in, Rod," I said.

He walked in and closed the door. He leaned against the office door. Jam sat back down on the couch and I handed him a paper towel.

"What happened?" Rod asked. "What I missed?"

"He talked to Moms this morning," I said.

"It was bad," Jam said.

"What did she say?" Rod asked.

"I just asked her if all of this shit was true. Did she try to pimp Deja and now Mariah? Did she really treat y'all like trash? Is she really this low-down person? Of course, she can't answer truthfully because she's locked up and they listen to the calls. But the way she answered my questions confirmed it was all true. She made the excuse of doing what she had to do to survive.

I just went off because that's not the mom I've known for the past nineteen years. She didn't like me checking her. She brought up my court case saying my dumb ass should rot in prison. She was so evil and cold, and I'd never heard her talk like that. And I kept saying it's your son, Jam, to make her come back and realize who I was. And she disowned me and said my punk ass wasn't her son."

"Sounds like Moms. She lashes out and says foul shit." Rod said. "I know y'all close and this is hurtful. Me and

Rell been through this same shit with her. You have to take the lick and keep pushing."

"She's not even sorry for the shit she's said or done. It's wild." Jam said. "Jay said Momma lashed out at her and I didn't want to believe it. Growing up, Jay and I thought y'all were so mean for the way y'all treated her. Now, we finally see and understand. Sorry for not always understanding."

"Y'all were kids and didn't know," I said. "Momma was a crackhead, felon, scammer, and drug dealer for ten years, that was before you and Jay were here and of age to understand."

There was a knock at the door.

"Who is it?" Rod asked.

"Carlos." the raspy voice said.

Rod opened the door.

"Yo, there's a dude here with a bunch of other dudes asking for Rell," Carlos said.

I knew it had to be Chauncey. I quickly ran out of the office.

"No. Chill!" Rod yelled.

Chauncey stood by the front door with four other dudes. That didn't intimidate me.

"Let's take it outside," I said.

We walked outside with his entourage following us.

"Yo, I don't want to fight," Chauncey said.

I didn't hear anything. All I saw was red. I threw the first punch and tackled him to the ground. We scrapped for a little bit. Rod and Jam got me off of him and pushed me to the side.

"It ain't worth it, bro," Rod said holding me back as I charged towards him.

"I just wanted to talk, Rell," Chauncey said out of breath.

"Ain't no talking. You know how I get down. You been talking so much shit to everybody else now you want to talk to me?" I said.

"I fucked up, Rell."

"I ain't do shit to you. You put hands on my daughter and baby momma. That's beyond fucked up. You keep telling folks I abused drugs and alcohol like you haven't done the same. I'll never do you like you did me. The fame got to your head and you switched up."

Chauncey doesn't say anything and I take time to catch my breath. Just seeing him made me angry. This was my guy, my right hand and now we're here.

"You good?" Rod asked.

"I'm good," I said.

I walked back into the restaurant and went to the office with Jam and Rod.

"Man, I hate losing my cool like that!" I yelled.

"Nah, he was asking for that," Jam said.

There was a knock on the door.

"Wassup?" Rod said.

"It's Carlos again. Chauncey wants to talk to Rell."

This dude wasn't giving up.

"Tell him to come to the office," I said.

"Aight," Carlos said.

A few minutes later, Chauncey walked into the office. I sat behind the desk and Rod and Jam excused themselves and left the office. Chauncey sat in the chair in front of me and drummed his fingers on the desk. We don't look at one another and we don't say anything to one another.

After minutes of us sitting around, Chauncey finally speaks up.

"Yo, you going to talk to me or do you just want to fight?" Chauncey asked.

"I ain't got much to say. You the one with so much to say." I said.

"I can admit I was wrong for talking shit about you."

"You ain't just talk shit, you tried to ruin me. In this business, your name is your brand and it means everything. You got people calling me a crackhead, a deadbeat, an alcoholic, and a bum. You ain't did shit to clear up anything."

He nodded his head. "Sorry ain't going to help but I apologize for doing that to you."

"But what did I do to you, bruh? I ain't steal your shit or fuck yo bitch. I needed time to myself and you took that as me being fake and started all of this shit."

"And that's my bad. After the injury, I saw a different side to you that I didn't like. I didn't understand it."

"Yeah, I was angry as shit back then so I get why you didn't want to fuck with me. My problem is you taking our issues to blogs and social media. You did a lot of fucked up shit that I can't rock with. I wouldn't do you like that."

"Let me talk to you about yesterday."

"Go ahead."

"Lay is only eight but she got the mouth and attitude of a grown woman. Porsha lets her get away with it. She laughs at Lay and thinks it's cute. Yesterday, I told Lay to clean up a mess she made, and she got smart with me and called me a bitch. I popped her two times and shit went left."

"She got a Daddy. You could have called me to handle it."

"True. And again, that's my bad."

"Why you got with my baby momma?"

"It wasn't on no petty shit. We started talking on the gram and it went from there. She's cool but she never felt right about the whole thing so we fought a lot."

"All these bitches out here and you chose my baby momma?"

"I was wrong, bro."

"And to top it off, you linked up with Chloe to spite me and Porsha."

"Hearing this shit back is crazy."

"Imagine how I feel. I can't believe you switched up like this. We went to college together, got drafted on the same night, and played pro ball together. You were like a brother to me. You know I don't let a lot of people in my circle. You knew better than anyone what I was going through."

"I'm sorry, Rell. I'm going to clear all of this shit up. I know we'll never be bros again but I don't want to fight whenever I see you. I don't want no beef with you."

"It wasn't no beef. You started acting mad shady like I did something to you."

"Nah, you ain't do nothing. It's all me. I'm getting help so I can be better and handle shit differently."

"I appreciate you pulling up so we can finally talk about this shit."

"I appreciate you listening to me. I'm going to fix all of this shit."

Chapter 48

Get Home

I was back home watching the news and working on the channel with Jam. The news reporter spoke about a killer virus that shut a whole country down.

"That's wild," Jam said, "You think it'll come to the States?"

"They better get ahead of it," I said.

"I see Chauncey put out an apology video."

"Now we can finally move on and these wack-ass trolls can get off my dick."

"Chloe reached out to me and I blocked her."

"Why is she reaching out to you?"

"Trying to get in touch with you. I told her I ain't in it and blocked her. I don't see her the same after what she did to you and Jay."

"Have you talked to Jay?"

"Yeah, and she's good. She's supposed to be coming by in a little bit. Dad is driving her crazy."

"Does he know she's pregnant?"

"Not yet. You know if he knew, he would have cussed us all out for not telling him."

I chuckled. "You right. I can hear him now fussing at us."

"Unc, I'm home!" Marley said. Then we heard the front door close.

"Living room," I said.

He walked into the living room smelling like smoke and barbeque.

"Where's Junior?" I asked.

His eyes danced to avoid eye contact. "He's on the way."

"I thought y'all got off at the same time," I said.

"Nah," Marley said.

"Guess I'm trippin'. How was work?" I asked.

"It was cool. I told Pop Pop I only want to work the weekends so I can focus on my work and soccer during the week."

"And if that gets to be too much, you can just work during the summer. I knew Junior wasn't going to do it without you."

"I know. That's why I don't mind working."

"You can go take a shower and change out of your work clothes. I'm 'bout to make dinner."

He walked out of the room and I texted Junior.

```
Me: Where are you?
Junior: Work. Be there soon.
Me: You got off at 2 today?
Junior: nah 4. Be home soon
Me: GET HOME NOW
```

I saw he read the message but didn't respond.

"Have you talked to Kennedy?" Jam asked.

"Nah, she's still mad at me. Marie said she'll come around." I said.

Jam looked at his phone shocked at whatever he saw.

"What?" I asked.

"Somebody sent a clip of you and Chauncey fighting to a blog and now it's everywhere," Jam said.

"Shit. People always got their phones out. I know my lawyer, Clay, is pissed as hell."

"Have they dropped the other charges?"

"Nope. They were just happy to arrest rich semi-famous people."

"Of course. Police ain't really here to serve and protect."

"Right, but we knew that."

"Where's Junior? He's commenting on the blog post so he must be off work now."

"But he can't respond to my text. What did he say?"

"That he got next. Junior don't play 'bout you."

I smiled. "That's my right hand there. He's always been like this."

"I like to see y'all getting close again. He needs you and I know you've missed him."

"I hate he's about to go away for thirty days."

"He's going to be good, bro. He's going to get all of the help he needs to kick that nasty drug habit and become a better person."

There was a knock at the door.

"I got it. I think it's Jay." Jam said.

Jam rushed to the front door.

"Jam!" Jay squealed.

"What's good, Jay?" Jam asked.

A few minutes later, they appeared in the living room. She had on an oversized shirt and leggings.

"Yo dad ain't suspicious with you wearing these big ass clothes?" I asked.

She smiled. "Not yet. I'm sure he's happy I'm not wearing my usual tight clothes."

"How's everything going?"

"It's going. I have an appointment next week." Jay said.

"I'm coming with you," Jam said.

They joined me on the couch.

"What y'all got going on?" Jay asked.

"We're working on these channels. I'm trying to get our channel monetized so we can start making money." I said.

"And I'm trying to upload another video," Jam said.

"Your first video was funny. I ain't never seen Rod that mad." Jay said.

"I got to prank him," Jam said.
"Be careful. You know how he is." I said.
"What's your next video?" Jay asked.
"I went to a party on Friday," Jam said.
Jay looked at me. "You let him go to a party?"
"He was hosting and making money," I said.
"Don't tell Dad. I don't need him on my back." Jam said.
"You know he watches your videos?" Jay said.
"I'm sure I'm going to catch it more than you," I said.
"How much you made?" Jay asked.
"I made two thousand dollars," Jam said.
"That ain't bad. I miss my club days sometimes." Jay said.
"I don't. I'm glad you ain't working in that strip club anymore." I said.
"Is Sam still acting crazy?" Jam asked.
"Yeah. I got a restraining order. I still can't sleep at night." Jay said.
"Is he out of jail yet?" I asked.
"Yeah, his bro, Shawn, bailed him out. He's staying with his girlfriend, Keya."
"She's pregnant too, right?" Jam asked.
"That's what she's saying. They can go be happy together and leave me alone."
"Is Chloe still bothering you?" I asked.
"Nah, that ass whopping Chantel gave her shut her right up."
"I didn't know Chantel had it in her," Jam said.
"She ain't nothing to play with. People underestimate her because she's small but she can handle her own." I said.
"The way Chloe talked, I didn't expect it to be that easy," Jay said.
"Hell, the way she tried to beat my ass, I expected something different," I said.

"She was probably tired as hell. She was fresh out of jail and hella drunk." Jay said.

Marley walked into the living room in a pair of sweats and a T-shirt.

"Hey Jay," Marley said hugging her.

"Hey baby, you getting tall," Jay said.

"Can I go to the mall?" Marley asked.

"Nah, I got a text from your teacher that you have a packet to do," I said.

"Come on, Pops. I can do it later." Marley said.

"Do it now," I said.

He stormed out of the room.

"What you going to do with these teenagers?" Jam asked.

"I don't even know," I said.

"Where's Junior?" Jay asked.

"Your guess is as good as mine. He's lying and saying he's at work." I said.

"Yo kids bad. I called Lay the other day and she got a lot of mouth. It was like talking to one of my friends." Jay said.

"I haven't seen that side of Lay. Porsha's soft with Jack and Lay so I'm not surprised."

"Chantel was telling me about the reality show."

"Yeah?"

"She said it's some shit she regrets but didn't go into details. She's worried about how the show will make her look."

"When does the show air?" Jam asked.

"Monday," I said.

"Just know I got your back, bro. I ain't letting nobody talk crazy about you." Jay said.

"Don't stress yourself about me, Jay. I want you to be okay. I can handle it." I said.

I heard the front door creak open.

I'm home, Pops," Junior said.

"Come here," I said.

He appeared in the living room with bags in his hands. "I brought dinner."

"Where ya been?" I asked.

"You want the truth?"

"Always."

"I was with my girl."

"Uh-huh. Y'all being safe?"

He looked away. "Of course, Pops. Where's Ava?"

"With your mama. Surprised you asked about her."

"I'm trying to do better."

"How was work?"

"Pop Pop wasn't there so it was a good day."

"You and Pops still bumping heads?"

"You know how he is. Where's Marley?"

"He's upstairs doing his work. Take the food to the kitchen. Thanks for bringing dinner."

"I'm going to take a shower then I'll join y'all."

Chapter 49

Close Call

Jay, Jam, and I went into the kitchen to see what Junior brought home for dinner. He got barbeque ribs, fried chicken, hot wings, yams, cornbread, creamed corn, mac and cheese, and baked beans.

Marley walked into the kitchen. "I smelled food so here I am."

We sat at the kitchen table with our plates.

Coby and Rod walked through the front door and took off their shoes.

"Come join us," I said.

They walked into the kitchen a few minutes later. Coby sat at the table and Rod fixed plates for him and Coby and then joined us at the table.

"This is like old times," Jam said.

"All we're missing is Deja," Jay said.

"We got to go pay her a visit. Rell, you should come with us." Rod said.

"I don't know, Rod. I'll think about it. How was work?" I asked.

"It was cool. We got new business thanks to the video of you and Chauncey fighting plastered everywhere."

"I want to apologize for doing all of that there at the Juicy Boil," I said.

"You ain't mess up the restaurant so I ain't trippin'. I'm glad it's handled and now he can shut up and stop talking about you." Rod said.

"I see he's trying to clean up the mess he created," Jay said.

"Trying but the damage is done. All I can do is move forward." I said.

Jay's phone rang. "It's Daddy." She put the phone on speaker. "Hey, Daddy!"

"What ya doing?"

"I'm over at Rell's house having dinner with everyone," Jay said.

"Sam called and asked about a baby."

We all almost died at the table.

"You know Sam is always talking crazy, Daddy." She put her fork down and fidgeted with her hands.

"Are you pregnant?" Eric asked.

"No." Jay lied.

I knew I had to step in.

"Hey, Eric," I said.

"You good, Rell? You getting arrested one day and fighting out in public the next day." Eric said.

"I'm good. They arrested me for no reason and Chauncey had to catch that fade." I said.

"You can't be doing the same shit that you were doing when you were younger. You ain't a kid anymore. Remember you're a grown man with kids." Eric said.

"I hear you but I had to defend myself. I've let Chauncey get away with a lot. I've lost a lot of deals because of him."

"Y'all used to be best friends. What happened?"

"He got in his feelings."

"Y'all good now?"

"Yeah."

"I talked to y'all mom today and she goes to court next week for a bond hearing."

"She got a lawyer?" I asked.

"She's using a public defender," Eric said.

"But Ted got a good ass lawyer. What was she thinking?" I said.

"His family got him that good lawyer," Eric said.

"Moms stole all that money for his fees and a lawyer for no reason. Should have saved some of that money for herself." I said.

"I said the same thing. Ted ain't looking out for her like she looked out for him. It ain't hit her yet how much trouble she's in." Eric said.

"I don't think she cares. She ain't sorry for none of this." I said.

"This whole thing is draining. I'm ready to close this chapter and move on."

"Is the divorce final yet?"

"Her lawyer said she signed the papers under emotional distress so we're having her sign again. I finally sold the old house."

"You sold it for the price you wanted?"

"Yup, got the price I wanted."

"I got to get my home ready to sell."

"If you need help, let me know."

"I'll reach out."

"I'll let y'all get back to eating and talk to y'all later. Love y'all."

"Love you too."

I ended the call and handed Jay her phone.

"That was close," Jay said.

"He's going to be watching you like a hawk now," Jam said.

"I got to find my own spot."

"You can move in with me. I got space." Rod said.

"I might take you up on that offer because Dad treats me like a little kid," Jay said.

"That's why I ain't there," Jam said.

"I get it now. I got to get the hell on." Jay said.

Chapter 50

Like Old Times

On Sunday, Porsha and Chantel had a brunch meeting so they brought the kids to the house. Marie was traveling out of town for a few days so I also had Kennedy. She still ain't talking to me even though we're in the same house. I was in the yard with Jackson, Lay, Ava, Junior, and Life. Mariah walked out of the house.

"What's Kennedy doing?" I asked.

"She's taking a nap," Mariah said.

She kicked around a soccer ball.

"Junior, you ready for this program?" I asked.

"I guess. My baby boy is coming this week."

"Dang, it's time already?"

"She's having a C-section on Tuesday."

"You going to be there for her?"

"Yeah, I got to see my baby boy before I leave."

"Y'all got a name?"

"Not yet." He bounced Ava in his arms. It was the first time I had seen him interact with Ava. "My girl trippin'."

"Why?"

"She don't want me to go away."

"She should want you to do better."

"I told her she needs to get help too. Her baby daddy's talking about taking her little girl from her."

Junior sure knew how to pick them. "She's on drugs too?"

"Yeah, but she don't want help and she don't want me to get help either."

"She got to do better and so do you."

"I had to break up with her. It hurt cuz I liked her a lot. But I know once I get clean, I can't be around that."

"That's how it is, Junior. Not everybody can go on this journey with you."

"I'm seeing that now. I had to cut my cuz off too. He's mad I ain't on the block. I paid him all this money to get him off my back."

"How much money?"

"I gave him ten stacks."

"Whoa! Where you get the money?"

"Jam and Momma."

"Man, you got to start coming to me about this shit."

"I was scared but I'm going to tell you everything from now on, Pops. I have to see my PO tomorrow. He wants to make sure I stay on my shit while I'm away."

Jam drove down the driveway and parked next to my Jeep. He climbed out of the car.

"What you doing driving?" I asked.

"I had to go help Jay move into Rod's place," Jam said.

"I'm glad you made it without being stopped. I'm guessing something happened for Jay to move out."

"Her and Dad had a huge fight and she left."

"She's good?"

"Now that she's away from Dad, she's good."

"Thanks for helping out Junior. I'm going to deposit it back into your account. Just remind me."

"We're family. I ain't want nothing to happen to him."

Junior smiled and it was my first time seeing him smile in a while. Life fussed and whined as she tried to get out of her jumper. I picked her up and rocked her in my arms.

"Bro, you want any more kids?" Jam asked.

"Nah, I think I'm good. Junior got me raising my grandkids so I don't need anymore."

Junior laughed. "I appreciate you, Pops, and I love you."

"I love you, Junior."

Now, the kids and I were having dinner at Pops' house. Rod, Coby, and Jam were also here. Pops and Stephanie cooked a feast. They had set up a kids' table in the living room and we adults sat in the dining room.

I bounced Life on my knee as she chewed on her toy. Chantel and Porsha both decided I should keep the kids overnight.

Pops was smiling from ear to ear glad to have us here and I liked seeing that. "I appreciate y'all coming by for dinner. And Jam, thanks for joining us. I haven't seen you in a while."

"I've been trying to lay low and stay out of trouble," Jam said.

"Stephanie, how you feeling?" I asked.

"This pregnancy is kicking my ass. I've been sick all day." Stephanie said.

"That's how Chantel was when she was pregnant with Life. By the end, she hated me and hated being pregnant." I said.

"I know it'll be worth it in the end so I'm not going to complain too much and try to enjoy it," Stephanie said.

"Pops, you worked today?" I asked.

"I'm taking a much-needed break," Pops said.

I knew something was wrong with Pops if he was taking a break. "I know this dude, Sunny, and he'll be a great manager for your restaurant."

"Let me meet him and I'll decide that. Is he a young dude?"

"He's my age. When's a good time for you?"

"I'll be there tomorrow. Tell him to come around ten in the morning."

"Aight, we'll be there."

I fed Life yams and she kicked her legs in excitement.

"She's eating good," Pops said.

"She's so big now," Stephanie said.

"She's going to be tall like you," Pops said.

"Yeah, she's already off the charts for height," I said.

"What's going on with you, Rod? You're quiet." Pops said.

"I'm just enjoying the food and being around y'all," Rod said, "Ain't nothing going on with me. Just working and taking care of Coby."

"You're doing a good job with him. He's so respectful." Pops said.

"You want any more kids?" Stephanie asked.

"I don't but Coby been asking for a sibling. I told him he got enough cousins and didn't need a sibling." Rod said.

"That ain't the same as having a brother or sister in the house with you," Stephanie said.

"Rod, how is it having Jay at the house?" Pops asked.

"It's cool. She stays out of the way and been baking like crazy. Coby likes having her there."

"Is it true she's pregnant?"

Jam, Rod, and I almost choked.

"Where did you hear that?" I asked. I was just buying time to get my lie together.

"Eric called me asking if I knew anything. I told him ain't nobody told me nothing. If Jay is pregnant, I hope y'all encourage her to tell her dad. She can't hide it forever." Pops said. "Y'all grown now. He's going to be mad but he ain't going to beat y'all."

"He might," Jam said, "He just pulled off his belt on me the other day."

And our laughter broke the tension in the room.

"Jam, when are they going to make the decision about school?" Pops asked.

"Sometime this week. I don't want to go back." Jam said.

"You don't like college?" Pops asked.

"Seems like a waste of time. I ain't found a major that interests me." Jam said.

"Did you even get to the major classes yet?" Rod asked.

"I took a couple of major classes to get an idea of what to major in and I hated those classes too."

"You can always go back," I said.

"That's what I did," Stephanie said.

"What did you major in?" Jam asked.

"Business administration."

"Are you using your degree?"

"I am. I work in human resources. It's not what I'm passionate about but it pays the bills."

"And you got a nice side hustle," I said.

"Yeah, I love knitting and making stuffed animals, blankets, or whatever."

"Speaking of, I need you to make something for Jay when you get a chance. Growing up, she had this giraffe and it got misplaced." Jam said.

"I remember that giraffe. She loved it." I said.

"What color was it?" Stephanie asked.

"It was blue and yellow," Jam said.

"If you got a picture, I'll try my best to make it."

"Cool, and I'll send you the payment."

"You don't have to pay."

"I want to," Jam said.

"How you making so much money?" Pops asked Jam.

"Well, my savings is keeping me afloat. I also host parties and Dad gives me money from time to time."

"And your channel's about to take off," I said.

"You got me looking crazy on there," Rod said.

"I watched that video. Y'all are a trip." Stephanie said.

"They've been like this since they were kids," Pops said.

Chapter 51
Not Me

On Monday, I dropped everyone off at school. Marley, Ava, and Life were hanging out with me.

Chantel got arrested late last night after a fight with Ty. According to several blogs, she stabbed Ty. I don't know how true everything is because I haven't talked to anyone. I just saw the blog Porsha forwarded me. I hate she let that man get her to that point.

"Marley, you want breakfast?" I asked.

He was in the backseat leaning against the window.

"Yeah," Marley said.

"What you want?" I asked.

"Mickey D's," Marley said.

"You done with all of your work?"

"I got a couple of worksheets left."

"You ready to go back?"

"Yeah, I miss soccer. Thanks for talking to Coach."

"Of course. I didn't want you to get kicked off the team. Don't blow your second chance."

"I'm not. I had a dream about Momma."

"Yeah?"

"We were just hanging out but she was telling me she was proud of me and to keep taking care of Mariah. She looked just as beautiful. She hasn't come to me in a dream in forever. I wish I could go back in time and hug her."

I blink back tears. "I feel the same way, Marley."

"She's missing so much."

"She ain't missing it. She's watching over us."

"I don't get why He took her when we still needed her."

"It's not for us to understand. We can't pick how or when we leave. I hate she had to go out that way, she didn't deserve it."

"I want to play football, Unc."

"Now you do?"

"Yeah, Coach saw me in PE and told me I got skills."

"You used to play football and soccer when you were a tyke and liked soccer a little more. If you need me to train you, let me know. I'm sure we can find you a team but it might be hard to do both soccer and football."

"That's what Coach told me. I still like soccer and I think I got a better chance at getting a scholarship for that."

"Me and you can just play football for fun."

"I would like that."

I pulled into the Mickey D's parking lot.

"What ya want?" I asked as I drove to the speaker.

"Two chicken biscuits, a sausage biscuit, hash browns, and orange juice."

"Boy, you can eat."

I repeated his order to the speaker and pulled to the next window.

"You paying or I'm paying?" I asked.

"I'm broke," Marley said.

"How you broke already?"

I gave my card to the cashier. She looked at me star-struck but didn't say anything. I grabbed my card from her and drove to the next window.

"Why you broke?" I asked Marley.

"Food, weed, games, and clothes," Marley said.

"So, you spent your weekly allowance already?"

"Basically."

"Didn't I tell you they drug test athletes? You need to stop smoking."

"I already know when they drug test. I just got to cleanse before it happens."

"And why you spent more money on clothes? You got a closet full of clothes you don't even wear."

"I needed a few things."

I grabbed the bag of food and orange juice. I make sure everything is in the bag before handing the bag to Marley. I made my way to Pops' restaurant. I had to meet up with Connie and introduce Sunny to Pops.

"Learn how to save your money, Marley. I give you more than enough money to make it through the week."

"Yes sir."

My phone rang interrupting our talk.

"Wassup Porsha?" I said.

"I just bailed Chantel out of jail," Porsha said.

"Where's Ty?"

"He's in the hospital."

"What's his condition?"

"He was just moved from critical to stable condition."

"How's Chantel?"

"She's at my house taking a nap. She's exhausted and knows she made a huge mistake. Ty is always beating on her and she just snapped. Her daddy is coming to town too."

"Oh hell. Crazy Joe needs to stay where he's at."

"She made me talk to him and he's pissed."

"Man, I wished she would have walked away. That man ain't worth her life."

"That's what I told her. Hell, we were going through the same shit. I wanted to stab Chauncey plenty of times but he ain't worth my freedom."

"Have you talked to Chauncey?"

"Yeah, he apologized. I got to tell you something crazy."

"What?"

"I'm pregnant."

"Nah, you lying. It better not be his bitchass baby."

Porsha laughed uncomfortably.

"You taking this clown back?"

"Hell nawl."

"You keeping the baby?"

"I don't know."

"You can get rid of a baby?" Marley asked.

"Shit. I forgot you were in this car."

"Who's that? Junior?"

"Nah, Marley. He got suspended for fighting so he's home."

"Hey, Marley."

"Hey, Ms. P."

"Rell, I don't know what to do."

"No matter what, I got you."

"I thought you were going to be pissed."

"I can't change it and it ain't my situation. I want you to be happy."

"Well, I'm definitely not happy."

"Not right now but one day you will be."

"I want you to take the kids for the next month. I need to get my life together. They've been seeing me crying and sad and they don't understand. I don't want them to go through this with me."

"I got you."

"I'll bring their things to your house."

"Aight. I'm not at the house but Jam should be there if you stop by."

"Okay. I will pack their bags and head to your place to drop everything off. I'll call you later."

"Aight, talk to you later."

I ended the call.

"So, how can you get rid of a baby?" Marley asked.

"You don't forget nothing," I said.

"Junior told me his girl could have gotten rid of the baby but he didn't explain how."

"A woman can have an abortion and the doctor takes it away and the woman is no longer pregnant. Some women wait too late and can't get rid of it."

"Oh. Sounds like murder."

I almost choked. I couldn't believe he said that. "You don't need to worry about that. We've had this talk. If you're having sex, always wear a glove. We don't want you in the same situation as Junior."

"I don't ever want a baby. I'll double up on the condoms to prevent that."

I laughed out loud. "Man, these babies must be driving you crazy for you to say that."

"All they do is cry and they're expensive."

Chapter 52

Trash Talking

I walked into Pops' restaurant with the double stroller and Marley following me. Connie was sitting at a booth in the middle of the restaurant.

She stood and we hugged. Marley scoots into the booth and I sit beside him. Marley put his earphones in his ears and ignored us.

Connie opened her notebook. "Rod and I have found you six different opportunities."

"Oh really? That was fast." I said.

"Some of these companies have wanted to work with you for a while. You need to engage more on social media and you'll have even more opportunities."

"What opportunities do you have for me?"

"An athletic wear clothing company will send you clothes and you just post what they send in an IG story and post. We're still working on the pay for this one."

"It doesn't sound like they're asking for too much so I'm down for that," I said.

"We also have a sunglasses opportunity."

"I don't even wear shades like that so I'll pass on that."

"We have a commercial opportunity where you say a few lines."

"I can do that. I haven't done a commercial in a long time."

"We have a brand ambassador opportunity for a new clothing boutique. It's fashion-forward, flashy, and quality clothing."

"I'll pass on that."

"Why?"

"That ain't my thing. You know I like my sweats and T-shirts."

"This could be a way to step out of your comfort zone."

"I'll think about it."

"There's an opportunity to interview on a morning show and you will also have a cooking segment."

"Now that sounds dope and I can promote the businesses while I'm there."

"Exactly."

"Just tell me when and I'm there."

"So, there's also this protein shake that -"

I hold up my hand. "You can stop right there. I don't like advertising those types of things."

"Rod said you would say that. I want to see meal planning and healthy meal ideas on your channel. It'll bring a new audience to the channel and would be interesting."

"Good idea. I've been slacking on healthy eating but I know a lot of good recipes."

"And y'all are finally monetized. I worked everything out. The payments will go to the business account and you have to pay Jay, Jam, and Rod."

"Cool. Send everything to my email."

"I got you."

"When are you going to let me take you out?"

She rolled her eyes. "You don't want these problems?"

"How you know I can't handle it?"

"You just got out of a situation and shouldn't be rushing into anything new."

"That shit with Chloe doesn't even count as a situation."

She laughed. "What's going on with Chantel?"

"Hell, you tell me. Porsha and Chantel are going through it. And the show is coming on tonight."

"Is she out of jail now?"

"Yeah, Porsha bailed her out."

"They're best friends now, huh? I remember breaking up a couple of their fights."

"It's crazy how things have changed. Chantel better hope her job doesn't catch wind of this arrest."

"She's a nurse, right?"

"Yeah, she's been out here wilding like she ain't got a professional job."

"I can't wait to see this show and them cutting up. I know they're acting a fool."

"Is it true you're quitting your job here?"

"It's true. I've been here eight years and it's time to move on. I told Pops I would wait a few months to train the new shift manager and of course, the store manager has to get adjusted."

"What you doing when you leave this gig?"

"My side hustle is going to become my full-time job. I'm managing two YouTubers, a popular lifestyle blogger and, now you. Once I leave here, I'll have more time with Sassy."

"Sassy's going to love having that time with you. Porsha got to get her life together so I will have Layla and Jackson for the next month. I'm kind of nervous. Those two are wild because Porsha let them get away with everything and they're spoiled. A weekend is all I can take with Layla and Jackson."

"You're going to be fine. You now have the opportunity to get them in line."

It was later in the day and all the kids were either asleep or in their rooms not wanting to be bothered. I still had Life with me because Chantel had a day and needed time to herself.

Jam and I were in the living room getting ready to watch this reality show. I had it saved to watch later. I haven't been on social media because I didn't want anything to spoil the show.

"Press play, big bro," Jam said opening his bag of chips.

I started the show and quickly paused it when Kennedy walked into the room.

"Wassup?" I asked.

"Can I get a snack?" Kennedy asked.

"Yeah, go in the pantry and get yourself a snack. You still hungry?"

"Yeah."

"You want me to make you something?"

"No, I'll just get a snack."

"You good?"

"Yeah." She turned around as she was walking away. "I love you, Daddy. Goodnight."

"Come here, baby girl." This was her way of coming around and throwing in the white flag. This is the most we've said to one another in days. She walked over to me and I pulled her into my lap. I held her in my arms.

"I love you, baby girl. I don't like when we're fighting." I said.

"Me either. It makes me sad."

"Me too. Go get yourself a snack and have a good night." I kissed her on the cheek and helped her up. She practically skipped out of the room.

I picked up the remote and pressed play. The first scene was Porsha and two other women meeting for lunch. They introduced themselves and discussed their baller husband, baby daddy, or boyfriend.

And then Chantel appeared and you can tell one of the women didn't like her. My ears perked up when I heard my name. I was on the edge of the couch catching every word and insult. It was hurtful, not gonna lie.

"Damn, they dogging me," I said.

"It's me," Junior said announcing himself as the front door creaked open.

"We're in the living room," I said.

He appeared in the living room seconds later and sat on the couch beside Jam.

"Oh, this the wack ass show that got everybody dragging you," Junior said. "People on your page in your comments talking crazy."

"They can say whatever. I'm more pissed that Chantel and Porsha would say all of this shit when our kids can one day see it. They're even insinuating that I cared about drugs more than the kids."

"I don't care what no one says, you're a good dad," Jam said.

"That's why I posted this," Junior said showing us his phone.

He posted a photo of me with all of my kids with the most beautiful caption showing his love and appreciation for me. I had to wipe away tears after reading his caption.

I hugged him. "I appreciate you, son. I love you."

"I love you too. You mean the world to me, Pops."

I smiled. "You mean even more to me."

"I got to go to the hospital tomorrow morning at nine. My son is on the way."

"Jam, can you watch Marley, Ava, and Life tomorrow?" I asked.

"I got you. Junior, you excited?" Jam asked.

"Nah, I'm scared but ready to see him."

"You really a grandpa, Rell," Jam said.

"Don't remind me," I said.

We tuned back into the show when we heard arguing. It was Chantel and Ty going at it.

"Now, I see why she stabbed his ass. He's disrespectful." Jam said.

"Man, she deserves better. I know Joe is pissed if he's watching this." I said. I looked at Junior. "You better never treat a woman like this."

"I'll leave a girl before I do all of that. You taught me better than that, Pops."

"And keep your hands to yourself. It ain't worth you sitting in a cell."

"Yes sir."

"And I ain't saying let a woman just beat on you. You can restrain her and push her away. Walk away when it gets heated and take time to cool down. Don't handle any situation when you're angry."

"I got it, Pops."

"Rell, I got to know what's going on with you and Connie," Jam said.

"Ain't nothing. She's managing me and helping me secure brand deals. I asked her out and she ain't with it. I ain't going to press it." I said.

"Well, I'm going to bed," Junior said.

"Night son," I said.

"Night Junior," Jam said.

Junior walked out of the room. I heard the front door close seconds later. Jam and I tuned back into the show. Porsha and Chantel were shopping and discussing their relationship drama. It made me sad that these beautiful women were going through so much hell.

"What's crazy is that these two trash-talked you in the beginning but going through all of this shit with Ty and Chauncey. You never did them like that." Jam said.

Chapter 53

Great Man

I have a grandson! Aaron Jerrell, our little AJ, is here and he's perfect. The momma, Jada, was in the bed resting and Junior and I were sitting on the couch. I cradled AJ in my arms giving him a bottle.

"He's so chunky and already bigger than Ava," Junior said.

"It ain't easy having kids at your age, Junior. It's going to be a long road. Shit is going to be different now. You got two little ones depending on you and looking up to you. You got to care for them and protect them. They didn't ask to come into this world so you can't lash out at them because of your own mistakes."

"That's why I'm going to this program so I can be present and be a good dad to Ava and AJ."

"Reem wants to meet for lunch. You down?"

"Yeah, it's been a minute. And I know Kennedy has already reconciled with him and I want to do the same."

"How was your meeting yesterday with your probation officer? You didn't talk about it."

"It was good. We just talked about the program and community service. I have to do my hours when I get back from the program. Once I'm done with the program and the hours, I'm off probation."

"And you can move on with your life."

My phone lit up and it was an incoming video chat from Marie.

"It's your mom," I said.

I answered the call.

"Aw, is that our new baby with his chunky self?" Marie said.

"Mama, this is AJ," Junior said.

She dabbed at her eyes with a tissue. "I wish I was there."

"When you coming back?" I asked.

"I'll be back Wednesday night and can't wait to see y'all. Rell, how's Kennedy treating you?"

"We're back on good terms," I said.

"How's Jada? How was labor?" Marie asked.

"She's asleep. She had a scheduled C-section and everything went quickly." I said.

"It was wild seeing them pull the baby out," Junior said.

"He's beautiful. Are her parents there?" Marie asked.

"Her mom was here earlier but she had to go to work," Junior said.

"Is AJ living with y'all too or is he going home with Jada?"

"Right now, he's going home with Jada. Her mom pulled me to the side and told me they were financially struggling and wouldn't be able to properly care for AJ. It's all up to Jada on what she wants to do."

"Junior, you sure know how to pick them."

He laughed and shook his head.

"I got to get ready for work. Put the camera on AJ."

I flipped the camera and put the phone in front of him. AJ looked right into the camera.

"Look at that little face. He's so adorable. Let me see y'all. I don't want to start crying again."

I put the camera on me and Junior.

"Aight. I got to get ready for the day. I'll talk to y'all later. I love y'all."

"We love you, Mama," Junior said.

We ended the call.

After feeding and burping AJ, I handed AJ to Junior. Junior looked at him and AJ stared right back.

"Hey, little man," Junior said rubbing AJ's cheek.

It was beautiful seeing Junior bond with his son. It brought me back to when Marie had him and I held him for the first time.

"You're going to be a great father, Junior," I said.

"Just like you, Pops," Junior said.

I picked up Ava, Marley, Jam, and Life from the house and headed to lunch. We walked into the pizza restaurant. Reem was already there waiting up front for us. We joined two tables together so we could all sit together. Junior and Reem don't say anything to one another.

"Junior, that's your baby girl?" Reem asked pointing to Ava in the stroller.

"Yeah, that's Ava," I said when Junior remained quiet. "His son, AJ, was born this morning." I showed him a picture.

"Congrats, Junior. Your kids are beautiful. Still can't believe you're a dad." Reem said.

"Thanks," Junior said.

"What y'all want? I'll go put in our order." Jam said.

"I want a small buffalo chicken pizza and a meatball calzone," Marley said.

"Did you eat breakfast?" I asked.

"I made eggs, grits, bacon, and toast for him. He smashed it and was still hungry after." Jam said.

I shook my head. "You can put down some food, Marley. Just get me two pepperoni slices and a salad."

"I want a small pepperoni pizza and ten buffalo wings," Junior said.

"Reem, you ordered?"

He held up his number. "Yeah."

I handed Jam a couple hundred bills and he walked away to order the food.

"Junior, what's been going on with you?" Reem asked.

"Well, I'm a dad now. And I have to go to rehab." Junior said.

"When did you start using drugs like that? I knew you smoked weed but I didn't know about the pills and shooting up."

"I've been smoking weed since I was thirteen. About a year ago, I started using heavy drugs. A lot was going on and I couldn't take it."

"Was it the divorce or something else?"

"It was a little of everything. Me and Pops weren't talking. The divorce changed you and Mom. Y'all were angry and argued a lot. It was hard to see y'all be so mean to one another when there was so much love there."

"I'm sorry we put y'all through that. Y'all saw the ugliest sides of us and I hate that. I want you to know that you never had to pick sides between me and your mom. I was going to be here for you and Ken no matter what."

"I felt bad for Mom and her anger became mine."

"I understand that and don't fault you for looking out for Moms. I wasn't the nicest person to her and I'm sure you only wanted to protect her. I want us to get back cool. I want the best for you and to see you win, Junior. You know that."

"Yeah, I do."

"I've been in your life since you were five years old. It's been a decade of knowing you. I've watched you grow over the years and wiped your tears and I still want to be here for you. I love you, Junior."

Junior and Reem hugged.

"I love you too," Junior said.

I couldn't have asked for a better stepdad than Reem for Kennedy and Junior.

"Marley, you ready for school tomorrow?" I asked.

"Not for school but ready for soccer."

"Don't blow this second chance."

"I'm not. Look at what Eric sent me."

He showed me a picture of me, Eric, and Deja. Deja was holding a baby Marley in her arms.

"Wow, that's a throwback. Where did he find that picture?"

"He's going through all the pictures he had in the garage."

"That's a nice picture of Deja."

"What were y'all doing?"

"I think Moms took that picture. I just got home from practice. Your mom was on the way to an interview. It was a job she wanted at this clothing store. Eric was going to watch you and I was taking her to the interview. We were all in a good place in this photo."

Jam returned to the table and Marley showed him the picture.

"Look at Deja looking as beautiful as ever. Where did you find that photo?" Jam asked.

"Eric is going through the photos," Marley said.

"He's probably reminiscing and drinking Henny right now," Jam said.

"You know it. You got us something to drink?"

"Yeah, she's going to bring the drinks in a second. You want your change?" Jam asked.

"Nah, keep it."

"Man, look at this photo Dad sent me," Jam said.

He showed us a photo of a younger us. Rod, Deja, and I were in our teens. Jay and Jam were little kids.

"Aw man, look at us," I said.

"Mariah looks like Mommy," Marley said.

"Just like her," Jam said.

"Jam, you look bad as hell with that grin," I said.

He laughed. "Not nearly as bad as you and Rod."

A server brought over our drinks.

"Jam, you got a decision from school?" I asked.

"Eric went to the meeting because I didn't care what decision they made. I'm suspended for the rest of the semester." Jam said.

"How ya feeling?"

"It's whatever. I don't want to go back. Dad wants me to get a plan together. I got an interview tomorrow. Hopefully, that's good news so he can leave me alone."

"You went to the doctor with Jay the other day. How did it go?"

"They did an ultrasound and everything looked fine. I'm trying to convince her to tell Dad and she ain't hearing it. She thinks she can tell him on the day she delivers."

"Nah, that's crazy. I'm going to talk to her. She ain't going to listen but I'll try."

Daddy duties called as Life gets fussy and lets out a loud wail. I took her out of the stroller and I dug around her bag for her bottle. I sat her on my lap and handed her the bottle.

"Rell, are the things I'm seeing about Life's mom true?" Reem asked.

"Yup," I said.

"I've met her a few times and she was so sweet."

"Chantel, sweet? She's always been a firecracker."

He chuckled. "Well, I ain't see that side of her. Now if Porsha was on the blogs for stabbing her man, I wouldn't be shocked."

I burst out laughing. "You a fool for that but you right. Porsha don't play."

Chapter 54

You Got This

The next day, I drove Jam to his interview with Jay sitting in the backseat for moral support. Eric and Pops were at the house watching Ava and Life.

Jam's right leg was shaking and he was drumming his fingers on his left leg. He was so nervous about this interview.

"You got this, bro," Jay said.

"We've prepared all week for this. Just be yourself and be confident." I said.

I pulled into the parking lot and parked near the front. Jam took several deep breaths before getting out of the car. We watched him walk into the building.

"Come up here, Jay," I said.

"Coming." She climbed into the passenger seat moments later.

"How's it going?" I asked.

"I have good and bad days. I get sad sometimes because I never wanted to bring a kid into this mess. I should have been more careful but none of that matters now."

"Is Sam staying away?"

"Yeah, he doesn't want to get locked up again. He talks crazy about me on social media but I ignore it."

"Your life is not over, Jay. This is not a death sentence. You're twenty-two and own a bakery. That's a big accomplishment and you will accomplish a lot more.

You got your whole family behind you. You ain't going to raise this baby alone."

She wiped her tears. "I was so worried about how y'all would react and y'all have been so supportive."

"You got to tell your dad. We can't keep lying for you."

"Will you be by my side when I tell him?"

"Yeah. Have you talked to Momma lately?"

"That relationship is strained. I don't like how she did Jam. Maybe one day we can sit down and talk about everything. Right now, she needs time to think about the fucked-up things she has done. I struggle with loving her and being angry with her. She stole from all of us. She robbed Mariah of her innocence. She cheated on my dad with this awful guy. And she lied for years that this awful guy was her brother. The worst part is she's not sorry for any of this shit."

Jay cried even harder and I rubbed her belly. I held her in my arms and she cried into my chest.

"I'm going through my first pregnancy without my mom and child's father. I never imagined it being like this."

"I know it's hard, baby girl. But you got a whole village here for you and your baby."

"I think about how much of an ass I was to Deja at times. I guess I thought I was better than her. I remember her telling me your life can be up one minute and down the next. She told me that one day I'll understand that we don't plan for the bad and that shit happens. I remember being young and thinking I knew everything and nothing bad could ever happen to me. I was popping, getting money, and somewhat had my life together. Man, life came at me fast."

"It happens to us all, Jay. In life, you deal with the good and the bad. Just know the bad doesn't last forever. You'll be okay again."

"I'm scared, Rell."

"And that's okay."

"I'm not ready to be somebody's momma. I don't have it all together yet."

"You don't have to. I wasn't ready to be a dad when I had Junior. I had to figure it out and learn how to be a parent. I had Eric, Pops, and Poppa as guides and leaned on them for support. I knew the type of bond I wanted with my kids which is the same bond I have with my Pops, stepdad, and granddad. I promise you it's all going to come to you. You ain't got to be perfect to be a good parent. You have to be able to love, protect, and provide for the child. That's the basics."

"I don't even know how to love myself, Rell."

"Well, you're about to go on a self-love journey. You're going to learn a lot about yourself. Don't stress about all of this right now. As soon as the baby is here, it'll all come to you."

"I think I want to go back to the bakery part-time."

"It'll be good for you. It'll give you something to do to keep your mind off of things."

"I want to create more videos for the channel too."

"We can do that."

She looked in the mirror. "Ugh, I'm a mess."

I went into the glove compartment and passed her a pack of tissues.

"Thank you for everything," Jay said.

"Of course, Slim. I got you forever. I love you."

She smiled hearing her childhood nickname. "I love you, Relly."

We hugged and I kissed her on the cheek.

No matter what, that's baby sis. I can't stay mad at her for too long. We fuss and fight but at the end of the day, we got a lot of love for one another.

I looked down at my phone and read a text from Rod.

Rod: **Moms just posted bail**
Me: **They giving anybody bail. Who got her out?**
Rod: **her friend Julie**

```
Me: oh wow
```

"Moms just bonded out of jail," I said.

"Really? I thought they weren't giving her a bond." Jay said.

"Judge must have had a change of heart. I'm surprised she's out too."

"Where is she staying?"

"No idea. Rod said her friend, Julie, bailed her out so maybe Moms is staying with her."

"You think she's going to stay out of trouble?"

"I doubt it."

Chapter 55

Secret's Out

Jay, Jam, and I walked into the house joking and laughing. We walked into the living room where Ava and Life were fast asleep and Eric and Pops were on the couch chillin'.

"Wassup, y'all?" Pops asked.

"Tell 'em, Jam," I said.

"I got the job!" Jam said.

Eric jumped up and hugged him.

"That's what I'm talking 'bout!" Eric said.

"Congrats Jam," Pops said.

"Can we go to the kitchen? I got to tell y'all something." Jay said.

Jam and I looked at one another not ready for this conversation. Eric and Pops followed us to the kitchen. I grabbed bottled water out of the fridge. Pops and Eric sat at the table. Jay stood between me and Jam.

"Did someone die?" Eric asked.

"No. Did you hear Moms bonded out of jail?" I asked.

"Yeah, I got to talk to you about that," Eric said.

"Jay, what you got to tell us?" Pops asked.

She took a deep breath and used the softest quietest voice to tell them she was pregnant. I watched their faces process the news.

"You're what?" Eric asked.

"I don't think we heard you right," Pops said.

"I'm...pregnant," Jay said.

Eric slammed his hand on the table making us all jump.

"Are you serious?" Eric yelled. "Don't tell me that little nappy-headed boy, Sam, is the dad."

"Yes," Jay said meekly.

Eric stood to his feet. "Wow." He paced the floor making us all nervous. Pops was still too shocked to respond. An awkward silence fell over the room.

"And y'all knew?" Eric asked pointing to Jam and then me.

Jam looked down at his feet and said nothing.

"Yeah," I said.

"And y'all been lying to my face when I asked about it?" Eric said.

"It wasn't my place to tell," I said.

"Don't blame them, Daddy. I wanted to tell you myself." Jay said.

"Come outside with me, Jay."

She looked over at me terrified.

"It's okay," I said.

Eric and Jay went outside to talk. Jam and I sat at the table.

"I knew it," Pops said.

"How?" I asked.

"I know when y'all lying to me. And she's wearing baggy clothes now, that was the first clue. Y'all shouldn't keep things like this away from us." Pops said.

"She's grown. I'm not going to put her business out there when she didn't want anyone to know." I said.

"How would you feel if one of your kids had something going on and no one told you? It's cool y'all sticking together but she needs her dad for this situation."

"You right. I didn't think about it like that."

"Sunny is a cool dude."

"He got the job?"

"Yeah. Everybody liked him and he jumped right in making sure everything was good. I feel good about leaving him in charge."

"And you know I'll pop in often to check on everyone and everything. You need to take time off and get healthy."

"I am. Everybody has been preaching for me to do that and I'm finally listening."

"And you need to eat better too."

"I will."

"If you want me to help you with meal prep, I will."

"I would like that."

"Have you talked to Momma?"

"She called to let me know she's out."

"Is she staying with Julie?"

"That's what she said which means getting high and getting into mischief."

"Man, she was doing so good."

"She wants to talk to you."

"That ain't happening."

"I think it would be good to hash it out and go y'all separate ways."

"I don't know, Pops. I can see her making me mad especially if she don't own up to her shit and pretends to be a victim. And I don't like how she's doing Jay and Jam."

"What did she do?"

"She's just been talking crazy lately," Jam said.

"She ain't herself, that's for sure. But I think she finally realizes she fucked up. All the scamming and low-life shit catching up to her." Pops said.

"What made you leave Momma?" I asked.

"I don't like mess. The police were at the door constantly asking for her. She was doing a lot of shit I wasn't cool with or trying to stay away from. It wasn't worth the headache. I was staying for you, Rod, and Deja but I realized it would be better and healthier to leave and get custody of y'all. Me and Deja's dad, Carlos, were cool and I could do a little more than he could so he let Deja come with y'all if he couldn't take her in for whatever reason."

"Carlos was a great guy," I said.

"Yeah, he was. He worked hard to provide for his family. And just when things were about to take off, someone killed him. It's sad."

"Why they killed him?" Jam asked.

"Robbery gone bad. He had this taco stand and he was popular. I guess this dude thought he had a lot of money on him. Carlos wanted to one day own a restaurant and Deja wanted to do the same to honor her dad's memory and she never got the chance to do that." Pops said.

"Man, I forgot she wanted to open a restaurant," I said.

"Carlos left behind all these recipes for her and she was going to use them to create her menu. We had so many talks about this." Pops said.

"You still got that notebook?" I asked.

"Yeah, I was going to give it to Mariah or Marley when they're a little older."

Jay stormed into the house with tears down her cheek.

"You okay?" I asked.

"I hate him!" Jay yelled.

She walked down the hall to Jam's room. I stood up.

"I'll go," Jam said.

I sat back down as Jam went to his room.

Eric walked into the kitchen.

"Now, why would you upset her? She's pregnant." I said.

"I wasn't trying to upset her. I was giving her a real talk on this situation and she couldn't take it." Eric said.

"Now wasn't the right time for that," I said.

"Stay out of it, Rell. You can't tell him how to parent his child." Pops said.

"That's the point. Jay is not a child, she's grown." I said.

"She ain't too grown that she can't hear what I got to say," Eric said.

"You're just pushing her further and further away," I said.

"Nah, she's mad right now but she'll come around," Pops said.

"Cool, y'all know everything," I said.

"Why you getting mad?" Pops asked.

"Ain't nobody mad. Y'all ain't got to like that she's pregnant, just support her and be there for her." I said.

"Watch your tone now," Pops said.

"This is the shit I'm talking 'bout. We ain't kids no more." I said.

"Let me get out of here. I'll talk to y'all later." Pops said.

"Now we can't have a conversation? Aight cool." I said.

I walked away to the living room and Pops walked out the front door.

"I'll be back," Eric said following Pops.

Ava stirred in her bassinet and I ran to the kitchen to get her a bottle. I took her out of the bassinet and sat on the couch cradling Ava in my arms. I found something to watch as I gave her the bottle.

I answered an incoming video call from Rod. He was in the kitchen at the Juicy Boil.

"What the hell is going on?" Rod asked.

"Man, what you heard?"

"Jay called me crying hysterically. I'm guessing Eric wasn't happy to find out she's pregnant."

"Nah, he's pissed."

"And Pops just called me talking 'bout get your brother and hung up."

"Pops trippin'."

"What now?"

"I just told Eric he ain't have to upset Jay. I wanted him to be mindful that she was pregnant. She don't need all of this stress, she's stressed out enough."

"True."

"And Pops jumped in like you can't tell him how to parent."

"How did it go left?"

"He was trying to check me like I'm a kid."

"Y'all been bumping heads lately."

"I'm telling you, Pops trippin'. He's stressed about this new baby on the way and worried about Stephanie because she's sick all of the time."

"You know I forgot they're having a kid."

"At our big age, we're about to have a little brother or sister."

"I still can't believe it. What's going on with you and Connie?"

"Ain't nothing, bro."

"She likes you, you like her. What's the problem?"

"I didn't know she liked me. She don't act like it."

"Everybody knows she likes you."

"I think she's scared to get hurt again. She saw me play women and scared to take that chance. I made my move and she was acting funny. Ya feel me?"

"I feel you. Chloe reached out to me in my DMs. She wrote this whole essay and I'll forward it to you. Basically, she wants me to tell you she's sorry."

"I got to call that crazy girl so she leaves y'all alone. She reached out to Jam too."

"You done, bro? I know you like them crazy."

I chuckled. "Hell yeah, I'm done. I'm not going to be going through all of that with Chloe. I'm too old for the bullshit. She didn't want to be in a relationship for real."

"Yeah, I can tell. She's been in a lot of situations and it's nothing but drama. Are y'all getting custody of AJ too?"

"Yeah, Jada's momma wants her to focus on school and Jada said she's not ready to be a mom. She told me she would have gotten the abortion if she didn't find out so late."

"You 'bout to have three babies in your house crying all the time."

"I'm not ready, bro. I got to hire a nanny. Life is already getting into everything."

"You got to put Life in a preschool program. How long you keeping Life?"

"For the next week or so. Chantel's in a lot of legal trouble and got to handle her business."

"What about her job?"

"She still got her job. Her Pops is here handling everything."

"Oh, she 'bout to get a slap on the wrist if Joe is handling everything."

Chantel comes from money and her dad is a well-known politician. Rod might be onto something.

Rod walked out of the kitchen and into his office. I could tell my bro wasn't good but I wasn't sure if he would open up to me.

"How's everything, Rod?" I asked.

"Everything is everything."

"But how are you?"

"I ain't going to lie to you. I've seen better days."

"What's going on?"

"Just thinking about my past, bro. All the shit I've been through. Sometimes I can't believe I'm still here."

"I'm glad you're still here, bro. I'm glad you got a chance to turn it around. You even have your own restaurant which was your dream."

"Moms reached out to me. It was weird. I ain't talked to her in a long time. I realized I'm angry and hurt by all the shit she's done to us. I couldn't even have a conversation with her."

"What did she want?"

"She just wanted to see how I was doing. She wants to get together and talk. But there ain't shit she can say to me."

"You never know, bro. It might be what you need to heal from this shit and move on."

"What about you? You going to sit down and talk? You'll come with me?"

"Yeah bro, I'll come with you."

Eric walked into the living room and sat on the couch.

"Wassup Eric?" Rod said.

Eric looked at the phone. "Yo Rod, what's good?"

"I got to get back to the kitchen y'all."

"Hold ya head, bro. I'm going to come by and see you later."

"Aight, I'll see you soon, bro."

I ended the call.

"How's Pops?" I asked.

"I just had to get his blood pressure down before he headed home," Eric said.

"It wasn't that serious," I said.

"He got a lot going on," Eric said.

"We all do," I said.

"You talked to Jay?"

"Nah, she's back there with Jam."

"Should I go back there and talk to her?"

"At your own risk."

He chuckled.

"I appreciate you watching the little ones, Eric."

"Don't mention it. Thanks for taking Jam to his interview."

"When's his next court date?"

"Next month. Got me stressed but I got to stay positive for him."

"It's all going to work out."

"I just want him to get his license back."

"Rod said Momma reached out to him."

"Ah, that's why he looked a little down."

"Yeah, he worries me because he holds everything in and never wants to talk about how he's feeling. You would never know if Rod was struggling. He's been like this since he was a kid."

"I remember. I'm going to reach out and make sure he's straight."

"What did you say to Jay to make her so upset?"

"She didn't like the fact that I told her I was disappointed in her and that she was bringing a child into a fucked-up situation. Y'all can be happy about this but I'm not. She's twenty-two and she ain't ready and she knows she ain't ready. She's immature and selfish and she likes to have a good time. She has a lot of maturing to do in the next few months. You know this."

"She ain't at the place to receive all of that. She's stressed and she needs our support."

"I'm going to support her but I still don't like it."

"That's fair."

"It's the same as you supporting Junior but don't like some of the choices he has made. Kids, grown or not, need tough love and to be checked sometimes."

"Aight, I see your point. I don't like y'all at odds."

"I don't like us being at odds either. That's my baby girl."

Chapter 56

Not Okay

It was nine at night and I called Rod to check on him.

"Wassup?" Rod asked.

"Where you at? I'm 'bout to pull up on you."

"I'm at the house, bro."

"I'm on the way."

I walked into Jam's room. He was lying in bed watching television.

"Hey. Can you watch the house for me? I'm 'bout to go to Rod's real quick. Life is in her room and Ava is in my room. They shouldn't get up while I'm gone."

"Aight, I got you."

"And Marley is at the guest house with Junior. Ken needs to be in bed by ten. If she gives you any problems, call me."

It was only a fifteen-minute drive to Rod's house and I got there as fast as I could. I walked into his dark house and down the hall to his living room. He was on the couch with his head resting between his legs.

"Where's Jay?" I asked.

"She's already asleep," Rod said.

I noticed a bottle of pills and empty alcohol bottles on his coffee table.

"Rod, what you got going on?" I asked.

"I'm chillin', bro." He lifted his head and his eyes were low.

I picked up the pills. I read the label. "What the hell are these? You poppin' pills now?"

He dropped his head.

"What's wrong with you, Rod? This is why your ass is always out of it."

"I'm dealing with a lot of shit, bro."

"Bro, you ain't dealing with it if you high. Your ass watched me struggle with addiction and you do the same shit. I'm already worrying about Junior and now I got to worry about you too. I don't want to lose you, bro."

"Stop trippin'. I can quit whenever, bro."

"You can? Cool."

I left the room with the pill bottle in my hand.

"What you doing, bro?" Rod asked.

"Getting rid of this shit." I ran to the kitchen at the end of the hall with Rod on my heels. I poured the pills down the sink and turned on the water. Rod started swinging.

"Come on, bro!" I yelled ducking his hits. I tackled him to the floor and restrained him. "I don't want this for you, bro. I love you too much to see you go out like this. And we're brothers. You could have told me what was going on."

"What's wrong?" a timid voice asked.

I looked up and saw Coby and the panicked expression on his face. I stood to my feet. Rod sat on the floor with his back against the wall. I walked over to Coby. He stepped back. I'm sure Coby seeing me pin his dad on the floor scared him.

"Nothing is wrong. Go back to bed, baby. I'll come up in a second." I said.

He turned and walked down the hall. He glared at me as he walked back upstairs to his room. Rod stood to his feet. I stood against the counter and he stood by the refrigerator.

"My life is a mess," Rod said.

"Tell me about it."

"Vanessa is fighting for custody."

"The same Vanessa that said she'll kill Coby?"

"The same one, bro. She said she wanted nothing to do with him and now she wants joint custody. I'm trying to keep it from happening. Coby don't want nothing to do with her."

"Can you blame him? She held a knife to his throat."

"I feel like the judge 'bout to give in and grant this crazy lady visitation rights. I feel horrible that I can't protect Coby if that happens."

"You got to get my lawyer to handle it. This is why you got to reach out to me and let me know what's going on. Jordan Waters will make sure Vanessa doesn't get visitation, custody, or none of that."

"Send me his information. I need all the help I can get."

"Do you even have a lawyer?"

"Nah."

"Bro, you can't ever go to family court without a lawyer. I bet Vanessa's crazy ass got a lawyer."

"She does."

I throw my hands up. "See? How long y'all been battling this in court?"

"About four months."

"Call my guy, Jordan, and it's all going to work out."

"I've been thinking about my life. Man, we came from the bottom. Shit was so rough. I knew if I ever had kids, I wanted things to be different for them. I didn't want them to feel pain, have an abusive parent, or none of that. I don't want Coby to worry if his mom will come after him. I tell him I got him but I know I can't protect him from everything."

"Nope, we can't protect them from everything. We just got to be there for them and guide them. I couldn't protect Junior from a life of drugs. All I can do now is pray, support him, and get him help."

"I got a little one, bro."

I looked at him like I heard him wrong. "Huh? You got a what?"

"You remember Tiffany?"

My eyes widened. "No, bro! You got a baby by her? I ain't seen her in years."

"She texted me outta the blue that she got my baby. She said when we broke up, she was pregnant and never told me."

"How old is this baby?"

"She's three years old."

"You got a DNA test?"

"Got the results today and I'm sick, bro."

"That's why you going crazy. I would be poppin' pills too if I knew Tiffany was my baby moms."

He smiled. "She's already asking for all of this money in child support and saying she's going to drain my pockets."

"Damn, she couldn't wait. You got a picture of your baby girl?"

He pulled his phone out of his pocket and showed me a picture. I looked at him then at the picture then back at him.

"Yup, that's your baby alright. Jordan can help you with this too. Where is Tiffany living? She got baby girl looking rough."

"She's in New York somewhere, slumming it. I don't like her lifestyle. I heard she's doing coke and tricking for money and leaves baby girl by her lonesome. Like how I picked the worst moms for my kids?"

"You picked toxic ass females like Momma. Ashley, Vanessa, and Tiffany are all crazy as hell just like Momma."

"Wow, that's crazy."

"I told you that you got to stop running and deal with that shit. It's going to follow you until you do."

He put his head in his hands thinking about what I said.

"It's going to get better, Rod."

I embraced him and let him cry on my shoulder. Rod didn't have a lot of vulnerable moments. He kept everything inside and wanted us to always think he was okay.

"Bro, I can't take this shit anymore. It's always something. I've been having thoughts of leaving here. I keep thinking about everything I've been through. I've been feeling strange and just out of my mind. For Coby, I keep going."

"Nah, you can't leave here. It's gonna get much better. I promise I ain't leaving your side. Shit, I'm going to stay with you tonight."

"You ain't gotta do all of that."

"I ain't leaving you like this, bro."

"I got to hop in the shower."

"If you ain't out in fifteen minutes, I'm knocking the door down."

He smiled sheepishly and walked out of the kitchen. I called Jam.

"Wassup bro?" Jam said.

"I got to stay with Rod tonight," I said.

"Is he okay?"

"Yeah and no. I'll explain later."

"I got the kids, don't even worry about it. Can I stay in your room?"

"Yeah, that's fine."

"Yes! I'm 'bout to sleep like a King tonight in your King-sized bed."

I shook my head. "The kids ain't going to school tomorrow. We got to drop Junior off at his program and they're tagging along."

"What time?"

"Twelve fifteen. You coming with us?"

"Yeah, got to make sure nephew straight."

"Call me if you need anything."

"I got it over here, bro. Just take care of Rod."

I walked up the carpeted steps to Coby's space-themed room. He sat up in bed with his knees to his chest and his head resting on his knees. I sat on the bed and looked up at the galaxy-painted ceiling.

"What's going on?" I asked.

He sniffled. I pulled him close to me and let him cry into my chest.

"What's wrong, Coby?"

"I'm scared," Coby mumbled.

"You heard us talking?"

"A little. I don't want to lose my daddy and I don't want to see my mom."

What could I possibly tell him to comfort him?

"Am I a burden?" Coby asked.

"No, don't ever think that. What would your dad do without you? You're his whole world and I like having you in my life too."

He smiled.

"Coby, I need you to get some rest. You got school in the morning."

I tucked him in and kissed him on the cheek. "I love you, Coby."

"I love you too, Uncle Rell."

I walked into Rod's bedroom as he walked out of the bathroom.

"You got something for me to wear?" I asked.

He passed me pajama bottoms and a T-shirt. I changed clothes and lay down at the foot of the bed.

"I appreciate you, bro," Rod said.

"You can't leave me, bro. I need you. We all need you." I said.

"You know me better than anybody. A lot of shit in my life traumatized me. I escaped death at fourteen when that dude shot me three times. I've been in and out of the system since I was fifteen. I couldn't even be there to send Deja off because I was locked up. And the shit Moms put me through ruined me. The world's just so cold, bro. I can't smile and I'm always looking over my shoulder. We weren't supposed to grow up seeing our mom snort coke, bodies on the ground, and all of that shit."

"Nah, we weren't even supposed to survive. They counted us out before we could even count. That's how it is when you from the bottom."

"It's fucked up."

"That's why I reach out to these kids and let them know they're bigger and better than their present circumstances. It's up to us to save them, make them believe their dreams are valid, and show them somebody cares about them."

"That's why I feed every kid who comes into the restaurant even if they don't have a cent to give me. They know they can come to the Juicy Boil and fill their bellies."

"We've been through so much, Rod. Did you ever think we would get this far?"

"Nah, we were constantly told dreams didn't come true."

"But Poppa made me feel differently. He made me feel like I was bigger than life."

"I hate that I disappointed Poppa and Pops so much."

"You ain't disappoint them, bro. They understood your journey and supported you through it. They knew you would be okay."

Chapter 57

Checked In

The following day, we gathered around Junior, said a prayer, gave him encouraging words, and let him know how much we loved him.

I grabbed his suitcase. Marie, Junior, and I walked into the facility while everyone went back to the rented Sprinter van. We walked to the front desk for intake. Junior looked down at the floor as Marie talked to the lady at the front desk.

"Hold ya head up. You a soldier." I said.

We filled out the paperwork and it was time to say goodbye. Man, I wasn't ready. I couldn't cry because I didn't want him to see me upset. Marie wrapped her arms around him.

"We're going to miss you so much, baby boy. Stay strong and get through this. I can't wait to see you loving on Ava and AJ." Marie said.

Junior smiled. "I'm going to miss y'all."

"This month is going to fly by. You gonna be back at the house begging me to make lunch." I said.

He laughed. "I love you, Pops. I love you, Mom."

Marie let him go and wiped away her tears.

I hugged him. "You got this, Junior. I'll talk to you on the phone and visit you as soon as I can. Don't worry about nothing. I got the babies. Just get better for you and them."

"I will, Pops."

And it was time for him to go. I knew this would be hard on him but I also knew this was the best decision for him. I held Marie in my arms as she broke down.

Junior was our baby and to see him being led to the back was hard. Man, we ain't see the day of checking our child into a rehab program coming at all. Marie got herself together. We walked out of the facility hand in hand. Rod and Jam stood by the van waiting for us.

"He's all checked in," I said.

"How ya feeling?" Rod asked.

I didn't say anything and looked away. And my brothers embraced me knowing I wasn't good.

"Marie, make sure the babies are good," Rod said noticing her looking worried.

She climbed into the van and Rod shut the door.

"He's going to be straight," Rod said.

"I know what it's like to be in one of these facilities. It's lonely as shit and the withdrawal is the worst part. The throwing up, the shakes, sweating like crazy, and all that shit. It feels like you're about to lose your mind when you're trying to get the drugs out of your system. I want to be right with him as he goes through it. But I know he got to do this without me. Junior didn't say a lot but I know he's nervous."

"Junior is going to be okay. This is the best place for him. He's addicted to pills, coke, and heroin. He needs serious help and he's getting it. He can't continue on this dangerous path."

"Rod, you're right."

I looked back at the facility and took a deep breath. This was going to be the longest month of my life.

Chapter 58

I Told You So

It has been two weeks since that day and Junior is doing great. Jay is back at the bakery on a part-time basis. Pops has officially retired and left Sunny in charge. Connie is still there keeping an eye on things.

Life is back home with Chantel and Joe is still in town helping her out. Jam is still fighting his case. Rod checked into a recovery program after an overdose left him stuck at a red light. Instead of going to jail, he's going to this program. I'm watching Coby while he gets clean.

I was currently at the house with Jackson, Ava, and AJ. As Ava and AJ napped, I worked on social media campaigns and the channel. My recent video of meal prepping was an overnight success that brought a lot of subscribers to the channel. I sat at the bar on my laptop looking at analytics proud of our growth in a short amount of time.

I answered an incoming call from Boss.
"What's going on, Boss?" I asked.
"Not too much. What's good with you?"
"It's all good, bro."
"Everything is set for Saturday. Thanks for renting the bowling alley for Honey's coming home party."
"Of course. I'm glad she's back home."
"Me too. It's been a few days and she's adjusting. The kids love having her home. I wake up next to her not believing she's home."

"I can't wait to see Honey."

"Is Rod going to be home by then?"

"Yeah, he gets out of the program tomorrow."

"His program was short as hell."

"It's a week in the facility and he has weekly appointments for treatment and therapy."

"That's good. I'm just glad he's getting off that shit. You know that virus is here now?"

"You serious?"

"Yeah, it's at some nursing home in Washington state."

"What does that mean for us?"

"Nothing yet. We just have to keep watching and see what happens. It's going to spread everywhere soon."

"I ain't ready for that. You think we're going to go on lockdown like these other countries?"

"Shit, I don't know. It's probably going to come to that as soon as it hits the other states."

"I'll keep watching the news then. That's all we can do."

"True. You and your fam need to stay away from drugs. I watched your mom go through it. I watched you go through it. Now, I got to watch Junior and Rod go through it."

"I know, Unc. I pray nobody else in the fam goes through this shit. Every time Junior calls, I want to break down. I can't help but feel that I failed him."

"Nah, he made his own choices. You and Marie are good parents. Hell, he even had a great stepdad in his life. Junior is hardheaded and you can't tell him nothing. He had to fall on his own."

"I was the same way. I thought I knew everything and life happened and I realized I didn't know nothing."

"That's how it goes. I talked to y'all mom earlier. You and Rod going to meet up with her tomorrow?"

"That's the plan. Eric, Pops, Jam, and Jay are coming to the sit-down too."

"Where are y'all meeting?"

"At this new Italian restaurant. It's about time for all of us to sit down and talk about everything."

"I pray y'all get what y'all need from it so y'all can move on."

"I need an apology. I don't want nothing else from her. The money is already gone and she can't pay me back so an apology is all I can get."

"She's facing twenty years behind the fence."

"You think she'll get that much time?"

"I don't know. They already dropped some charges. She was looking at forty or so years in prison."

"Jeez, they're ready to throw the book at her."

"I mean she was told years ago, if she ended up back in court, she would get the maximum punishment. It scared her enough to stop her shit but she got caught up."

I heard somebody talking to Boss in the background. He got back on the phone.

"Aight Rell, I'll see you at the gym later."

"I'll be there at seven."

I ended the call and continued working. Now, I was getting a call from a number I didn't recognize.

"Hello," I said.

"Please don't hang up." a familiar voice said.

It took a minute to figure out who it was then it hit me. *Chloe*.

I took a deep breath. "You ain't supposed to be contacting me."

"I know. I know. I just hate the way things ended between us."

"You attacked me then got in a fight with my baby moms."

"I was just shocked at the things you said during that lunch."

"Shocked that I caught you in a lie?"

"Rell, I didn't call to fight. I'm tired of fighting with everyone."

"Why you calling then?"

"I wanted to fucking apologize but you won't let me."

"Just say what you got to say."

"I feel horrible about everything. I never wanted it to go down like that. I got angry and lost it. I should have kept my cool that day. I hate that I caused all of this drama when I was trying so hard to change. Rell, you were great to me and I appreciate you. I wasn't ready for a serious relationship and I should have been honest with you. I'm sorry for everything."

"Yeah, you should have told me that from the jump."

"I didn't realize you wanted a wife until much later. I thought we were just having a good time. I ain't ready to be someone's wife."

"I get it. I wish you the best, Chloe. Ain't no hard feelings."

And she could only cry. A part of me felt bad but I didn't know what to say. I liked her a lot and I'm not sure she ever felt the same way.

She ended the call without saying anything else. I tried to call her back and it went straight to voicemail. Nothing else I could do. Before I could put the phone down, I got a call from Marley.

"Wassup Marley?" I asked.

"Coach just announced a surprise drug test."

"When is it?"

"Today. You got to come get me from school. I ain't going to pass no drug test."

"Didn't I tell you this would happen?"

"Yeah, now I'm screwed."

"Just because you don't take it today doesn't mean you won't take it tomorrow."

"I just need a day to detox."

I don't know what kind of detox he was going to do in a day to pass the drug test. He's just talking nonsense at this point. "What happens if you don't pass the drug test?"

"You get suspended for a few games or kicked off the team."

"I think you need to stay and take the test. I tried to warn you about smoking and you acted like I didn't know what I was talking about. I think you're way too young to be smoking the way you do."

"So, you making me stay?"

"Yeah. You need to face that and deal with the consequences."

"Man, I thought you were the cool one. I'll call Jam."

"Don't you dare! He's not even allowed to drive. Just take the test and tell me how it goes. I told Coach to give you another chance and I hope this doesn't mess it up."

"Man, fuck you."

Even though he mumbled this under his breath, I heard him.

"What you just say?"

He got quiet as he realized I heard him.

"Marley, you going there with me for this? I warned you so many times that this would happen. You just got to deal with it."

The call clicked. I looked at the phone knowing good and well he didn't hang up on me. I called him back and he didn't answer.

Jackson walked into the kitchen.

"You got to go to the potty?" I asked.

He nodded his head.

"Come on."

I grabbed his hand and we went to the bathroom down the hall. I set his potty seat on the toilet. I checked his diaper and saw poop. I don't get mad. It was my fault for not checking on him and getting him to the bathroom.

"Accidents happen, Jackson. When you feel it coming out, you got to rush to the potty, okay?"

"Okay," Jackson said.

I cleaned him up and sat him on the toilet. I put the soiled diaper in a plastic bag. I had to take this stank bomb to the trash can outside.

"I peed," Jackson said.

"Good job, Jack. You think you want to put on your big boy underwear now?"

"No."

I helped him put on a pull-up and washed his hands at the sink. We walked out of the bathroom.

"Here, let's take this to the trash," I said handing him the bag.

"Ew," Jackson said pinching his nose. He grabbed the bag.

We walked out the door and put it in the trash. We walked back into the house.

"I'm hungry," Jackson said.

"Again? I'll make you something."

He hung out with me in the kitchen as I made him a PB&J sandwich. I decided to also cut up a banana for him. I set the plate and glass of milk on the table. I sat him in a chair and he went right for the bananas. This little boy could eat.

I heard AJ crying and I rushed into the living room and scooped him out of his bassinet before he woke Ava. They're only a month apart and I've been trying to sync their schedules because they've been wearing me out. I made his bottle and joined Jackson at the table.

"Jack, you having fun with Daddy?" I asked.

"I play with toys," Jackson said.

"What's your favorite toy?"

"I'm a superhero. I go fast, Daddy."

Jackson was always talking in riddles.

"What kind of superhero are you?"

"I fly and invisible too."

"Wow, that's cool, man."

He didn't say anything else and continued eating. I took a picture and sent it to Porsha. I know she's missing her babies. She sent a text right back.

```
Porsha: I miss his little face. I'll call them later.
Me: He misses you. How ya doing?
Porsha: Not great
Me: Y?
Porsha: I went to the doctor and she confirmed I'm pregnant. I don't know how to tell C.
Me: Just gotta tell him
```

There was a knock at the door at 4:30 PM. I opened the door and all of the kids filed into the house. Eric was busy getting things out of his trunk.

"If you have homework, I need you at the kitchen table," I said. "And Marley, I need you to go to my room."

Jam walked into the house and seeing him in a button-down and slacks was weird.

"How was your first day?" I asked.

"It was straight. We ain't do nothing too crazy. I'm 'bout to take a nap." Jam said.

"Aight. I'll call you when dinner is ready."

I walked into the kitchen and Jam walked to his room. Jackson ran into the kitchen excited to see everyone. Layla, Coby, and Mariah were seated at the table ready to do their homework.

Eric walked into the house carrying Coby and Layla's backpacks.

"Hey. What's going on?" I said.

"Not too much. You cooking dinner?" Eric asked.

"Yeah, I'm baking chicken and veggies right now," I said.

"It smells good."

"I got to go check Marley. Did he tell you about the drug test?"

"Nope."

I jogged up the stairs to my room. Marley was sitting on the edge of the bed.

"How did it go?" I asked.

"I failed," Marley mumbled.

"Now what?"

"Coach is making me write two papers. One on why drugs are bad and the other on the history of soccer. And he suspended me for five games. He wanted to kick me off but Coach Sam saved the day and was like I'm a good player and give me another chance. I told them I quit smoking and the next time I get a test, I'll pass."

"I'm glad you didn't get kicked off the team."

"I'm 'bout to miss five games though."

"That's called consequences. You know every action has a consequence."

"Yeah."

"I want to talk about how you disrespected me earlier."

"C'mon, Unc. You know I ain't mean it. I was frustrated."

"Don't talk to me crazy when you're frustrated."

"Yes sir."

"You got homework?"

"Always."

"Go downstairs and do your work."

"That's it?"

"I'm going to give you time to correct your behavior because you ain't never gotten out of line with me."

"I love you, Unc."

"I love you too. C'mon, I got to finish dinner."

We walked downstairs to the kitchen. Eric and I stood by the stove.

"How ya handling these two babies?" Eric asked.

"Barely. I'm tired as hell. Marie is getting Ava this weekend so that's a little break. I'm ready for Junior to come home and take over. I'm trying to sync their schedules so they're eating and sleeping around the same time."

"Yeah, that would make things easier."

"What time are you getting Rod tomorrow?"

"Eleven in the morning. Then we'll meet y'all at the restaurant."

Jam walked into the kitchen holding Ava.

I grabbed a bottle out of the fridge and handed it to Jam.

"Y'all ready to see Momma?" Eric asked.

"Nope," Jam said.

"It's whatever," I said.

Chapter 59

You Not Sorry?

The following day, I went to the restaurant for this sit-down with Moms. I sat at a table with Jay, Jam, Pops, AJ, Ava, and Jackson. We were waiting for Moms, Eric, and Rod.

"I'm sleepy," Jackson said rubbing his eyes.

"Come here," Pops said.

Jackson hopped out of his chair and walked over to Pops. Pops picked him up and rocked Jackson in his arms. I peeked into the stroller and Ava and AJ were fast asleep.

Eric and Rod walked through the front door of the restaurant. It was good seeing Rod. I stood up and hugged them both.

"Janet still ain't here?" Eric asked.

"Nope. You think she's coming?" Jam asked.

"She texted me a few minutes ago that she's on the way," Eric said.

Rod sat beside me and Eric sat across from me.

"Well, let's go ahead and order," Eric said.

We all took a moment to look over the menu. I got the waitress' attention. She walked to the table and we went around the table telling her what we wanted. The waitress walked away from the table a few minutes later.

Moms walked into the restaurant and uneasiness was now at the table. Moms looked different. She was dressed in tight jeans and a bright pink crop top. She had her hair down her back and I've only seen her hair in buns and puffs. She sat down at the table.

"Hey," Eric said looking her up and down.

"Hey y'all," Moms said.

"How you doing?" Pops asked. "You looking good."

"I'm good. These are my girlfriend's clothes." Moms said. Whelp, that explained the look.

"Look over the menu. I'll call the waitress over when you're ready." Eric said.

The tension was thick at the table. Eric called the waitress over to the table five minutes later. Moms ordered her drink and food. Once the waitress left, Eric started the conversation.

"Aight, I didn't come to have a silent lunch," Eric said.

"I'll start," Moms said.

We all looked at her ready to hear what she had to say.

"I get y'all upset with me but I want y'all to know I ain't mean to hurt y'all," Moms said.

"Nah, we can't start like that. That's bullshit and you know it. You say you didn't mean to hurt us but intentionally said and did hurtful things to us." I said.

"What do you want me to say?" Moms asked.

"I'm sorry would be a start. Hell, you stole twenty g's from all of us and didn't start off apologizing." I said.

She rolled her eyes. Moms didn't like being checked by no one so I'm not shocked.

"You serious right now?" Jay asked. "You dismissing what Rell said like it's nothing. On top of stealing from us, you tried to get me caught up in your shit. You said I had a clean record and could take the fall. You tried to pin the robbery and the stolen money on me when you knew I had nothing to do with it."

"You tried to blame Jay for the robbery? That's news to me." Eric said.

"She was running her mouth to investigators to save her own ass. And you know more than anyone that I wasn't with Sam and hadn't seen him in a month. So, you knew I didn't plan that shit with Sam as you tried to say to the officers." Jay said.

"Come on, Janet. You can't keep doing shit like this. You got to one day grow up and be accountable for the things you do." Pops said.

"I got a lot of growing to do, I know. They were asking questions and said if I said some shit about certain situations and people, I would get a lesser sentence. I folded because I knew I was looking at some serious time. I talked to Sam and he said you were in on the robbery and you were the one who told him Rell wasn't home. I went with the story too." Moms said.

"Sammy was mad I wouldn't get back with him so he lied to hurt me. You knew I was pregnant and you put me through that shit. I was detained for hours then I had to sit down and talk to investigators and be interrogated like I was a criminal. It took days to clear my name and reveal you and Sammy's lies against me."

"Jay, you should have told me," Eric said.

Jay wiped her tears. "I wanted to forget. It was humiliating." Jam rubbed Jay on the back as she cried harder.

Moms looked away then looked at Jay. "I'm sorry, Jay. I shouldn't have done you like that. I was being selfish and only thinking about myself."

At least, somebody got an apology.

"Excuse me," Jay said walking away from the table. Eric excused himself to make sure she was good.

"You got anything to say to us?" Rod asked.

"Y'all always tell me how bad of a mom I am. Y'all tear me down constantly but y'all had food, a place to stay, and clothes on your back." Moms said.

"Thanks to Poppa, Pops, Carlos, and Eric," I said. "Remember you smoked and snorted all your money?"

"Rell, you always want to go there with me. I was clean for fifteen years until recently. I wasn't an addict your whole life."

"But, for most of my life, you were. I was nineteen when you got clean, remember? I remember you caring about the drugs more than us. You took us to the crackhouses. Hell, we saw you cook crack in the kitchen. You tried to sell your twelve-year-old for a gram." I said.

"And you tried to pimp Mariah and you act like it's nothing wrong with that," Rod said.

"What else y'all got? I'm a strong bitch. I can take it." Moms snarled.

"We ain't trying to beat you down, Ma. But you got to admit you ain't always been the best mom to us." I said.

"I can't change the shit I've done. What do you want from me?" Moms asked.

"I want you to say you fucked up as a mom and apologize for the fucked-up things you did. You know you did Deja wrong. That's why you didn't go to her funeral. You couldn't even face it." I said.

"You always going low like a little bitch," Moms said.

I jumped up. "Man, I knew this shit would go like this. You the same evil person. You ain't never changed. You just got better at hiding your ways."

"Sit down," Pops said noticing the looks and stares from others in the restaurant.

I sat back down with my leg shaking. Moms knew how to press my buttons.

"Every game, I was there. When you needed money to go out of town for a tournament, I made it happen." Moms said.

"You made it happen one time, Moms. And you constantly told me not to play ball and that I wasn't good enough to make it as a professional football player."

"You needed a plan B, Rell. All you had was football and you didn't think about anything else. What if that shit didn't work out?"

"I would have figured it out. I didn't need you discouraging me. On signing day, you weren't there.

You were mad I made it happen and you couldn't take credit for my success. You didn't get me to this point of my life, Ma. I got it outta the mud and made something out of nothing. You were a bad mom to me and you know that."

"I know I'm not perfect. I was a young mom and had to figure it out on my own. All I knew was the streets and I got caught up a lot. I was on drugs because I didn't want to deal with the pain or think about the things I went through. You don't even know half of what I've been through."

"Why put your kids through the same hell?" Jam asked.

"Yeah. Why not make it better for us?" I asked. "We didn't ask to be here and you acted like you hated us or we were a burden."

Moms got quiet and didn't say anything for a few minutes. "You know what, I fucked up a lot in my life. When it comes to you, Rod, and Deja, I didn't do right by y'all. I admit I didn't know how to love or be a mom. We were struggling and I was doing whatever to make money. I wasn't around much because I was in and out of jail."

"You abandoned us, Momma, whenever you could," I said.

"I'm sorry, Rell."

I was shocked by the apology. No excuses attached, just an I'm sorry. All I wanted from Moms was to acknowledge she wasn't the greatest mom and apologize.

"Momma, I loved you even when you didn't love me. I loved you despite everything. I was the only one who thought one day you would come around. I loved you no matter the beatings, how you spoke to me, and the fucked-up things you did to me. You ain't make me cold-hearted like you. I loved you because you were my momma. I figured if I did this or that, I could get you to love me back.

You stealing from me was the last straw. You knew I would give you the shirt off my back. And the fact that you stole the money to protect some low-life who harmed your granddaughter is a new low even for you. That's when I knew it was time to close that door and move on with my life without your love or approval. I realized I didn't need it. You were my inner voice for years that made me doubt and question everything good that came into my life. I can't get close to anyone and have a hard time trusting others because of how you did me. These are the problems you caused for me."

I looked down at the table, glad I could tell her exactly how I felt. Two waitresses brought the food to the table.

Rod put his arm around my shoulder. I pinched my eyes and tried to think about something else. Momma's body shook as she cried and I've never seen her so emotional.

"Y'all about to make me cry too," Pops said.

Jay and Eric returned to the table.

"Damn, what we missed?" Eric asked.

Pops caught him up to speed.

Eric turned to me. "You aight?"

"Yeah." I croaked still trying to get myself together.

Moms looked at me. "I'm so sorry, Rell. I've always loved you. I was just bad at showing it. I wish I can go back and change all this shit."

I don't say anything.

Rod spoke up next. "Ma, at fifteen when we got caught up, you pinned all the charges on me thinking they wouldn't try me as an adult. But they did and I spent a few months away. When I got shot at fourteen, you ran but didn't get me help. I could have died that day and you left me in the dirt like I meant nothing. Another time, I was facing thirty years and you didn't come to court to see my fate. You never had my back. You taught me the game and left me out there to die."

Moms wiped her eyes. "I fucked up your life, Rod. I shouldn't have shown you that shit. You were only twelve years old, a kid, and I got you caught up in that life. I wasn't thinking. I'm sorry, Rod."

"I didn't think I would ever get an apology from you," Rod said.

"A part of my bond agreement is going to therapy and it's rough. My therapist taught me a lot. I'm not always the victim. I'm learning a lot about myself and how to be a better person. I've hurt people because of my own pain. Y'all didn't deserve it."

"Did you mean the things you said to me?" Jam asked.

"No, I was angry. I'm sorry for saying those things to you. How's the case?"

"Still fighting."

"You're going to beat that, Jam. Don't even worry about it."

Jam just smiled.

"You're a great grandma now," I said pointing to the stroller.

She looked at Ava and AJ. "They are beautiful. I ain't going to see none of my grands get big."

"Why you say that?" I asked.

She shook her head. "I got a lot going on."

"You straight?" Eric asked.

"You live by the gun, you die by it. That's just how it is." Moms said.

"Somebody wants to kill you?" I asked.

"Someone didn't like what I said about them to investigators," Moms said.

"You serious?" Rod asked.

"Yeah, that's why I wanted to meet up, make up, and make sure y'all good. I couldn't leave here with us on bad terms." Moms said.

"Man, this world is so cold," Rod said. "I pray that you stay safe out here."

"Yeah, where ya staying?" Pops asked.

"I'm staying with my sis, Macy. I had to leave Julie's place because it was getting crazy."

Chapter 60

What's Wrong?

At nine o'clock at night, I got a frantic call from Pops. I was frozen in the kitchen not believing what he just told me.

"Wait. What happened, Pops?" I asked.

"There was a shooting. Your moms was hit." Pops said.

"What's her condition?"

"Critical."

"Do you know what happened?"

"Some folks shot up Macy's house. They don't know if she was the intended target."

"Was Macy there when it happened?"

"Nah, just her and some other woman. The other woman is in stable condition. She's not cooperating with investigators."

"Tell me how it's looking, Pops."

"It's pretty bad, Rell. I'm at the hospital now with Eric trying to make this decision."

"Just keep me updated."

"You got to tell Jam."

"Did y'all tell Rod and Jay?"

"Not yet. I'm going to call Rod and Eric will call Jay."

"I don't know how to feel."

"It's a lot to take in. If you need anything, call me."

"Aight. I'll talk to you later."

I walked down the hall to Jam's room. Jam was sitting on his bed playing the game. I sat down at his desk.

"Uh-oh, what's wrong?" Jam asked pausing the game.

"I don't even know how to tell you this news," I said.

"Just tell me, bro."

"Moms is in the hospital."

He turned to me. "Why? Is she okay?"

"She was shot and she's in critical condition."

"Damn, we just saw her. Who did it?"

"Hell, she's been in this game so long, it could have been anybody."

Jam buried his head in his hands unable to say anything else. It wasn't anything I could say to make him feel better.

"You want me to leave?" I asked.

"I just need a moment. Got to wrap my head around this." Jam said.

"I'll be upstairs if you need me."

I left the room and walked upstairs to check on the kids.

Mariah and Marley were up in the family room watching a movie.

"Y'all did all of y'all homework?" I asked.

"Yes," Mariah said.

"Make sure y'all take a bath and get to bed by ten," I said.

"Okay," Marley said.

I checked on Jackson and Layla in their shared room and they were both sleeping wildly in their beds. Then, I went to the nursery to check on the babies. They were both asleep in their cribs. I walked down the hall to the master's bedroom. I plopped on the bed.

I picked up my phone when an incoming video chat request from Kennedy popped up on the phone. I smiled when I saw her face.

"Hey Ken Ken," I said.

"Hey, Daddy," Kennedy said.

"What you doing?"

"Just finishing up some homework."

"Don't stay up too late."

"I'm not. I'm almost finished. I talked to Junior earlier."

"Yeah, I'm sure you liked hearing from him."

"I did. I miss him."

"Aw, two more weeks, and y'all will be back together getting on each other's nerves."

She laughed.

"Your mom said you got detention."

"It was for dress code."

I side-eye her. "What were you wearing?"

"A shirt and leggings. They were trippin'."

"What shirt?"

"It was just a regular shirt."

"You got a picture."

She flipped the camera and showed me the photo on her laptop. Ken had a figure so that's probably why she got the violation.

"That ain't a regular shirt, look like a crop top. You need a longer shirt next time. Why you got your stomach out at school?"

"Daddy, don't start."

"I know you got your own swag and I like that. But you got to cover up a bit, especially at school. A longer shirt wouldn't have killed you."

"You're just used to the way Mariah dresses."

"All of her outfits are age-appropriate. You can do the same."

"She's a tomboy and I'm a girly girl. Of course, we dress differently."

"Being a girly girl means showing your ass and belly?"

"We're not going to agree on this."

"How's school going?"

"Back to straight A's."

"That's what I'm talking 'bout! You like school now?"

"Yeah, because I go to school with Mariah."

"Let me see your room."

She panned around the room and she had a mess everywhere. She turned the camera back to her face.

"It's a little messy right now."

"A little? Clean that room."

"I got it this weekend. I got something to tell you."

"What?"

"There's this boy I like."

I cringed hearing that but I'm glad she felt comfortable enough to share with me.

"What's his name?"

"TJ."

"Are you telling me you have a boyfriend?"

"No. He's mean to me."

"Like I need to pull up on him?"

She chuckled. "No, Daddy. I just want to know how I get him to like me back."

"This is something you should ask your mom."

"She blows things out of proportion."

"You can't make anybody like you. Either they do or they don't. If he's not interested, there ain't nothing you can do to change his mind. You're not supposed to chase a boy anyway, he's supposed to chase you."

"What do you mean by chase?"

"Let him approach you. Have you asked him if he liked you?"

"He said no and that I was ugly."

"And after he told you that, you still like him?"

"Not anymore. How do I get a boy to like me?"

"Be yourself, Ken. At this age, y'all ain't that focused on boyfriend and girlfriend. One day, you'll find a guy who likes you and won't be afraid to say it and show you. Just be patient, Ken."

"Thanks for not wilding out."

I smiled. "Don't forget the talk we had."

Her eyes doubled in size. "I'm not ready for that."

"I got some news about Grandma too."

"What?"

"She was shot and in the hospital."

"I don't like the way she did Mariah."

"None of us do. I know you and Grandma were close at one point. That's why I'm telling you this."

"I haven't talked to her in months."

"Yeah, she's been going through a lot so she ain't been around as much."

"Are you sad? You seem fine."

"No, I'm not sad. She prepared us for this since we were young. She was living a certain life and always told us if they take her out, there's paradise on the other side and she's good."

"Is she going to die?

"I don't know."

"Ken, you need to get off that phone and go to bed!" Marie yelled in the background.

"It's Daddy!" Kennedy yelled back.

"I don't care if it's the president. You can't be up all night."

"Ugh, you're annoying. It's the weekend, Mom. I have nowhere to be in the morning."

"Don't talk to your mom that way," I said.

Kennedy rolled her eyes and smacked her teeth.

"Fix your face before I drive thirty minutes to your house to fix it."

"I got to go."

"I love you."

"I love you too."

She ended the call. I sent her an uplifting text message. I didn't want her to go to bed angry. Jam walked into my room.

"You okay?" I asked.

"Can I crash here tonight?" Jam asked.

"Yeah. I'm 'bout to take a shower. Listen out for my phone."

He lay at the foot of my bed and I handed him the remote.

I walked into the bathroom to take a shower and clear my head. I just felt so numb. I got out of the shower twenty minutes later feeling refreshed.

Jam was wide awake watching the news.

"Anybody called?" I asked.

"Nope. I can't believe this virus is locking down countries. Them folks can't go nowhere."

"Shit, our president needs to get ahead of it so we don't have to go through the same."

"He ain't. You know that. He's acting like it doesn't exist and it's just a little flu."

I dressed in pajamas and sat in bed with my back against the headboard.

"After y'all left the restaurant, me and Dad stayed behind to talk to Mom," Jam said.

"How did that go?"

"She told us about her therapist and how therapy is going."

"I'm glad she's going to therapy because she needs it. It's just crazy that she just escaped death after getting into it with police officers and now somebody tried to kill her."

"I didn't think she would live after the fight with the police."

"Me either. I prepared myself for the worst."

"Mom was saying she needed to change and do things differently."

"She sounded genuine?"

"Yeah. She seemed a little down like she had a lot on her mind. She mentioned being tired and that she can't live the same way forever."

"I saw a different side to her today. I think it's finally hit her all of the shit she's done and how much trouble she's in. She can't get out of it this time."

"She doesn't want to be in prison for the next twenty years."

"Who does? Nobody wants to be in there for a day. But she got to face the consequences."

"That's what Dad told her. She was bawling her eyes out and saying her life was a mess."

"She screwed over everyone and now she has no one. She ruined so many lives. This whole situation makes me numb. I love her but I can't feel anything for her."

"I wish I didn't feel anything."

"It's okay to feel hurt, sad, or whatever. Y'all were close as hell."

"I talked to Jay and she's doing okay."

"That's good. Her pregnant ass can't take too much more."

He chuckled. "I try to think about the good times with Momma but now it's all clouded with the evil things she's done to everyone."

"You got a good heart, Jam."

"It can't take too much more."

Chapter 61

You Don't Understand

Jam and I stayed up all night talking and reminiscing. Neither one of us could fall asleep. It was eight o'clock in the morning on a beautiful Saturday.

Momma slipped into a coma at two this morning and it doesn't look like she's going to pull through. Marie came by a few minutes ago to pick up Ava and drop off Kennedy. Kennedy went straight to bed. Layla, Jackson, Life, and AJ were all up with lots of energy. Jam, Mariah, and Marley were all asleep.

I leaned back on the couch and watched the news talk about this killer virus. It was spreading across the States and I was worried about how this would impact life. My phone vibrated and I looked down to see who was calling.

"Hey, Connie," I said.

"Hey, Rell. You sleeping? You sound tired."

"Nah, the kids got me up early this morning."

"I found the perfect nanny for you."

"How old is she?"

"Thirty."

"She got kids or a husband?"

"Nah, she's single. You're going to like her. Her name is Alix and she's been a nanny for ten years. She started as a babysitter in her teens and then became a nanny. She has worked with two different families. I called them and they had nothing but good things to say about Alix."

"I can't wait to meet her."

"I had someone reach out to me regarding a radio interview. The only thing is that it's for the morning show."

"That means I got to be up early. You know I'm not a morning person."

"I figured you would already be up with one of those babies."

I chucked. "When is this interview?"

"Monday."

"This Monday?"

"Is that not a good time for you?"

"I don't know, Connie. My mom got shot yesterday."

"Rell, I'm so sorry. Why didn't you call me?"

"I've been trying to process it."

"I can call them back for another day and time."

"Nah, it's best I go ahead and do it. I need an opportunity to clean up my image and promote the businesses."

"I told them no questions was off-limit."

"Oh boy, it's going to be nothing but drama."

"No, it's going to be you clearing the air so you don't have to answer those questions again. Any other interview going forward will have limits on what they can ask you."

"I appreciate you, Connie."

"Of course. If I find any other opportunities, I'll let you know. Make sure you're posting on social media, going live, and all that jazz."

"I got you."

"I'll talk to you a little later. I got to make Sassy some breakfast."

I put the phone beside me with a smile on my face. Just talking to her put me in a better mood.

Lay skipped into the room.

"You finished your breakfast?" I asked.
"Yes. Can I go play in my room now?" Layla asked.
"Yeah."

She ran upstairs to her room. Life and Jackson were playing together on the living room floor and I could only smile as I watched them. Jackson was so good to his little sister.

Jam staggered into the room.

"Morning bro," I said.

"Morning," he said groggily.

"Go get yourself some breakfast."

"Aight. Any news on Momma?"

"Nothing new. We just got to wait for her to come out of this coma or make a tough decision to let her go."

"Let me go eat."

He left the room and went to the kitchen. A call from the facility Junior is at popped up on my phone and I hurriedly answered the call.

"Hello," I said.

"Hey Pops, it's me," Junior said.

"How ya feeling?" I haven't been able to talk to Junior because he has been sick.

"I'm better," Junior said, "It's kicking my ass."

"You got this, Junior. I talked to your nurse the other day and it had me worried about you."

"I felt like I was going to die."

"Your body got to get used to not having the drugs. You were using heavy drugs for the past year."

"I didn't think it would be this bad. I feel like I'm going crazy in here."

"But you sound better."

"How are AJ and Ava?"

"They're good. I got to take them to the doctor next week."

"What's wrong?"

"They're good. This is a check-up appointment. Your little boy can eat. And Ava is finally gaining weight."

"That's cause Momma getting her every weekend. She's probably sneaking her some food."

I laughed. "She's spoiling Ava rotten. She's going to start getting AJ too. She's loving her grandbabies. Your siblings like having the babies at the house too."

"I appreciate y'all for loving on them and holding it down while I'm away."

"What you up to today?"

"I got an art class in a little bit and therapy a little later."

"How's therapy going?"

"It's cool. It's hard for me to open up, ya know?"

"Yeah, I know. What y'all talk about?"

"Not much. She wanted to know why I started using drugs thinking I had some sort of childhood trauma. But my childhood was straight. I missed you when you were on the road but I didn't feel abandoned. I just felt like nobody understood me. And when I didn't want to go to school, nobody cared to know why. I felt distant from everything and everyone.

And then you got injured and wasn't yourself and it was hard to talk to you. Reem and Mom got divorced and it was so much drama. I didn't know how to deal with it. My cuz reached out to me and was like I got a way for you to make money and you ain't got to go to school and the rest is history."

"Your cuz took advantage of you."

"Yeah, I know that now. Here I was thinking he was looking out for me. I always looked up to him and thought I could trust him. He was the one to introduce me to the heavy drugs and I thought nothing of it."

Hearing Junior's story made me sad. The people he needed most weren't there when he needed them and he found comfort in the streets and drugs.

"You live and you learn, Junior. Not everybody will look out for you, be loyal to you, or have the same heart as you. You just have to be careful."

"Pops, my guard is up. I ain't trusting nobody."

"That's how I am. I've been hurt by so many. Dealt with so many snakes. I just take the L, learn the lesson, and keep it moving."

"Right."

"I got to tell you something."

"What?"

"Grandma is in a coma."

"What happened?"

"Somebody shot up her place."

"Is she going to be okay?"

"We don't know. I didn't even want to give you this bad news right now."

"It's okay, Pops. I can handle it. How's everyone taking the news?"

"Me and Rod are good. Jam and Jay taking it the hardest."

"Does Ken Ken know?"

"Yeah. She's still upset about how Grandma did Mariah so she don't feel no type of way."

"Me and Grandma used to be so close but I can't get over how she treated Mariah and Marley. I didn't realize she treated them differently."

"She treated Jam and Jay better than me, Rod, and Deja."

"That's messed up. She didn't even try to hide the fact she has favorites."

"Son, I've been through so much in my life. I tried to prevent you from going through the same hell but you never listened to me. I realized some lessons you got to learn on your own."

"I didn't think y'all understood what I was going through."

"Man, I felt the same way when Pops and Eric tried to teach me about life. I just want you to get better so you can be better and do better."

"My therapist wants me to write down goals. And the hardest thing is figuring out my goals."

"Think about all of the things you want to accomplish. Goals don't have to be big, Junior. It can be saving twenty dollars from every paycheck. Send me your list of goals. I'm curious what's going to be on your list."

"Thanks, Pops for always having my back. It means a lot to me."

"Of course, Junior. I ain't never leaving your side. Don't let this world make you cold. It's okay to have a good heart."

Chapter 62

Clear The Air

On Monday, I headed to the radio station. I wasn't in the mood for this but knew it would be good for the businesses. I wasn't sure what questions they would ask which made me nervous.

I climbed out of the car and walked into the building. I signed in and waited to go on air. About thirty minutes later, the producer prepped me for the show.

I sat in front of the microphone and adjusted my headphones. The hosts Ryan, Nia, and DJ Mars were across from me.

"Welcome back to the hottest morning show. It's yo boy, Ryan, and we got a special guest in the building."

"We have Jarrell "Money" Duncan in the building!" DJ Mars said.

"What's good?" I said into the microphone.

"We got a lot to get into this morning," Nia said.

"Let's do it," I said.

"We miss you out on the football field. You were one of the best receivers in the game." DJ Mars said.

"I miss being out there," I said.

"It seemed you disappeared after you got injured," Ryan said.

"Man, that injury broke me. I got the news that I wouldn't play football again and I didn't know how to take it. I thought I could get better and get back on the field, but my injury would prevent me from ever playing again. I didn't know how my life would be without football."

"How has life been without football?" DJ Mars asked.

"It was hard at first. Football was my entire life at one point. It was all I knew. I had to find something else to be passionate about and find ways to occupy my time." I said.

"And what did you do to occupy your time?" DJ Mars asked.

"I went into business with my family."

"Oh really? What kind of business?"

"I opened up the Juicy Boil with my brother, Rod. It's a crab and seafood restaurant. I have a bakery, Jay's Sweets, with my sister. And I have a juice bar. I'm now taking over my Pops' restaurant slash record store."

"I know all of that keeps you busy," Ryan said.

"Most definitely," I said.

"I want to talk a little about the drama," Nia said.

"What drama?" I asked like I didn't know what she was talking about.

We laughed and that broke the tension in the room.

"We see that your baby mommas are on a new reality show. They bashed you and made you seem like a deadbeat." Nia said.

"That ain't cool," DJ Mars said.

"They were angry and frustrated. It was at a time when I couldn't be there how they wanted me to be there. I hate they took the drama to the show. Everything is cool between us. People all in my comments coming at me and telling me to take care of my kids. I want everyone to know that there wasn't a time my kids weren't straight."

"What's crazy is that all of these years we didn't know your personal business. You stayed to yourself and kept a low profile. And then yo boy started talking crazy. You never came out to say anything until recently." DJ Mars said.

"What happened between you and him? Y'all were like brothers and played on the same teams." Ryan said.

"I don't know what happened. I've known this dude since middle school. We went to different colleges and linked back up when we got drafted for the same team. He was like a brother to me. My brother was locked up and even though we kept a bond, he wasn't physically by my side. When I'm going through things, I need time to myself. Some people don't understand that and take it wrong."

"Man, this man made you out to be a crackhead," Ryan said.

"And he got with your baby momma," Nia said.

"He did what?" DJ Mars asked.

"It's crazy." That's all I could say.

"Now I see why you handled him the way you did. Man, when I first saw that video, I was shocked to see y'all fighting." DJ Mars said.

"I don't do that talking social media beef. I'll pull up on you and handle it. But it ain't no beef between us. I see how he moves and I'm good on that." I said.

"Before we go, I want to know what happened between you and KoKo. Honestly, I never thought you two of all people would ever be together. Like Mars and Ryan said, you like a private life and you got with someone who loves attention and is always in the limelight." Nia said.

I didn't want to talk about Chloe. "I don't know what I was thinking. I like to give people the benefit of the doubt."

"How did y'all meet?" DJ Mars asked.

"At the club. She was hosting a party. She looked good and I stepped to her. She was cool and we had a good conversation. I heard a lot about her but I didn't know her. People kept telling me to be careful but I didn't listen. And that's nothing against her, she's just always in drama and wasn't ready for a serious relationship."

"Bro, what did you really expect from KoKo?" Ryan asked.

I chuckled. "Bro, I don't even know."

"And it ended with you two having a physical altercation in a restaurant and mugshots," Nia said.

"I've never cleared this up and she didn't either. I never hit her. She released those photos of her face after getting into a fight with someone else. And everybody thought I did that to her." I said.

"What happened at the restaurant?" Nia asked.

"I wanted to end things with her and thought we could do that over a nice lunch. Things went left and she attacked me. She was getting into it with the police and I was trying to get her to calm down. She was still on ten and they arrested her. When she tried to reach for me, I pushed her away and got arrested too."

"That's wild. We will have more with Jerell "Money" Duncan after this song." Ryan said.

We talked off the air for a bit and I was glad I got this chance to clear my name. And the interview was going great.

"We are back. Jerell is still hanging out with us. We told y'all to submit questions so let's answer some questions from the fans." Ryan said.

"CoolFan said there are reports of your mom being killed and is there any truth to these rumors?" Nia asked.

"I didn't hear these rumors," DJ Mars said.

"I haven't had a chance to say anything publicly regarding this. This story aired on the news and people put two and two together that was my mom. People have been sending me the story asking if she's okay. My mom is still with us. That's all I can say."

"I had no idea. Sending prayers to the fam, bro." Ryan said.

"And we appreciate that," I said.

"There are so many people saying I love you and that they miss you on the field," Nia said.

"I love y'all too and I miss being out there. Some of the best moments of my life were on the football field." I said.

"LottieLon asked, do you see yourself being a sportscaster?" DJ Mars asked.

"That ain't my thing," I said.

"Shortknot asked, growing up, did you play any other sports besides football?"

"I played basketball and soccer. My niece and nephew are soccer stars and it's been cool to practice with them."

"Finebyme23 asked, where's Junior," Nia said.

"Yeah, Junior has been missing from the gram," Ryan said.

"That's another thing I haven't addressed. My son was battling demons, struggling with drug addiction, and is away getting the help he needs."

"Bro, you're going through so much and still came out to do the show. I appreciate that." Ryan said.

"I'm here to support, bro. We went to the same college. You used to tell me and Mack that you wanted to be on the radio. I'm proud of you and glad you made it happen." I said.

"I didn't even think you remembered me. That means a lot to me." Ryan said.

"I didn't know y'all went to school together," Nia said.

"I didn't want to mention it in case he didn't remember," Ryan said.

"It was good times. We got to link up with Mack and hang out." I said.

"I have a fan asking if you're single," Nia said.

"I'm single," I said.

"Do you want to get married?" Nia asked.

"Yeah, I'm ready to settle down."

"It took you long enough. Someone asked do you have any tea on Chantel and Ty. We have some messy fans this morning." Nia said.

"I don't know nothing. Not my household, not my business."

I answered a few more questions from fans. They were more invasive than the hosts.

"Yo Rell, it's been cool having you here this morning. I'm glad you stopped by. Don't be a stranger." Ryan said.

Now, I was headed home to check on the kids and then I had to head back out to meet a client at the gym. Jay was sitting on the living room floor surrounded by Life, Jackson, Ava, and AJ.

"How's it going?" I asked.

"It's cool. I feel like I'm running a daycare though. I heard you on the radio."

I sat on the couch. "How did I do?"

"You did good. I'm glad you cleared your name. People were talking mad crazy about you and it had me tight."

Even if we're fighting and mad at each other, we always got each other's back. It's us against everybody.

"The nanny's coming around one o'clock. If I'm not back by then, please start the process without me."

"What do you need me to do?"

"Interview her and just see how she interacts with the kids. I'll send you some questions to ask her. You're good at reading people so I trust your opinion. Just don't be mean."

She smiled. "I'll be nice, bro."

Life crawled over to me and pulled herself to a standing position. She held up her arms and I picked her up.

"She's going to be walking soon," Jay said. "We video chatted with Chantel earlier. Life was happy to see Mommy."

"How's Chantel doing?"

"Just worried about the case but she's back at work."

"That's good."

We talked for a few more minutes and then I left for the gym.

My new client, Marsha, was at the gym when I got there. We shook hands.

"What are you needing the most help with?" I asked.

"I've packed on several pounds since getting married and having six kids. I currently weigh two hundred and eighty pounds."

"And how tall are you."

"I'm five four."

"Do you have any health problems?"

"I have high blood pressure."

"Why are you looking for a personal trainer?"

"I need someone to motivate me. I've had so many gym memberships and I quit after a month. I'm serious now and I want to get healthy. I want to love my body again. My youngest is four and I can't even run behind him."

"This is going to be a whole lifestyle change for you. First, let's discuss diet. What do you eat a lot of?"

"You don't even want to know. I love fatty and fried foods."

"And you can have those things in moderation. Marsha, I want to help you reach those fitness goals. I want you to love looking in the mirror."

She smiled. "I'm excited to get started."

"Today, we will do several tests and develop a workout plan. We will create a menu so you have an idea of what to eat for breakfast, lunch, and dinner. You ready?"

Chapter 63

Life Changing

Two weeks later, life changed completely. The virus was here in Georgia and taking people out across the country. Our governor just signed a shelter-in-place order and the kids' schools announced closures. We weren't sure if they would return to finish the school year. We had to figure out how to work these businesses because we could no longer offer dine-in services.

I was now on the highway rushing to get Junior. I answered a phone call from Stephanie.

"Wassup Stephanie?" I said.

"Not too much. You free to talk?" Stephanie asked.

"Yeah, I'm just on the road to get Junior."

"Who got the kids?"

"Eric. How's everything going with the baby?"

"I'm still sick but I'm getting through it. I'm just worried about this virus."

"Don't stress yourself too much. I'll stress for the both of us."

"They say it's going to be bad for older people and those with underlining conditions."

"Yeah."

"I'm just worried about hubby, your Pops. He doesn't want anyone to know this but he's sick. They found a tumor a few months ago and recently removed it. The cancer scans are clear but it doesn't mean it can't come back."

"What? You telling me Pops had cancer and didn't even tell his fam?"

"He didn't want anyone to know and worry about him. I told him that he should tell y'all but he didn't think it was a good idea."

"Man, that's fucked up. Now, I'm going to be stressed like hell about Pops."

"He also has high blood pressure."

"Keep his ass in the house. I'll get y'all groceries, medicine, and whatever else y'all need. Just reach out to me and stay inside."

"You know that old man is stubborn. He's worried about the restaurant and just left to check on things."

"Man, he better let me and Sunny worry about the restaurant."

"What's the plan, Rell?"

"I'm talking with Boss and Kadeem to see how we move forward. Our restaurants have to be strictly to-go and delivery. With the gym being closed, I don't know if the juice bar will survive this. It was already struggling."

"My job is scrambling to figure out how we can work from home."

"I got a lot to figure out. I got to homeschool all of these kids now. I can't hire the nanny because she doesn't want to commit to being a live-in nanny since she takes care of her grandma. It's just insane they hit us with this out of nowhere."

"Think about the people who aren't in your financial position. I know those people are going through it."

"Most definitely. I got to figure out how to reach out, donate, and help where I can. I'm 'bout to order masks and hand sanitizer before it all sells out. Make sure you and Pops always wear a mask when going out."

"Of course. Can you call your Pops and tell him to get home?"

"Yeah, I'll talk to you later, Mama."

I ended the call and called Pops.

"Wassup Rell?" Pops asked.

"What ya doing?" I asked.

"I'm just at the restaurant talking to the team getting a game plan together."

"That's what me and Sunny are going to do. You need to get home and stay there until they flatten this curve for the virus."

"I ain't scared of no virus. I don't want to lose my business."

"Pops, I'm going to make sure that doesn't happen. Stephanie just told me that you had cancer and have high blood pressure. This virus can kill you."

"I don't know why Stephanie is telling you my business."

"Don't be mad at her. She's pregnant and you could take the virus back home to her and your unborn daughter. You're being stubborn and selfish. Take your ass home, Pops."

"I know you ain't talking to me like that. You ain't too old to be put over my knee."

"C'mon Pops, just stay in the house. I'll bring your groceries and meds to the house. Just stay home."

"You can't tell me what to do."

And Pops hung up on me. Next, I called Rod.

"Yo Rod, what you doing?" I asked.

"I'm stressed, bro. I got to fly to New York to get my daughter. You know they got an outbreak there and she's living on the streets with her mom. I'm flying out tomorrow and need to know if you can watch Coby. You have to keep him for the next two weeks. We have to quarantine for a few days since we're coming from New York. I don't want Coby to get sick. You know he has asthma."

"It's so much going on, bro."

"I know but we're going to get through it."

"I got Coby for you. We got to figure out how to keep Pops in the house."

"You know his ass ain't staying in the house."

"Rod, he had cancer."

"What!"

"Stephanie told me they removed a tumor and that the cancer scans are clear for now. He also has high blood pressure. This virus could kill him."

"He's going through it and didn't even tell us. Where is he now?"

"He's at the restaurant. And Stephanie is pregnant and already sick enough."

"Rell, we got to hide his car keys."

"Nah, I'm going to take his car. He got to stay home."

Chapter 64

Cool Dad

Junior climbed into the car. He had gained weight and needed a haircut.

"How ya feeling?" I asked.

"Good. I can't wait to see everybody." Junior said.

"We're on lockdown," I said.

"I heard."

"I got to go to the grocery store before we go home."

"Who's at the house?"

"Eric and all of the kids."

"How's Grandma?"

"She ain't came to yet."

"But, how is it looking?"

"According to doctors, she's already gone."

"They don't know who did it?"

"Nope. I don't know if we'll ever know. Nobody saw or heard anything. You know how that is. School is going to be virtual. You got to check in and submit your assignments online."

"I didn't want to go back to school anyway."

"Why?"

"You told the world I was in rehab. That's embarrassing."

"Ain't nothing embarrassing about that. Everybody is happy you got help before it was too late. I doubt anybody would have talked shit about you. People have been showing you so much love."

He looked out the window. I could tell he wasn't happy with me telling the world he had a problem.

"Junior, my bad for telling your business. I just couldn't lie about where you were. I've had people message me telling me they finally got their child help after listening to my interview. I should have let you tell your own story and that's my fault."

"It's cool, Pops. I know you meant no harm."

"You hungry?"

"Nah, I'm good. I'm just ready to sleep in my own bed."

"I hear ya."

"Are we about to lose everything?"

"No, why you ask that?"

"I read an article that this lockdown will take a toll on small businesses. It had me worried."

"The businesses aren't my only income so we're going to be okay. The only business that worries me is the juice bar. We're going to take a hit financially from all the businesses but I'm hoping we don't have to close any of them."

"The juice bar is my favorite spot. Boss is going to make sure we don't lose it, I'm sure."

I smiled because even Junior knew how much Boss does for the businesses. "Yeah, we're about to come up with a game plan." An incoming video chat from Marie appeared on the phone screen. "That's your momma." I handed him the phone.

"Hey, Momma," Junior said answering the call.

"Hey, baby. How are you doing?" Marie asked.

"Don't you start with that baby voice. He ain't no baby." I said.

"He's my baby. I'm about to cry just seeing you." Marie said.

"I'm good, Momma," Junior said.

"What y'all doing?"

"We're about to go to the store."

"That's a bad idea. I just left the store and it was nuts. There was no hand sanitizer, no disinfectant wipes, and people were buying out the toilet paper."

"It's that crazy?" I asked.

"Man look at IG and you're going to see. We had to wait two hours to be checked out." Marie said.

"I'm 'bout to stop at a store in this small ass town before I head to the city," I said.

"That's probably best because the stores here are empty. I got to go to another store tomorrow because I couldn't find everything I needed." Marie said.

"So, folks shopping like it's a hurricane or snowstorm coming?" I asked.

"They're shopping like the world is about to end."

"And this is just the start, Ma."

"I'm staying my ass inside. My job is getting the work-at-home procedure together. Reem is moving back in to help with the kids and we'll be quarantined together so the kids don't have to go back and forth between houses."

"Oh shit, y'all 'bout to be remarried with a baby on the way."

She chuckled. "Nah, ain't no funny business. We're doing this for the kids. Kennedy wants to be with you so she can be with Mariah. You know they need one another."

"That's cool. Pack her bags and send her over."

"You got all of your kids?"

"Life is going to be with Chantel and her grandpa. I don't know how we're going to work out the back and forth through this."

"Video chat her every day."

"Got to. I'm going to have everybody else though. I know they 'bout to drive me crazy. They're saying we can't go nowhere."

"Nope, essential trips only. Everything is closing like bowling alleys, children's attractions, parks, and gyms.

Reem bought the kids laptops and tablets to do their work and keep them entertained."

"I need to do the same for mine."

"Junior, what did you think about the program?" Marie asked.

"It was cool. I learned a lot. I got to keep doing therapy and check-in for the next few months." Junior said.

"All of these years I've tried to get you therapy and you never wanted to do it."

"I didn't think I needed it."

"Convince your daddy to go to therapy while you're at it."

"Haha, very funny," I said.

I merged over and took the next exit. I looked around for a grocery store.

"I can't wait to see you, Junior. You seem much better and I'm so proud of you."

He smiled. "Thanks, Ma. I feel better."

"What are your plans moving forward?"

"I got to stay focused. I'm going to finish school, work, and take care of Ava and AJ."

"And stay away from those fast-tailed girls."

Junior just laughed.

"I've been spoiling the babies rotten. I know I got to stay away for the next few weeks but if they need anything, let me know. Make sure to video chat me every other day so I can see my babies and you."

"Ma, I'm going to call you every day because I know that's what you want."

She laughed. "Yeah, don't let a day go by and I don't hear from you. I want to make sure you're good."

I finally found a big box grocery store and pulled into the full parking lot. I wasn't ready to deal with this crowd.

Junior and Marie finished their conversation and we headed into the store. It was pure chaos as soon as we stepped into the store. There were a lot of people, long lines, and barely any carts.

"This is wild," Junior mumbled grabbing the last cart.

"Make sure you wipe down the cart," I said handing him a wipe.

We walked into the store and started filling the cart with food and essential things we needed. While in the store, I ordered toilet paper, masks, hand sanitizer, and gloves from an online store. I wanted to get these things before they sold out.

We were now in the vitamins aisle and they had a low stock of Vitamin C. I grabbed two big bottles of Vitamin C, a big bottle of Vitamin D, and kid multivitamins. I've heard the key to fighting this virus was building your immune system,

"I'm happy to have my favorite snacks again," Junior said throwing cookies and chips into the cart.

"Make sure you get snacks for everybody else too."

"I will."

I looked around for tissue and hygiene products. I'm not trying to go back into the stores for a long time. Luckily this store still had tissue, hand sanitizer, and hand soap.

I met back up with Junior in the meat section and it was looking a little slim with only a few packs of meat left. I would have to go to my local butcher to get meat. I found chicken breasts and ground turkey. And I also got hot dogs for the kids.

We spent two hours shopping and filled two separate carts. It took about an hour to check out and I spent a thousand dollars. This shit better last for a month.

Junior and I were outside packing the trunk. I'm glad I decided to drive the SUV and not the sports car.

"Yo, is that Money Duncan," an older Black gentleman asked.

I turned to him. "It is."

"Man, I'm a big fan. It's good seeing you."

"Thanks for supporting. You want a picture?"

He looked like he wanted to cry. His wife took the photo and I signed a piece of paper for him. I handed him five hundred dollars. That was all the cash I had on me.

"Aw man, we appreciate this. My wife just got laid off and we're caring for three grandchildren. My oldest son is in prison so we have his babies."

"I'm sorry to hear that. Things are crazy right now. I pray it gets better for y'all."

"We appreciate you, man. You're a good guy and one of the best the league has seen. We miss you out there, Money."

"Thanks. That means a lot."

We bumped elbows and they walked into the store.

"That was cool of you, Pops," Junior said.

"You just now realizing your Pops is cool? I'm the coolest person you know."

Chapter 65

Shocking News

Late at night, I was up watching the news. I answered a call from Jay happy for the distraction. The news was making me depressed.

"Hey Jay," I said. "What you doing up so late?"

"I can't sleep. Thinking about the business."

"Don't stress, Jay. We're going to get a game plan together."

"People are canceling orders left and right. Most of the orders were for graduations, weddings, and birthdays."

"It's going to be tough for a little bit. Not everyone is going to cancel so don't fret about those cancellations. We're going to offer takeout and delivery. You have to create a limited menu, things you sell a lot so we're not wasting a lot of product and money."

"I'll get that together for tomorrow's meeting."

"I know Rod is going out of town for a couple of days and Coby is coming here, are you going to be okay in that house all alone?"

"I should be. No one knows I'm here."

"If you need to come here, you can. You know I got plenty of room."

"I appreciate that. Daddy said he will pull the plug if Mom's not any better by Tuesday. They are starting to limit visits at the hospital. Daddy said if she doesn't make it, he wants to have a beautiful funeral for her before they start the restrictions for funerals. I can't even go visit her because I'm high-risk."

"I haven't even had the time to visit her."

"I still hope she recovers. We weren't on the best of terms but I was hoping we could repair things and she could be there for me when I have my baby. I can't imagine not having my mom by my side when I give birth."

"I hope she gets better too."

"You don't sound so sure about that."

"I still don't know what to feel, Jay."

"That's fair. I can tell it's affecting Rod even if he says it doesn't."

"Rod got a lot going on."

"I just know he's not himself."

"Nah, he's not. But he's dealing with life sober and feeling everything at once. He's been worried about his daughter. Now that he has custody, he should be back to himself."

"I think he's worried about his business too."

"We all are but this is the time to start the blog on the website and push out YouTube videos. The world is at a standstill and we have their attention. We just got to create our way through this."

"That's a good way to look at this."

"When you're baking or cooking, prop up the phone or camera and make a video. Send the video to Tanya. She'll edit and I'll upload. Also, I need you to type up a couple of recipes for the blog. We're going to be bored as hell so we might as well create content."

"True." She gasped.

"What's wrong? Your water broke?"

"No, sorry."

"Girl, you almost gave me a heart attack."

She giggled. "Sorry, Rell. I read a story about you giving a couple five hundred dollars. The guy shared a tear-filled video about what that encounter meant to him."

"He's a good guy. His oldest son is incarcerated and they are taking care of his kids."

"That was nice of you, bro. My pregnancy hormones are making me cry while watching this story so if you hear me sniffling that's why."

"You have become such a crybaby, Jay."

"I know. I hate it but I'm still a G don't get it twisted."

I bust out laughing.

"It ain't that funny, Rell."

"Nah, that was hilarious."

"I'm getting sleepy."

"Get some rest, baby girl. I'll see you at the bakery tomorrow."

"I love you, bro."

"I love you, Jay."

I end the call and lay back on the pillow. I didn't know what was ahead but I had to remain optimistic. I've been through so much in life and I know this was just another obstacle. I had my whole family on my back, so I was feeling the pressure.

The house was so quiet. We moved Ava and AJ into the guesthouse and now Junior is fully responsible for his little ones.

A shocking text from Eric had me on the edge of the bed in seconds.

Eric: **Your mom passed. Will call you later.**

I took a deep breath. That wasn't the news I expected. I ran downstairs to check on Jam. He was in his bed crying hysterically. I held him in my arms.

"I'm so sorry, Jam," I said.

"She was supposed to wake up," Jam said. "She was finally getting her life right and now she's gone. Mommy's gone, bro."

I let him vent without saying much. This was the worst news to get. Man, I thought she was going to come out of it.

Chapter 66

Next Mourning

I couldn't even sleep after I received the news about Moms. I stayed in Jam's room to make sure he was good. I looked at the time on my phone and it was six in the morning. I walked down the hall to the kitchen and made a cup of coffee.

I sat at the table and held my head in my hands and all I could do was cry. No matter what, I had so much love for Momma. I wanted to see her come out of that coma and be a better person. I feel guilty for not visiting when I had the chance. I'm glad we were on good terms and my last words to her weren't cruel.

I read a text from Rod that he was on the way. I got myself together, drank my coffee, and worked on business plans.

My phone vibrated on the table and I answered the call.

"Wassup Eric?" I asked.

"Y'all good? I know we could only talk briefly earlier." Eric said.

"It was a rough night but we got through it," I said.

"Me and Pops been making her arrangements. Shit is sad but hopefully, she's at peace."

"What happened?"

"The doctor said she went into cardiac arrest and they were unable to save her."

"Wow."

"Take care of yourself, Rell. I know this news is not easy to digest."

"Nah, it's not. I just got to tell the kids and go from there."

"What you up to today?"

"I got to go to the businesses and get a plan together for each spot."

"Who's watching the kids?"

"Jam."

"He ain't in no condition to watch anybody. I'll come by and watch the house."

"Thanks, Eric."

"Now, tell me how you're doing?"

"I'm down but I'll bounce back."

"If you need me, I'm here."

"I know, Eric."

"Let me get ready and I'll be there in a little bit."

"Okay, I'll see you soon."

I ended the call with a heavy sigh.

"Daddy!" Jackson yelled from upstairs.

I ran up the steps. Jackson was sitting in the middle of his bed wide awake. I picked him up.

"Good morning," I said.

He smiled. "Morning."

I took him downstairs. I held him in my arms as I made oatmeal for breakfast. I sliced him a few strawberries too. I sat him down at the table and put the bowl in front of him.

There was a knock at the door and I jogged to the front door. I looked through the peephole and it was Coby and Rod.

"Coby, why you looking so mad?" I asked.

He stormed into the house. I gave Rod a puzzling look.

"He got smacked for talking to me crazy," Rod said.

"Oh boy," I said.

"This is his bag."

He handed me a suitcase.

"Damn, this is heavy. Is he moving in?"

Rod chuckled. "It's everything he needs for the next two weeks. His asthma pump is in the front of the bag."

"Is Jay at the house?"

"She's staying with Eric. After getting the news about Momma, she was a hot mess. How did Jam take the news?"

"Woo, it was a mess."

"I'll try to video chat him later."

"What manager is going to be at the Juicy Boil today? Got to get these plans together."

"Nick should be there."

"I'll talk to you about everything when you get the chance. What time is your flight?"

"Elven thirty. I'm going to get breakfast and head to the airport."

"You got a mask?"

"Couldn't find any in stores."

"Come in for a second."

He walked into the house and I ran to the pantry. I grabbed him a box of masks and a small bottle of hand sanitizer.

"Thanks, bro," Rod said grabbing the items.

"How you taking everything?" I asked.

"I'm okay. I prayed for the first time in a long time. Wish we could have gotten back close but I'm glad we were on good terms before she left here."

"I'm just glad she finally admitted her shortcomings in raising us. That's all I ever wanted from her. I also learned they brought a new charge against her that carried a life sentence."

"Dang."

"But we'll talk. I don't want you to miss your flight."

"Coby, I love you and I'll talk to you later," Rod said.

"Whatever," Coby said.

"Coby, tell your Pops you love him."

"I love you," Coby mumbled.

Rod and I hugged.

"I love you, bro," I said.

"I love you," Rod said.

I walked him to his car. I watched him drive away and said a prayer for safe travels. I walked into the house and joined Coby and Jackson at the kitchen table.

"Coby, you need something to eat? I made oatmeal." I said.

"No, I'm good," Coby said.

"What's wrong with you?" I asked.

He huffed. "Nothing."

"Don't catch an attitude now. I'm trying to make sure you're good."

"Can I go upstairs?"

"Yeah, take your bag upstairs."

He hurried upstairs to the guest room. Layla walked down the steps.

"Good morning," I said.

"Morning," Layla mumbled.

"You want to eat?" I asked.

"Yes."

"What you want? I made oatmeal."

"Cereal, please."

She sat down at the table and I made her a bowl of cereal.

"Y'all want to call Mommy?" I asked.

"Yes," Jackson said.

I started the video chat with Porsha, and she answered after a few rings.

She smiled. "Hey, babies."

"Hi, Mommy," Layla said.

"Mama!" Jackson said.

"Can you see us today?" Layla asked.

"I have to stay away because of the virus. I can get really sick."

Layla sighed and looked down at the table. "I hate this virus. I can't go to school and now we can't see you."

"I'm only a call away."

"Mommy, are you pregnant?"

Porsha and I were shocked to hear her ask this.

"Why you ask that?"

Layla shrugged. "You look fat."

"That's not nice," I said.

"I'll tell you the truth, I'm having a baby."

"See? I knew it!" Layla said.

"You made a decision?" I asked.

"Yeah. I went to the appointment and I couldn't do it."

"Does C know?"

"Nope, he doesn't want to talk to me. He blocked me on everything so I have no way to contact him."

"I bet if you announced it on the gram, he would be blowing your phone up."

"Is it a girl baby?" Layla asked.

"I don't know yet," Porsha said.

"I want to be the only girl."

"I know but we can't control that. We want a healthy baby."

"And healthy mama," I said.

"How are you going to homeschool all of those kids?"

"Shit, I don't know. They haven't sent out any info yet on how they are doing everything."

"I'm just looking at the news and it's like the world has gone mad. I haven't even gone to the store. I'm scared to go out."

"Send me a list and I got you. What's going to happen to the beauty shop?"

"Right now, I don't know. I'm hearing they're about to close everything down so I'm just playing it by ear."

"I got to tell you some news too."

"What?"

"Momma's gone."

She grabbed her chest. "Are you serious? I thought she was getting better."

"We did too."

"You're not even distraught. You seem so nonchalant."

"I've prepared myself for the worst since I heard she got shot."

"I know Jay and Jam are going crazy. I'm praying for y'all."

"Thanks, Porsha."

"I want to go to the funeral so let me know the details when you get them."

"I'll text you."

"Jackson, what ya eating?" Porsha asked.

"Apple," Jackson said proudly.

"Tell Mommy you're eating oatmeal and strawberries," I said.

"You got to feed him sausage, bacon, or something to fill him up."

"He's going to be full with the oatmeal. And he's having a fiber bar for a snack."

Kennedy walked into the kitchen.

"Morning," Kennedy said. She busied herself in the kitchen.

"What you making?" I asked.

"I'm making a bowl of cereal."

"Y'all, I got to get ready for work. I love y'all." Porsha said.

"I love you, Mommy," Layla said.

"Bye Mama," Jackson said.

I sent a text to Eric asking if he was on the way. Kennedy sat at the table with her bowl of cereal.

"How did you sleep?" I asked.

"Good," Kennedy said.

Then she got on her phone.

"Are you going to be here today?" Kennedy asked a few minutes later.

"Nah, I got to go check on the businesses. I'll be back by four." I said.

"You're never here."

"I got to handle business and have these meetings. I'll be in the house more starting next week."

"We'll see about that."

"You woke up with an attitude, I see."

She rolled her eyes and I shook my head. I didn't get Kennedy sometimes.

"Daddy, can we go to the park?" Layla asked.

"I don't know if we can. They are closing everything down. You can play in the backyard."

"That's boring," Layla said.

"Don't be ungrateful. Millions of kids wish they had a big house and spacious backyard. I got to hire somebody to clean the pool so y'all can swim. I have someone installing a swing set and playground. Y'all finish eating and put y'all bowls in the sink. Come on Jackson, time to get cleaned up and dressed for the day."

Chapter 67

Down To Business

I walked into the juice bar and joined Kadeem and Boss at a table in the back of the restaurant. We opened our notebooks ready to discuss our ideas.

"According to the governor's order, we can provide takeout and delivery. The issue is that most of our customers are from the gyms in the area and the gyms are closing." Boss said.

"If we don't get much business, we will close until the shelter-in-place is lifted," I said.

"What about the employees?" Kadeem asked.

"We're going to take care of everyone. We want everyone to be safe and healthy." I said.

"How long can we really pay these people?" Boss asked.

"We're going to pay until we can't anymore. This is just a wait-and-see situation." I said.

"I'm going to try and be here as much as I can but Honey works at a grocery store and is getting a lot of hours. I have to be home with the kids." Boss said.

"Take care of the kids, Boss. We should be able to work mostly from the house. Kadeem, do you think you can hold it down? I know you've only been a manager here for a few weeks." I said.

"Yeah, I got it," Kadeem said.

"We have to remove the seating or tape it off," Boss said.

"We only have a few tables and chairs. Let's move those to the backroom. We also need to come up with a limited menu. What do people get the most?" I asked.

"That's going to be the vegan salad, strawberry banana smoothie, kale salad, and green juice," Kadeem said.

"I would add smoothie bowls and sandwiches to the limited menu. The chicken wrap is also popular. If we offer delivery, we'll have an opportunity to get more business." Boss said.

"Do we go through a delivery company or are we going to have our employees be the delivery drivers?" I asked.

"We need to see if anyone here is willing to take on that role," Boss said.

"This is a lot to think about," I said.

"Are you offering delivery at the other restaurants?" Boss asked.

"Pops doesn't want to offer delivery. I don't think we'll do it for Juicy Boil or the bakery. But I still have to meet with everyone and see what they want to do."

We continued talking about the business and getting our game plan together. Things were about to be much different for us and we had to prepare for the unexpected.

It took about thirty minutes to get a concrete plan together. Kadeem went to the front of the restaurant and gathered the staff to tell them the plans.

"How ya feeling, Rell? I got the call at two this morning. I can't believe she's gone." Boss said.

"Yeah Unc, it's crazy."

"We grew up together. She was eight years older than me. She always looked out for me and considered me a little brother. Her mom and my mom were like sisters and they raised their children together. When her mom passed, my mom took her in but she did her own thing and got kicked out. We remained close and she was the closest person to me. I ain't like all of her decisions but I always tried to be there for her. She was a good person who made a lot of mistakes."

"Boss, you always see the good in people."

"I try to. We would all be considered monsters if people only focused on the bad."

"That's true. I'm struggling with breaking down and being strong for Jam and Jay."

"You can do both."

"No matter what, I loved that lady. When it was good, it was really good. When it was bad, it was really bad."

"Just hold your head up, nephew. We're going to get through this."

After a long day, I was finally home. I now had a game plan for each business and I felt optimistic. I was busy in the kitchen cooking dinner for the family. Eric went home a few minutes ago. Jam was sitting at the kitchen table editing a video. Layla walked into the kitchen.

"Can I get juice?" Layla asked.

"Not before dinner," I said.

"Please."

"You can beg until you're blue in the face. I already said no, now go play."

"You're mean, Daddy."

"I'll be that. Now, go play."

"I hate you."

"And you still not getting juice."

She spat at me. That was the last straw and I popped her.

"Go sit at the table and chill out!"

She cried as she walked over to the table.

"Don't you ever disrespect me like that again! Hush up that noise."

I checked on my chicken breasts in the oven. I looked into the pot on the stove and my pasta was done cooking. I turned off the stove. I took the garlic bread out of the oven.

Kennedy walked into the kitchen.

"Daddy, what ya making?" Kennedy asked.

"Baked chicken. I also made a tomato and mushroom penne pasta."

She scrunched up her face. "No mac and cheese?"

"Nope, not tonight."

"Can I make a sandwich?"

"You don't want what I made?"

"I don't like flavorless baked chicken, tomato, or mushrooms."

"Flavorless? You can't insult my cooking like that. I promise the chicken has a lot of favor. Ask Jam. He loves my cooking."

"I ain't getting in between you two. But Ken, give the food a try. The pasta is good."

She gave Jam a disgusted look.

"I want you to at least try it. If you don't like it, make a sandwich." I said.

"Fine."

"Go tell Junior that dinner is ready."

She stormed out of the kitchen. I heard the front door slam shut and I wanted to go after her but I stayed calm.

"Jam, you ready to eat?" I asked.

"Yeah," Jam said closing his laptop.

I made plates for everyone. I took plates to Jam and Layla.

I called Jackson, Coby, Mariah, and Marley to the table. Kennedy walked into the kitchen.

"He's coming," Kennedy said sitting at the table. She got right on her phone.

"No phones at the table," I said.

"Dang, what can we do?" Kennedy asked.

"You can eat dinner and talk to your family."

Jackson ran into the kitchen and climbed into a chair. I took two plates to the table for Kennedy and Jackson. About five minutes later, everyone was seated at the table enjoying dinner. I sat at the head of the table. We were cramped at the kitchen table. Maybe we should have had dinner in the dining room.

"How was your day, bro?" Jam asked.

"Stressful," I said, "You had a good day?"

"Yeah. I filmed a cooking video and kept busy to get my mind off things."

"All you can do."

"Poppa E told us the news," Junior said.

"Yeah, I told Eric to break the news to y'all. Are y'all okay?" I asked.

"A couple of years ago, I would have felt differently about her death," Junior said.

"Same," Marley said. "I'm going to miss our smoking sessions."

I looked at him shocked. "I didn't know she smoked with you."

"It used to be me, Grandma, and Junior on the porch smoking good gas. She always had the best weed." Marley said.

"I don't feel no way. She was awful and made my life hell." Mariah said.

Jam and I didn't know what to say.

"I didn't know her," Coby said.

"I'm just mad someone killed her and we'll probably never know who," Kennedy said.

"I pray we get justice but ain't nobody talking," I said.

I read a text from Stephanie that Pops left the house again. I knew it was time to take the car. He was being so stubborn. I sent Pops a text.

Me: **GO HOME**
Pops: **mind ya business**

"Kennedy, I don't see you complaining about my cooking now," I said.

"Nah, she's over here smacking and enjoying the food," Jam joked.

We laughed.

"Fine, it's not so bad," Kennedy said.

"It's good, Unc," Marley said.

"I like the chicken," Junior said.

I looked down at Ava in her rocker and she kicked her legs. Junior held AJ in his arms.

"Did AJ and Ava's mommas check on them while I was away?" Junior asked.

"AJ's momma, Jada, has been checking up on him and video chatting. Ava's momma, Q, don't want nothing to do with the situation so I stopped bothering her." I said.

"That's Q for you," Junior said.

"She might come around," I said.

"I don't care if she does. I'm going to raise Ava on my own without her." Junior said.

"Yeah, fuck her," Kennedy said.

I gave her a look.

"I'm sorry. Forget her." Kennedy said.

"She's a deadbeat mother," Mariah said.

"Y'all got to be careful talking about the other parent in front of the kid. That's never cool. She's a baby now but she don't need to grow up hearing y'all talk crazy about her mom." I said.

"Are we really about to do virtual school?" Marley asked.

"It looks that way," I said. "So, y'all butts better be up early to do y'all work."

Chapter 68

New Normal

On Monday morning, a bunch of emails about virtual school flooded my inbox. After reading all of the emails, I was overwhelmed. I sat at the kitchen table with my coffee mug.

"Bring down y'all laptops and tablets!" I yelled.

Jackson ran into the kitchen from the living room with his toy firetruck in hand.

"What's that?" I asked.

"Truck," Jackson said excitedly.

"What are you doing?"

"Play."

Mariah was the first to appear with her laptop. I went to the email her principal sent and got everything set up. I handed her the laptop and she browsed through her online classroom.

"We already have work," Mariah said with a pout.

"Yup. You better get started. You have a couple of video conferences too."

"Can I go to my room and do it?"

"Yes, don't get distracted."

Marley and Kennedy were next to arrive. Kennedy sat at the table while I got Marley squared away.

"Look at all of this work," Marley said.

"Good luck. Lunch will be ready at noon. If you need me, call me." I said.

Marley left the kitchen with a scowl on his face.

"This is stupid," Kennedy mumbled once I got her set up.
"You got it, Ken. Just stay focused and do the work."
"I will."
She took her laptop and left the kitchen.
Layla appeared with her tablet.
"Go get paper and a pencil," I said.
She ran back out of the room. I downloaded the apps and signed in so she's all set to use them. Lay returned to the table with a pencil box and paper.
"Sit down," I said.
"Why can't I go to my room?"
"You might need help."
Coby walked into the room with his tablet and sat at the table. I looked at the emails Rod sent me and got him squared away.
I called Junior. He answered the phone and I could hear Ava wailing in the background.
"Wassup Pops?"
"Hey, Junior. What's wrong with Ava?"
"Nothing, she's waiting on her bottle."
"I'm 'bout to send you some info so you can access the virtual assignments. If you need help, I'll come over."
"Aight, send it over. I'll get started on it once I feed Ava."
I ended the call. I showed Layla how to navigate her virtual classroom. We worked on the first assignment together.
"Now, can I go to my room?" Layla asked.
"Nope, I need to watch you."
She pouted for a moment and then continued doing her work.
I started uploading videos to the channel. We had enough content for the next three weeks. I answered a video chat from Jay.
"Hey," I said completely distracted.
"Hey, bro," Jay said.

I looked at her. "You okay?"

"I'm in my feelings but I'm okay."

I stepped away from the table. "What's wrong?"

"I'm just thinking about life. Everything is so crazy and I feel overwhelmed."

"Just take a deep breath, Jay. We don't need you stressing."

"I keep thinking about Momma and I get sad. We were so close and when we weren't as close, it hurt me. And now she's gone forever."

"Jay, it's going to get better. Just give yourself time."

"Rell, it's just not fair. I'm never going to be okay after this."

"Where are you?"

"I'm in the basement at Daddy's house."

"Is he there?"

"No, he went to the Juicy Boil for a little bit."

"You want to come over?"

"Yeah."

I walked back to the kitchen and Coby needed help with an assignment. I helped him and sat back in front of my laptop. My phone rang and it was Rod. I paced around the kitchen as I talked on the phone.

"Wassup bro?" I said.

"Not too much. Headed to the airport in a few." Rod said.

"How's baby girl?" I asked.

"Jahzara is still scared but she's opening up a little. She's so frail, bro. Tiffany had her living in horrible conditions and starving her. I had to take her to the barbershop for a haircut because it was that matted."

"I bet she looks just like you now."

He chuckled. "Yeah, she's my twin for sure."

"You got full custody?"

"Yup, full custody. And Vanessa was denied visitation and joint custody of Coby."

"See what happens when you have a lawyer?"

"Yeah, Jordan is the truth. I appreciate you, bro."

"Anytime."

"When is the funeral?"

"We're waiting to get the body back. Eric wanted an autopsy done. Her body will be turned over to us by tomorrow. And Eric wants to have the funeral soon before everything shuts down. He wants a proper burial for Momma."

"How soon?"

"Like Friday soon."

"Wow, this shit is really real."

"I ain't going to accept it until I see her in that casket."

"Same, bro. I talked to Jay and Jam and they are so torn up over this. Wish I can take the pain away."

"Me too. Jay is headed over here now and I made Jam go to work. He just started the job and couldn't take that time off."

"Work will be good for him and Jay needs to get out of that dark basement. Did you get my message about how to set up the virtual learning for Coby?"

"Yeah, he's working on his assignments now."

"Let me talk to him. He ain't answering his phone."

"Coby, it's your dad," I said handing him the phone.

He takes it but doesn't say anything. He then looked at me. "I don't want to talk to him."

He handed the phone to me and I got back on the phone with Rod.

"Rod, I'll get him to call you later."

"It's cool. I'll talk to you when I land."

"I got to take Pops' car. He's been going out too much."

"Let me know and I'll help you out."

"We'll talk about it when you get back."

"Cool. I love you, bro."

"I love you. Be safe."

I sat at the table across from Coby.

"Why you ain't talking to your dad?" I asked.

He shrugged.

"Use your words and talk to me," I said.

"He only cares about my sister now," Coby said.

"He cares about both of y'all. He's been worried about her well-being because she was in a bad situation."

"I want to be with him and he sent me away."

"There's a virus spreading across the states. The people most at risk have underlying conditions and older people. Your dad and sister are coming from a state with a lot of cases and must stay inside for two weeks. Your dad doesn't want you to get sick. You have asthma and if you get this virus, it could be bad for you. Your dad didn't want that so he sent you over here. Call your dad and tell him you love him."

He pulled out his phone and called Rod.

"Hey, Daddy...Yeah, I know...I just want to tell you...uh...I love you."

Chapter 69

Work Too Much

Jay was now at the house and helping me make tacos for lunch. It was an easy meal and would fill the kids up until dinner.

"I posted a selfie of me being here on the gram and Daddy just texted me asking why I was out of the house," Jay said.

"He got to understand that it's hard for you to be in that house alone."

"Exactly. He's going through all of the photos and reminiscing. There are all these memories that I don't want to relive."

"He's trying to have the funeral on Friday."

"Everything is happening so quickly. I'm not ready to say goodbye."

"You'll never be ready, Jay."

Mariah walked into the kitchen.

"Ugh, I hate virtual learning," Mariah said.

"What's wrong?" I asked.

"They expect us to do all of this work in one day. We don't even do this much work at school."

"What class is giving you the most work?"

"Science and Reading."

"You want me to reach out to your teachers about the workload?"

"Please. They are killing me."

"I got you. What is Kennedy doing?"

"She's asleep."

"She's been sleeping this whole time?"

Realizing she slipped up, she looked away from me. "No, we've been working on our assignments together. I told her it was time for lunch and she wanted to take a nap."

Mariah was a horrible liar.

"You lying to me?"

"No."

"Look at me."

She couldn't bring herself to look at me.

"That's what I thought. Go sit at the table. Lunch is almost ready. Jay, finish up for me."

"I got you," Jay said.

I ran up the steps. I walked into the room Kennedy and Mariah shared. Kennedy's laptop was closed and she was knocked out sleep. She didn't just go to sleep as Mariah said.

"Get up now!" I yelled.

Kennedy jumped up startled out of her sleep. "C'mon Daddy. You could've given me a heart attack."

"Why aren't you working?"

"I've been working. I'm just taking a nap."

"Let me see your work."

She opened up her laptop and clicked away. I could see her trying to type up something. I take the laptop and she hasn't done anything. All of her modules were still at 0.

"You haven't even started. You're better than this." I said.

"It was a lot of work," Kennedy said.

"And it's going to be even more if you don't start."

"You're so annoying."

"I'm annoying because I want you to do your work? You told me you were going to work on your attitude."

"I don't have an attitude. If you leave me alone, I can do my work."

"You're going to do your work downstairs where I can keep an eye on you."

"You don't have to do that. I'll do my work."

"Yeah, you'll do your work downstairs with Coby and Layla."

She lay back down in bed. "I'm good. I'll do my work later." She pulled the cover over her body.

Man, she was trying it. I took a deep breath. I pulled the cover off of her.

"Ugh!" Kennedy yelled.

"Get downstairs now!" I said.

She crossed her arms.

"Let me go get my belt because you think I'm playing."

"Fine, I'll go."

She climbed out of bed and stomped out of the room and down the steps.

I checked on Marley next. He was watching a math lesson.

"Good to see you working," I said.

"It's a lot," Marley said.

"I know. I think they are still trying to figure things out and see what works and what doesn't."

"Well, this doesn't work. There's so much work to do."

"Mariah just said the same thing. I'm going to reach out to the principals and get it all sorted out. Is working on the laptop fine or do you need a desktop?"

"I like the laptop."

"Lunch is ready. When you're done, come down and join us."

"What did y'all make?"

"Tacos."

"I'll be downstairs after this lesson."

I walked down the stairs to the kitchen. Everyone was at the table talking and eating. I made a plate and joined them.

"I talked to Jam a few minutes ago," Jay said.

"Yeah, how is he?" I asked.

"He's good and glad he went to work. His job is thinking about teleworking. He has to buy a computer and get a router in his room."

"We can make that happen. It would be easier for him to work from home instead of me driving him to work and picking him up."

"With this virus, it's going to take forever for his case to go to court."

"And he's so ready to put that behind him."

"Rod texted me a picture of his baby girl."

"She looks just like him, doesn't she?"

"Just like him. She's so pretty."

"You made a decision about the bakery whether you want to stay open or close until the order is lifted?"

"I'm going to play it by ear and then decide. We have a lot of canceled orders and I'm not sure about things right now. And my team is worried about the virus and their jobs."

"That's understandable. We're all worried and everything is up in the air."

"Sam reached out to me on Facebook."

"Yeah?"

"He was saying it was no beef, he's sorry for this and that. He even asked if I could drop the restraining order so he could be involved in the pregnancy. I told him I wasn't doing it because I didn't trust him. He's threatened my life too many times. After I told him that, he proved to be the same old Sam."

"What did he do?"

"He was called me a ho, cursed me out, and threatened to kill me."

"His crazy ass."

"I blocked him."

"Good. You need to stop talking to him."

"You're right."

"I'm serious, Jay. I don't want to bury another sister."

Chapter 70

Just A Friend

I pulled out of the driveway and headed to Jam's job. Jay already went home so I brought Jackson, Layla, and Coby with me trusting the older kids to be on their best behavior while I'm away.

"Coby, you got a chance to video chat with your sister?" I asked.

"Yeah, she's shy," Coby said.

"In a little while, she's going to be talking up a storm and getting on your nerves."

"I thought she was a boy because she's bald."

"She's not bald. She got a low cut."

"I'm happy I have a sister."

"I know it. You've been asking for a sister for the past three years."

"And now I want a brother."

"Did y'all finish y'all work?"

"Yes," Layla said.

"I finished everything," Coby said.

"Was it easy or hard?"

"The math was hard but you helped me. Everything else was easy." Coby said.

"Reading was hard for me," Layla said.

"Your teacher suggested you read for fifteen minutes every night. You're going to be a better reader in no time."

"Books are boring."

"You can't think like that. Reading is fun."

I looked at the clock as it struck 5:30. The traffic was bad and Jam got off in thirty minutes. I answered an incoming call from Connie.

"Hey," I said.

All I heard was sniffling.

Now, I was worried. "Everything okay, Connie? Say something."

"No, they had a fire at my apartments," Connie cried.

"Are you and Sassy okay?"

"Yes. It was so scary to see the building engulfed in flames and people being rescued. And it's the worst time for this to happen. I'm not low on funds but money ain't coming in like it used to. I'm just frustrated."

"You got a place to stay?"

"They're trying to put us in this crappy hotel. I can't stay with my mom because I don't want to make her sick."

"Come stay with me. I have another guest room."

"Are you sure?"

"Yeah, come around seven tonight. I'm not home right now since I got to get Jam from work."

"That's perfect. I'm packing up my apartment to take everything to storage. I appreciate you, Rell."

"Anytime. I'll talk to you later. I'm in traffic."

"Okay. Talk to you later."

I hung up the phone.

"Who's moving in?" Coby asked.

"You so nosey," I said, "I have a friend moving in."

"We already have a full house," Layla said.

"We got more than enough space so it's not like we're all on top of one another."

A notification popped up that Mariah was going live. I had to see what these kids were up to but I couldn't join the live with my profile.

"Coby, you got an IG?" I asked.

"Yeah, I don't use it," Coby said.

"You follow Mariah?"

"Uh-huh."

"She's live. Let me see your phone so I can see what your cousins are up to."

He passed me his phone and I joined the live from Coby's account. I propped up the phone on the dashboard and sneaked glances at the screen. It was just Mariah and Kennedy. They were blasting music and having a good time.

"Hey everybody. I'm going to wait for a few more people to join." Kennedy said.

Marley and Junior appeared in the frame.

"Junior's home," Kennedy said.

"Dare us to do something. We're bored." Mariah said.

And the suggestions came in.

"Ken Ken, go get an egg," Mariah said.

Kennedy ran off-screen and returned with four eggs. They had all this schoolwork to do but instead, they were doing this foolishness. Ken cracked an egg on Marley's head. Mariah and Kennedy laughed hysterically. And then, Mariah threw an egg at Junior. All I could think about was my carpeted floor in the living room.

"Pops is going to be pissed. It got everywhere." Junior said.

"Ken Ken, somebody dared you to twerk," Mariah said.

"She better not," I mumbled.

"Nah, my sis don't do that," Junior said.

"This my song too," Ken said. She started gyrating and Junior snatched her away from the screen and I'm glad he did. I could hear him fussing in the back.

"Take a shot," Mariah said.

"A shot of what?" I asked out loud as if they could hear me.

"I'll take a shot. Unc got some Henny." Marley said.

It was time to put an end to this. I sent a request to join the live. I'm sure she didn't read the name and just accepted the request. When my face popped up, they froze.

"Hey," Mariah said nervously.

"Hey, nothing. Clean up that mess before I get home. Get off live and sit down somewhere. Y'all have work to do."

Ken tapped the screen to take me off live.

"He's so lame." Kennedy huffed.

I got off the live before my blood pressure spiked. I've never been more pissed in my life. I handed Coby his phone back.

I called Junior and he didn't answer. I kept calling until he answered.

"Why you ain't answering my calls?" I asked.

"I didn't have my phone," Junior said.

And I knew that was a lie but I let it slide. "Why y'all ain't doing y'all work?"

"Pops, we're just taking a little break. Can't we have fun?"

"That's fun to y'all?"

Mariah and Kennedy were laughing in the background. It didn't sound like they were doing work.

"Are they still on live?" I asked.

"Nah, Pops."

"You my right hand, Junior. I need you to get everyone in line and not join in with the foolishness."

"I'm handling it, Pops."

"Where's Ava and AJ?"

"AJ is in the rocker wide awake staring at me and Ava is asleep in the bassinet."

"How is she sleeping with all that noise?"

"She's probably used to it. Her momma was at every party while pregnant."

"Connie and Sassy are going to move in for a little while. They had a fire at their apartment."

"Are they okay?"

"Yeah, they just need a place to stay."

"That's your girl?"

"Nah, she's just a friend."

"Whatever you say, Pops."

I chuckled. Connie and I were getting closer but she was still scared to give me a chance.

"Do some work, Junior."

"Okay. I'm almost finished with everything."

"That's good. Make sure they finish everything too, especially that Kennedy."

"I got you."

"I love you, Junior."

"I love you, Pops."

I pulled in front of Jam's job right at six o'clock. I looked in the rearview mirror and the kids were fast asleep. It's been a long day and it's only the first day.

Jam walked out of the building talking to a pretty young woman. He climbed in the car once saying bye to her.

"I see you, Jam," I said.

"Stop," Jam said.

"How was work?"

"Nice distraction. They're trying to transition everything so we can work from home. They gave me a checklist to get my room ready."

"When do you start working from home?"

"They're saying as early as next week. They're waiting to see what the governor will say next."

"We're waiting on that too. So, what's her name?"

"Morgan."

"You like her?"

"She's cool and a good friend."

"Already a good friend? You just met her."

He laughed. "That's my answer and I'm sticking with it."

"Speaking of friends, Connie and her daughter are moving in."

"You serious?"

"Yeah, their apartments caught fire."

"Aw man, that sucks especially now with all of this other stuff going on."

"That's why I told her to move in with us until she can find a new place."

Chapter 71

Full House

The kids were at the kitchen table working on their assignments. I went straight to the living room to inspect the carpet. I don't know what they used but my carpet looked good as new.

Coby, Layla, and Jackson climbed on the couch and continued napping. I walked back to the kitchen.

"I don't like that y'all acted a fool as soon as I left. I'm glad y'all are doing the work now." I said.

"It was just a break," Mariah said.

"And y'all could have spent that break doing something other than acting a fool for the world to see."

I looked in the fridge and decided to make spaghetti and meatballs for dinner. All of the kids loved that.

Jam walked into the kitchen after taking a shower. He helped me cook dinner.

"Daddy, we're going viral," Kennedy said.

"What you talking 'bout?" I asked.

"They posted a clip of you from the live on a blog," Kennedy said.

"I'm probably looking crazy as hell," I said.

Jam walked over to the table to see the video. He cracked up laughing once he saw the video.

"Man, you done become your Pops and my dad," Jam said.

"I understand them now," I said.

I took a break to check out the blogs. Though the comments praised me for being a good dad, I didn't like how some comments trashed the kids.

"Do y'all read comments?" I asked.

"I don't care what people say," Mariah said.

"Yeah, they don't know us," Kennedy said.

"They're just saying we're bad like we don't know that," Marley said.

And that made everyone laugh.

"Marley, you didn't take a shot, did you?" I asked.

"Nah, I was joking," Marley said.

There was a knock at the door and I walked to the door wiping my hands on a towel. Connie and Sassy were there each with a suitcase and backpacks on their back. Connie looked so good and I had to stop myself from staring. I showed them upstairs to their room.

"If y'all want something to eat, dinner will be ready soon," I said.

Connie smiled. "I appreciate you so much."

"Don't mention it."

I left the room and walked down the stairs. Jam pulled the dinner rolls out of the oven. I began to make plates for everyone.

"Put y'all devices away," I said. "It's time for dinner. Coby, Jackson, and Layla, come eat!"

"Coming," Coby said groggily.

Marley, Mariah, Junior, and Kennedy put their things away. Sassy walked down the stairs.

"Sassy, you ready to eat?" I asked.

"Yes," Sassy said.

"Go sit at the table. I'm bringing dinner over now."

Jackson ran into the kitchen and climbed into a chair. Jam took plates to the table. Speaking of tables, I got a bigger table for the kitchen. The kids hated eating in the dining room, saying it felt too fancy. Coby and Layla raced into the room and found a spot at the table.

Connie walked down the steps and joined me in the kitchen.

"I need a drink," Connie said.

"I got wine, vodka, and Henny," I said.

"I'll have some wine. You drinking?"

"Nah, I'm good."

She poured a glass of red wine and I handed her a plate. Jam came back over to grab a plate.

"You sweating, bro," Jam said.

"It's hot in this kitchen," I said.

"Uh-huh. And you say she's just a friend." Jam said singing it like the song.

"Boy, go eat."

He walked away laughing. I'm not going to lie. I have feelings for Connie. I took a deep breath and joined everyone at the table.

"Who started the fire?" Jam asked.

"Our upstairs neighbor. They were frying chicken and went to sleep." Connie said.

"Man, why would they go to sleep while frying anything?" I said.

"They said they were tired after work and just fell asleep on the couch," Connie said.

"If you're tired, don't start cooking. That's just dumb." Jam said.

"It caused a huge fire with three buildings being affected. Thirty families are now displaced."

"Were you able to save anything?" I asked.

"Yeah. The fire only spread to the living room and kitchen. Our bedrooms were spared so I was able to get all of our clothes, Sassy got her toys, and personal things like photos and important documents. I have to move our furniture out another day."

"We'll help you move the furniture," Jam said.

"How are y'all dealing with everything?" Connie asked.

"Just taking it hour by hour, day by day," I said. Truth was I wasn't dealing with it.

"When are the services?" Connie asked.

"Friday. Pops and Eric are planning the service." I said.

"Are y'all going to see her before Friday?" Connie asked.

"Me and Jay are going to see her tomorrow," Jam said.

"I don't know yet," I said, "How was homebound learning for you?"

"A mess. Sassy don't listen. I don't know how her teacher does it." Connie said.

"Sassy, you have to listen. What grade are you in?" I asked.

"Kindergarten," Sassy said.

"Daddy had us in boot camp all day," Kennedy said.

"Nah, tell the whole story. Ken went upstairs and went to sleep instead of doing her work." I said.

"I saw the clip of you on live and I'm like Rell, don't play," Connie said. "And young lady, don't be shaking your butt like that again. You don't know who's watching."

"Yes ma'am," Kennedy said.

"Her momma called and got her together. Make sure y'all eat the salad too." I said.

"Unc, don't nobody want salad every day," Marley said.

"It ain't every day. Y'all need to stop eating so much junk food and fast food." I said.

Chapter 72

Just Right

I woke up the next morning with a headache. It was seven in the morning and I had to wake up all the kids for virtual learning.

I jumped up when I realized Connie was in the bed. I peeked under the sheet and her breasts were looking right back at me. All she had on was a thong. What the hell happened? All I remembered was Jam, Connie and I drinking, playing cards, and talking about life. I shook her gently.

"Yeah," Connie mumbled.

"What happened?" I asked.

Her eyes popped open. She sat up and wrapped the sheet around herself. "I'm sorry."

"Did we do anything?"

"We wanted to but we didn't."

I kissed her on the lips. It was just so tempting. She kissed me back.

"What you 'bout to do?" Connie asked.

"First, I got to take Jam to work. Then, I'll come back and make sure the kids are doing their work. I got to find time to work on the channel. What ya doing today?"

"Just getting campaigns for my clients and helping you with the kids."

I wrapped my arms around her. I could get used to this. She leaned her head into my chest. I dropped another kiss on her lips and our tongues intertwined.

I cupped her breasts in my hands and caressed them as we kissed.

I lay her down on the bed and kissed her from her head to her toes. She was such a beautiful woman. I climbed on top. She removed my boxers with her feet. I took off her thong and gently entered. She gasped. She matched my strokes and I removed myself before I exploded. She leaned over and sucked me until I erupted. I held her in my arms and pleasured her until she exploded all over my fingers. My alarm sounded interrupting our good time.

"Shit," I mumbled. "Let me go hop in the shower."

Connie was lying down on the bed exhausted. I rubbed her ass and wanted another round but I knew we would never leave the room if we did. I walked into the bathroom and took a shower. This was the best way to start the morning. I got out of the shower twenty minutes later and walked back into the room.

"Guess I better get ready too," Connie said.

"I'm going to take Jam to work and I'll be back," I said.

She kissed me on the lips. "I'll get everybody up and make breakfast."

She walked into the bathroom. I got dressed and headed downstairs. Jam was eating a bowl of cereal at the kitchen table.

"Did you sleep?" I asked.

"Barely. I'm still fucked up from last night."

"What were we thinking?" I asked.

He grinned. "Did you hit?"

"That ain't your business."

"It's cool. I already know. I was coming upstairs to see if you were up and I heard y'all."

I shook my head. "Don't let Connie know that you know."

"I won't."

"That's what you're wearing to work? Your shirt is wrinkled."

"You sound like Dad. I haven't done laundry. I used to take my laundry to Momma and she would do it for me."

"Moms really babied you and Jay. I'm going to see if I have a shirt for you. You can't wear that." I ran back up the steps and got him a shirt. He changed his shirt and continued eating.

"You need to do laundry when you come in and iron your shirts," I said.

"I'm going to take my clothes to a laundry service."

"You would rather do that than just do it yourself?"

"You know I'm lazy, bro."

"I see that now. The internet company is coming later to install a router in your room. I got to get you a computer and you're good to go."

"Thanks, bro."

"Don't mention it. Jay is getting you from work, right?"

"Yup going to see Momma today."

"Is Eric meeting y'all there?"

"Yup, we can't do it alone."

Connie walked down the steps carrying Jackson.

"Daddy," Jackson said with his arms out.

"He came in the room looking for you," Connie said.

I took Jackson from Connie.

"Good morning, Jacks. You want some cereal?"

"Yes."

"I'll make it," Connie said.

I put Jackson down and he sat at the table. He talked to Jam about trucks.

"Porsha's pregnant!" Jam said out of nowhere a few minutes later.

"How you know?" I asked.

"She announced it on the gram," Jam said.

I looked at my feed and Porsha shared an ultrasound picture and a picture of her growing belly. She also threw shade at C in her caption by calling him a deadbeat.

"Is she really pregnant by Chauncey?" Connie asked.

"Yup," I said.

"What a hot mess," Connie said.

"She wanted to hurt me for hurting her and he was on some get-back shit now look at them," I said.

"People are talking so much shit too. I couldn't be famous like y'all." Connie said.

"What are they saying?" I asked.

"It's a lot of people calling her a ho and disloyal. The show already makes her look horrible for sleeping with her baby daddy's best friend." Connie said.

"It is what it is."

"You and C were best friends and seen everywhere together. Y'all fell out and then your baby mama popped up with him. It looks crazy." Jam said.

"There are rumors that Ty and Chantel are back together and they dropped the charges against her," Connie said.

"I don't know if I believe the rumor that they dropped the charges," I said.

"And there are rumors she's pregnant," Jam said.

"These blogs make up the wildest stories so I don't know what to believe. I haven't talked to Chantel in a while. I've been talking to Joe so I can talk to Life." I said.

"Why didn't you keep Life?" Jam asked.

"Chantel wanted her and I didn't want to deal with the drama of fighting for custody right now."

"She's a nurse, right?" Connie asked.

"Yup, that's why I wanted Life with me," I said.

"Rell, you ready to go?" Jam asked.

"Ready when you are."

I kissed Jacks on the cheek. "Daddy will be right back." He pouted. "Okay."

Jam and I walked out the door and climbed into the sports car.

"So, are you and Connie together now?" Jam asked.

"We ain't nothing right now," I said.

"She's wife material, bro."

"You think so?"

"I know so. And I also know you like her."

"We've known each other for so long. It just seems it ain't never been the right time."

"I think it's the right time now. Hell, y'all are going to be stuck together for the next few weeks. Either y'all are going to love one another or hate one another."

"That's true."

A call from Rod interrupted us.

"Sup Rod," I said.

"Sup Rell."

"Not too much. I'm driving Jam to work."

"Wish I was headed to work."

"You don't know how to sit still, bro."

"Stephanie left the car keys in the mailbox. I think it's best to take the keys and not the car. You know Pops will report it stolen and it'll be all bad."

"You right. I'll get the keys before I drop Jam off at work."

"Just tell Stephanie you got the keys."

"I will. Where's Jahzara?"

"She's knocked out sleep. I'm just up and bored as hell."

"She's going to have you running around that house soon."

"I can't wait. It'll give me something to do."

"Send me your grocery list too."

"I got you. I saw a selfie of Connie and couldn't help but notice she was at your crib."

"And he smashed!" Jam yelled.

Jam and Rod cracked up laughing.

"That's your girl now?" Rod asked.

"We're just seeing where life takes us," I said.

"It's about time. Y'all were supposed to be together years ago." Rod said.

"It wasn't the right time," I said.

"Why is she at your place anyway?"

"Her place caught on fire."

"So, her and Sassy are staying with you?"

"Yup, until they find a new place."

"I got to reach out to Connie and make sure she's good. I also saw Porsha's announcement."

"It's embarrassing, bro."

"Not for you. They're dragging her."

"I don't like that. Porsha is still a good friend."

"Nah, bruh. She ain't that good of a friend if she fucked the homie."

"You know Rell got a good heart. He ain't cold like us." Jam said.

"I just want to see the good in everybody," I said.

"I can't see the good in Porsha. Shit makes me mad. Chauncey was like a brother. It was wrong for him to even step to her and Porsha was weak as hell for playing right into his hands." Rod said.

"I hear ya, Rod. I can't cut her off. We got kids together."

"And it needs to only be about the kids. You be sending her flowers and shit like that's your girl. She trashed you on national television while sitting in your homie's lap."

I abruptly ended the call. Jam looked over at me with his brows furrowed.

"You good, bro?" Jam asked.

"I'm good. I just don't want to hear that shit right now."

I pulled in front of Pops' house and Jam got the keys out of the mailbox. I texted Stephanie that I got the keys.

"Pops is going to be pissed," Jam said.

"He should have stayed in the house," I said.

Chapter 73

Parenting Woes

I'm back at the house and all the kids were awake and doing their work. Connie sat at the table with Coby, Layla, and Sassy and helped them with their work and video calls. I was in the living room watching Jackson slam his toy cars together.

I decided to go live on IG since I received so many messages and comments about Porsha's announcement.

"Wassup, y'all? I have a lot to say so I'll wait for a few more people to join." I said.

I read the comments.

"Y'all always asking about Junior. He's good and will be back on the gram soon. He's busy taking care of his little ones and finishing school." I said.

Jackson climbed on the couch and sat beside me.

"Say hi," I said.

He looked confusedly at the phone and waved.

"Cool, enough people are on here. So many people are hurting because of this pandemic and it's just the start. I will be helping the community so if you want to donate canned goods and non-perishables, drop them off at Juicy Boil, Jay's Sweets, JuiceIt Bar, and Poppa's Soulfood.

I'm going to put boxes together to feed families in my old hood. I'll get a flyer made so you all can know the different addresses of where to drop things off. I will also be giving the date and time that I will be giving away these food boxes. I want to help as many people as I can. I'm going to be buying things as well for the boxes."

I took time to read the comments.

"Yeah, you can donate money to Deja's Hope Foundation, and the link to do that is in my bio. I saw a report about an increase in domestic violence cases and it makes me sad. My sister was killed by her ex-boyfriend in front of her kids. I started the foundation in her memory."

I continued to read the comments.

"I appreciate y'all watching the channel. We got more videos coming. Jam has been working but he's going to put out more videos soon."

The comments were going so fast.

"A lot of y'all are mentioning Porsha. What y'all want to know?"

I waited for questions to appear.

"Am I mad? Mad about what? That's Jacks and Lay's momma so I ain't going to air her out. I don't do people how they do me. Karma always takes care of people."

Connie brought me a glass of Henny and Jackson a juice box. She knew exactly what I needed. She exits out of the room.

I tuned back into the live and saw a bunch of 'who's that' questions.

"Y'all so nosey. Don't worry about it. What should I make for lunch? I'll make a video for y'all."

I declined Rod's request to join the live. I didn't want to talk to Rod.

I read the suggestions.

"Salmon sounds good. Give me a side. My kids don't want salad." I said.

Everyone was suggesting rice.

"Are y'all going to watch a salmon and rice video?"

A comment that said, we just want to see you Zaddy made me chuckle.

"Y'all are wild. Are y'all cities locked down yet? My state hasn't done a full lockdown yet."

I see a mix of yes and no.

"Y'all stay safe and healthy. Only go out when necessary."

I saw a question asking why I haven't posted about my mom's passing.

"I didn't want to talk about my mom's passing but I'll make a post soon."

Then I see a bunch of "your mom died" comments and someone wondering if she died from the virus.

"No, my mom didn't die from the virus. My mom was murdered."

I took a sip of my drink and read more comments.

"Yeah, I have all my kids but my baby girl, Life. My kids are doing virtual learning. My oldest kids are stressed because it's a lot of work."

People were going back and forth in the comments about how many kids I have. When I saw someone say ten kids, I had to comment.

"I have five kids and I take care of my niece and nephew. I also have a granddaughter and grandson. Y'all can't believe everything y'all read and hear. I take care of my kids. Always have. Always will."

Kennedy walked into the living room.

"Wassup?" I asked.

She sat next to me.

"You on live?"

"Yeah."

"This is my daughter, Ken Ken. Y'all are used to seeing Mariah and she's my niece. Yeah, they do look alike. They both look like my sister, Deja."

I saw a comment that was out of line asking if she's the one shaking her ass for a few likes.

"Yo, don't get on this live talking crazy and being disrespectful. I don't want to pull up on nobody. I got to get off of here before I say some real shit that hurts feelings. Watch my page for details on how to donate. I'm about to make a food video for y'all."

I ended the live.

"What's going on?" I asked Kennedy.

She covered her face and cried. I wrapped my arms around her.

"What's wrong, Kennedy?"

"Grandma came to me in a dream." She sucked up the tears. "She said she was sorry and never meant to hurt any of us. When I asked why, she disappeared. I woke up crying and Mariah was up too. She said Auntie Deja visited her in her dreams and told her she was okay and that Mariah would get through everything."

This shit was deep. I had no idea what to say. What a coincidence for them to have these dreams. Momma wanted to clear her conscience one last time and Deja was letting us know that she was at peace. I text Mariah to come downstairs.

"I hate death. I wish we didn't have to die." Kennedy said.

"I feel the same way, Ken. It gives me comfort to know that my momma is at peace. I don't have to worry about her behind bars or none of that. She's been through so much and I don't think she had it in her to fight. She was ready to go."

Mariah walked into the room. "What I do now?"

"I want to make sure you're okay," I said.

She sat next to Kennedy.

"Yeah, I'm good," Mariah said.

"I heard your mom came to you in a dream," I said.

"Yeah, she did. It was good to see her again. I don't really remember her. I just know the stories y'all share about her." Mariah said.

"She loved you and Marley so much," I said.

"She didn't love us enough to leave," Mariah said.

"When she finally got the courage to leave, he killed her."

"She waited too late."

"Mariah, don't feel that way. It wasn't easy to leave. She never wanted this man to hurt her or y'all. Y'all mom loved y'all and died fighting for y'all. I know because I had to go to the house to see the crime scene. Her bloody handprints on the wall where she blocked this man from getting to you and Marley."

Mariah ran out of the room unable to deal with what I told her. Kennedy ran behind her. I couldn't believe Mariah had questions about her mother's love. I couldn't even check on her because I was getting a call from Pops.

"Yo, where are my keys?" Pops yelled.

"What are you talking about, Pops?" I asked.

"I feel like your sneaky ass is behind this."

"Pops, I don't know what you're talking about."

"I can't find my keys, not even my spare keys. They told me it's going to take two months to get new keys because everything is slow with the virus. And I don't even want to spend all this money on a new key."

"Where was the last place you put the keys?"

"I put my keys in the same spot every day." He was getting frustrated.

"Yo, why you mad at me?"

"This got your name written all over it. Boy, if you got anything to do with this, I'm whooping your ass."

Then the phone clicked. Boy, Pops was crazy.

"Jacks, I got to cook lunch now," I said.

"Okay," he said lying down on the couch without taking his eyes off the television.

I walked to the kitchen and set up the camera. I looked in my cabinets and refrigerator. I decided to make Tuscan butter salmon with asparagus and red potatoes.

"I don't want to do this," Layla whined.

I turned to her. "What you complaining about?"

"I don't want to do any more work. I want a break." Layla said.

"What do you have left to do?"

"She has to read a book, two worksheets, and a video," Connie said.

"You can finish that," I said.

"I don't want to."

I knew Layla was acting out because she missed her mom. I started the camera and ignored her. She let out a scream and threw herself on the floor.

"No ma'am. Get up." Connie said.

I stopped the camera and walked over to them.

"Sit down and finish your work," I said.

She knew my tone meant business so she quickly got up and sat in her chair. Connie helped her read the book. I turned the camera back on.

Raising kids is something else.

Chapter 74

Run Away

Thirty minutes later, I called everyone to the table. I called Junior on the phone to come over and get lunch.

"You got to go live again. You had thirty thousand people on that live." Connie said.

"For real? I didn't even pay attention. They were there to hear me trash talk Porsha." I said.

"I'm glad you didn't. She has enough going on. Chauncey just came out saying she's a ho and slept around and he doesn't know if that's his baby. He's even claiming you could be the dad."

Mariah walked down the stairs and sat at the table sulking.

"Where's Kennedy?" I asked.

"She's coming," Mariah mumbled.

"You still mad?" I asked.

"I don't want to talk about it."

"Jackson, come eat."

"Coming," Jackson said.

Jackson ran into the kitchen a few seconds later. He climbed into a chair and Connie made sure he didn't fall.

I took plates to the table. Junior walked in holding the babies. Connie took Ava and Junior sat down with AJ in his arms.

"You got a chance to do your work?" I asked.

"Yeah, I got a lot done," Junior said.

Kennedy walked into the kitchen.

"You okay?" I asked.

"Yeah," she mumbled.

I continued taking plates to the table until everyone had a plate in front of them.

"Where's Marley?" I asked.

"In his room," Mariah said.

"Why he ain't come down?" I asked.

"I don't know," Mariah said sounding annoyed with me.

Boy, these kids and their attitudes. I walked up the steps to Marley's room. I knocked on the door. When he didn't answer, I opened the door and walked into the room.

He was gone and his window was open. I leaned out the window and didn't see him in the yard. I walked down the steps.

"Where the hell is your brother?" I asked Mariah.

"In his room," Mariah said.

"I'm not stupid. I just went up there and he's not there. Junior, you know anything?"

"Nah, I video-chatted him earlier and he was in the room. He didn't say nothing about going anywhere." Junior said.

"Mariah and Kennedy, where is Marley? I'm sure y'all know." I said.

"I don't know shit," Kennedy said.

"Who you talking to?"

"I don't know anything."

"His window is open."

"What that got to do with us?"

"You need to watch how you talk to your dad. Marley could be in trouble and you are withholding information on his whereabouts. If anything happens, you're going to feel guilty." Connie said.

"He went out," Mariah mumbled. I knew she would crack first.

"Out where?" I asked.

"Outside," Kennedy said smartly.
"He said he was going to the park," Mariah said.
What park?" I asked.
"He didn't say. He said he was going to race and be back."
"You saying too much," Junior said.
"Nah, she's telling me exactly what I need to know," I said.
"What kind of race?" Connie asked confused.
"I don't know," Mariah said scared to say anything else.
"I'm sure it's street racing. Junior, what do you know?" I asked.
"I don't know nothing about nothing," Junior said.
I sat at the table with my food. I called Marley and it went straight to voicemail. I cursed under my breath.
"Don't stress, boo," Connie said.
"Boo?" Kennedy questioned.
"You know I call everybody boo," Connie said.

Around one o'clock in the afternoon, I got a call from an officer about Marley. I was now headed to get him from the police station. I had Jackson, Layla, and Sassy with me because they begged to come with me. I just picked up Jay on the way to the station because she wanted to get out of the house.
"What have you been doing today?" I asked Jay.
"Trying out new recipes and making videos," Jay said. "I saw you pop into Connie's live. Y'all cute."
"Did you check out my live?"

"Yup. Them people were wilding and asking all types of crazy questions."

"I'm used to it."

"Could Porsha's baby be yours?"

"Nope, C is talking outta the side of his neck like always."

"I figured. I talked to Porsha to make sure she was good. The comments bothered her but she's handling it. She doesn't want C in her child's life so she's not going to force him to be a dad."

"C is being childish right now but I know he's going to come around."

"He's showing his ass. I feel bad for Porsha."

I pulled into the parking lot of the police station. Jay looked around confused.

"I thought you were going to the grocery store and wanted me to watch the kids while you went inside," Jay said.

"I got to pick up Marley from here and then we'll go to the store."

Jay's eyes widened. "What the hell did he do?"

"Drag racing and disorderly conduct for a fight. He snuck out of the house to pull this stunt. I'll be back."

I walked into the police station, introduced myself, and signed the paper so Marley was released to me. Marley and I walked out of the station fifteen minutes later.

"What were you thinking?" I asked.

Marley shrugged.

"What does that mean? You don't have nothing to say?"

"My boys said pull up. I was bored so I did."

"How did you get to that part of town?"

"I got a ride."

"How are you bored with all of that work?"

"I just wanted to get out of the house."

"It was irresponsible for you to leave the house and be around such a big crowd. There's a virus that is killing people and you could have brought that back to the house."

"I wasn't thinking, my bad."

"Yo bad huh?"

I pulled off my belt.

"C'mon Unc. I know I messed up. I'm sorry."

I pulled him behind the truck and wore his behind out. He got in the car with a frown on his face. I climbed back into the driver's seat.

I GPS a grocery store near me and follow the directions to the store. The parking lot didn't seem full so hopefully, I can be in and out. I pulled up the text message with Rod's list and made my way around the store getting everything he needed. It took about an hour to finish shopping and get checked out.

When I returned to the car, Layla and Sassy were up front with Jay singing along with the radio.

"Y'all having fun," I said through the window.

"Two carts? What did Rod need?" Jay asked.

"He had me do a month's worth of grocery shopping."

I handed her a chocolate candy bar and bottled water.

"Aw, you love me," Jay said.

"You never have to doubt that. Marley, come help me."

Marley reluctantly got out of the car. I opened the trunk.

"We got to wipe everything down and put everything in these cloth bags," I said.

"You serious?" Marley asked.

"Deadass."

I squirted hand sanitizer into my hands. I wiped down the groceries with a disinfectant wipe and put things into the cloth bags. Marley worked alongside me not saying a word.

"I know I come off as strict sometimes but I know you're better than this. I want more for you, Marley. You snuck out of the house. You out here fighting in the streets like you have no home training. And on top of that, they caught you behind the wheel of a car. They can't confirm if you were racing or not, but you had no reason to be driving at all."

He doesn't say anything and I stopped lecturing because he wasn't listening anyway.

"Get in y'all seats," I said when we were on our last bag.

Marley climbed back into the car. I took the carts back and climbed into the car.

"That wore me out," I said.

"Were you able to find everything on his list?" Jay asked.

"Yeah, this store ain't as empty as most. Just had a limited stock of toilet paper."

"That's everywhere. It's flying off the shelves."

I backed out of the parking space and drove to Rod's house.

"Call Rod and let him know I'm dropping off the groceries," I said pulling into his driveway next to his Range Rover.

I climbed out of the car, took the groceries out of the trunk, and put them on his front porch. Rod walked out of the door with a mask on his face.

"Thanks, bro," Rod said.

"Of course," I said.

I kept taking bags to his front porch and he took things inside. Jahzara stood at the door sucking her thumb. I waved and she waved back. I closed the trunk and waited for Rod to get everything inside. We said bye to one another once he was done taking everything inside. I took Jay back to her house.

We were able to get back home around four o'clock in the afternoon. Connie was on the couch cradling Ava and rocking AJ's rocker with her foot.

"Where's Junior?" I asked.

"He was tired so I told him I would watch the babies while he got a little rest," Connie said.

"Where's everybody else?"

"Coby went to sleep. Mariah and Kennedy are playing video games upstairs."

"Hey, Marley," Connie said.

"Hey," he grumbled.

He went upstairs to his room. Sassy and Layla sat on the couch with Connie.

"Your Pops called me angry about his car keys. He wanted me to look around the house for them. He thinks you have something to do with his missing keys."

"He ain't wrong."

She side-eyed me. "What did you do?"

"I took the keys."

"And I was defending you like hell."

"Pops is sick and needs to stay inside."

"You know your Pops is stubborn and can't sit still."

"And that's why I had to take the keys."

"You want me to make dinner?"

"If you want."

I excused myself and answered an incoming call from Porsha. I walked into the kitchen to take the call.

"Wassup?" I said.

"Who you got around my children?" Porsha asked.

"Ma, you got enough drama in your own life. You ain't got to stir up drama with me."

"I told you about having your women around my kids."

"You know Connie. Why you trippin'? Her apartment caught fire and she's here with me until she gets a new place."

"I didn't know that was her. My girlfriend said there was a woman on your live. So, you with Connie now? You've been telling me for years it was nothing between y'all."

"What I do don't concern you. Take that energy to C."
"Y'all men are trash."
"You calling to talk to your kids or to get in my business?"

Porsha ended the call.

I walked back to the living room.

"Who was that?" Connie asked.

"Porsha," I said.

"Sounds like she's trippin' about me being here."

"She can get over it. She got too much other shit going on to be worried about my business."

Jackson whined and held his arms up. I picked him up and he rested his head on my shoulder. I rocked him to sleep. It was too late for his nap, but I knew he would be cranky if I forced him to stay up.

I heard the kids arguing upstairs. I knew they would figure it out.

"Jeez, who's doing all of that yelling?" Connie said.

"That's Kennedy. Marley's probably mad at them for telling on him. But he got locked up so I was going to find out anyway."

Chapter 75

Mixed Feelings

Friday came too quickly. I can't believe today is the day we lay Momma to rest. I sat in the back pew with Rod. Eighty of us were in this small church waving paper fans as it quickly heated up.

Boss, Honey, and their kids were seated in the front of the church. Pops and Stephanie were in the front pew with Eric, Jay, and Jam. Connie was also here for moral support.

Pastor Neal began the services with a powerful prayer for forgiveness and comfort. Jam was the first speaker and he looked sharp in his tailored black suit. He looked over at the casket before speaking.

"The day I've been dreading is here. I have to say goodbye and I'm not ready. I wrote a speech but I don't want to say what's on paper. My mom was my best friend. Anytime I needed her, she was there. I consider myself blessed because not everyone got to know the Momma I did. We had our ups and downs but I knew she loved me and I'll always love her. When Pops whopped my butt, Momma was there with open arms and a candy bar. She wasn't perfect and made a lot of mistakes. But, she had a beautiful heart and she was genuine." He stopped himself and held back tears. "Yeah Momma, I'm going to miss you. I pray you're finally at peace." He wiped his eyes and sat back down.

Jay walked up to the podium. Her belly poked through her black dress. She took off her dark shades revealing her red puffy eyes.

"Hi everyone."

The congregation said hi back.

Jay adjusted the microphone and spoke. "My rock. My best friend. My superhero. That's what my mom meant to me. I don't harp on the bad moments because we shared so many good moments. I will never understand why you had to go so soon and why someone did this to you. I don't know if I'll ever get over losing you. I know you're with me forever and I'm forever grateful to have an angel looking over me. I love you. Rest easy, Momma."

She completely broke down when she looked at the casket. Eric rushed to her side and led her back to her seat.

Rod and I walked to the podium. I held back tears seeing Momma in the casket. It hit me at that moment she was gone.

"I don't know where to start," Rod said, "We weren't close when she passed. But before she left here, I got closure and got the chance to understand why she was the way she was. Our best moments were hanging out on the block. She taught me things at a young age that many wouldn't have exposed a child to but that was her way. I learned a lot about life and I appreciate all the lessons she taught me."

He looked at me. I was stuck. I couldn't move or say anything. I looked down at the floor regretting coming up here.

"Come on, Rell." Pop encouraged from his seat.

I looked up and stared at a wall in the back of the church. "I don't have any words to describe what I'm feeling. I'm hurt. I'm mad. Me and Momma had a rocky relationship. Nobody understood it but us."

I looked over at the casket and stopped talking. I couldn't finish my speech. I was at this podium with people staring at me. I had to say something. "When it was good, it was good. When it was bad, it was really bad. I don't know what to feel. I'm stuck. I'm numb. She'll always be Momma and I'm going to struggle with this for a while."

I looked over at Rod unable to say anything else. He thanked them for listening and then led us back to our seats. I sat down and bawled my eyes out. All of my feelings hit me at once. Rod wrapped his arms around me and I cried on his shoulder.

Boss walked up to the podium.

"Can't believe this day is here. Janet was like a big sister to me. Boy, the stories I can tell." He looked at the casket. "I remember the day you and your brother moved in. Your brother was tragically murdered two months after that. You lost your mom and brother around the same time and you took it so hard and I'm not sure if you ever got over their deaths.

I knew you like nobody else. You confided in me when you didn't have anyone else to turn to. We were best friends. I was the only one who could tell you that you were dead wrong and you would listen. And you're the only person I could give my pain to and you didn't judge me. We understood one another and had each other's back. I don't know how I'm going to do this without you, Netta. I've been trying to be strong but this broke me.

I remember that time when you were twenty-two and I was fifteen and I had to rescue you from a pimp's house and he almost killed us both. I hated seeing you being misused and abused. I stood by your side through the toughest times. We went through drug addiction together and you never told a soul I had a problem and nobody knew my struggles but you. We'll forever have a connection and a piece of me is still with you.

At my lowest moments, I could call you. At your darkest moments, you could call me. I was your first phone call every time you got locked up and I always had to find a way to get you out. When Honey got sentenced and sent to prison right away, I cried in your arms. I had no idea how I would raise five kids on my own and you kept me encouraged. I knew everything about you. You admitted your flaws, wrongdoings, and regrets to me.

I kept pushing you to make things right and told you to stop hurting those closest to you. You always had the habit of pushing away people who loved you most. You couldn't push me away. You understood my pain and I understood yours. Netta, I ain't going to forget you and I'm going to get justice for you. I know you're happy to see your mom and your brother, Terrell, again.

I know one day, I'll see you again. Until then, I'll mourn you and keep our memories alive. You in my heart forever, big sis. Rest easy, my angel."

Boss' speech was beautiful and I learned a little more about Momma. Pops hugged Boss on the way to the podium.

"Janet was my first wife. My high school sweetheart. When I met her, she already had a kid and was doing whatever she could to provide for her child. We grew up in the same projects. It was always drama with Jan but it was a lot of love too. She had been struggling with drugs since she was fifteen. I thought I could be there for her and help her get clean.

Most people don't know this but Jan had a beautiful singing voice. She would win all the talent shows. I wanted her to do music but she wasn't interested. We went to the studio and recorded a song together called Rainy Days. We got the song on the radio but nothing happened after that."

They played the song for us to hear. A melody started and the most beautiful voice blared out of the speakers.

I couldn't believe it was Momma singing. The chorus spoke to me because Momma struggled with doing right and doing what she knew all her life.

Rainy days don't last forever
My life's been full of pain
I know this is not the end
I got a lot of sunny days ahead of me
I'll say bye to the rainy days for now
I hope trouble don't find me again

Pops sang along to the chorus at the end. I knew Pops could sing but I haven't heard him sing in a few years.

"Man, we thought we had a hit with that song. I remember us sitting in the car hearing it on the radio thinking we were about to be superstars. She was so disappointed that her music career stalled and she started using more and more and just gave up on her music career dreams. And in turn, I gave up my dreams of being a music producer. I took over the family business and that's when our love story turned into a nightmare.

We were fighting a lot and we didn't want to raise our kids in a toxic environment so we divorced. We developed a good friendship over the years. She caused a lot of trauma for my kids so it was hard not to be angry with her. We had a conversation recently and I forgave her for putting them through so much. Jan never got a chance to heal from her own childhood trauma and she repeated the cycle.

I don't know if my sons know this but Jan loved y'all. She shared a journal with me that she's been keeping her whole life. And she shared her last entry with me and there were notes she wrote to her kids and grandkids explaining her actions, apologizing, and how she wanted to make it right. It was hard for Jan to be vulnerable and she always had a wall up.

Man, I wish she got the chance to tell her kids and grandkids those things because they might think differently about her. Anyway, I just wanted to talk about my friend, Jan, and share her song. I'm going to miss you, Jan. We love you forever."

Pops stepped away from the podium. I was learning so much about Momma. She didn't seem like such a bad person.

Eric was next to speak.

"All of these beautiful stories about Janet got me in my feelings. We went through a lot together. If you asked her about me, she would tell you I changed her life. My folks didn't understand why I was so interested in her and wanted to be with her. They only saw a drug addict but I saw more. She was smart, had a good heart, and was just easy to talk to.

I met her on the block smoking a blunt. When I learned she had three kids, my heart ached for them. Five months after meeting her, me and Boss enrolled her in a program and she got sober. I don't know if her oldest kids ever saw the difference in their mom. When she got clean, she was completely different. She went to church regularly, got an office job, and found a legal way to provide for her kids.

What I didn't realize was that Janet was living two separate lives. A life I knew nothing about. But once I learned, we got a divorce. I'll always hate how things ended. But being in that hospital room holding her hand and enjoying those final moments meant a lot to me.

Her journey ended before she could truly change and do right by the people she wronged. But Janet lived one heck of a life and I'm sure she's smiling from above at all these crazy stories we're telling about her. I love you Janet and I'll mourn you forever."

Eric walked away wiping his eyes with his handkerchief.

Momma's longtime friend, Mary, walked with a limp up to the podium. She had a cast on her arm.

"Me and Netta went through everything together. The world only saw us as crack whores. I've been clean for ten years now and she was there for me every step of the way. I was the last person with her. She gave me an envelope and told me to give it to her oldest son, Jerrell."

I looked up wondering what was in the envelope.

"Janet went back on the block to what she knew to make things right with her son. This same lifestyle led to her untimely demise. I kept telling her it had to be another way but as you all know Janet does her own thing and you can't tell her nothing when she has her mind made up. On that night she was shot -" Mary paused for a second.

"On that night, she shared suicidal thoughts with me. I never heard her talk like that. She told me they added new charges and that she would never come home again. I held her in my arms as she vented to me about how unfair life was. She broke down and I didn't want to leave her side. I told her we were going to beat the charges even though I didn't know how. Her pimp, Teddy, put her as an accomplice to his crimes and she felt like life was over.

We talked for hours and she felt a little better so she went to the kitchen to fix something to eat. I went upstairs to the bedroom to watch television. She was on her way up the stairs with food and drinks. We were going to make the best of her last night free because we weren't sure when she would come home again. Then there was popping noises that sounded like fireworks. I thought they were shooting up another house until a bullet came my way. I heard Netta screaming out in pain. I had to stay low and couldn't get to her right away.

When I found her, she was in a pool of blood. I opened the front door yelling for help. I had been hit too and in so much pain but I was only worried about her. I had to crawl to my phone as I was bleeding out to call for help. I was right next to Netta until they came. I didn't think I would make it and I didn't want my friend to die. The fact that she died and I lived kills me. I feel guilty and I have to live with this nightmare forever.

How did I survive and she didn't? She had way more to live for than I did. Netta had so much love for everyone and she loved the wrong people too much. I pray her family finds peace, gets justice, and doesn't harp on the bad. We had our ups and downs and plenty of fights in the streets. But she was like a sister to me and I loved her." She looked at the casket. "Girl, I'm going to miss you and I'll never forget you."

Hearing Momma's last moments broke me. It was so much that I didn't know.

Mary walked away from the podium and beeline her way to me with an envelope in her hand. It seemed all eyes were on me. She handed it to me and limped back to her seat. I looked inside the envelope and there was cash and a note. I burst into tears after reading the note.

I love you baby boy forever. I'm so sorry, Rell. I'll do better.

Chapter 76

Keep It Moving

We had a chance to view the body before they closed the casket and that was the hardest part. Mariah, Marley, Junior, and Kennedy got emotional seeing Momma in the casket. Momma looked like herself and at peace.

Pops, Eric, Boss, Jam, Rod, and I carried the casket out of the church to the horse-drawn carriage. We rode to the graveyard in several different cars. It was a ride full of grief, tears, anger, and pain. I lost it when they lowered her casket because I realized she was never coming back.

Now, I'm back home trying to cope and process what happened. Jam and I were on the back porch grilling. The kids were enjoying a game of tag in the backyard. Eric, Pops, Stephanie, Connie, Jay, and Rod were in the kitchen. Boss had to go check on the businesses so he couldn't come back to the house.

I took a sip of my beer and sat down in the chair. Jam sat in the chair beside me. I decided to go live. I shared a photo of Momma earlier and so many people have reached out. I haven't had a chance to return the many calls, texts, and messages I received today.

"Wassup, y'all? It's me and my bro, Jam." I said.

The comments started coming in.

"Yeah, that is my real bro. He's the baby of the family. Make sure y'all support the Jay's Cooking Channel and Jam's World on YouTube. Jam does vlogs and pranks. And if you're already supporting, thank you. We appreciate it."

People commented that they donated money or items.

"Thank y'all for donating. I'm going to start preparing the boxes. I want to feed as many people as I can. I know people are going through a tough time."

I kept reading the comments.

"Man, thank y'all for the condolences. It's been a rough day. That's why me and Jam got on these shades. If you've followed my story, you know me and my mom had a rocky relationship. But that was Moms and I loved her."

Jam went to check on the food on the grill. I knew he didn't want to talk about or hear about Momma right now. I looked at the comments and a lot of people were asking how was the funeral.

"The funeral was a beautiful ceremony. I learned so much about her. Before today, I never forgave her for the things she did to me. And while they lowered her casket, I forgave her and let go of so much pain. I wish I would have done that sooner."

I poured myself a glass of Henny and took a sip.

"Jam, how's everything looking?" I asked.

"Everything looks good, bro," Jam said.

I stood up and showed what I was cooking on the grill. I sat back in my chair and continued reading the comments.

"Yeah, you can only hold onto that pain for so long. I'm drinking Henny. I need it after the day I had."

Connie walked out of the house and I pulled her into my lap.

"What y'all cooking?" I asked.

"They in there cooking everything. I'm watching Ava and AJ. Just wanted to come to check on you."

"I'm good."

We kissed and she walked back into the house. I almost forgot about the live.

"What y'all talking 'bout?" I started reading the comments. "Nah, I don't have a type. If you got a good heart and patient with me, I'll see where things lead."

I read the comments and people were talking badly about Chloe and Porsha. Some of the comments made me laugh.

"Y'all got to stop. Chloe has a good heart. She's not as evil as y'all think and she's a sweetheart. She just wasn't meant to go on this journey with me. And Porsha means well, it just falls short sometimes."

The comments were coming even faster now.

"I've known Connie for a long time. Don't y'all go looking for her and stalking her page. She's a private person."

I drink my Henny and read comments trying to reply to as many people as I could.

"Yeah, my step-momma still makes the stuffed animals. Go to her page, Steph's Creations."

Jam sat back down.

"Jam, somebody asked if you single?"

"Nah, I'm not," Jam said.

I looked at him shocked. "You wasn't going to tell big bro?"

He laughed. "I don't want you in my business."

"But you always in my business. Who is it?"

He leaned over and whispered 'Morgan'. She was the fine young chick from work.

"Oh shit," I said giving him dap. "You told Eric?"

"Nope, and you better keep your mouth closed."

I gave him a sly grin. Rod walked out of the house and joined us.

"Rod, say hi to the live," I said.

Rod adjusted his shades and looked at the screen. "Wassup, y'all?"

We saw nothing but heart eyes and heart emojis.

"You single, bro?" I asked.

"Yeah," Rod said.

We read the comments.

"Nah, I have two kids and two baby mommas," Rod said. "But it ain't no drama with the mommas."

Jahzara ran over to us and stood next to Rod.

"Why you not playing with everyone else?" I asked.

She shrugged. "She called me a boy."

"Who?" Rod asked.

"Layla," Jahzara said.

"It would be Layla," I said. "Come here, Lay." She looked in my direction and I waved her over.

"Hold my live," I said to Rod handing him my phone. "They talking to you anyway."

Lay ran over to me. "Yes, Daddy."

"Why you being mean to Zara?" I asked.

Lay looked down at her shoes. "I'm not."

"Zara is family. Be nice to her."

"I don't want to play with her."

"Sassy!" I yelled waving her over.

"You don't have to play with her but you don't have to be mean to her either."

Lay looked at Zara. "Why you tell on me?"

"You're still being mean. Apologize."

Lay crossed her arms. "No."

I popped her and she stormed into the house crying. Sassy ran over to me.

"Sassy, this is my niece, Zara. Can you play with Zara for a little bit?" I asked.

"Come on, Zara," Sassy said grabbing her hand and they ran off to play.

Rod handed me back the phone and I looked at the comments.

"Yeah, Lay is a mess. Sometimes you got to get them back in line."

"Spare the rod, spoil the child," Rod said.

"That's right. Rod, somebody asked when you gonna give them a chance."

He looked at the comment and laughed. "That's Skyy's crazy ass."

"From the bakery interview?"

"Yeah, bro."

"We got to talk offline. What else y'all want to ask us?"

"Nope, ain't hosting no parties no time soon," Jam said, "They're canceling all of my gigs."

"My son is nine and my daughter is four," Rod said.

We answered a few more questions before I ended the live.

"So, when you and Skyy started talking?" I asked.

"I ran into her at the grocery store. She has a food truck selling cookies, cakes, and shit."

"That's good for her," I said.

"We've been talking and she's cool. We ain't had the time to meet up yet."

"Maybe once this is all over, y'all will get the chance to link up."

I stood to my feet and walked over to the grill. It was time to take everything off the grill. I had barbeque ribs, hot dogs, burgers, and fish. Pops brought all of the sides they cooked outside.

"What y'all cooked?" I asked.

"Mac and cheese, potato salad, greens, baked beans, and rice. Jay made cookies and a pound cake." Pops said.

"Everything ready?" I asked.

"Yup, everything is ready. So Rell, where are my keys?"

"You not letting up, Pops."

"Because I know you're behind this. Now I got to be chauffeured around like some kid."

"You gonna be aight, Pops."

"If I find out you have those keys, I'm whopping your ass." Pops walked back into the house.

Jam, Rod, and I cracked up laughing.

"Pops is going to kill you," Rod said.

Chapter 77

Two Weeks Later

There was a new shelter-in-place and you had to be an essential business to remain open. All bars and clubs have been ordered to close. There goes my hosting money right there. Cases were spiking and the world was going mad.

We had to shut down the bakery because two employees got the virus. I was now at the Juicy Boil taping papers on the door to show we were an essential business and only open for takeout. Boss was installing Plexi glasses around the front counter and cash register. Another employee and I put the chairs on the table. I had someone coming through all the businesses to sanitize and disinfect.

Rod walked into the restaurant.

"I put all the donated food in your trunk," Rod said.

"Thanks, bro. You got to close at three today. I have a cleaning crew coming at four."

"I'll put a message on our social media page about it. Where ya going after this?" Rod asked.

"Got to pick up the other donation boxes. We had to sanitize everything in the bakery box just to be on the safe side. Me and Connie are getting everything together for next weekend."

"I'll be there to help you out."

"Bro, we got so many donations. We're going to be able to feed hundreds."

"People need it."

"I have a farmer donating fruits, vegetables, and milk too."

"That's wassup. Coby misses you."

"I miss him too."

"He told me about all the fun he had at your place. You got a playground, a swimming pool, and a game room. Me and Zara were stuck in the house bored."

"Y'all needed that time though."

"Yeah, we did but my mind was racing. I've been thinking about Momma."

"Yeah, she's been on my mind too. Connie brought the envelope to me this morning. I've been avoiding opening that envelope again, even touching it. I feel bad she went back on the block just to repay me."

"Don't feel guilty about that, bro. That just shows how much she loved you and how badly she wanted to make it right with you."

"We counted the money and it was twenty bands."

His jaw dropped. "Damn, she made that money fast."

"Hell yeah."

"What are your plans with the money?"

"I deposited it into the business account. I started a new foundation in her honor and donated money to Deja's fund."

We all turned to the television when the newswoman mentioned a proposed stimulus bill.

"Hell yeah, they better pass that," a cook, Jerome, said.

"I think they will," Lynn, the cashier, said.

"People need that," Boss said.

I went outside to took a call from Jam.

"What's good, Jam?"

"It's not a good day, bro," Jam said.

"Talk to me," I said.

"This death ain't easy to get over. I haven't talked to Momma in weeks and I used to talk to her every day, even if it was for a couple of minutes. For the first time, I went back and listened to recorded calls and voicemails. I broke down just hearing her voice again."

"I'm sorry, Jam. I know this ain't easy. You never really get over it, you learn to live with the fact that the person is never coming back. Are you on break?"

"Yeah, I'm on my lunch break."

"You need to get out of that room and take a walk. Marley will walk with you. You ain't been out of the room in two weeks. Have you talked to your therapist?"

"Not in a week. I can't bring myself to talk about it anymore. I don't want to accept the fact that she's gone. I replay Mary's speech in my head and think about how horrible Momma's last moment were. She was on the floor bleeding with drinks and food all around her. I can vividly hear her screaming and I can't save her."

"You weren't there, Jam. You can't feel guilty for not saving her. It's going to take you some time to heal so stop rushing the process. See if you can get a couple of days off from work. You can help me and Connie put together the food boxes. I'm sure helping others will make you feel better."

"I'm emailing my boss now. I didn't know working from home would make me feel so isolated."

"That's because you don't leave the room."

"I don't want the kids to see me like this. I'm the fun uncle, not the depressed uncle."

I smiled. "They'll always see you as the fun uncle. Rod is too strict to ever be considered the fun uncle."

He laughed and it was the first time I heard him laugh in weeks. "My girl is trippin'."

"Why?"

"I've been distant."

"She has to be understanding. You just lost your mom. It's not something you can just get over."

"And you need to wife Connie. The kids love her. She's holding it down while you've been busy with the businesses. She takes care of all of us, even me. She's been bringing meals to my room and little notes to get me through the day."

I smiled. "She's a special woman, for sure. All the things I've been seeking and wanting in a woman."

"Take that step, bro."

"I don't think it's time. She already told me she's not ready for marriage."

"She wasn't ready to date you either now look at y'all."

He had a point. "I don't like when you're right, bro."

He chuckled. "I'm going to go take a walk with Marley."

"Good. You ain't seen outside in two weeks."

I ended the call and I walked back into the restaurant. Rod and I walked to the back to discuss the menu.

"Jam just called me," I said.

"Yeah, he aight?"

"He's getting there. He 'bout to take a walk."

"Good, he needs to get outta that room."

"That's what I told him."

"I ain't used to seeing Jay and Jam down."

"Me either. Wish I could take the pain away."

"Same, bro. We've been like this since we were kids. We don't want to see each other hurt."

I nodded my head. "Do you think Momma loved us?"

"Yeah, she just had a horrible way of showing it. She wanted the best for us but didn't always guide us or show us the best routes. I'm in counseling now for this shit because it's a lot to wrap my head around."

"Yeah?"

"At the funeral, I learned so much about Momma. I guess I've been blocking out the good because of all of the bad. But I remember her teaching me so much. I was running the streets before Momma had me out there.

She took me under her wings because she always thought it would be better for me to run the streets with her than some of the shady dudes out there. Now she could have made sure I didn't run the streets at all but this was her way. She didn't have much guidance growing up and didn't guide us correctly. You know what I found out?"

"What?"

"While I was locked up, she was putting money on my books. Pops brought over a bunch of letters Momma wrote me but never sent. And now I see shit differently. I've been mad for years and it only hurt me."

"I'm glad you're letting that pain go, bro."

"Got to so my kids don't have to deal with the shit. I got counseling after I realized Coby would rather be with you than me. I thought I was just being strict but I was taking my frustrations out on him. Coby told me he didn't know if I loved him and told me I was mean. That made me want to change because that's how Momma made me feel."

I give him dap. "I'm proud of you, bro."

Chapter 78

By Y'all Side

I didn't get home until ten o'clock at night and I left the house bright and early this morning. I've been busy getting all of these restaurants together. We were prepared to work as essential businesses and that made everything worth it. Connie was watching a movie in the living room.

"Hey, baby," I said.

"Hey. I made you a plate. It's in the refrigerator."

"Thanks. How was virtual schooling?"

"We've had a lot of video conferences today with their teachers and classmates. Layla was so happy to see her friends. Everybody did their work without giving me attitude so it was a good day."

"That's good."

"The county is switching to a four-day work week next week so the kids can better manage the workload."

"I know Kennedy and Mariah are happy to hear that."

"They are. They have the most work out of everybody. How was your day?"

"I've been sorting through the donations. I got to take everything to the dining room. My entire car is filled."

"That's awesome. We have a shipment of noodles, crackers, and rice arriving tomorrow."

"Is everybody asleep?"

"I think Marley is up playing video games."

"Let me go check on everyone and I'll be back. I appreciate you holding it down."

I walked up the stairs and changed out of my clothes and then I checked on the kids. Mariah and Kennedy were fast asleep in the same bed. Layla and Jackson were knocked out sleep in their room.

I peeked into Marley's room, and he was sitting in his desk chair with eyes glued to the television playing his game. I sat on the edge of his bed.

"Your charges were dropped," I said.

He paused the game. "Fa real? I'm not going to jail?"

"Not this time. But if you stay on this path, you will. You got to get back focused. You're such a hothead and you have to learn that everything doesn't need a reaction. It's okay to walk away sometimes. You get what I'm saying?"

"Yes sir."

"It's my job to keep y'all outta the streets and the system. It was set up for us to fail and we can't fall victim to that trap. You're better than that."

He said nothing and looked at the floor.

"You finished your work today?"

"Yeah."

"How's everything going?"

"It's going."

"What does that mean?"

He stood to his feet and stood by the window. "I have good and bad days. I miss soccer and my friends. We got to stay at the house because everything is closed. I can't race with my friends or nothing."

"You got a roof over your head. You got a huge backyard. I just got you and Junior ATVs and dirt bikes."

"Yeah, me and Junior rode them today."

"It don't have to be boring just because you're at home."

"You don't let us do anything."

"I don't let y'all do anything illegal, you're right."

He huffed. "You don't understand."

"Help me understand."

"Our lives completely came crashing down. It's a lot to deal with and then I had to deal with Grandma's death too. I struggle with missing her and hating her for what she did to Mariah. I'm angry someone murdered her and no one wants to say anything. Everybody I love and everybody I get close to dies. Mom, Dad, and now Grandma. How am I -"

He couldn't even finish his statement before he broke down completely. I was by his side in seconds. I didn't know what to say to him. He's been holding this in for some time and dealing with this alone.

"I know your life hasn't been easy, Marley. You've been through so much. You're the strongest and smartest kid that I know. After everything, you're still standing. I promise you that it won't rain forever, Marley. Just hold yo head, stick that chest out, and keep moving forward."

Jam was at the entranceway of the door.

"I was asking Connie if that was you after hearing the door close. I came up here looking for you." Then he noticed Marley. "Marley, you good?"

Marley shook his head no.

He walked into the room and we both held Marley and encouraged him. We moved away from the embrace a few minutes later.

"Yo, we went walking earlier and just talked about life. Me and Marley always bumped heads and never got along. But today, I got to know him and he got to know me." Jam said.

"That's good. We need each other." I said.

"Yeah, we do. I wouldn't be able to get through any of this without y'all." Marley said.

That almost made me cry. "I love you, Marley."

"I love you, Unc."

"I love you, nephew," Jam said.

"I love you, Jam," Marley said.

"I want y'all to know that as your uncle and your oldest brother, I carry y'all pain. When y'all hurt, I hurt. I don't like to see y'all down. Wish I could make it all go away and make things right but I can't. All I can do is be right by y'all side. Don't hesitate to call or text me even if you think I'm busy. I'll always have time for y'all. Whatever y'all need, I got y'all. You're my nephew. You're my baby brother. Family's all we got."

Chapter 79

Hit Home

At four in the morning, I was awakened out of my sleep by a phone call. I scoot to the edge of the bed so I don't wake Connie.

"Hello," I said groggily.

"Hey Rell," the voice said. I looked at the caller ID and it was Stephanie. Her voice sounded strange like she had been crying.

"Everything aight?"

"No."

When she said that, I stood to my feet. "Something happened to the baby?"

"We're fine for now."

"What's going on?"

"Around two this morning, your Pops complained of chest pains. He's been sick all day, lying around, with no energy, and had this ugly cough."

I knew where this call was going and I didn't like it. "Where is he?"

"We thought he was having a heart attack so we called for an ambulance. About an hour ago, he was rushed to Emory Hospital. I couldn't go with him and that hurts the most."

"Was he breathing when he got in the ambulance?"

"He was struggling to breathe so they gave him oxygen."

"Is he still at the hospital?"

"His fever spiked so they're keeping him. They think it's the virus."

I didn't want to hear that.

Stephanie continued. "So, they gave him a test and we're just waiting on the results. They told me I have to quarantine for fourteen days in case I have the virus too."

"They won't give you a test?"

"No. Because I don't have any symptoms, I can't get a test. I told them I was pregnant and I needed to know. By the time I show symptoms, it might be too late for us."

"And what did they say when you said that?"

"They just told me the criteria to get the test and that I don't qualify. It's frustrating."

"We'll have you test at a private lab and you won't have to worry about that."

"It's expensive."

"I got you. Have you talked to Pops yet?"

"No, they said he's resting and it's best to let him sleep. I'm going crazy."

"Try to get some rest, Stephanie. You need to be well-rested and healthy to fight this virus if you have it. Let me do all of the stressing."

"I'll gladly pass that on to you."

"Goodnight, Stephanie. Text or call me with any updates."

"I will."

I called Eric and conferenced Rod so I could tell them the news.

"Hello," Rod said groggily.

"What's going on?" Eric asked.

"Yo, I got y'all on this call because I got to tell y'all something."

"What is it?" Eric asked.

"They just admitted Pops to the hospital and think he has the virus," I said.

"Shit," Rod said.

"How is he doing?" Eric asked sounding more awake now.

"He's having trouble breathing but resting now," I said.

"I know Stephanie's going crazy," Rod said.

"Yeah, she's stressed out," I said.

"Is she sick?" Eric asked.

"Not yet. They won't give her a test to see if she has it though." I said.

"They're so selective on who they give that test to," Eric said.

"What hospital is he at?" Rod asked.

"Emory," I said.

"He's at a good hospital. They're going to take good care of him." Eric said. "I'll check in with Stephanie and make sure she's good."

"Y'all think he's going to survive this?" I asked.

"I don't know. This virus is nasty but Pops is a fighter." Eric said.

"I've already had a long night. Been up thinking 'bout the businesses." I said.

I walked downstairs to the kitchen.

"Yeah, how's everything looking? I've been out of the loop since I'm not working at the restaurant and home with Jay making sure she's good." Eric said.

"It's just a lot going on. New things are passed daily it seems. We just got to figure it all out. I don't want to cut staff at this time. Since these third-party delivery companies want a thirty percent commission, I'll see if the staff wants to deliver. It takes a lot of money to run a restaurant so I got to be on top of it.

This pandemic is cutting into profits. I've already had to close the bakery so we ain't making no money there. Rent and bills are due for all of these businesses. We got to close at eight o'clock at night. All restaurants are in different cities and counties so there are different rules to follow depending on where we are."

"That sounds stressful as hell, Rell. We can't control what's happening in our world. We just got to let go and let God. Make a plan and live day by day. It's all going to work out." Eric said.

"Bro, what you doing today?" Rod asked.

"I'm preparing the boxes. I'm adding an envelope of twenty dollars to each box. It's not a lot but I hope folks appreciate it." I said.

"Hell, twenty dollars is all somebody needs sometimes. That could be gas money, the little extra they need to pay rent or bills." Eric said.

"True," I said.

"I'm going to drop some donations off to you a little later. In my area, the stores have lots of hand sanitizer, masks, and toilet paper. Jay and I have been making kits to put in the boxes. How many kits should we make?"

"We got enough donations and things to feed at least five hundred families."

"We've made two hundred kits so far. We'll make three hundred more."

"And whoever we can't give a box to, we're handing out cash and gift cards. Nobody's going to show up and leave empty-handed."

"I had somebody donate 70 twenty-dollar gas cards so I'll bring those by," Rod said.

"Man, that's a blessing. And gas is so low right now so that might fill up a lot of cars." I said.

I busy myself in the kitchen making breakfast.

"Yo bro, did you hear they're thinking about cutting the school year short?" Rod asked.

"Nah, I haven't heard that."

"They already went to a four-day work week so the kids only have to work Monday through Thursday and catch up on Friday if they need to," Eric said.

"Man, my kids are happy about that. Mariah, Kennedy, and Marley have been complaining about the workload. Now they have these scheduled web conferences with their teachers and classmates. Me and Connie had to get a calendar to keep up with everyone's meetings." I said.

"Same for Coby. I'm his personal assistant now. He got a meeting three times a week." Rod said.

"Imagine that times five kids," I said.

"Nah, I can't imagine that, bro. But Connie got that shit organized."

"She's on it when it comes to this virtual learning. Couldn't do it without her."

"So wassup with you and Connie?" Eric asked.

"She's my girlfriend," I said.

"Oh shit, you claiming her now?" Rod said.

"You and Jam are the worst," I said.

Eric and Rod laughed.

"If you're happy, I'm happy. I hope you'll get married in my lifetime. Both of y'all." Eric said.

"I don't know if marriage is for me. That short-lived marriage with Ashley was hell." Rod said.

"Don't do that tough guy shit with me. I know you're ready to settle down." Eric said.

"I'm talking to somebody. I just got my guard up because of what I've been through." Rod said.

"I understand that. But you got to realize you can't make others pay for what someone else did." Eric said.

Chapter 80

Just A Mess

All of the kids are up, had breakfast, and now doing their work. Connie, Jackson, Ava, AJ, and I are in the dining room. Connie and I were busy packing boxes while the little ones watched us.

"Any word on Pops?" Connie asked.

"Stephanie called about nine to tell me she talked to him and he seemed weak and not himself. Stephanie doesn't sound like herself either."

"I hope she ain't sick. That would be horrible for her and the baby."

"She's supposed to be getting a test today. I had to pay a private lab to do it since everybody giving her the run around saying she needed to have symptoms to get the test."

Connie shook her head. "Everyone should have access to the test."

"It's just a shitshow. How are we the United States and everybody divided? This state doing this and another state doing that. And there's no leadership to guide anybody."

"And the president acting like it doesn't exist or the numbers are exaggerated."

"It's a mess. We just got to see how this is going to play out."

"I'm watching what happened in Italy and I can't believe how this virus is weakening and crippling people. It's sad to see the crowded hospitals, the overworked nurses, and all of the despair around the world."

"Yeah, it's something else. Look at what's happening in New York right now."

Connie shook her head. "I try not to watch the news but with this virus, I can't keep my eyes away from it. How is Chantel doing?"

"Oh, I meant to tell you. Her Pops, Joe, is bringing Life to the house. Chantel is going to New York to work at a hospital."

"More power to her. That's a brave thing to do."

"She always wants to help others. That's why she became a nurse."

"What time is Life coming?"

"They're getting her things together now. She'll be here around one o'clock. Her first birthday is coming up too."

"When is it?"

"Next week."

"You're just now telling me! We have to do something."

"We had this huge party planned but we had to cancel it. And now Chantel is going away."

"We're going to do something anyway."

I turned on cartoons for Jackson.

"Let me go make sure Sassy is starting her meeting," Connie said leaving the room.

I continued packing the boxes. We have prepared fifty boxes so far and have so many to go. Every day shipments were dropped off at the front door and I was grateful for the support and donations. Kennedy walked into the room.

"Wassup Kennedy?"

Kennedy sat on the floor beside me. "Nun much, Daddy."

"You doing your work?"

"Yeah, I just need a break before my meeting."

"I reached out to your teachers about the workload."

"They listened because the workload is much lighter now. Have you heard from Pops yet?"

"Not yet. Stephanie said he's doing okay. Eric took the tablet up there so hopefully, we get to see him a little later."

"Is he going to die?"

"I don't know, Ken. It can go either way at this point."

"I don't want to lose Pop Pop."

I wrapped my arms around her. This pandemic was putting the kids through it.

"None of us want to lose him. We just have to pray and be his strength."

The doorbell rang.

"I got it," Connie said.

"Okay," I said.

"It's Lifey," Connie said a few seconds later.

"Coming," I said. I turned to Kennedy. "You okay?"

She wiped her face with her hands. "Yeah."

"You can help us pack the boxes. It will get your mind off of things."

"Okay."

"I love you, Ken." I dropped a kiss on her forehead and jogged to the front door. Lifey was in Joe's arms with her head resting on his shoulder.

"Hey, big girl," I said.

She reached her arms out and I took her from Joe.

"What's going on, Poppa Joe?" I asked.

"Man, too much. My baby girl is stressing me out. You know how Chan is."

"How is it looking for Chan?"

"It's still looking pretty bad but we're going to fight these charges."

"Are you going to New York with Chan?"

"Nah, I'm too high risk to be going to New York. I'm going to stay at my place here. My oldest daughter and two grandkids left Cali and going to stay in my basement to ride out this virus."

"Yeah, I've heard it's bad in Cali and New York."

"Ma, they can't hear me!" Sassy yelled.

"Duties call. Nice meeting you, Poppa Joe." Connie said.

"Nice meeting you too."

Connie walked away. Joe turned to me and smiled.

"I like her for you."

I smiled. "She's a great woman and I'm happy."

"She seems like it and you seem happier. That's what matters most. I'm going to get Lifey's suitcases out of the car."

"Is Chan already in New York?"

"Yeah, she left early this morning. I'm going to be worried sick about her until she comes home."

Chapter 81

Tough Call

We gathered in the living room around a tablet to video chat with Pops. Eric, Stephanie, and Rod were also on the call from their homes. It was seven at night and I couldn't wait to see him.

It sucks hospitals are not allowing visitors but I also understand they want to stop the spread. I would be right by Pops' side if it wasn't for this virus. I don't want him to feel alone or go through this alone. The nurse was fully covered from head to toe wearing a hazmat suit, an N95 mask, and face shield. Pops appeared on the screen.

"Wassup Pops?" I said.

It was hard seeing him so weak and lying in a hospital bed. This is why he didn't tell us about his other problems because he never wanted us to see him like this.

Everyone else on the call said hello to Pops.

"It's good seeing y'all," Pops said with a raspy voice.

It looked like that sentence knocked the wind out of him. Another nurse put an oxygen mask on his face. Pops didn't look well and looked like he was in a lot of pain.

"It's good seeing you," Eric said holding back tears. Eric and Pops were so close so I know seeing his good friend like this was hard. "Stay strong, brotha. You got this. I'm going to hold it down for you. Don't worry about the fam, the business, or nothing. I got it. Just focus on yourself and get better."

"Thanks, brotha. I know you got me." Pops said.

We talked for a few more minutes before he was too tired to continue the conversation. We ended the call and put the tablet away.

"Y'all want to watch a movie?" Connie asked.

"Yes," the kids chorused.

I walked away to the kitchen. The reality that I could lose Pops just hit me. I wasn't ready to lose him. I remember when we lost Poppa. He was good then the next day, we got the call he had a heart attack and didn't survive.

Poppa was an Atlanta staple, an advocate, and well-known. The funeral was packed with thousands to show their respects. I couldn't believe how many people showed up for him.

I poured Henny in a glass and took a swig from the bottle. Junior walked into the kitchen and we sat at the kitchen table.

"That was tough," Junior said.

"Yeah, it was," I said.

"I didn't think this shit was real, Pops. Seeing him in the hospital bed with an oxygen mask made me realize how real it is."

"That's how it is. It ain't real until it affects you personally."

"We just put Grandma in the ground. I ain't ready to bury Pop Pop."

"None of us are. I think he's going to pull through, Junior. I have to believe that or I would be losing my mind. We have to stay positive and pray."

"This virus is killing so many people, Pops. The funeral homes are full and they got bodies in trucks."

"I know. It's sad. It doesn't matter if you're old, young, rich, or poor, this virus coming after everybody. That's why we're doing these Blessing Boxes."

"Can we go pack some boxes?"

"Yeah, come on."

I grabbed my glass and we went to the dining room. I flipped on the light. There was stuff everywhere. We packed three hundred boxes today and had a lot more to go. Junior sat on the floor and started putting things in boxes.

"Don't forget to put the envelope of money and restaurant coupon in the box."

"Aight Pops."

"Remember to always be good to people, son. It'll come back to you."

"What's something Pop Pop taught you?"

I smiled. "He taught me everything from how to ride a bike to how to drive a car. He trained me for football and made sure I ate right and stayed in shape. He would cook all of these healthy meals and I used to hate it. I'm like I want fried chicken like Rod and Deja. But he was teaching me discipline, organization, and structure, things I needed for life and to play the game."

Junior smiled.

"He made me a better football player. He knew what he was doing even if I didn't understand it at the time. I can hear his lessons in everything that I do. I can't make a decision without hearing his voice. Pops is always threatening a butt-whopping too. But Poppa was the same way. They don't think you are ever too old."

"When I was working in the kitchen, Pop Pop would come in and just talk about life. Of course, I didn't want to listen and I thought it was annoying. But he knew what he was talking about. He used to tell me constantly, boy, you got to lay off those drugs. The drugs making you slow as hell."

I laughed. "That sounds like Pops."

"I could talk to him 'bout whatever. If I couldn't call you, I called him. Y'all got me through that program. I was thinking of ways to escape and then y'all called and

I knew I had to see it through and finish the program. And I'm glad I stuck with it because I'm happier and less depressed."

"Just keep talking to us. You ain't alone. I'm always here for you."

"I love you, Pops. You never gave up on me."

"And I'm never giving up on you."

I sat beside him. "I love you." I kissed him on the cheek and he didn't push me away.

Marley stood at the doorway.

"You good?" I asked.

"I'm afraid," Marley said.

"You want to talk about it?" I asked.

He looked away. "I wasn't prepared to see Pop Pop like that. I thought he would be sitting up in bed cracking jokes and laughing." Marley shook his head trying to make sense of it. "I've never seen Pop Pop so weak. I've seen this before and I'm afraid he's going to die."

"Me and Junior were just talking about this. I know it was hard to see and you don't want to lose anyone else. We have to pray and stay positive."

"Unc, God don't listen to my prayers. I asked him not to take Daddy and he was gone two weeks later."

"Sometimes you have to pray for strength, peace, and comfort. We're not promised to live forever, that's the reality. God has His reasons even if we don't understand it.

Your daddy is no longer in pain. That cancer took a toll on him. Your momma was a beautiful person who fulfilled her Earthly duties. Grandma is finally at peace and no longer dealing with this cruel world. Pops has lived a good life. We have to accept whatever outcome comes from this."

Marley sat on the floor and covered his face with his hands. These kids were experiencing so much pain. Growing up, we said we didn't want our kids to feel any pain or go through what we did.

Even though I was in pain myself, I had to take the pain from Junior and Marley and comfort them. I didn't even know how to deal with all of this. I'm still mourning the death of Momma. Now, I could possibly lose my Pops and I wasn't ready.

Chapter 82

Can't Be Time

The next morning, Pops requested to talk to me and Rod. I stared at him on the screen not believing this frail man was Pops.

"Hey, Pops," I said.

"Wassup Pops?" Rod said.

"Hey," Pops said weakly.

"Pops, I never thought I would see the day you would be in a hospital bed like this. I can't make it without you, Pops. You got to keep fighting. We need you." I said.

Connie rubbed me on the back.

"Listen to me, Rell and Rod. I ain't never too far. Y'all can always call on me even if I'm not here. I don't want to leave y'all but if it's my time, it's my time."

I shook my head not wanting to accept that. "Nah Pops, it can't be your time."

"Pops, what are we going to do without you?" Rod asked.

"Y'all going to keep living. I want y'all to be there for Stephanie and my baby girl. I know y'all ain't happy about the baby but look out for her."

"We got you, Pops," Rod said.

"This can't be it," I said.

"I don't know if it is but I wanted to talk to y'all. Let y'all know I love y'all. Y'all the best things to ever happen to me and I'm proud of y'all." Pops said.

Even though I wanted to cry, I held it in because I wanted to be strong for Pops.

"Don't stress about nothing out here. We're holding it down. We're taking care of the business and Stephanie. Just focus on getting healthy." Rod said.

"This a different beast. I ain't gonna lie, I'm nervous as hell. I beat cancer and this shit is a different fight." Pops said.

"You got it," I said.

"My Pops, y'all Poppa, came to me and told me to hold on and keep fighting. I was probably imagining things but it felt like he was here holding my hand. I've been having crazy thoughts and I don't feel like myself. I'm going to write a letter to each of the grandkids. I just got to prepare for the worst."

"They would like that, Pops. Junior and Marley were very upset after seeing you." I said.

"I know they're taking it hard. Just tell them to hold their heads up and pray for Pop Pop. That's all we can do."

"Yeah, Coby had a rough night too after seeing you yesterday," Rod said.

"I'm going to record a song for Coby. It's our favorite song and I used to sing it to him at bedtime when he spent the night."

"He would like that, Pops."

"I got to get some rest, Rell and Rod. I just wanted to talk to y'all. Let's pray."

We closed our eyes and Pops prayed. We ended the call after saying our goodbyes. Connie sat in the chair beside me. She rubbed me on the back without saying anything.

"I wished I would have taken the keys sooner," I mumbled.

"Don't you dare blame yourself! The news is now saying there are asymptomatic people with no symptoms unknowingly spreading the virus."

"There's just so much we don't know about this virus."

"We learn something new every hour."

"I just want to be by his side. Just like I'm scared, I know he's just as scared. I can't hold his hand. He's going through this shit alone. I got to see my Pops on a tiny screen. These could be his last moments. I know the nurses are taking good care of him and I appreciate them for being his support. I just wish I could be by his side."

"Yeah, his team is amazing. When does Stephanie get her results back?"

"Should be today or tomorrow. I pray she doesn't have it but she's not herself."

"She texted me yesterday saying she felt sick."

"She was already having issues with the pregnancy. If she gets this virus, it's going to be bad."

"I don't wish this virus on my worst enemy. Let me get up and make breakfast. Rell, what you doing today?"

"Going to pick up donations at the restaurant then I'll come back to finish packing the boxes."

Jam walked into the kitchen.

"You clocked in yet?" I asked.

"Not yet. I got an hour before I clock in." Jam said.

"How's it going?" I asked.

"We're not getting a lot of calls so it's boring. I'm just blessed to still be working and getting a check. People are getting laid off left and right."

"Yeah, that unemployment rate is through the roof. I pray we don't have to lay any of our employees off."

"Did you get people to sign up to be delivery drivers?"

"At every restaurant, we have people wanting to be delivery drivers. That'll help with keeping jobs and getting business during this pandemic. Once the employees from the bakery get out of quarantine, they will have the decision to be furloughed or work in one of the other restaurants."

"They say with this new stimulus package, people are going to get an additional six hundred dollars weekly in unemployment benefits," Connie said.

"That's not bad at all. That'll help a lot of people." Jam said.

"The only thing is it might be hard to get unemployment. Those people in them offices barely worked before the pandemic. I don't know how they're going to handle it now." Connie said.

"It's always something," I said.

"I was in my room watching the news not believing how out of control things are," Jam said.

"Blame the poor leadership. They're not giving the governors any direction on how to handle this." I said.

"He's a joke. Our last president would have handled this." Jam said.

"Most definitely. How's your girl?"

"Morgan is good. It's just weird we can't go on a date or hang out. We just be on the phone talking for hours. I can get emotional about shit without her calling me gay or judging me. I ain't gotta be this tough guy all the time around her."

"What! You letting down your guard?"

"I'm trying, bro. It ain't easy."

"Nah, it's not. Me and Rod talked to Pops this morning."

"Yeah? How was that? I missed the call yesterday. I was knocked out sleep."

"You ain't miss much, bro. He's weak and not himself. He seems tired and like he's ready to leave here."

"You know they say people know when it's their time."

"I don't want to think it's his time."

Chapter 83

Downhill Fast

At around three o'clock in the afternoon, I got a call from Pops' nurse. I knew if she was calling, it was serious.

"Hello," I said into the phone.

"Hi, Mr. Duncan."

"You got some bad news for me?"

"We don't want to look at it that way. Your dad was so talkative and laughing earlier and we thought he was improving. Over the past hour, things have rapidly declined and his condition has worsened."

I plopped down on the couch in the dining room. Connie looked over at me worriedly. I didn't have the call on speaker so she had no idea what was going on.

"Is he still with us?" I asked.

"Yes. With his condition, we are thinking about putting him on a ventilator."

That meant things were really bad and Pops might not make it.

"Let me talk to my fam and we'll make a decision."

I ended the call feeling numb.

"What's wrong?" Connie asked.

"They want to put Pops on a vent," I said.

Connie gasped. "He seemed fine earlier."

I called Eric, Stephanie, and Rod on a conference call and we discussed everything. We decided to go with the vent so Pops is comfortable. He's struggling to breathe and it's painful for him and this might provide some relief and make things better. We also know the risk that the ventilator carries and that he might not come out of this alive.

I called the nurse back with our decision. They would see how he progressed before they made the final decision to put him on a ventilator. The hardest part was not being there and making all of these life-or-death decisions over the phone.

I ended the call not sure how to feel.

"Guess what?" Connie said.

"What? I can't handle too much more." I said.

"Stephanie tested positive for the virus."

"Lawd, let me call her."

I called Stephanie.

"Hey, Rell," Stephanie said sounding winded.

"How are you feeling?" I asked.

"I'm not great. I'm eight months pregnant and I don't want to have this baby without my husband or this early."

"I'm coming to see you," Connie said.

"I would appreciate that. I hate being in this house all alone."

"You better wear your mask," I said.

"I'm going to be extra safe. She needs someone."

"Stephanie, try to rest until Connie gets there."

"I'll try." I hung up the phone. "Connie, I'm afraid for you to go over there. I don't want you to get sick."

"I'll talk to her from the front yard and she'll be on the porch. I'll have on my mask and she'll have on hers. I also have gloves in case I need to get anything for her. She can't be alone at a time like this."

Connie kissed me on the lips and left the room to get ready. The food drive was this weekend and I had so much to do. Jackson ran into the room and sat beside me. I decided to get on live to get my mind off of things. I propped up the phone so they could see me.

"How y'all doing? Y'all safe? Check in with me." I said.

I read the comments.

"If you lost anyone to this virus, I'm sorry. If you know anyone fighting, I'm praying for you and praying your loved one survives. My Pops is in the ICU fighting for his life."

Prayer hand emojis and hearts appeared on the screen.

"This has taken a toll on my family. Yes, the food drive is still this Saturday. I'm packing boxes right now."

I turned my camera and panned over the room filled with boxes and food. I turned the camera back to my face and set the phone down.

"If you know anyone that needs food, tell them about the drive and share the flyer too."

I read the comments and saw a comment that said the virus isn't real.

"I don't know how you're going to say it ain't real with all of these people sick and dying. What I know for certain is that we don't have all the information on this virus. Every day we learn something new, a new symptom, a new fact that contradicts what was said previously. They 'bout to put my Pops on a ventilator and he was just fine earlier."

I continued reading the comments.

"Wait, why y'all saying don't put him on the vent?" I kept reading the comments. "The vent is killing folks? I didn't know that. Oh hell, they already put him under so y'all pray for me and the family. I got on here to clear my mind and y'all got me more worried. Ask me some questions."

The questions started coming in.

"How many children do I have? I have five kids and two grandkids. I also take care of my niece and nephew."

"Do I miss football? Man, I used to miss it so much but now I'm good. It's still my favorite sport and I'll always love it. It was just a lot of wear and tear on my body."

I kept reading the comments.

"Did I hear what about Chauncey?"

The questions continued.

"What's my favorite food? Catfish is my favorite. My bro, Rod, can fry the hell out of some catfish and he has this secret batter. Man, I want some now."

I looked at the comments and multiple people said Chauncey was in a bad car crash.

"He was in a car crash? I didn't even hear anything about this. Prayers to him for a speedy recovery."

The comments were coming so fast now.

"All of our restaurants are open. Jay's Sweets is closed until further notice. We want to make sure the staff is healthy. And my sister is pregnant and still dealing with the loss of our mom. JuiceIt Bar, Juicy Boil, and Poppa's Soulfood restaurants are open for takeout and delivery. Go to my page for directions and hours. We're getting the website together so y'all can order online."

The positive reviews for the different restaurants made me smile. I'm glad people enjoyed our businesses and supported us.

"How am I handling the death of my mom? I have good and bad days. We didn't have the greatest relationship but we were working on it. I think about the good times and it makes me sad. I see how hard it is on my sister and brother and I feel their pain. It's hard losing a parent especially if y'all had a good bond."

I answered a few more questions before ending the live. I called Porsha to see if she heard the news about Chauncey.

"Hey," Porsha said.

"Hey. How ya doing?" I asked.

"I'm aight."

"You heard about C?"

"Yup. His friend just called to tell me the news."

"Do you know his condition?"

"Critical. He's on life support and had to be airlifted to the hospital. I saw photos from the crash and his car was totaled. I don't know how to feel. I'm carrying this man's baby and he might lose his life."

"Think positive."

"I'm sorry about your Pops too and praying for y'all. I saw your post earlier and cried."

"They put him on a ventilator and we'll see how he progresses."

"Is his wifey okay?"

"She tested positive for the virus too and stressed out."

"Man, that's my biggest fear."

"We ain't talked but I hope you're good."

"Yeah, I'm good. I'm just in a fucked-up situation with the world judging me. I had to close the salon and take care of my stylists."

"I'm in the same boat. I don't want to let employees go but this pandemic is cutting into our profits. Sales are going to be down for a while. We had to close the bakery since a couple of employees caught the virus. I'm just glad Jay tested negative for the virus. She's still taking time off to get herself together."

"I don't blame her. I reached out to Jay to check on her. I know her and Jam were super close to y'all mom. She was sad but she's taking it well."

"Her and Jam are trying."

"It's not easy losing a parent. When I lost my dad at sixteen, it broke me. It's been years and I still have moments of sadness when I miss him and wish he was here. I know he's so disappointed in me and that hurts the most."

"Nah, he's proud of you. You own a salon, doing well for yourself, and a good mom."

"I wish he could have met Lay and Jackson and even my new baby. I know he's watching over us but sometimes I wish he was still here."

At two in the morning the following day, I got a call from an unfamiliar number. They have called a couple of times and I finally answered because it had to be serious if they kept calling.

"Hello," I said groggily.

"Hey, you don't know me. I'm Stephanie's sister, Kendra."

"Uh-huh," I said still asleep.

"I came to town because she said she needed me."

"Yeah?"

"I had to rush her to the hospital."

I sat up in bed with my heart racing. "Is she okay?"

"No. She gave birth to a baby girl via C-section and she's now in a coma."

"My girl saw her earlier and she seemed okay."

"She declined quickly."

"How's the baby? Does she have a name?"

"What's ironic is that we were coming up with names today because she felt she would have the baby soon. I didn't think it would be this soon. We decided on Serena Michelle. She's four pounds and an ounce and she's fighting. We haven't gotten her test results back."

We talked for a few more minutes and she promised to keep me updated. The call ended and I looked at my phone in disbelief. My life was falling apart. I shook Connie awake.

"What's going on?" Connie asked rubbing her eyes.

"You got to sit up for this news," I said.

She sat up and I wrapped my arms around her. Her and Stephanie were best friends.

"I just got a call from Kendra."

"Stephanie's sister?"

"Yeah."

"She made it to town?"
"Yup."
"What did she want?"
"She wanted to tell me that Stephanie's health declined."
"Please don't tell me she passed."
"She gave birth to a baby girl and is now in a coma."
Connie immediately started bawling.
"How could this be? I just saw her. She was up laughing and talking and just fine."
"Kendra said it all happened quickly."
"How did she give birth?"
"Emergency C-section."
"How is the baby?"
"Serena is four pounds and fighting. She's not allowed to be with her so she doesn't have a lot of details about what's going on. I gave her your number so she can call you with updates."
"Poor Serena. Both of her parents are fighting to live."
"This virus is turning my life upside down. We can't even be with Pops and Steph to hold their hands, tell them it'll be aight or nothing."
"It sucks. We just have to sit here waiting on the news."
"Basically. We probably won't get an update until later in the morning. I can't even go back to sleep."
"Stephanie was so excited about her first baby and for it to be like this is devastating. Can we pray?"
We grabbed hands and I said a prayer. I pray that God heals Pops, Stephanie, and Serena. I pray that he protects our family. I pray for comfort. And I don't forget to thank him for what he's already done and our many blessings.

Chapter 84

Giving Back

It was Saturday and time to kick off the food drive. We had hundreds of boxes in a moving truck and fifty volunteers all wearing masks and gloves. We are praying for a great turnout. Rod, Jam, Junior, Boss, and Eric were all with me. Connie stayed home with the kids.

My mind was elsewhere but I couldn't cancel this food drive. Stephanie and Pops were still fighting to live. And every day they don't come to, I lose hope that they'll ever recover.

Little Serena is breathing on her own and doing better than anyone thought she would. Her test results were negative so that's a blessing.

I looked at the clock as it struck 11:00 AM. The food drive is starting and we only had a few cars lined up. When we thought it would be a low turnout, more cars pulled up. By noon, cars were wrapped around the corner and down the street. It was a good feeling to be a blessing to others.

I grabbed a box and took it to a car. I put the box of food in the trunk and closed the trunk. I talked to the person inside for a little bit before they drove off. The lady in the car was a single mom of four who lost both of her jobs and taking care of her elderly mother.

All day, I've been hearing stories of despair, struggle, and pain. This pandemic was hurting a lot of people.

I went back to the tent. Junior was getting back at the same time. I could tell something was on his mind.

"Yo, you okay?" I asked.

"This dude I talked to is a single dad of five and he lost his restaurant gig. He does taxi services but business is slow. He just lost his dad to the virus. He's only twenty-three going through all of this." Junior said.

"Dang. Twenty-three with five little ones?"

"He took in his two sisters because his mom passed a few years back."

"Did you get his contact information?"

"Yeah, because I told him I wanted to help him out. He's struggling with rent and getting tablets for his sisters so they can do their work. The libraries are closed so they have to share a device."

"Damn, the libraries being closed is going to affect a lot of people, even college students that had to come home. That gives me a good idea of how to help people."

Boss walked over to me.

"Boss, how ya doing?" I asked.

"I'm okay. I'm hearing so many stories of how people are struggling, and I wish I could do more. I'm happy they passed the stimulus and hopefully, that helps people."

"Junior just told me about a young man that lost both parents, lost his job, took in his two younger sisters, and is taking care of his three children on his own."

"How old is he?"

"Twenty-three."

"Wow, that's a lot on his shoulders. I had kids young and I wouldn't wish that struggle on anyone. I just talked to a family that's living in a hotel. I gave them four hundred dollars to pay for the week and the mom and dad cried. It just makes you realize it was a crisis before this crisis and the current crisis only magnified it."

"That's true. We grew up poor so we know the struggle. But at the same time, we're removed from it because we haven't struggled in a while."

"A lot of people were living paycheck to paycheck with little to no savings."

I shook my head. "Things have to change in this country. It took a pandemic to showcase what's wrong with this country. And if they don't address it, it will only get worse."

Rod walked over to us. "Media wants to talk to you."

I excused myself and Rod and I walked over to the news anchor, Shelia, and the cameraman. I stood in front of the camera.

"We have Jerrell Duncan who coordinated this food drive today. You may know him as a popular football player but today he's giving back." Shelia said. "What made you want to have this food drive?"

"A lot of people are hurting and I wanted to help out. I figured out that the greatest need is food. The schools are out and that is sometimes the only place a child gets food. We have been packing the Blessing Boxes for the past week. We've had several companies reach out and donate food and basic essentials. Thanks to local farmers, we were able to give out milk, bread, and eggs."

"There are so many cars in line. The line goes back for several blocks. Are you afraid of running out of boxes to give away?"

"I think we have more than enough for everyone in line. Even if we run out of boxes, no one is leaving here empty-handed."

It was three o'clock in the afternoon when Junior and I returned home. I took a shower and joined my family in the living room.

I sat on the couch beside Connie. Life crawled to me and I picked her up. She rested her head on my shoulder and I pat her on the back.

"How was it?" Connie asked.

"Exhausting but it felt good to help others. It got my mind off of my own problems. How were the kids?"

"They wore me out. Ava and AJ must be going through growth spurts because I've been making nonstop bottles. Life and Jackson have so much energy. Chantel video chatted Life to check on her."

"How's Chantel?"

"She just told me it's hard to see so much death at once every single day. She seemed down and I have never seen her that sad before."

"I got to reach out to Chantel and make sure she's good."

"At any rate, Life was happy to see her."

Marley walked into the room with his laptop.

"Wassup nephew?" I said.

"I've been working on something."

"What is it?"

"Me, Junior, Kennedy, and Mariah made a song. I made the beat."

"Y'all rapping or singing?"

"Kennedy and Mariah are singing the hook. Me and Junior are rapping."

"Let me hear it."

He played the song and I nodded my head to the beat. Marley was the first one rapping and his timing and flow were sick. Then Kennedy and Mariah harmonized and sounded soulful singing the hook. Junior's spit game was crazy. He rapped a little faster than Marley. I couldn't believe the talent.

The song ended and Connie and I clapped.

"I love it," Connie said.

"That was dope. Would you put that out for the world to hear?"

"I don't know. We were just playing around."

"Y'all are talented and got something to say. Upload the audio to a YouTube channel and see what happens." I said.

"That's a good idea," Connie said.

"And I'll see how I can get it on other platforms if that's what you want," I said.

"That would be cool," Marley said.

"Send me the song."

"Aight, I'm going to send it to you."

"How's the schoolwork now?"

"The workload is better. I can get everything done in a day. I miss soccer."

"Your sis said the same thing the other day about missing soccer."

"We went out to the backyard earlier and kicked around the ball and had a one-on-one game. We worked on her footwork and speed. It cheered her up a little bit."

"You're a good brother. Thanks for looking out for her."

"Of course. I don't like to see her sad."

"Is she open to doing therapy yet?"

"No. I'm trying to talk her into it."

"How's therapy going for you?"

"I like that it's virtual and Allen is easy to talk to."

"What y'all talking about?"

Marley sat on the arm of the couch. "Just life. I talked to him about the murder of my mom. I wished I had the opportunity to know her. And then we talked about the death of my dad. I realized I wasn't over it until we talked about it."

"Michael, your dad, was a good dude. He took y'all in at a time when he was recovering from drugs. He changed his life around for y'all. Got a new job, nice place, and provided a good life for you and Mariah."

"I remember my dad telling the best stories."

"Yeah, Mike always had the wildest stories. He lived one hell of a life, I tell you."

Chapter 85

Celebrating Life

Today is Life's birthday and we were having a barbecue. It's not a huge celebration like we planned but it's still a nice celebration for Life's first birthday. Life started walking a couple of days ago and she's already into everything.

Rod and I stood by the grill. Zara wasn't so shy anymore and was now running around and yelling with the other kids. Connie was inside setting up the balloons and decorations.

"Rod, what's going on with you and Skyy?" I asked.

"We finally got a chance to link up. We went to the park with the kids and had a little picnic. Then we walked the nature trail. We had on our masks and couldn't get close to one another. I guess this is the new normal with dating."

"I wish I could take Connie out on a date. What you think about Skyy now that y'all linked up?"

"Skyy is a cool chick and a good person. She's easy to talk to and doesn't seem crazy. Coby likes her and she's good with the kids."

"That's big. He don't usually like anyone."

Rod laughed. "You right. You should have a car date with Connie. I saw someone on the gram post about doing one with their lady."

"What's a car date?"

"Just you and Connie go somewhere, order takeout, and chill out in the car with the food and drinks. Y'all can even go to a drive-in movie or something. I bet Connie would like that."

"That sounds dope. We had a candlelight date the other night after the kids went to bed."

"Y'all getting close, bro. Is she getting her own place or what?"

"She's trying to get out of her lease. I know this might sound crazy but I'm going to ask her to marry me."

Rod stopped what he was doing and glared at me. He then felt my forehead for a fever. "You're serious, bro?"

"I'm deadass. I know Connie is my soulmate and I want her to be my wife."

"Me and Pops been trying to get y'all together for years."

"The timing has always been wrong but now is the perfect time."

Sassy and Zara ran over to us.

"What y'all doing?" I asked.

"Playing," Zara said.

"Can I show her my room? I want to show her my dollhouse." Sassy said.

"Yes, but come right back," I said.

"Can we bring dolls outside?" Sassy asked.

"Yes, just don't forget to take them back inside."

"Come on, sissy." Sassy grabbed Zara's hand and they ran inside.

"They're going to be best friends," Rod said.

"They already are. Sassy and Lay fight all day."

"Because Lay is mean as hell."

"I don't know when she got like this. I think she's missing her momma."

"When is Porsha getting them back?"

"When this shit gets better, hopefully, June sometime. She only wants to get them on the weekend."

"I heard C is out of the coma."

"Yeah? I ain't been following the story for updates."

"Blogs are saying he's paralyzed from the waist down."

"Word?"

"That's what they're saying. And Ty and Chantel were spotted in New York together."

"You serious?"

"Yeah, but she's saying they're not together so who knows?"

We took the food off the grill and put them in different pans. Rod took the food inside while I cleaned up everything. Junior walked over to me holding Ava and AJ in his arms.

"They liked being in the sun?" I asked.

"Yeah, they were just chilling on the blanket. I kept them in the shade."

"Take them in for a little bit. Did you put sunscreen on them?"

"Connie did before we came out here."

"The food's ready. I know you're ready to eat."

"I'm starved."

A few minutes later, we gathered around the back door. Connie lets us into the house now filled with pink and purple balloons. And she even had Life spelled out in big silver balloons.

Connie had two rectangular tables set up in the kitchen, one with a pink tablecloth and the other with a purple tablecloth. On the counter, there was a three-tier princess cake with a tiara on top and also a princess smash cake.

Rod and I fixed the plates as the kids sat at the table. Connie put Life in her highchair. I took the plates to the kids.

We said grace and everyone enjoyed the food.

We gathered around Life's high chair after we were done eating. We sang Happy Birthday, both versions, and watched Life smash the cake and get it everywhere.

Then we cut slices of the other cake, and it was a delicious vanilla and strawberry marbled cake. Jay did her thing with these cakes.

There was a knock at the door and the kids screamed when they saw the popular characters. We gathered in the living room and interacted with the characters from their favorite shows and movies. After that, there was a magic show. Connie went all out for this party.

We talked, danced, and laughed the night away. Even in the midst of turmoil, we found a way to celebrate and enjoy life.

Chapter 86

Pandemic Exposed

It has been about a week and we were still waiting on Pops and Steph to come to. Serena is at their home with her Aunt Kendra. I just got a call from Boss that he tested positive for the virus and was quarantined at home.

I was in my home office preparing for a video chat with a television daytime show. The hosts were Tina, Kim, and Trent and they seemed like cool people. They introduced me and I turned my sound on to talk.

"Wassup?" I said.

"How are you doing?" Tina asked.

"I'm great. Hope y'all are safe and healthy."

"Thanks. We're trying to stay as healthy as possible. This is not how we wanted to do this interview and we definitely wanted to see you in person." Kim said.

"I know. I wanted to see y'all too. I'm just glad we're still able to do the interview." I said.

"Bro, I know you're in a different sport but we lost one of the biggest and greatest basketball players this year. Did you ever meet him?" Trent asked.

"Man, that was a sad day for me. That was someone I watched and admired. I was sad to hear the news even though I didn't know him personally. I only met him in passing, got a picture with him, told him I looked up to him and that's it."

"I think you shared that photo on your social media," Kim said.

"I did. That moment meant a lot to me."

"You have been doing a lot to help those out here struggling. You hosted a huge food drive, been giving back in different ways from buying tablets to paying bills. You are even making sure your employees stay employed and paid." Tina said.

"I'm just one person doing what I can. I can't just sit back and do nothing. I have struggled and had nothing and now I'm able to be a blessing to others. I heard domestic violence cases were going up and my organization pays for hotel rooms, gives to local charities, and buys flights and bus passes to get the heck away.

I started a fund in my mom's honor to give back to the community. My mom was big on that. I remember my mom making sandwiches for the homeless or peanut butter and jelly sandwiches for the kids in the hood. My granddad and Pops always gave free food to anybody who needed it. It's just something I'm used to seeing and doing."

"That's beautiful. How do you have time to manage all of that and the YouTube channel too? You're really consistent and a new video is always posted." Kim said.

"I have a great team. We recorded several videos beforehand and just wanted to provide relief from all the news coverage. Jam and Jay have been working the hardest to get content out."

"I love watching Jay make her crazy pregnancy cravings. Keep the content coming." Tina said.

"We got you," I said.

"We know you have been personally affected by this virus. Do you want to talk about it?" Trent asked.

"Yeah. My Pops and stepmom are both on ventilators. My uncle is back home and recovering. He has an oxygen tank and lost a little weight but will make a full recovery." I said.

"Your family is in my prayers. I hope your Pops and stepmom pull through and make a full recovery." Trent said.

"Thanks, bro," I said.

"We also know you found love in quarantine," Kim said.

I smiled. "It's wild how this happened. She had a fire at her place, and I told her to come stay with me and the rest is history. She's my best friend and has been in my life for years."

"Aw, that's so sweet. Do you see yourself marrying her?" Kim asked.

I paused. "Yeah, I do."

"What! I never thought I would see the day Jerrell 'Playa' Duncan would want to settle down." Tina said.

I chucked. "When you find the one, you have to hold onto them."

"I know that's right," Kim said.

"Are you in a good place with your babies' mothers? Two of them are on a reality show dogging you out." Tina said.

"We weren't in a good place when they filmed that. As you can see from my social media posts, I have all of my kids with me. So, we're all in a good place." I said.

"How's homeschooling?" Trent asked.

"Bro, you know how it is. My girl is handling that because I don't have the patience. I got to stay on my oldest kids to make sure they stay focused." I said.

"I have four little ones and it's a hot mess in our house trying to figure out this virtual learning," Trent said.

"Y'all going to get there," I said.

"I read on your social media that you think this pandemic is a blessing in disguise. Care to explain that?" Kim asked.

"People are getting a break from the day-to-day grind and spending more time with their families. We're valuing the small things in life. We're taking time to smell the roses and appreciate life. It's exposing the problems in this country that have been swept under the rug like healthcare and paying people a livable wage. This pandemic exposed that we're a rich broke country. And it seems they would rather bail out businesses than the people." I said.

"You said a mouthful there. With the new stimulus, they have small business loans. Will you be applying?" Trent asked.

"Nope, we don't need the money as badly as these other companies. I hope the mom-and-pop shops that need it most get the money. We're staying afloat and paying employees. We have had a lot of business lately and I'm grateful. Make sure y'all support local and small businesses."

"I agree. I've been supporting Juicy Boil and Poppa's Soulfood." Trent said.

"I appreciate you supporting us. You've been shouting us out and sending a lot of business our way." I said.

"Your juice bar is up the street from me and I always go there when I want to get out of the house. I didn't know that was your spot until I did the research for this interview." Kim said.

"A lot of people don't realize that's my spot because my mom was the one holding it down. What's your favorite thing to get there?" I asked.

"I like the smoothie bowls, tea sandwiches, blueberry smoothie, and kale shot. When I want a light lunch, I go there." Kim said.

"That's wassup. I like the blueberry smoothie too with honey." I said.

"I'm trying that next time I go," Kim said.

"Bro, shout out all of your projects so people can support," Trent said.

"Yo, I got a lot going on. My kids got a song titled Mental on YouTube. They call themselves Choppy so check them out. Check out Jam's World and Jay's

Cooking Show on YouTube. Follow me on the gram as moneyrell. I'm always going live and posting.

Support my restaurants, Juicy Boil, Poppa's Soulfood, and JuiceIt Bar. Jay's Sweets, our bakery, is closed right now. Go to my website allmyspots.com to see menus and order online. We just got the site up and running. Thank y'all for supporting me. It doesn't go unnoticed."

Chapter 87

Back To It

Two months have passed and I'm at Juicy Boil with Rod filling orders. The news was on and they were talking about the process of reopening the state.

"Oh boy," I said.

"It's too soon for us to fully open back up," Alicia said.

"And they're opening everything at once too. Beaches, restaurants, beauty salons, malls, nail salons, and you name it. He don't give a damn about us." Rod said.

"We're not going back to full operations right now. We're going to wait and see." I said.

"I think they're doing this because they don't want to keep paying unemployment," Alicia said.

"That's what it is," Johnny said.

I handed Alicia three orders.

"These should be in the same area. Junior gonna ride with you because this area is a little rough." I said.

"Okay cool. Come on, Junior."

They walked out of the restaurant.

"When do the kids get out of school?" Rod asked.

"Next week. They're ending the school year two weeks early." I said.

"Same for Coby. The kids need a break."

My phone rang and I stepped away to take the call. It was the nurse and I was scared to hear the news.

"We have good news," Nurse Jackie said.

I breathe a sigh of relief. "Let me hear it."

"Your Pops is up and off the ventilator. He's just on oxygen right now. We'll try to video chat later. He's a little out of it."

"I appreciate y'all so much. Tell Pops we love him and will talk to him soon."

"I will let him know."

I thanked her again and ended the call. I wiped the tears from my eyes and smiled. Pops is still with us.

I walked back to Rod and told him the news. He just grabbed me in a hug and we held one another. We weren't expecting him to come out of this even though we were praying and staying as positive as possible.

"He's going to call us later, bro," I said.

"I can't wait to talk to him. Let me go to the office and get myself together."

He walked away and I called Eric to give him the news.

"Praise God," Eric said after I told him the news.

"What ya doing?"

"I'm doing delivery for Poppa's Soulfood today."

"You must have needed to get out of the house."

"Yeah, I did. Your sister's pregnancy hormones are driving me up the wall."

I chuckled. "That baby is going to look just like you, the way you two are always fighting."

"She's ready for her own place but doesn't want to live alone. I told her I'll just go out and deliver food for a few hours to give her some space."

"And she's going to be calling you to come home because she hates being alone."

We laughed.

"You know your sister so well. She needs to get back to the bakery. You heard the governor is reopening the state?"

"Yup, he's a fool for this."

"We ain't even got the virus under control yet. Y'all 'bout to let people dine in?"

"Nope. I think it's too soon for all of that. The cases will spike and we might have to shut down again. What's going on with Jam's case?"

"By the time they tested him in jail, his alcohol level wasn't above the limit so they dropped the DUI charge. The only charge that stuck was the disorderly conduct charge and we paid the fines for that. He has to finish this course and reinstate his license. No jail time."

"Boy, he got lucky."

"That's what I told him. We had a good lawyer and this pandemic helped him out. We had to fight though, you know this system ain't fair for us."

"Nah, it's not. I just heard these two white men killed a black man for jogging in his own neighborhood."

"Shit, we can't do nothing. I got to read up on this case."

"I just heard about it on the radio. I'm going to let you focus on the road. I'll send you the link to join the call when Pops is up to it."

Pops was ready to talk to us around five o'clock in the afternoon. I was back home surrounded by my family.

"Wassup Pops?" I said.

Pops smiled.

"It's good seeing you," Rod said.

"I thought I was dead," Pops said sobbing.

I wasn't used to seeing him like this. I grabbed the phone and went to the kitchen so the kids wouldn't have to see him like this.

"It's okay. You're going to be out of the hospital soon and back at home." I said.

"It's okay, OG. We've been praying for you and it's good to see you up." Eric said.

I heard Connie's phone ring. I heard her talking one minute and sobbing the next. I looked at her puzzled. I muted the call with Pops and waved her over. She sat in the chair beside me and I put my arm around her shoulder.

"What's wrong?"

"Kendra said she was on the phone with Stephanie's nurse. While she was updating her, Steph went into cardiac arrest and they're trying to save her life. We're waiting to see if they're successful."

She cried on my shoulder. I got back on the phone.

"Sorry, y'all. We got an emergency. I got to get off the call. I'll talk to everyone later. I love you, Pops." I said.

I left the call and held Connie in my arms. Eric called a few minutes later.

"Yo," Eric said.

"Wassup?" I said.

"I got Rod on the call too. What's going on?"

"Kendra just called Connie with an update on Stephanie."

"Did she pass?" Rod asked.

"We're waiting to hear the news. She went into cardiac arrest." I said.

Eric went straight into prayer mode. His prayer made me feel at ease and like it would be okay. We talked a little more before ending the call. Now we wait for the news.

Around eight o'clock at night, Kendra called to let us know that they were successful in saving Stephanie's life. She's alert and on oxygen. We've been waiting three hours for this call. She was so out of it and doesn't even remember being pregnant, let alone having a baby.

"I need some wine," Connie said getting up from the couch and going to the kitchen.

I rocked Jackson in my arms. I texted Eric and Rod the news. Jam walked into the living room and plopped on the couch beside me.

"His badass finally asleep?" Jam said.

"He was fighting it," I said, "Stephanie is up and alert."

"Thank God. It's been a long two months and three weeks of not knowing what would happen to Pops and Stephanie."

"Yeah, it was. I hope they will be released soon and can go home to their daughter, Serena."

"Serena looks so much like Pops."

"Yeah, that's his twin."

"What you trying to do with this song? It's blowing up and going viral."

"I can't believe it. The kids want to make a music video. I figured we could set up something in the backyard."

"I can help film it. I also have a friend that films music videos."

Connie walked back into the room holding a glass of red wine.

She changed the television to the news where they discussed our state reopening too soon and a second wave coming if we're not careful.

Lawd, we're barely surviving the first wave and they're talking about the second wave will be worse. When things open back up, everything will look a little different. I guess we just had to get used to our new normal.

Chapter 88

Missing You

A week later, I could walk into a store and find disinfectant wipes, hand sanitizer, and toilet paper. These things have been sold out for months. The stores now had a limit on how much you could buy at once.

I was in the grocery store buying things for Pops. I was just so happy he was finally back home.

I looked around at the crowd in the store, no one was standing six feet apart or wearing masks. It was like this deadly virus didn't exist. I continued shopping for personal care items and groceries. I got stopped a couple of times for pictures.

I walked out of the grocery store an hour later. I stood in the parking lot wiping everything down and putting everything in reusable cloth bags. I couldn't risk Pops getting this virus again.

I climbed in my car and drove to Pops' house. I unlocked the door with my key. Kendra and Serena were on the couch in the living room.

"Hey," Kendra said.

"How's it going?" I asked.

"Good. He's been sleeping for most of the day. He got up to eat some soup and went back to sleep."

"How is his breathing?"

"He's still needing the oxygen and gets winded quickly. He's talking out of his head though."

"Still? Does he know he's home yet?"

"Not really."

"I'm going to put everything away and go check on him. You need me to fix you something to eat?"

"Yes, please. I haven't had a good meal in forever."

I put everything away and walked upstairs to see Pops. I sat in the recliner beside his bed. Pops had lost thirty pounds. He was thin, frail, and swallowed whole by the king-sized bed.

"Wassup Pops?" I said.

He opened his eyes, reached out, and held my hand.

"Hi, son. Your Poppa just visited me and we had a good laugh. I got to cook him a burger later."

"Yeah, he would like that."

"I know it."

"Your wife gave birth to a beautiful baby girl and we named her Serena."

He looked at me confused.

"Did you eat?" I asked.

"Uh-huh."

"You still hungry?"

"No, just tired."

"How's your chest feeling?" I asked.

"My chest?"

"Does your chest hurt?"

"No. Poppa visited me today."

"Yeah, you told me. I'm sure it was good seeing him."

Seeing Pops like this was hard, and I had to hold back tears.

"I got to go make lunch. I'll stick around for a bit. If you need me, call me. Just try to rest."

"Okay, tell Poppa I'll see him later."

"Okay."

I left the room and closed the bedroom door. I leaned against the wall and slid down to the floor. I held my face in my hands and cried. This wasn't the Pops I knew. It was like I didn't know him at all.

The doctor said it would take him some time to get back to himself but I wasn't expecting Pops to be like this. And on top of everything, today is Deja's birthday. She would have been thirty-six years old if that coward didn't take her life. Man, I wish she was still here.

"You good?" a voice said.

"Rod, I'm good. I didn't know you were coming by." I said.

"I told Pops I would come see him," Rod said.

He sat on the floor beside me and put his arm around my shoulder.

"He's not himself, bro," I said.

"I know. I sat with him yesterday. He kept repeating things and didn't remember much. Stephanie finally remembered she was pregnant and asked to see Serena."

"Yeah, she's not out of it like Pops."

"He'll get back to himself soon and back to getting on your nerves."

"Let me get downstairs to fix lunch."

"I'll help you out, bro."

"It's Deja's birthday."

"Me, Mariah, and Marley are going to visit her today."

"I'll come with y'all."

We walked down the steps and into the kitchen.

"What are we making?" Rod asked.

"Kendra said she hasn't had a home-cooked meal or time to cook. I'm going to make cabbage, mac and cheese, cornbread, and fried chicken. You got to make the chicken." I said.

"You get started on everything else. I'm going to give Kendra a little break and watch Serena."

I took things out of the cupboard and refrigerator to make the meal. Rod walked in a few minutes later holding a fussy Serena.

"It's smelling good in here bro," Rod said.

"That's the neck bones," I said.

"You know where her bottles are?"

I went into the fridge and grabbed a bottle. He walked back to the living room with the bottle.

I turned on the radio and got in my zone. I decided to record a cooking vlog for the channel. As long as I was working, I could keep my mind off things.

I now stood in front of Deja's grave. Rod, Mariah, and Marley were walking back to the car.

"Happy birthday, Deja. I haven't been back because I was expecting you to come back to me. I didn't want to believe you were truly gone and never coming back. It's been hard to accept. You were my best friend. I could go to you about whatever. If I had a problem with a girl, you handled it."

I chucked. "I know you would have loved Connie. I got your kids and they're straight. I miss you out here but I know you up there holding your baby girl and looking down on us. Deja, continue to rest easy."

I touched her headstone and looked down at the grass. I still can't believe she's gone but I know she's in a better place.

"I love you, Deja. Keep watching over us, my angel."

I walked back to the car and climbed into the passenger side.

"You good?" Rod asked.

"I haven't been back since we buried her. I like the photo they put on the headstone. That's how I remember Deja with that big smile and dimples. It's like I was able to talk to Deja." I said.

"We did that for Mariah and Marley so they don't forget her face. They were so young when everything happened." Rod said.

"As long as I'm alive, they'll never forget her face or forget about her."

Chapter 89

Better Days Ahead

A couple of days later, Stephanie came home and Pops was more like himself. He's more mobile and not getting winded as quickly. We were on video chat watching Stephanie meet Serena for the first time.

She was sitting in a rocking chair in Serena's room. Pops was in a chair beside her. Kendra brought Serena into the room. Steph cried as Serena was placed in her arms.

"This is so beautiful," Connie said wiping away her tears with a tissue.

"Aw, Pops understands now," Jam said.

We noticed Pops looking over at Serena with a smile on his face. He's been around Serena but has been so confused about who she was.

"I have a daughter with me again," Pops said.

I smiled hearing him say that. Deja was like a daughter to him and he was devastated when she was killed. I know I gave him a hard time about having a kid at his age but he seemed truly happy.

"She's beautiful," Pops said.

"Isn't she?" Jay said wiping her eyes. Eric and Jay were at their house watching the video chat.

"Pops, I'm going to come by later and bring you some crab legs," Rod said. He was at his house with Coby and Zara.

"I would like that," Pops said.

"Jay, I need a banana pudding cake," Stephanie said.

"I got you," Jay said.

"I can't believe we've been down almost three months," Stephanie said.

"Do y'all remember anything?" Jam asked.

"I just remember Kendra dropping me off at the hospital. I don't remember giving birth or anything else." Stephanie said.

"Everything happened quickly," Kendra said.

"Yeah, I remember being in the hospital feeling like I was about to die. Everything else is a fog." Pops said.

"Yeah, you've been out of it, Pops," I said.

"I haven't felt like myself," Pops said.

"I put your car keys on the table in the living room," I said.

"You could have kept them. I ain't going out for a while." Pops said.

I smiled. "The world was praying for y'all."

"Kendra showed me all of the messages on the gram. I also saw a post about C being paralyzed from a car crash." Stephanie said.

"It's been a lot going on. He moved in with Porsha and Porsha is taking care of him. They think if he does physical therapy, he'll walk again. I don't know why the blogs are saying he'll never walk again." I said.

"What! Porsha is taking care of C? That's wild." Stephanie said.

"She's a good person with a good heart. He didn't have anyone else so she stepped in to help." I said.

"Y'all kids are so big now. Y'all got to come see Pop Pop." Pops said.

"We will," Marley said.

"And y'all got a song too? Y'all sound good. It was on the radio and Kendra told me it was y'all." Stephanie said.

"I got to hear this song. We got to catch up since we missed so much." Pops said.

Chapter 90

Will You?

A few days later, I went to the park to have a picnic date with Connie. It was just me and her. Connie took a sip of her wine.

"This is nice," Connie said.

"I had to do something special for you, Connie. I want you to know I appreciate you so much. It's crazy how this pandemic brought us together. I don't know if I could have made it through this without you." I said.

"And as much as you needed me, I needed you. I needed your company, companionship, and strength."

"We've been friends for years, Connie. I'm glad we're together now."

"Me too."

We kissed.

"I can't see my life without you in it. You mean a lot to me. You're going to think I'm crazy for this." I pulled the ring box out of my pocket and she screamed. I opened the box and presented a 13-karat white gold engagement ring. "Will you marry me?"

"Am I just as crazy if I say yes?"

I smiled. "Probably."

She squealed. "Yes. YES!" I put the ring on her finger. "It's beautiful, Rell." She looked at her hand in disbelief.

I kissed her so happy that I would be spending the rest of my life with her.

"I'm so excited to spend the rest of my life with you, Connie. You're special to me and I can't wait until we become one. I also bought Sassy a promise ring." I showed her the ring and she could only cry. "We are about to be one soon and I accept all of you." I wiped away her tears. "I can't imagine being on this journey without you."

It took a tragedy for me to come back to reality and realize what's important in my life. The first wave made me appreciate life and learn that in an instant, life can change. I've been up. I've been down. One thing I know for certain is that it will always work out in the end. I have to keep pushing forward and know better days are always ahead.

Just like football, no matter how hard you prepare and plan for a good game, shit happens. You win some and you lose some. But you stay in the game no matter what. You never know what will happen and sometimes you have to pivot. Keep your head in the game and focus on getting the win. Don't concern yourself with the when. Because you will eventually win and it doesn't matter how long it takes. And there's nothing like that victorious celebration to enjoy that glorious win. This is how we survived the first wave.

It has been a month since the governor reopened the state. We have reopened our dining space at limited capacity with tables being spaced out. Things looked a little different but this first wave taught me to accept this new normal.

I just hope we all survive the second wave. Sometimes things change and it's not always a bad thing. Maybe we all needed this change to be better and do better.

THE END

Also By Joshlyn Nicole

About the Author

Joshlyn Nicole is an indie author from Atlanta, GA. Her passion for writing started at a young age and she has dreamed of being a published author since she was twelve years old. Now, she is doing just that releasing books about life ranging in topics from relationships to grief. Her goal is to take the world by storm through her writing which can hopefully impact others and inspire change. Her biggest inspirations are life itself and learned experiences. Besides writing, Joshlyn enjoys being a mom to two rambunctious boys, creating content, and enjoying time outdoors.

Made in the USA
Columbia, SC
24 February 2025